FLING WITH HER HOT-SHOT CONSULTANT

KATE HARDY

FAMILY FOR THE CHILDREN'S DOC

SCARLET WILSON

MILLS & BOON

First Published in Great Britain 2020
by Mills & Boon, an imprint of HarperCollins*Publishers*
1 London Bridge Street, London, SE1 9GF

Fling with Her Hot-Shot Consultant © 2020 Pamela Brooks

Family for the Children's Doc © 2020 Scarlet Wilson

ISBN: 978-0-263-27974-0

MIX
Paper from
responsible sources
FSC® C007454

This book is produced from independently certified FSC™ paper
to ensure responsible forest management.
For more information visit www.harpercollins.co.uk/green.

Printed and bound in Spain
by CPI, Barcelona

FLING WITH HER HOT-SHOT CONSULTANT

KATE HARDY

MILLS & BOON

To Scarlet—always great fun working with you!

PROLOGUE

GEORGIE HAD BEEN secretly haunting the website for a week now.

Job swap.

The idea was that you'd swap your job and your house with a stranger for six months. Various health trusts across the country had signed up to the initiative, so all you had to do was find a match. Someone who did the same job as you; someone who maybe wanted some experience in a different place to enrich their working life.

Was it running away? Or was it just what she needed to give her a fresh start?

It wouldn't be without complications. She'd be letting Joshua down, for a start. Her elder brother was a single dad who relied on her for help with childcare for his daughter Hannah—and Georgie loved her brother and her niece dearly. She didn't want to let them down.

But over the last year London had become more and more of a prison; and she was oh, so tired of being seen as Poor Georgie, widowed at twenty-nine and being so brave about carrying on. Poor Georgie, who hero husband Charlie had been part of a team of emergency doctors helping after an earthquake and had been killed trying to save someone.

Poor, poor Georgie…

If only everyone knew the truth about Charlie. But how she could shatter everyone's illusions? His family and friends didn't deserve that. The way she saw it, they should be able to mourn the man they'd loved without seeing the side he'd kept hidden. Which meant she had to keep his secrets. So far, she'd managed it, because in a weird sort of way keeping that secret was protecting her, too; but she was getting to the point where she felt as if she'd explode if she didn't get away from all the memories and the pity.

So today she'd look at the website again to see if there was a match. If there wasn't a suitable match for her, she would take it as a sign to stay exactly where she was and stop being so pathetic and just get on with things. If there was a match, then it was a sign she should leave.

Location.

That meant hers: west London.

Position.

So far, so good: paediatric registrar.

Desired location.

That was harder. 'Anywhere' meant just that. And, even though she wanted to get out of London, she didn't want to go somewhere really remote. Not, she supposed, that there were that many remote hospitals. That field was probably meant for the GPs—ones who maybe wanted to swap an isolated rural practice to gain experience in the fast pace of a city practice; or maybe those who were burned out by inner-city medicine and craved a country idyll for a while.

Somewhere by the sea...

No. She could've run away to her parents' at any time, but she hadn't taken that option then and she wouldn't take it now. This was the chance to make a fresh start. She shook herself and chose the 'anywhere' option.

Time frame.

That was an easy one. Now.

Then she clicked the 'Find Your Match' button.

The system thought about it. And thought some more.

Clearly there wasn't a match, or perhaps the system was down. Georgie was about to give up and close the page when the screen changed.

One match found.

She clicked on her result. Edinburgh? She'd never been to Edinburgh.

All she really knew about the place was that it was the capital of Scotland and it had a castle, a very famous comedy festival and an amazing Hogmanay party.

One match. Meaning that this was fate giving her a little nudge to keep trying.

She clicked 'connect' and wrote a short email, doing her best to sell her job in London. And everything she wrote was true: the Royal Hampstead Free Hospital was a great place to work, her colleagues in the paediatric department were utterly lovely, and her comfortable flat in Canary Wharf with its balcony and fold-back doors overlooking the Thames was only a short walk from the Tube station.

Put like that, it would make anyone wonder why she wanted to leave. What wasn't she telling? What was the catch in what looked like a perfect life?

The whole truth wasn't something she wanted to tell anyone, let alone a complete stranger. 'Personal reasons' was too vague and likely to net her a rejection. So, instead, she stuck to a simplified version of the truth.

I was widowed almost a year ago and I feel I need a fresh start, away from the pity.

Pity that would be so much worse if people knew the truth. Charlie had been cheating on her with Trisha for months; his mistress, who had been killed in the landslide with him, had been pregnant at the time.

In Georgie's view, nobody, but nobody, needed to know about Trisha and the baby.

She stared at the words for a while. And then she took a deep breath and pressed 'send'.

It didn't mean she was definitely going to leave. The other paediatric registrar might not want to live in this part of London, or might change his or her mind about doing the job swap. But she'd made the first move. If this didn't work out, her next attempt would be easier. And then, for the first time since she'd learned the truth about her husband, Georgie could stop feeling as if she was weighed down by the whole world.

CHAPTER ONE

Two weeks later

GEORGIE COULD STILL hardly believe it had all happened so quickly. Clara Connolly had been happy to swap her job in the paediatric department of St Christopher's Hospital in Edinburgh for Georgie's job at the Royal Hampstead Free in London, and she too wanted to start the swap as soon as possible.

Perfect.

Telling Joshua had been the hardest part. Her brother had been so upset. He'd accused her of bailing on them when he and Hannah really needed her. In the end, Georgie had been forced to tell him why she needed to get out of London, and the truth about how Charlie had cheated on her and lied both to her and to his mistress. Joshua had been horrified that she'd kept it to herself for so long, then guilty because he felt he hadn't supported her well enough for her to tell him the truth earlier. But they'd pretty much worked it through, he'd promised to keep it to himself, and she was going north with his blessing.

Though her brother's insistence that she should send him a text every time she stopped for a break was driving her crackers. Why did he have to fuss so much? OK, so she hadn't driven that much for a while—in London, she didn't really need a car—but she was perfectly capable of driving the seven or so hours from London to Edinburgh on her own. Actually, she was enjoying it hugely. She'd hired a bright orange convertible Mini for a fortnight, to give her enough time to work out whether to buy a car for the rest of the job swap or extend her lease; driving on the motorway on the bright autumn day, with the roof down and the stereo turned up loud with a playlist of happy, bouncy music, was the most fun she'd had in months. And she stopped every two hours at a service station to stretch her legs, grab a coffee and text Joshua that she was absolutely fine.

The navigation system was working well; not that she really needed it on the motorway, because it was pretty obvious she was just heading north up the M1 to Scotland. Apparently Clara's cottage was at the edge of a village outside Edinburgh, about thirty minutes away from the hospital; although Georgie was pretty sure she'd be able to pick up supplies in the village, she decided to get some bread, milk and instant coffee on her last stop, just to tide her over in the first minutes when she arrived.

Edinburgh.

Her new life.

Freedom.

She'd still be doing a job she loved and trying to make a difference to the world, but she would no longer have to pretend all the time. And, just in case Charlie's ghost was listening, she instructed the car's sound system to play The Proclaimers' 'I'm On My Way' and sang along with it at the top of her voice. She was definitely driving away from the misery she'd felt in London, and nothing was going to stop her enjoying her new life in Edinburgh. Being *happy*.

An hour later, she revised that.

The persistent rain had made her put the hard top on the car. It was already dark—a good hour before it got dark in London—but there were no street lights in sight so she had to rely on her headlights, and the narrowness of the road and the multiple bends meant she was driving at practically a crawl. The satnav didn't seem to have a clue where she was and kept telling her, 'You have reached your destination,' when she clearly hadn't. And she'd reversed down what felt like the same narrow, muddy track *twice* now.

Clara had said that her cottage was on the edge of the village. Obviously Clara's definition of 'edge' wasn't the same as Georgie's. Possibly neither was 'village': a pub, a church, a school, and a renovated courtyard of barns, which was apparently a farm shop and in whose car park she was now sitting as she tried to make sense of her bearings. How on earth was that a village?

Everything seemed to be firmly closed at seven o'clock on a Saturday evening—even the pub, which she could hardly believe—so she couldn't ask anyone for directions. In London, her local shops were open before dawn and closed after midnight. Did that mean she'd have to drive for half an hour to get supplies if she ran out of milk?

According to the sign on the barns, they sold fruit, veg, award-winning dairy and meat. There was a bakery and a café, and local crafts and gifts.

All crammed into a few barns in the middle of nowhere.

This was starting to feel like a huge mistake rather than a fresh start. Saturdays shouldn't be this difficult.

And thank God she'd bought milk and coffee at the service station. The first thing she'd do when she got to her new house would be to put the kettle on and make double-strength coffee. Maybe treble.

OK. She'd make one last attempt to find the cottage; if that failed, she'd give in and call Clara and ask her just where the cottage was.

She drove up the narrow track as slowly as she could. And, this time, was it her imagination or was there a chink of light at the side of the road—something which might mean people? She drove even more slowly until she saw an opening that led into a yard, then carefully pulled in. There was a large four-wheel drive car already parked there, so obviously this wasn't Clara's cottage. But at least it looked as though there was someone in residence—someone who might know where Hayloft Cottage actually was and could give her directions.

She parked next to the other car, made her way to the door of the cottage and banged on it.

No answer.

But there was a deep woof. Definitely not Clara's cottage, then, because Clara hadn't said anything about a dog. A neighbour's, then. She hoped the neighbour was friendly. In London, you hardly even saw your neighbours. Would it be different here?

She knocked again. More woofing. And this time the door was dragged open by a man who looked very fed-up indeed and was wearing nothing but a bath towel slung round his hips.

Her mouth went dry.

He had pale skin, grey eyes, slight stubble and wild, slightly over-long dark hair. Add in the light dusting of hair on his chest and his perfect six-pack, and he could've been the star of an action movie. He was the first man who'd made her mouth go dry like that since Charlie, and it put all her senses on full alert: this was dangerous.

'What do you want?' he snapped.

Oh, help. He had that lovely Scots accent too. The sort that melted your bones.

And her brain cells must have been temporarily scrambled from the long drive to make her focus on his unexpected gorgeousness instead of solving her problem. What on earth was wrong with her? The man must think she was some kind of tongue-tied idiot.

'I—I'm sorry to bother you,' she managed to get out finally, cross with herself for being so pathetic. 'I'm a bit lost. My satnav has been telling me for the last five miles that I've already reached my destination, I've been on the road since nine o'clock this morning, and to be honest I've had enough. Could you please tell me where I can find Hayloft Cottage?'

'Hayloft Cottage,' he repeated. There was another woof behind him, and he turned to the dog. 'Shh, Truffle, it's all right,' he said.

Was he scowling because he hadn't heard of the cottage? Or maybe this place was like the village where her parents lived in Norfolk, where something had an official name but everyone local called it something completely different. 'Clara Connolly lives there,' she added, hoping it would help.

'And you are…?'

'Georgina Jones—Georgie.'

'You,' he said, 'aren't due to arrive until tomorrow.'

She couldn't quite process this. What did he mean? 'Tomorrow?' she asked, confused.

'Your job swap thing. Clara said you weren't coming until tomorrow.'

'You know Clara?'

'Aye.'

The penny suddenly dropped. He knew Clara. He knew she was expected. So this had to be Hayloft Cottage. 'Are you Clara's friend? The one she said might be staying?'

For pity's sake—he knew who she was, now. Couldn't he just let her in so she could get a cup of coffee and warm up a bit?

She realised she'd spoken aloud when he raked a hand through his hair. 'Yes. Of course. Sorry. I was in the shower. I'll get something sorted out.' His towel nearly slipped as he reached behind him to grab the dog's collar, and Georgie's pulse went up a notch. 'This is Truffle. She's a bit nervous, but she's friendly when she gets to know you.'

'Uh-huh,' she said warily.

'You're not a dog person?'

'I'd never hurt one,' she said. 'But, no, I'm not used to pets. And Clara didn't tell me to expect a dog.'

'I see.' He paused. 'Truffle's a rescue dog, so she's a wee bit shy with people she doesn't know. Ignore her and she'll come to say hello when she's feeling brave enough. She won't hurt you,' he advised. 'Though don't leave shoes or cake lying around. They'll be gone in three seconds. And please don't leave chocolate anywhere, even if you think it's out of her reach, because it won't be and it's poisonous to dogs.'

'Noted,' she said, slightly nettled by his tone. OK, so she wasn't used to dogs, but it didn't mean she was stupid. Plus it was raining and she was a little tired of being left on the doorstep by a man whose social skills seemed more than a bit on the skimpy side. So she couldn't help the sarcastic edge to her voice when she asked, 'So would it be possible to bring my stuff in, do you think?'

'Let me dry off and put some clothes on,' he said, 'and I'll help you bring your things in.'

She was perfectly capable of bringing her own things into the cottage. She wasn't a delicate little flower who needed a man to sort things out for her.

Before she could make the point, he said, 'The cottage is open-plan, so I'm afraid I can't shut Truffle in another room. Two of us bringing your things in means it'll be quicker and I won't have to keep her on her lead for so long.'

'Right.'

'Free feel free to make yourself some coffee,' he said. 'The mugs and the coffee are in the cupboard above the kettle.'

'Thank you.'

He stepped aside to let her in, then closed the front door behind him. 'Good girl, Truffle,' he said to the chocolate Labrador, then disappeared up the spiral wrought-iron staircase in the centre of the room.

So she was stuck in a cottage in the middle of nowhere with a complete stranger—one who didn't seem to be that pleased to be sharing his living space—and a nervous dog. What else hadn't Clara told her?

To be fair, Clara had said that her friend might still be there; but she'd also said that her friend would most probably be gone before Georgie arrived. And she hadn't even mentioned the dog.

Plus Georgie had no idea what her new housemate's name was. He hadn't even introduced himself. Grumpy

McGrumpface, perhaps? He might be gorgeous, but he seemed incredibly prickly. She really hoped there was a soft side to him, because sharing a place with someone difficult was going to be really wearing.

'I'm going to make some coffee,' she said to the dog, who was regarding her warily from the other side of the room.

At least with Grumpy McGrumpface leaving the room she had a chance to look round. Hayloft Cottage was compact and open plan, and utterly gorgeous. The windows all seemed quite deep-set, so Georgie guessed that the stone walls were very thick. The floors were pale flagstone, and at one end of the ground floor there was a kitchen consisting of cupboards painted sky blue, an old-fashioned butler's sink, a cream-coloured Aga and a plate rack on the wall. She assumed that the fridge, freezer and washing machine were hidden somewhere behind the cupboards. Opposite the cupboards was a scrubbed pine table and four matching chairs.

The wrought-iron staircase was the feature in the middle of the room, and there seemed to be a baby's safety gate fastened across it. On the far wall there was an old-fashioned wood burner and two comfortable sofas on either side of it with a thick rug and a coffee table set between them, plus a wicker basket with a soft blanket that clearly belonged to the dog. It was cosy and pretty, and Georgie tried not to think about the fact that it was in the middle of nowhere or how disconcerting it was not to hear any noise from passing traffic.

She headed to the kitchen area and filled the kettle. Just as Truffle's owner had said, the coffee was in a tin above the kettle, along with a shelf of mugs.

Should she make some coffee for him, too?

She was still dithering when he came downstairs. He was dry now—or at least *drier*, because his hair was still damp. And it wasn't dark, as she'd first thought: it was a deep auburn. Utterly gorgeous: but she knew that being handsome and being nice didn't necessarily go together. Charlie had been charming, but he had turned out to be far from the nice man she'd thought she'd married; and her new housemate wasn't even charming, let alone nice.

Cross with herself and knowing that she was possibly being unfair to him—for all she knew, he could've had the day from hell and the last thing he needed was a complete stranger turning up on the doorstep when he wasn't expecting her—she asked, 'Can I make you a coffee?' Once she'd downed a mug of the stuff, her head might be back in the right place again and she'd be her usual practical self. And hopefully she'd also stop reacting to him like a hormonal and star-struck teenager. She wasn't here to get swept off her feet by a handsome stranger; she was here to get her life back on some sort of track.

'Thanks. No milk or sugar.'

Did he mean he didn't take milk or sugar, or that there wasn't any? She'd organised a food delivery with a note telling Clara to use whatever she needed and to make herself at home. She'd left a bottle of decent Prosecco in the fridge and a box of her favourite truffles, with a sticky note saying 'Welcome to London'. As this was Scotland, she'd kind of hoped that Clara might have left her some shortbread as a 'welcome to the job swap' sort of thing. That hope was starting to feel a bit forlorn. And this place suddenly felt every one of the four hundred and so miles away from London, away from nearly everyone she knew.

'If you take it, sugar is in the cupboard next to the

coffee and there's milk in the fridge,' he said, as if her thoughts were written all over her face.

'Thanks.' She made two mugs of coffee, then added milk and enough cold water to her own mug that she could drink it straight down, as she often did at work.

He raised an eyebrow. 'That's how my colleagues tend to drink their coffee.'

His colleagues? 'Are you a medic, too?' she asked.

He nodded.

'Clara didn't really say anything to me about you. I'm afraid I don't even know your name.' She'd been at the cottage for long enough for him to introduce himself. The fact he hadn't bothered told her that he really wasn't going to welcome her staying here.

'I'm afraid I don't even know your name.'

It was a rebuke, and Ryan knew it was deserved; though at the same time it rankled that his new house-mate was judging him. He'd been thrown enough by the interruption to his shower not to think about introducing himself to her. He'd already had a really horrible shift; losing a patient always sat badly with him, and losing a patient in today's circumstances was as bad as it could get. Being polite to some posh city girl was at the bottom of the list of things he wanted to do.

'Ryan McGregor,' he said.

'Pleased to meet you, Ryan,' she said, not sounding pleased in the slightest—that made two of them, he thought—and held out her hand to shake his.

Though she was at least trying to be polite. It wasn't her fault that he'd had such a horrendous day. He ought to make the effort, too. He shook her hand, and immediately wished he hadn't when heat zinged through him.

He couldn't remember the last time he'd reacted to anyone like that, even Zoe. And he definitely couldn't afford to react like that to Georgina Jones. Especially as they were going to be sharing a house for the foreseeable future, until he could find an alternative.

The problem was, she was just his type. Petite and curvy, with green eyes and fair hair pulled back in a scrunchie, and the sweetest, sweetest smile. Gorgeous.

Dangerous.

The surge of attraction felt as if it had knocked him sideways, and he struggled to deal with it. What the hell was wrong with him? Was he going down with the flu or something? That must be why he was hot all over; clearly he had a temperature. 'Pleased to meet you, too,' he mumbled, feeling totally off balance.

'So do you work at St Christopher's?' she asked.

'Yes.'

She looked at him, her eyebrows slightly raised.

What was this, twenty questions? He stifled his annoyance. Again, it wasn't her fault that Clara had been a bit sketchy on detail. 'With Clara, on the children's ward,' he said. 'I'm acting consultant.'

Though he really wasn't in the mood for making polite conversation with a stranger. Especially one who was giving his dog wary looks. Was it the potential mud and hair she objected to? Because, in that case, she really wasn't going to enjoy a Scottish winter. Waking up to deep snow might look pretty and romantic in photographs, but the reality meant cold, wet, long journeys. Being fastidious didn't cut it, out here in the country. Designer clothing like the stuff she was wearing right now was no match for the wind and driving rain. You needed waterproofs and layers and strong boots. Had she even brought warm outdoor clothes with her? he wondered.

'I—um—wondered if you might be able to recommend a takeaway service,' she said.

'A takeaway?' Here? She had to be kidding. Did she really have no idea where she was?

'I don't mind whether it's pizza, Indian, Chinese or fish and chips. Anything,' she added, clearly trying to be helpful. Not quite snooty, then, but a bit posh and clueless. Sharing a house with her was going to be a trial, and he couldn't even let himself think about what it would be like at work. He was used to Clara, and he couldn't imagine anyone in her place.

Why was Georgina Jones even here? Did she think it would be romantic to swap her big-city lifestyle for a six-month sojourn in the romantic, pretty countryside? Maybe it'd be kindest to be a bit cruel now and burst that particular bubble. 'We're in the Pentland Hills, a good fifteen minutes' drive from the nearest big town. Even if you could talk someone into delivering it, the food would probably be cold before it got here,' he said.

'Oh.'

He knew he really ought to be nice and offer to cook something for her. But, after the day he'd had, he felt too miserable to eat. All he'd wanted to do tonight was curl up in front of the fire with his dog and maybe a small glass of single malt, and listen to the kind of bluesy rock that always soothed his soul.

Not that that was going to happen now. If he stayed down here with his new housemate, he'd have to make small talk. And Ryan wasn't particularly interested in small talk. Especially with someone he barely knew and who didn't seem to have anything in common with him.

'I'll bring your things in,' he said, a little more abruptly than he'd intended.

'I'm perfectly capable of bringing my own stuff in,' she said, lifting her chin.

'I'm sure you are, but Truffle is a bit of an absconder and I'd rather not risk giving her the chance to disappear into the hills or find the nearest bit of fox poo to roll in,' he said. He went over to the cupboard where he kept the dog's things, took out her leash, and then coaxed the dog over to him. 'It's OK, girl,' he crooned, kneeling down by the wrought-iron staircase, and scratched behind her ears with one hand while he slipped the end of the leash through its handle, securing it to the stairs. Then he clipped the leash onto her collar. 'It's just until we get everything indoors,' he said.

The dog's ears drooped.

'I'll take you out for a walk after, I promise,' he said. He hated seeing the disappointment in the dog's eyes, the way she suddenly looked cowed and scared. Yet again, he hoped someone would find her previous owners and make sure they never, ever, *ever* owned another dog again. Just as he hoped that the parents of the four-month-old baby he'd failed to save that afternoon would never have another child, or that if they did then social services would swoop in and give them the support they so desperately needed before it was too late.

With an effort, he pulled himself together. 'Let's get your stuff in.'

Georgina's car was completely unsuitable, all style and no substance. It would cope with the track for now, but when not when the surface had turned to liquid mud. To handle the narrow track to the cottage over the winter, she'd need a four-wheel-drive, not some pretty little convertible.

And just how many suitcases did you need to stay somewhere for six months? Had she brought the entire contents of London's shoe shops with her?

Not that it was any of his business.

It was still raining, and they were both wet by the time they finished bringing in her luggage.

And Ryan was feeling really guilty. She'd asked about a takeaway service. Just because he was too miserable to eat, it didn't mean everyone else was. Clearly she was hungry.

While Georgina was unpacking, he released Truffle from her temporary confinement, then rummaged in the freezer. Clara was going to kill him. She'd left him a list of the things she wanted him to get in to give a proper Scottish welcome to her job swap partner, but he hadn't had time to do it. He'd planned to do it in the morning, before the woman arrived. It hadn't even occurred to him that she might arrive early. There was half a loaf of bread in the freezer, some peas, a bag of chips, and an orange lump in a plastic box that might be home-made soup, except it didn't have a label and it was probably way past its use-by date.

The fridge was just as empty. It held milk and half a lump of cheese, and that was about it.

Grimly, he promised himself he'd go shopping for food tomorrow.

Georgina Jones had been on the road since nine this morning—and this wasn't the proper Scottish welcome his best friend had planned. He'd let Clara down.

Just as Clara had let him down.

He shoved the thought away. Clara had done what

was right for her, and he wasn't going to stand in his best friend's way. OK, so she felt like the only stable thing in his life right now apart from Truffle, but that wasn't her problem. And after all these years he should be used to being on his own. Used to the fact that people in his life tended to leave him—and that was his fault, too, because he couldn't let people close. He couldn't trust them not to leave him; his mother had died when he was six, her family hadn't wanted him and a string of foster parents had given up on him. He'd thought at one point that Zoe might be the one to change things; but he'd ended up pushing her away, too, and she'd left him—which pretty much proved he'd been right in the first place. Relationships weren't for him.

Though now wasn't the time for a pity party. He was absolutely fine on his own. He had his job, he had his dog—who was pretty much his whole family—and he had friends. He shook himself mentally. What did he call this woman, anyway? Georgina? Georgie? Dr Jones? *Hey, you*, was definitely wrong.

And why the hell was he worrying so much about this? Nothing fazed Dr Ryan McGregor. Well, almost nothing. Social niceties hadn't bothered him for years. Why should a woman he hadn't met until a few minutes ago put him in such a spin? How utterly, utterly ridiculous.

'Dr Jones?' he called. 'I can make some cheese on toast.'

She appeared halfway down the stairs. 'Seriously?'

He understood why she sounded so snooty. Cheese on toast wasn't exactly a proper meal. But then, if she'd wanted a proper meal she should've turned up on the day she'd agreed, not the day before. 'I was expecting you tomorrow,' he said. 'I haven't had time to go shopping.

Cheese on toast—or just toast, if you don't eat cheese—
is all I can offer.' He resisted the temptation to add, 'And
you're lucky I'm offering that.'

For a moment, she looked shocked, even dismayed.
But then she recovered and gave him a very professional-
looking smile. 'That'd be good. Thank you.'

This really, really wasn't what he'd promised Clara
he'd do, and guilt prickled through him. 'I might have
some soup to go with it.' He crossed his fingers, hoping
the orange gloop from the freezer really *was* home-made
carrot soup. He couldn't think what else it would be.

'Can I do anything to help?'

He wasn't sure whether she was being polite, or assuming that he was as useless at preparing meals as he
was at organising them. In either case, he didn't want her
under his feet. He didn't really want her here at all, if he
was honest; he just wanted to be on his own so he could
decompress. 'No. You've just driven up here from London. A day early,' he couldn't help pointing out.

'It's the day I agreed with Clara.'

No, it wasn't. He suppressed a sigh. 'You're meant to
be here on Sunday the sixth.'

'Saturday the fifth,' she corrected.

'Clara wrote it on the kitchen calendar. The one where
we write our shifts so we know when each other's working.' He walked over to the pinboard next to the cabinets,
the dog trotting at his heels. 'See? Sunday the— Oh,
crap.'

'What's wrong?' she asked.

'I assumed the calendar was like the one on my phone
and started on a Monday, not a Sunday. So at a glance
it told me you were arriving on Sunday, not Saturday.'
He groaned and raked a hand through his hair. What the

hell was wrong with him? He paid scrupulous attention at work. Nothing got past him. So why, when it came to his home life, was everything such a mess? 'I apologise.'

'It's OK.' Though the look she gave him could've curdled milk.

The next six months were going to feel very, very long indeed.

Thankfully she left him alone to make the food, though he also noticed that she didn't go and make a fuss of Truffle. Not a dog person, then. Her loss.

He thought of his nightmare case earlier and wished he could've turned the clock back. To the point where someone had noticed what had been going on in that house and given them enough support to stop it happening, or removed the baby into temporary care before it was too late. OK, so his own experience of foster care had been less than great—but foster care was still better than living in a house where someone might hurt a child.

The orange gloop in the box wasn't soup. It turned out to be mango sorbet. 'Oh, crap,' he said when he tasted it.

'What's wrong?' she asked.

'I don't think mango sorbet is meant to be heated.'

'No.' The word was expressionless—as was her face—but he'd seen the slight contempt in her eyes before she'd masked it.

Christ. Why hadn't he just asked Janie at the farm shop to drop off some supplies for him today? Probably, he thought wryly, because he'd been in a bit of denial that Clara was actually going and he was going to have to get used to someone else as a housemate until he found a place of his own.

He'd keep his promise to Clara later and organise a welcome meal for her job swap partner. Though he hadn't agreed to anything about actually *sharing* said dinner with the new housemate, so he could get Janie to sort out a touristy dinner for him, stick it in the microwave to heat it through for Dr Snootypants, and then take Truffle out so he didn't have to see the woman sneering at the local delica—

The smell of singed bread brought him back from his thoughts and he yanked the pan from under the grill.

Crap, crap and double crap.

Not only was the orange gloop not soup, he'd managed to burn the cheese on toast because he hadn't been paying attention.

Annoyed with himself, he cut off as much of the singed bits as he could, and dumped the edible bits on a plate.

'Cheese on toast,' he said, handing her the plate.

'Aren't you having any?' she asked.

'I'm not hungry.' He thought again of the baby who hadn't made it, the mum who'd dropped to her knees as if felled by an axe and wailed her loss into the floor, the dad who'd been white-faced with guilt and shame and horror and mumbled incoherent apologies.

No. He really, really wasn't hungry.

'I'll leave you to it,' he said, knowing he was being rude but just not being able to face making conversation.

'Thanks.' She took a breath. 'Is it OK to have a bath after I've eaten?'

'You mean, have I hogged all the hot water?' he asked, nettled.

'No. I mean I've had a long drive, I'm tired, and I could do with a bath and an early night.'

'Oh.' He'd been oversensitive and assumed she'd meant something she actually hadn't. 'Sorry,' he muttered. 'Sure. There are towels in the airing cupboard next to the bathroom, and the water's hot.'

'Thank you,' she said.

'I'll leave you to it,' he said again. 'I'll take Truffle out.'

She didn't make any anodyne comment about seeing him later. Which was absolutely fine by him. He didn't particularly want to make conversation with her. He pulled on a waterproof coat and wellies, then clipped the dog's leash to her collar and left. And hopefully when they got back she'd be in bed and he could just sit down with his dog and a glass of single malt, as he'd originally planned on his way home from the hospital, and get his head back into a better place.

Without the man who was the walking cliché of a dour Scotsman and his equally unfriendly dog, the cottage should've felt larger. Instead, it felt smaller. How weird was that?

Georgie hadn't really expected a housemate; and to have one who was so abrasive *and* had a nervous dog was... She blew out a breath. It was something that she wasn't going to tell her brother about, because otherwise Joshua would worry. Maybe she ought to make more of an effort with Clara's friend; but then again, Grumpy McGrumpface hadn't exactly made a lot of effort to be friendly with her, had he?

He'd made her something to eat, yes, but he'd done it with bad grace and even worse ability. The so-called cheese on toast was utterly inedible. She wasn't even going to try to choke it down. Or the heated-up sorbet, which in other circumstances she would've found hilarious but right now she just found irritating. Ryan Mc-

Gregor might be pretty to look at, but she had the feeling he was going to be the housemate from hell.

She scraped the revolting mess into the bin with a grimace. Just as well she'd bought bread at the service station. She made herself a couple of slices of toast—which she ate dry, because there wasn't any butter in the fridge, let alone anything else to spread on toast—then headed upstairs for a bath. Tomorrow was another day. And maybe tomorrow she'd see the really pretty side of Scotland, the reason she'd moved up here from London.

Though, when Georgie peered out of the window after her bath, she saw complete darkness. Scarily so. She couldn't even see the shapes of the trees in the neighbouring field against the night sky. And it was so *quiet*. There wasn't so much as an owl hooting; then again, would an owl bother flying around in all this rain? It trickled down the windowpane relentlessly.

Scotland was so very different from London.

Didn't they say you should be careful what you wished for? Georgie had wished to be out of London, and here she was. So she should just stop whining and try to see the good side of things, the way she normally did, instead of staring into the darkness and wondering if she'd just made a huge, huge mistake. But it really did feel like a mistake, now she was sharing a cottage in the middle of nowhere with someone who didn't really want her here and found it an effort to be polite, instead of living in her luxury flat with its stunning views over the river, with her elder brother and her niece only a couple of floors away in the same building. Why hadn't she appreciated it more? Was work going to end up being difficult, too?

Though she couldn't just give in and go home. She'd have to make the best of it.

* * *

The next morning, she showered and changed into a sweater and jeans, then peered out of the window to see blue skies scattered with fluffy white clouds—and actual hills. The view from Hayloft Cottage was amazing, hills and heather stretching out as far as the eye could see; but it also made her wonder how Clara was getting on in London. Had Clara, too, had a rough first night— kept awake by the noise of the traffic and the river and the brightness of the street lamps, in the same way that Georgie had been kept awake by their complete opposite?

Ryan was nowhere to be seen when she went downstairs. Neither was his dog. OK. If she left now, she wouldn't have to put up with his dourness when he came back. She'd drive into the city, check out where the hospital was so she was prepared for her first shift tomorrow, and then grab something to eat, do a bit of sightseeing, and find a supermarket.

She scribbled a note to say she was going out and would be back later. Then she locked the door behind her, climbed into her car, and headed for the city.

She loved her first view of Edinburgh, when she drove down the Royal Mile in the Old Town, with the castle looming over it and the Palace of Holyroodhouse at the bottom, and then through to the New Town with its sweeping Georgian terraces that reminded her a lot of Bath. St Christopher's Hospital was utterly gorgeous, a Georgian building made from mellow golden stone, with huge sash windows and a big triangular pediment above the front door and columns flattened against the wall either side.

Hopefully her colleagues would turn out to be as lovely as the building.

Once she'd worked out where the staff car park was and was sure she knew where she was going first thing tomorrow, she headed back into the centre of town and parked.

The first thing she was going to do was tick off a couple of things on her tourist wish list.

Edinburgh Castle was a good place to start; according to the internet search she'd done back in London, it would give her amazing views of the city, plus a chance to see the Honours of Scotland—the Scottish Crown Jewels— and the firing of the gun on the roof at lunchtime. She thoroughly enjoyed wandering around the castle. Costumed interpreters and the 'court musician' made it even better, and she loved the huge medieval hall, the jewels, the ancient Stone of Destiny and the spectacle of the gun firing.

She took a few photos to send to her brother, her parents and her best friend with the caption:

How amazing is this? Right decision to come to Bonnie Scotland!

A sandwich and a cup of tea revived her, and then she headed to the supermarket.

Did she shop for one or two? She had no idea what kind of arrangement Clara had with Ryan, and she had no idea what Ryan ate. Was he vegetarian? Did he have any allergies?

Maybe she'd cook for him today, as a way of trying to reach some kind of understanding with him. She didn't need him to be her new best friend; but being on civil terms would make both their lives a lot easier.

She had no idea what his shift pattern was; he'd said

something about writing it on the calendar, but she hadn't thought to check the calendar before she'd left for the city. OK. She'd cook something that she could reheat quickly, if necessary. A chicken and vegetable stew, so she wouldn't have to bother cooking the vegetables separately, and she'd serve it with microwaveable rice. A jar of pasta sauce and some dried pasta, too, in case he didn't eat chicken, and anyway it was always useful having some store-cupboard essentials for a quick meal. She paid for her shopping and then drove back to the cottage.

There was no sign of Ryan's car; when she opened the front door, there was no sign of the dog. She put the shopping away, and then she noticed the note on the table.

At the hospital.
Truffle with Janie.
Back later.
R

Who was Janie? His girlfriend?

Not that it was any of her business.

She glanced at her watch. It was a mile down to the village. Hopefully she could have a quick look round and take some snaps to send home, and be back here before it was dark.

She was about to lock the front door when her phone pinged.

The text was from Clara.

Thanks for the bubbles, chocolate and food order! London's great. Sorry for not warning you earlier about Truffle. She's a sweetheart but keep your shoes locked up because SHE CHEWS.

Pretty much what Ryan had said.

Georgie texted back.

I'll remember.

Hope your welcome dinner was nice. Ry's not the best cook.

Georgie blinked. Welcome dinner? But then, it wasn't Clara's fault that Ryan was difficult. She didn't want to make her job swap partner feel bad. Though now she was seeing the funny side of the heated-up mango sorbet and burned cheese on toast, it would be nice to have someone to laugh about it with. She was pretty sure that Ryan wouldn't see the funny side.

It was lovely, she lied. It's very pretty out here.

And you're getting on OK with Ryan?

Oh, she really couldn't tell the truth about that one.

Just fine.

Time for some deflection.

Good luck with your first shift tomorrow.

You, too.

So Clara had asked Ryan to make her a welcome dinner? Even though he hadn't, Georgie thought that maybe she ought to ask Joshua to do something nice for Clara.

It wasn't her job swap partner's fault that her housemate had let her down.

She walked down to the village and took a few snaps, then followed up with a text to Joshua, complete with pictures to show him how gorgeous the village was, and asked him to sort out something nice for Clara; and then sent the same pictures to her parents and to Sadie, her best friend.

The farm shop was still open, so she decided to go and have a quick look around. It was an amazing place, full of fresh food, local artwork and jewellery, and even some locally made cosmetics; she picked up an adorable knitted dachshund for her niece Hannah, and some enamelled earrings and honey hand cream that she knew her mum would love.

But when she went to pay, she saw the dog curled up in a basket next to the till. 'Truffle?'

The dog gave a thump of her tail. Just one, but at least it was recognition of sorts.

The woman at the till looked at her. 'Now, lass, I don't know you, but you clearly know our Truffle, so would I be right in guessing that you're my new neighbour— the London doctor who's swapped jobs with our Clara for six months?'

'Yes,' Georgie said. 'Georgina Jones—though please call me Georgie.'

'Nice to meet you, Georgie,' the woman said. 'I'm Janie Morris. You might see our sheep peering through your window at some point.'

Georgie blinked. 'Sheep?'

'My Donald and I run the rare breeds farm as well as the shop,' Janie said, 'and our sheep are in the field next to Hayloft Cottage. They're a wee bit nosy. Welcome to

Scotland.' She rang Georgie's purchases through the till. 'My mum knits the dogs.'

'It's for my niece,' Georgie said.

'I hope she'll love it.' Janie took a thistle-shaped piece of shortbread and wrapped it deftly in greaseproof paper. 'Here. Something to have with your coffee. I made it myself this morning.'

'Thank you.' Georgie was shocked to find herself close to tears. This was the nearest thing she'd had to a welcome since coming here, and it made her feel ridiculously homesick.

'Now, I know Clara and Ryan work all hours, so I'm guessing you'll be the same. If you need milk or bread, or you want me to put anything by from the deli for you, just send me a text and I'll drop it off. I'm only next door and I've got a spare key, just as you and Ryan have mine, so it's no trouble. We can sort out the money side of it later.'

'That's so kind of you,' Georgie said. 'Thank you.'

'Ryan will give you my number,' Janie said.

And that was where this whole thing would fall down. Georgie couldn't imagine Ryan doing anything to help. He was way too prickly.

'He's a nice boy, Ryan,' Janie added.

Maybe in a parallel universe Ryan was nice, but Georgie smiled in lieu of contradicting her new neighbour. Least said, soonest mended.

'I assume you came to collect Truffle?' Janie asked.

How did she explain that she'd had no idea Truffle was here—Ryan had said the dog was with Janie, but not who Janie was—and she knew nothing about dogs? 'I, um—yes.' Then she thought of a nice way of saying no. 'That is, if Ryan left her lead?'

'He did.'

No excuses, then. She'd have to collect the dog, now. Janie smiled at her. 'And you've some poo bags?'

'No,' Georgie said.

'That's no bother. I have some here.' Janie took a couple of bags from a drawer.

'Thank you.'

'I often look after Truffle for Ry, when he's at work,' Janie said. 'She's a good girl. Shy, but a sweetheart.'

When she produced Truffle's lead, Georgie was left with no choice but to take the dog back to the cottage with her. And Truffle did the biggest poo in the world, halfway up the lane. Followed by another one about twenty steps later. Oh, great. This wasn't Bonnie Scotland, it was more like Pooey Scotland, she thought wryly. She left the two bags on top of the dustbin when she got back to the cottage—hopefully Ryan would tell her where to dispose of them when he got back—and looked at the dog.

'I have no idea what to do with you. I don't know if I'm supposed to wipe your feet, or anything. So just please, please, don't do anything that will upset Grumpy Mc-Grumpface, and I will do—oh, whatever it is that dogs like. Not that you can tell me. But I'll find out.'

The dog regarded her solemnly.

'All righty. Let's go in.'

Once inside the cottage, Truffle went straight to her bed. Though, when Georgie started making the chicken stew, the dog ventured into the kitchen area and lay down on the floor, looking hopefully at Georgie.

'I'm not sure if I'm allowed to give you anything,' Georgie said. 'How about I put a bit of chicken to one side for you? Then I'll ask your owner if you can have it.'

Truffle wagged her tail, just once. Obviously the dog didn't have a clue what she was saying, Georgie thought—but it was nice to kid herself. To feel that at least someone here wasn't totally averse to her presence.

Christ, what a day. Reliving everything from the previous day, taking the police through everything he knew and everything the team had done to try to save the baby.

Ryan still couldn't forgive himself for failing.

When he parked in the courtyard and walked into the farm shop, he was surprised not to be greeted by his dog.

'Young Georgie collected Truffle earlier,' Janie informed him. 'She's a lovely lass.'

Dr Snootypants, more like. But maybe she'd been nicer with Janie than she had with him.

'She bought one of Mum's knitted dogs for her niece,' Janie added. 'I think she'll be good with the children on the ward.'

She'd better be. Otherwise he was going to ask for a replacement. 'Right. Well, thanks for looking after Truffle for me. I appreciate it.'

'I know you do, and you helped Donald fix the fence last weekend. That's what neighbours are for,' Janie said.

When Ryan walked into the cottage, Truffle bounded over to him, wagging her tail. And the house smelled amazing. Whatever Dr Snootypants was cooking, it was fabulous. Way, way above his own skill set.

'Hi,' she said, looking up from the sofa, where she seemed to be reading a magazine.

'Hi.' She'd picked up his dog so he needed to be pleasant to her, even though he wasn't feeling it. 'Thank you for picking up Truffle. I wasn't expecting you to do that.'

'I just walked her back here. She's been asleep a lot of the time.'

'Uh-huh.'

'I left the poo bags on top of the bin, because I didn't know where to dispose of them.'

She'd picked up poo? Now, that he hadn't expected. 'I'll sort it,' he said.

'Um, and I cooked dinner,' she said. 'It'll take five minutes to heat through.'

'Thanks, but you don't have to cook for me.'

'I don't know what arrangements you had with Clara,' she said, 'but it would make sense for us to share the chores.'

He grimaced. 'I'm not a great cook.'

'Clara said.'

He felt his eyes widen. 'You've talked to Clara?'

'She texted me and said she hoped my welcome meal was good.'

He hadn't even looked at his phone. No doubt there would be a text from his best friend asking what the hell he thought he was doing. 'Sorry,' he muttered, guilt flooding through him. He'd let Clara down—and he hadn't welcomed her job swap partner at all.

'I said,' Georgie added, 'that it was lovely.'

Something else she hadn't had to do: lie, to save his bacon. 'It was terrible.'

'It was different.' Her lips twitched at the corners. 'It's the first time I've been offered hot mango soup.'

For a second, he wasn't sure whether she was laughing at him; and then he realised that she was laughing at the situation.

And she had a point. It *was* absolutely ridiculous.

Shockingly, he found himself smiling back. 'I'm sorry,' he said. 'Maybe we got off on the wrong foot. I'm Ryan McGregor. Hello.'

'Georgina Jones, but everyone calls me Georgie.' She

got up from the sofa, and an unexpected wave of lust surged through him. Her skinny jeans showed off her figure to perfection. Georgie Jones was *gorgeous*.

And, when she shook his hand, again he felt that weird connection. It scared him as much as it surprised him; he hadn't expected to react to her in that way. He didn't want to, either; what was left of his heart definitely needed protecting.

'Good day?' she asked.

The aftermath of yesterday. It'd been far from good. 'It was OK,' he lied. And, before she could ask for more detail, he needed to distract her. 'You got on all right with Truffle, then?'

'Yes. I wasn't sure if you allowed her to have treats, so I didn't give her any of the chicken when I made the stew. But I did cook some and put it aside for her, in case you said yes.'

Again, she'd gone above and beyond, side-swiping his expectations. 'That was kind of you. She'll love it. Thanks.'

She shrugged it aside. 'I don't know what to do with dogs. But I already know no chocolate, and keep her away from shoes.'

'Like I said, I've had to replace three pairs, so far.'

'I'll remember to keep my shoes out of her reach. We're going to be all right with each other—aren't we, Truffle?' Georgie asked.

God, her mouth was pretty when she smiled. Soft and warm and inviting. It made him want to reach out and draw his thumb along her lower lip.

He shoved the thought away. This really wasn't the time or the place. And it was completely inappropriate.

'So she's a rescue dog?' Georgie asked.

'Abandoned,' he said. And it still broke his heart when he thought about it. He hadn't meant to say any more, but suddenly it came spilling out. 'No collar, no microchip. She was about six months when she was dumped. We think her original owners couldn't cope with the demands of a puppy, so they brought her to the middle of nowhere and left her. She tried to find her way home; she was nearly hit by a car when she found the main road, but thankfully the driver stopped in time, coaxed her into his car and took her to the nearest dog shelter.'

'Poor thing,' Georgina said.

'Indeed,' he said drily.

'How long have you had her?'

'Just over a year.'

'So she's about eighteen months old now?'

'Nearly two years,' he said. And again he found himself explaining. Something about Georgie's serious green eyes made him want to talk; which was weird, because he never reacted to strangers like that. He rarely opened up to his friends, either. What the hell was going on?

'She was rehomed, but she's a chewer—I'm guessing her first owners didn't occupy her enough, and when she's bored or stressed she tends to chew things. The people who took her on really wanted to keep her, but they had small children who didn't enjoy having their teddy bears stolen and shredded, so they brought her back to the shelter after the first couple of weeks and she ended up with me.'

'It was good of you to take her on.'

Truffle had been just as good for him. It had been Clara's suggestion and his best friend had been right, because having the dog around had really helped him through his divorce. His dog was the only real family he had now. Not that he planned to tell Georgina about his divorce or his past. 'She's a good dog. But because of her past she has a few trust issues.' Which was why he understood her so well.

'The house I planned to buy fell through at the last minute, and most rental places don't allow pets—especially a dog who's known to chew. And I don't want to put Truffle in kennels where she'll think I've abandoned her.' Because he knew just how it felt to be abandoned: again, not that he was going to tell Georgina about that. 'She needs to know her for ever home is with me. That's why Clara offered to let me stay with her for a bit, though the stair gate's there to stop Truffle going upstairs,' he said instead.

'That's kind.'

'That's Clara. She's lovely.'

She tipped her head to one side. 'You're close to her?'

Closer than he'd been to most people. Which was why it hurt so much that she'd done the job swap thing without even talking to him about it beforehand. She hadn't trusted him with how she was feeling; and he hadn't been a good enough friend to notice something was wrong. 'She's my best friend. The sister I never had.' Like the family he'd never had—and they hadn't stayed with him, either.

Georgie thought about it. The sister he'd never had. Right now, she guessed that Ryan was feeling as frustrated and angry with Clara as her own brother was with her. But maybe this job-and-life swap thing meant that Clara would support Joshua if Georgie would support Ryan.

'I'm a stranger,' she said, 'and I know next to nothing about dogs. But Clara and I are pretty much swapping lives. She'll be getting used to my life in London, and I'll get used to her life here. We're going to have to make the best of sharing. If you're really the world's worst cook, then I don't mind doing the cooking for both of us—but then the washing up will be your department.' She'd spent years being the one who did everything, to keep life easy; from now on, it was equals or nothing.

'That,' he said, 'sounds fair. Clara and I have a rota. We can tweak it to suit.'

'That's fine with me.' She paused. 'I stocked the fridge a bit. I wasn't entirely sure what to get, because I didn't know if you're vegetarian or have any allergies. If chicken stew isn't OK, I can cook pasta with tomato sauce to-night.'

'Chicken stew,' he said, 'is absolutely fine. No allergies and I'm not fussy.' Foster care had taught him very quickly not to be fussy about food. 'Thank you. And either I'll give you half of what you spent in the shop, or you give me a list and I'll pay for the next shop, so it's fair shares.'

'OK. I'll heat the stew and the rice and serve dinner at six,' she said. 'I'll, um, see you in a bit.' And she disappeared upstairs to her room.

Ryan was quiet and a bit distant when they ate.

The last time she'd shared a house with someone she didn't know was more than a decade ago, when she'd been a student. Making conversation had been so much easier back then: you'd ask your fellow students about their home town, their A-level subjects and their course, and then you'd talk about music and TV and films and establish what you had in common. She couldn't really do any of that with Ryan; it felt too much like being nosy.

Still, she had a good excuse for an early night. 'I'm on an early shift tomorrow, so I'll head for bed.'

'I'm on a late,' Ryan said. 'I would offer to take you into the hospital tomorrow morning, but there isn't a bus back here, so you wouldn't be able to get home until my shift finishes.'

'I'll be fine driving myself in,' she said. 'I did a recce earlier today. See you tomorrow.'

'See you tomorrow.'

He wasn't quite as abrasive tonight as he'd been the previous day, but there was definitely something upsetting him, Georgie thought. Something that had made those grey eyes full of misery. And he barely knew her, so he was hardly going to confide in her.

She wasn't going to brood about it. Or start asking about him: because she didn't want her own past becoming common knowledge and gossiped about, either.

At least she was starting at the hospital tomorrow. Once she was actually doing her job, something she was familiar with, she'd feel a lot better.

CHAPTER TWO

THE JOURNEY INTO work was lovely, with the sky streaked with pre-dawn colour. Georgie managed to park without a problem, then was introduced to everyone by the head of the Paediatric Department, had a copy of her rota from the department's secretary, and got straight to work in the Paediatric Assessment Unit.

'I'm Parminder—everyone calls me Parm,' the nurse in the assessment unit told her with a smile. 'I'm rostered on with you in the PAU today. Welcome to St Christopher's.'

'Thank you.' So not everyone at the hospital was going to be as difficult as Ryan, then. That was a relief. 'I'm Georgina, but everyone calls me Georgie.'

'So are you settling in all right, Georgie?'

'I think so. It's very different from London—I wasn't expecting to be living somewhere quite so rural,' Georgie admitted.

Parminder smiled. 'At least you're sharing a house with Ryan. He's such a sweetie.'

Were they talking about the same person? Ryan most definitely wasn't a sweetie, in Georgie's experience. He'd opened up to her a bit about his dog the previous evening, but he didn't seem to have much of a sense of humour, and she felt as if she was treading on eggshells around him. 'Uh-huh,' she said, trying her best to sound non-committal.

'He's really good with the staff. All the students love him,' Parminder said.

Why? Just because he was really good looking?

As if she'd asked the first question out loud, Parminder told her, 'He's always got time to explain things to them, and he's really good with the kids. And he treats the nurses with respect instead of behaving as if we're much lesser mortals.'

Ha. He'd behaved as if *she* was a lesser mortal.

'Mind you, he's been so quiet, this last year. Ever since his divorce. And he doesn't seem to have found anyone to share his life since then.' Parminder wrinkled her nose. 'Sorry. I shouldn't be gossiping.'

'Don't worry. I won't repeat anything you said,' Georgie reassured her. Though she didn't quite feel up to explaining that she and Ryan weren't exactly saying much to each other.

'And he's had a horrible weekend—I don't mean with you arriving,' Parminder said hastily, 'but that poor baby on Saturday morning.'

'Baby?'

'Didn't he tell you?' Parminder winced. 'We had a little one in with a non-accidental head injury.'

'Oh, no.' Georgie went cold. That was the sort of nightmare case every paediatrician dreaded.

And it made things drop into place: everyone she'd spoken to seemed to think that Ryan was lovely. But nobody would be lovely after a case like that. It was the sort of thing that would make anyone short-tempered.

Perhaps that was why she and Ryan had got off to such a rocky start.

'He had to come in yesterday to talk to the police,' Parminder said. 'And I guess it's the sort of thing you think about over and over, wondering if you could've done something differently to change the outcome— even though I don't think anyone could've done any more than he did.'

This didn't sound good. She had to ask. 'The baby didn't make it?'

Parminder swallowed hard and shook her head.

'I'm sorry,' Georgie said, feeling guilty about the way she'd reacted towards Ryan on Saturday. *Grumpy Mc-Grumpface.* She'd had no idea. She would never have been so frosty with him if she'd known he'd had such an awful day. No wonder he'd seemed all over the place on Saturday night, incapable of even making cheese on toast. She'd just assumed he wasn't happy about sharing the house with her and was being difficult on purpose.

Then again, he hadn't told her what had happened, so how could she possibly have known? She wasn't a mind-reader.

'It's not your fault, hen.'

It still didn't sit well with her. But right now there was nothing she could do to solve it, and she had a job to do. 'Let's see our first patient,' Georgie said with a smile.

That morning's caseload was similar to those she'd dealt with at the assessment unit in Hampstead: rashes, head injuries, a Colles' fracture and the first of the winter's bronchiolitis cases. But Georgie found herself really struggling to understand her patients' parents. In times of stress, anxious parents often gabbled their words, but with a strong Edinburgh accent on top Georgie found herself needing to ask people to repeat themselves over and over again.

Her new colleagues were kind and asked her to go to lunch with them in the staff canteen, but again she found them hard to understand; was it her, or did *everyone* in Scotland speak really quickly? Nearly all the conversations seemed to revolve around football and rugby—things she knew nothing about—or about people she didn't know, and she found herself growing quieter and quieter as the break went on.

How was she going to cope with six months of this? And how could she learn to fit into such a different environment? Back in London, everyone talked about movies and music and gin. She knew what she was doing there. Here…she felt really out of the loop.

It seemed she was going to have to learn a bit about football, she thought. And maybe she could try a charm offensive tomorrow. Bring in some brownies—which maybe she should've done today.

She called in to pick up some ingredients from the farm shop on her way back to the cottage, and discovered that Truffle was there.

'Are you sure you don't mind taking her home, lass?' Janie asked. 'Ry mentioned this morning that you weren't used to dogs.'

'I'm fine,' she said with a smile. And she could always vacuum the dog hairs out of the car.

'I haven't had a chance to walk her, mind. If you could?' Janie asked.

It couldn't be any harder than the previous day. At least now she had a better idea of what to expect. 'Can I buy some poo bags as well?' Georgie asked. 'It's just I'm not sure where Ryan keeps them.'

'Don't worry yourself, lass. Here.' Janie handed her a roll of poo bags. 'They're on the house. And I'm guessing it would matter to you, so I can reassure you they're the biodegradable sort and not the ones that just clog up the landfill.'

'Thank you. That's good to know.'

Truffle didn't seem to mind jumping in the back of the car, and Georgie dropped the bits she'd bought back at the cottage before taking the dog out for a walk.

'It's as much to clear my head as to exercise you,' she told the dog. 'It was one hell of a first day, even though the patients were all easy. I like my colleagues, but half the time I can't understand what they're saying. They must all think I'm stupid.' She sighed. 'And Ryan. I had no idea he'd had that terrible case on Saturday. Maybe it'll be easier between us this evening.'

They were back at the cottage before it got dark, and Georgie made a fuss of the dog before baking a batch of brownies and making a veggie chilli. 'It's hard to make friends when you can't even follow what everyone's saying,' she said to the dog. 'And, apart from Parminder, I got the impression that none of them think I'm up to Clara's standards. Or maybe I'm just being paranoid. I guess we'll just have to get used to each other.'

The dog nudged her, as if to say, 'Like you and me.' Georgie smiled and scratched the top of Truffle's head. 'Yeah. You're right. Tomorrow is another day.'

She microwaved half a pack of basmati rice to go with her portion of the chilli, and fed Truffle a cup full of the kibble she'd found in the cupboard. The dog curled up on the sofa next to her while she flicked through the TV channels.

'I have no idea if you're allowed up here,' she said, 'but

if you don't tell Ryan, neither will I.' Having the dog lean-ing against her, sharing warmth, felt surprisingly good. If anyone had told her five years ago that she'd quite enjoy having a dog around, she would've laughed. But she was rapidly becoming very fond of Truffle. There was a lot to be said for quiet companionship.

Ryan came in a couple of hours later.

'Good evening,' she said.

'Good evening. Thank you for picking up Truffle. Janie texted me,' he said.

'It's fine.' She paused. 'I made a veggie chilli—there's a bowl in the fridge and half a packet of microwaveable rice.'

'Thanks. That was good of you.'

'It's what we agreed.' And, if she was honest with her-self, she'd missed cooking for two. 'And there's a brownie on the plate.'

'From Janie?'

'No. I made some for the ward tomorrow. But I kept the chocolate well away from Truffle.' She paused. 'Parm told me about your case on Saturday.'

His face shuttered. 'Yeah.'

'That's hard.'

'Yeah.'

She folded her arms. For pity's sake, would he give her a break? 'I'm *trying* to be nice.'

He shrugged. 'I'm a guy.'

She'd noticed, though she stuffed the awareness right back in the box where it came from. She wasn't ready to notice his masculinity. She didn't need any complica-tions in her life.

'And guys don't talk about things? That's so stupid.'

She shook her head. 'Talking's a good safety valve. It helps us cope when we have a case that breaks our hearts.'

He looked at her. 'Or it makes us relive it.'

'As you wish. But some food might make you feel better. I've fed Truffle, by the way. I looked on the pack and weighed out what they said was the middle of the range for a dog her size. I hope that was all right.'

'Thank you.' He looked surprised. 'That was kind.'

'I could hardly feed her veggie chilli,' she pointed out drily.

'No, because onions and garlic are toxic for dogs.'

'Did you used to take your bad days at work out on Clara?' she asked.

'I…' He closed his eyes for a moment. 'No. Sorry. That isn't fair of me.'

At least he admitted it. She pushed down the fact that Charlie had never admitted when he was in the wrong. Charlie was dead and buried, along with a lot of her hopes and dreams. 'Sit down,' she said. 'I'll microwave stuff, and you talk. Otherwise it's going to fester in your head and you won't sleep tonight.'

'You're bossy,' he said.

She inclined her head in acknowledgement. 'Sometimes you have to be.' She busied herself sorting out the chilli and rice while he sat down, then put the bowl in front of him.

'Thank you,' he said. And then he didn't speak for a while, except to mutter that the chilli was good.

When his bowl was empty, she folded her arms. 'No brownie until you talk. And, just so you know, I make seriously good brownies. You'd be missing out on a lot.'

'Uh-huh.'

'Unless you're holding out for a dipping sauce of hot mango sorbet to go with it?'

For a moment, she thought she might have gone too far, but then he laughed.

And oh, that was a mistake.

When he wasn't being grumpy, Ryan McGregor was the most gorgeous man she'd ever met—including Charlie, in the years when she'd been young and starry-eyed and hopelessly in love. Ryan's grey eyes stopped being stony when they were lit with amusement, his face changed entirely when he wasn't being all brooding and severe, and his mouth suddenly looked warm and soft and tempting.

And she'd better stop thinking that way, because she wasn't in the market for a relationship. This six months in Scotland was all about getting her head straight and finding herself again, getting back to a place where people would just stop pitying her.

'I'll pass on the hot mango. But yes, please, to a brownie.' He paused. 'Saturday was grim. I take it Parm told you that the baby didn't make it?'

She nodded.

'It's the worst thing ever, when a baby dies,' he said. 'And it makes you feel so angry and so helpless, all at the same time. The parents were young and they didn't get the right support.' He closed his eyes briefly. 'Part of me wants to see them locked up for ever—I hate losing patients, and circumstances like these make it worse—but it's not my job to judge them. When you've got a baby who won't stop crying so you haven't slept properly for weeks, and you don't know what to do to stop the baby crying, and you're frustrated and miserable and desperate, sometimes you react in a way you wouldn't do if you were in your right mind. If you don't ask for help, or you don't know how to…' He blew out a breath.

'Well. There's a young man right now who has to live with the consequences of what he did for the rest of his life. A family ripped to pieces. A funeral to plan. Everybody loses.'

'What happened?' she asked softly.

'The parents brought him in, saying he'd had a fit. They didn't know what to do. I was trying to find out if anything like that had happened before, or if there were any warning signs they hadn't known to look for, if there was a family history—and then the mum broke down. It seems the baby woke them a lot during the night and the dad went in when the baby started crying in the morning… And he shook the baby.'

Georgie felt sick. A momentary snap with life-changing consequences. How would they ever forgive themselves—or each other?

'The eye exam showed retinal bleeding, but the blood tests didn't show up any bleeding or genetic disorders,' Ryan continued softly.

She knew what he was going to say next. 'And the scans showed subdural haemorrhage and encephalopathy?' Together with the retinal bleeding, it was the triad that usually proved non-accidental injury.

'The surgeon tried a shunt to reduce pressure in the baby's brain, but…' He shook his head. 'We need to do more to support vulnerable parents. Teach them that it's fine to ask for help. That the crying won't go on for ever, even though it feels like it—and, when it gets too much, then you just put the baby safely down in the cot and walk away for ten minutes, give yourself a chance to cool down. Call someone. Do breathing exercises. Sing.

Throw a cushion. *Anything* that helps you cope and keeps the baby safe.'

'Agreed,' she said softly. She reached across the table and squeezed his hand briefly. 'I'm so sorry.'

'Me, too. And I'm sorry I wasn't very nice to you when you turned up.'

'You'd had the shift from hell, and you weren't expecting me. And I wasn't very nice to you, either.'

'Dr Snootypants.'

She felt her eyes widen. 'Is that what you called me? Well, *you* were Grumpy McGrumpface.'

'Grumpy McGrumpface?' He stared at her in seeming disbelief, and for a moment she thought they were about to get into another slanging match.

But then he nodded. 'You have a point. I was miserable after my shift, guilty because I'd got it all wrong about when you were supposed to arrive, and the whole thing just snowballed. The snootier you were with me, the angrier I got.'

'And the more you acted as if I was a nuisance, the more sarcastic I got with you. We both got it wrong,' she said. 'Maybe we should cut each other a bit of slack and start again.'

'I'm still not a great cook,' he warned. 'When it was my turn to sort dinner, I served up ready meals. I bought them from Janie, mind, so it was as good as home-cooked, but I do microwave dinners only.'

'We'll work something out between us,' she said, and finally handed him the plate with the brownie. 'Eat this. From what Parm said, nobody could have done any more than you did on Saturday.'

'That doesn't make it feel any better. I still couldn't save the baby.'

'We all get cases that haunt us,' she said softly. 'Things we can't fix, no matter how hard we try, because they're just not fixable.'

'Is that why you're here?' he asked. 'Because you needed to get away from memories in London?'

Yes, but not quite how he thought it was.

It seemed that Clara had respected her confidence, and Georgie was grateful for that. But what did she do now? On the one hand, she didn't want him to think that the move here was just an idle whim. On the other hand, if she told him even part of the truth, there was a risk she'd end up having to field all the pity here as much as she had in London. What was the point of coming four hundred miles to repeat your mistakes?

He was looking at her curiously, his amazing eyes full of questions.

'It's personal,' she hedged.

'Uh-huh.' But he didn't try to fill the gap with small talk. He waited.

In the end, she caved. 'All right. But, if I tell you the truth,' she said, 'I want you to promise me on your honour as a doctor that it stays confidential. And,' she added, 'most importantly, I want you to promise you're not going to start pitying me.'

He looked surprised, then nodded. 'All right. You have my word.'

Was that enough?

She thought about it. She barely knew him, and the fact she hadn't picked up on the fact that her husband was a liar and a cheat showed that her own instincts weren't so great. But she'd heard the way Ryan's colleagues and his neighbour spoke about him. They seemed to think he was a man who could be trusted; and that decided her in his favour. She'd take the chance.

'I love my job and I love my family and I love my friends. But, last year, my husband was one of the emergency doctors on a rescue mission after an earthquake, and he was killed in an unexpected landslide.' She couldn't bring herself to tell Ryan the rest of it. About the baby her husband had made with his mistress, though he'd come up with excuse after excuse not to make a baby with her. Better to stick to a simplified version of the truth. 'Everyone at work was sympathetic and kind, but I hate being seen as "Poor Georgie"—it's been weighing me down. I know everyone means well, but the pity just stifles me. And I needed to get a break from it all. That's why I wanted to leave London.'

Ryan could understand that. It was exactly how he'd felt after his marriage had crashed and burned. Everyone had been so nice, and he'd been so miserable. Clara had been his rock, offering him and Truffle somewhere to stay until he could buy another house—Zoe had bought him out of their home—but, oh, the conversations that had stopped when he'd walked into the room and the pitying glances. He'd hated being talked about, even though he'd known people were trying to be kind rather than judging him.

'I get that,' he said softly. 'And I won't pry. It's none of my business.'

'Thank you.'

Telling him about her husband's death had clearly been painful. But in some ways she'd done them both a favour: she'd given him another reason to keep a bit of emotional distance between them and not give in to the growing attraction he felt towards her. Physically, she was gorgeous, but it was more than just looks. Something about Georgina Jones made him feel hot all over, made him feel like a teenage boy having his first crush.

And that wasn't a good thing.

He wasn't good at relationships. He already had one divorce under his belt—and he knew that the break-up of his marriage was largely his own fault. He hadn't let Zoe close enough, and he hadn't been able to put his own feelings aside to give her the family of her dreams. As a widow, Georgie was clearly grieving for her late husband and she didn't need the complication of getting involved with a man whose own heart was a complete and utter mess.

'Given that I'm not Clara, will sharing a house with me be a problem?' she asked.

'Problem?' Did she mean because she wasn't Clara, or that he had a girlfriend who might not be happy about his new housemate? Unless someone at the hospital had filled her in, she wouldn't know. He took a deep breath. OK. She'd been honest with him. He'd be honest with her. Plus perhaps he needed to reassure her that he wasn't going to see her as easy prey. 'I'm divorced, and I'm not looking for another partner. So you'll be quite safe with me. You'll be staying in Clara's room and we both have our own bathrooms.'

'Thank you—though I'm not looking for another partner, either,' she said. 'You're safe with me, too.'

So why was it that he didn't feel safe in the slightest? What was it about Georgina Jones and her clear green eyes that made him feel he needed to build an extra barrier around his heart, and build it fast?

He shook himself. 'Well. Now that's out of the way, perhaps we can be good—' No, friends wasn't the right term. 'Housemates,' he finished.

She lifted her mug of coffee. 'I'll drink to that.'

Something reckless in him made him say, 'I have a better idea if we're drinking to something.' He went over to the cupboard and extracted a bottle and two glasses.

'I'm afraid I'm not really a whisky drinker,' she said when he brought them over to the table with a small jug of water.

'This isn't like the stuff you get in the supermarkets,' he said. 'It's a properly matured single malt. Try a sip—and then try it with a little water. It'll be smoother and let the subtle flavours come through.'

'Trust you, you're a doctor?' she asked wryly.

'Something like that.' He poured a small amount of the amber liquid into the two glasses, handed one to her and clinked his glass against hers. 'To housemates.'

'To housemates,' she echoed, and took a tiny sip.

When she grimaced, he added a little water to her glass. 'Try it now.'

'Oh—that's very different,' she said, looking surprised. 'It's quite nice. I can't believe that a little bit of water makes that much difference.'

'I won't bore you with the full details, but one of my housemates at university was a chemist,' Ryan told her. 'He wrote his dissertation on the smokiness of whisky and what affects the flavour, and he tested out his theories on the rest of the house.'

'Sounds like fun,' she said. 'So did you study in Edinburgh?'

'Yes, and I trained here, too. I assume you went to London?'

'Yes. I followed in my brother's footsteps,' she said. 'Actually, I work with him now. Technically, he's my boss.'

'And he was OK about your job swap?'

'We had a bit of a fight about it,' she admitted. 'He thought I was making a mistake.'

'And you don't?'

'No. I needed a change,' she said. 'Though I do feel bad about deserting him.'

'Clara's an excellent doctor and she gets on well with everyone. She'll do a great job,' Ryan said.

'I don't mean professionally,' she said. 'I'm Joshua's back-up for Hannah—his daughter,' she clarified. 'He's a single dad. He does have a nanny, but I'm there if he needs me. He lives in the same apartment block as I do, a couple of floors up.' She bit her lip. 'I feel guilty for being here because I've deserted them. But if I'd stayed in London I would've gone crazy.'

Yeah. He'd been there. Truffle had got him through the worst bits. The loneliness and the misery and wondering why he couldn't be the man his wife needed. But he'd come to terms with it now. He was who he was. And if that meant being alone, so be it. 'Sometimes you need to do what's right for you, even if it puts someone else out.' Which was, at the end of the day, all Clara had done, too. 'Your brother will forgive you. Since he worked with you, he must've seen how all the pity was getting you down.'

'Maybe.' She yawned, and blushed. 'Sorry. It's either the whisky or all this country air. And I'm on an early tomorrow. I'm off to bed.'

Ryan had to stifle a sudden picture of her curled up under the duvet, her hair spread over a pillow. *His pillow.*

For pity's sake. He was too old to start suffering from insta-lust. And he was just going to ignore the physical attraction. Nothing was going to happen between them. She was a widow. Still grieving. She'd made it very clear that she wasn't looking for a relationship. He didn't want one, either: he had no intention of setting himself up to fail all over again.

So he'd just have to look a bit harder to find a house that would suit him and Truffle, and put a little bit of distance between himself and Georgie as soon as he could.

CHAPTER THREE

'YOUR NEW HOUSEMATE's a bit on the quiet side,' Alistair, one of the junior doctors, said to Ryan on Tuesday morning when they grabbed a cup of coffee in the staff kitchen.

'Georgina's all right,' Ryan said.

'But she's not Clara, is she? She's not the life and soul of the party.'

'It's early days. Give her a bit of time to get used to us. Anyway, the most important thing is how she is with the children,' Ryan reminded him.

'Aye, and their parents,' Alistair agreed.

It made Ryan think, though, when he was back in his office, wrestling with paperwork. Being the new person in the department wasn't much fun. He hadn't made anywhere near enough effort at making her welcome; he hadn't even done the welcome dinner he'd promised Clara he'd sort out. Georgina had been really kind to him yesterday, when he'd opened up about his nightmare case. It was his turn to show some kindness and include her in the department a bit more. Maybe he could organise a team night out or something.

Georgina Jones had clearly had a rough year, being a widow. So he needed to do what Clara would do, and make his new colleague feel at home. He pushed aside the thought that it wasn't the only reason why he wanted to make her feel better. Yes, she was physically attractive. And the way she'd teased him about hot mango sorbet had made him feel lighter of spirit, a feeling he'd forgotten; part of him wanted more, but part of him was scared spitless at the idea. He'd failed in his marriage, and it wasn't as if Zoe was difficult. She wasn't high-maintenance or spoiled; she'd just wanted him to love her and make a family with her, to raise children with her. They weren't whims or wishes out of the ordinary.

Yet he hadn't been able to do it.

He'd loved his wife, but he just couldn't let down his barriers enough to let her properly close, the way a husband should. He didn't want children and he knew he'd be rubbish as a father—with his past, how could he be otherwise? He hadn't a clue how a real father behaved.

Having a family with his wife should've been the easiest thing in the world. He hadn't done it. His relationship had crashed and burned. And how much harder would it be to start a relationship with someone who'd experienced such a terrible loss already? Where he might not measure up against her late husband?

So it was better not to let his thoughts even go there. Whatever his libido might like to hope, it wasn't going to happen.

Georgie had a case that worried her. Baby Jasmine was a day and a half old, and had been feeding well so she'd gone home with her mum the day before; but, unlike most newborns, she'd slept completely through the first night. This morning she was lethargic, not opening her eyes. When the midwife arrived for her follow-up visit, Jasmine still wouldn't feed and then she started trembling. On the midwife's advice, Jasmine's parents had brought her straight into the paediatric assessment unit at St Christopher's.

Small babies could get very sick, very quickly; and Georgie really wasn't happy when she noticed Jasmine's breathing becoming more rapid.

It could be dehydration, it could be a blood sugar level problem, or it could be a virus. But, most importantly, she needed to keep Jasmine's breathing supported. She called up to the special care baby unit to get Jasmine ventilated and monitored, and ordered a battery of tests.

But later that morning all the tests came back clear. No dehydration, no blood sugar problems, and none of the other obvious things.

What was she missing? Some kind of allergy, perhaps?

She really needed input from someone with more experience. Even though the person she needed help from wasn't the easiest to deal with, her patient's needs came first. So she went to find Ryan in his office. 'Dr McGregor, do you have a moment, please?'

He looked up from his desk. 'What can I do for you?'

'I've got parents in with a very sick baby and I can't work out what's wrong. As you have more experience than I do, I was hoping you might see what I'm missing,' she said.

He nodded. 'Run me through it.'

She explained Jasmine's symptoms. 'I've got her on prophylactic antibiotics, in case it's a bacterial infection, but the SCBU says she's unresponsive, her face is swollen, she's deteriorating, and there just doesn't seem to be a reason for it because all the tests have come back clear.'

'A swollen face,' he said thoughtfully. 'Given that she's a newborn and there's progressive lethargy, it might be a urea cycle disorder. It's pretty rare—maybe one in a hundred thousand babies suffer from it, so that'd be six or seven each year in the UK—but try checking her for argininosuccinic aciduria.'

'So get her blood tested for ammonia?' she asked. At his nod, she added, 'I'm on it. Thanks.'

'Let me know how it goes,' he said. 'And it's nearly lunchtime, so would you like to grab a sandwich with me?'

That was the very last thing she'd expected. He'd done his best to avoid her at the cottage. Had he had some kind of sea-change and decided to make her feel welcome in Edinburgh? Or was this the real Ryan, the man she hadn't met yet—the man Parminder had said all the team adored?

She decided to give him the chance. 'If you could tell me everything you know about argininosuccinic aciduria, then yes, please,' she said. 'Otherwise, I'll be spending my lunchtime online, researching it.'

'Come and get me when you've ordered the tests,' he said. 'You've enough time for a sandwich and coffee before the results come back, and I'll fill you in.'

She sorted out the tests, then went to the canteen with him.

'How are you settling in, other than having a case that would make anyone panic slightly?' he asked.

'OK. I'm starting to understand more of the accent up here, provided I can persuade people to slow down a bit when they talk.' She gave him a rueful smile. 'And I think I'm going to have to learn a lot about football.'

He grinned, surprising her—and she was also shocked to feel as if her heart had just done an anatomically impossible somersault. When he was nice, he was very nice indeed. Then again, she knew his flip side: Grumpy McGrumpface.

Behave, she told her libido silently. *He's off limits.*

'Be very careful about which team you pick,' he said.

'London?' she asked hopefully.

He laughed. 'Which gives you at least fifteen to choose from.'

'I think,' she said, 'I'll have to find a list of them and toss a coin.' And she needed to concentrate on work, before her libido got the chance to have control of her tongue and came out with something inappropriate. 'So can you run me through argininosuccinic aciduria?'

'It's an autosomal recessive trait where the child lacks the enzyme argininosuccinic lyase,' he said, 'so that means either both her parents are carriers, or one of them maybe has the late onset form.'

'So between them they would have a one in two chance of a child being a carrier, a one in four chance of the baby having the condition, and a one in four chance of the baby not being affected at all,' she said.

He nodded. 'Symptoms usually start at birth, but might not be noticed for a few days. If it's less severe, it might start later in childhood or even adulthood. The lack of the enzyme causes excess nitrogen in the blood, in the form of ammonia.'

'Which damages the central nervous system. So that's why she'd be lethargic, refusing to eat, and her breathing's too fast,' Georgie said thoughtfully.

'I'd check her liver, too,' he said. 'And there's also a risk of neurological damage.' He paused. 'If it *is* argininosuccinic aciduria, would you like me to talk to the parents with you?'

'As I've never come across a case before, yes, please,' she said.

'I've only seen one case,' he said, 'when I was a student. But the baby was fine and he still comes in to see us regularly, so that should help reassure Jasmine's parents.'

'Is there a support group?' she asked.

'Yes, so we can give her parents the details.'

'Thank you.' She finished her coffee. 'Sorry to be rude, but I'd better get back. I won't be happy until I get those test results.'

The results provided the answer: there were indeed raised levels of ammonia in Jasmine's blood. Georgie went to the SCBU to update them and start treatment for Jasmine, then went to find Ryan. 'Thank you. Your diagnosis was spot on,' she said.

'Let's go and see her parents,' he said.

She introduced him to Jasmine's parents. 'Dr McGregor's the acting consultant in the department, and thankfully he's seen a case like Jasmine's before, so he was able to suggest different tests and we know what's wrong now,' she said.

'So is she going to d—be all right?' Jasmine's dad corrected himself, looking anxious.

It was the big fear of every parent with a newborn, and her heart went out to him.

'We're treating her now, so hopefully she'll start turning a corner today,' Ryan said reassuringly.

'So what's wrong with her?' Jasmine's mum asked.

'It's something called argininosuccinic aciduria,' Georgie said. 'It's caused by an enzyme deficiency.'

'When your body digests protein, the protein is broken down by enzymes into amino acids, and some of the acids turn into ammonia,' Ryan explained. 'Usually ammonia is excreted from the body when you urinate, but the enzyme deficiency means that Jasmine's body can't do that so the ammonia builds up in her blood.'

'Can you treat it?' Jasmine's mum asked.

'Yes. She's still very poorly and it's going to take a couple of weeks before she'll be able to come home again,' Georgie said, 'but we know what it is now, so we can give her the right treatment.'

'First of all, we need to filter her blood to get rid of the ammonia,' Ryan said, 'and then we need to find the right balance of milk protein feeds and medication to keep her ammonia levels under control.'

'And she'll be all right?' Jasmine's dad asked.

'There can be complications, but she should be fine,' Ryan said.

'Argin—' Jasmine's mum shook her head.

'Argininosuccinic aciduria,' Georgie repeated.

'I've never heard of it,' Jasmine's mum said.

'It's rare—about one in a hundred thousand babies get it—but there are children living perfectly normal lives with the same condition,' Ryan reassured her. 'When I was a student, I treated a baby with it here, and he's doing just fine. He's at high school now.'

'Is there a family history of any urea cycle disorders for either of you?' Georgie asked.

Jasmine's dad shook his head. 'Not that I know of—though my parents had a little boy about six years before I was born, and he died when he was a couple of days old. They thought it was cot death.' His face filled with terror. 'Oh, no. Does this mean he had the same thing that Jasmine has, this argino thing?'

'It's a possibility,' Georgie said, wanting to reassure him, 'but the difference is that we know what it is, so we're treating her and she's not going to die. If your brother had it, it sounds as if nobody picked up on it and he didn't get treatment.'

Jasmine's mum looked awkward. 'I'm adopted, so I don't know if there's anything in my blood line. I'm not in touch with my birth family.'

Georgie squeezed her hands. 'It's fine. We can offer you some tests to see if either of you is a carrier or has a problem with the enzyme, and if that's the case then if you have more children we'll know to test the baby straight after the birth.'

'I'm just so...' Jasmine's mum dragged in a breath to cut off the words.

'Of course it's scary,' Georgie said. 'She's a day and a half old. But she's in the right place and you both did all the right things. You brought her here in good time.'

'We're giving her the right treatment and we're expecting a good outcome,' Ryan said, 'but I do need to tell you that sometimes argininosuccinic aciduria can cause neurological damage. Right now it's early days so we can't give you a definitive answer, but it might be that because of what's happened Jasmine takes a little bit longer than average to reach the baby milestones—rolling over, sitting up, that sort of thing.'

'But we're keeping a very close eye on her,' Georgie said. 'Once we've got her stabilised, we can work with a dietician to find out the right amounts of protein and medication she needs. You can give her the medicine with an oral syringe, just as you would with infant paracetamol. Though you'll need to monitor every single thing she eats, and she'll need regular follow-up appointments as she grows to make sure that she's still getting the right amount of protein and medication.'

'It sounds a bit daunting,' Ryan added, 'but it's workable.'

'We'll do everything we need to, to keep her well,' Jasmine's mum said.

'Everything,' Jasmine's dad agreed.

'That's great. We can also give you an emergency plan to follow if she picks up a bug that makes her sick or gives her diarrhoea, which will obviously affect what she eats and how her body processes it,' Georgie said. 'The main thing is, you're not alone. We're here, and we can put you in touch with a support group so you can talk to other parents whose families have been through exactly what you're all going through, and they can re-assure you and give you practical advice.'

'We really appreciate that,' Jasmine's mum said. 'So can we see her now?'

'Of course you can. She's got a lot of tubes and can-nulas in,' Georgie said, 'but you can sit by her and talk to her and stroke her head and hold her hand. I know it's not quite the same as cuddling her, but she'll know you're there and it'll comfort her.'

'And our nurses are more than happy for parents to be involved in their babies' care, so you'll be able to help with things like washing her face and changing her nappy,' Ryan added.

'I'll take you up and introduce you properly,' Geor-gie promised.

'Thank you,' Jasmine's parents said, looking relieved.

'It looks scarier than it actually is,' Ryan said. 'But just remember that Jasmine will get a little bit better every day. Before you know it, she'll be back home.'

Georgie popped into the special care baby unit after her shift, too, just to see how Jasmine was getting on; and then she drove back to the cottage, pleased that her second day had gone well. Even though it was raining again, everything was fine until she was heading up the track to the cottage; then she felt a jolt, and after that the car started to pull strongly to the left-hand side.

Oh, no.

She was pretty sure that meant the car had a puncture. She'd never actually been in the car with a puncture before. Her dad had shown her how to change a tyre, but that had been years ago and she could barely remember how. The middle of a muddy track, in the rain, when it was starting to get dark and there was no place for anyone to pass her so she was completely blocking the road, wasn't exactly the best place to change a tyre for the first time.

Not that she had any other options. She'd just have to get on with it.

She stopped the car, put her hazard lights on to warn anyone else who might need to use the track that she was there, and used her phone as a torch so she could inspect the wheels on the passenger side of the car. Just as she'd feared, there was a hole in the front tyre; clearly she'd damaged it when she'd bumped through the pothole. Changing the tyre it was, then.

But, when she looked in the well of the boot, the spare wheel she'd expected to see wasn't there. All she could see was a repair kit with a compressor and a bottle of goo. According to the packaging, it would act as a temporary repair until she could get the car to a garage or tyre fitter to replace it, as long as the hole in the tyre was less than four millimetres in diameter and the side wall of the tyre was fine. Otherwise the kit wouldn't work and the tyre would have to be changed.

She went back to measure the hole. Six millimetres. She blew out a breath. Great. The repair kit wouldn't work and she didn't have a spare wheel. Now what?

The rain was coming down a lot faster now, and the wind was getting up, driving the rain right into her. She was soaked to the skin—and she was stuck here until she could get that tyre changed.

Shivering, she climbed back into the car. Please let there be a signal for her phone, so she could call a roadside assistance service. She wasn't sure if they'd come out to people who weren't actually members, but she hoped at least they'd be able to put her in touch with someone who would come out and help.

Then she noticed the sticker on the corner of the windscreen: it seemed that the hire car came with membership of a roadside assistance service. One hurdle down.

Though her relief was short-lived. When she rang them, they advised that they couldn't come out to rescue her for three hours.

Three hours.

She was tired, she was wet, she was cold, she was starting to get hungry, and right at that moment all she really wanted was a hot shower and a cup of tea. Clearly she was going to have to wait for a lot longer than she wanted to. But other people had much worse to contend with; she was lucky, she reminded herself, and she had a lot to be thankful for.

A few minutes later, she became aware of headlights travelling up the track behind her, and then she heard the sound of a car horn.

Time to upset the neighbours, she thought ruefully, and jumped out of the car, ready to apologise for the fact that she couldn't move her car and it was still going to be another couple of hours before the assistance company could rescue her.

Then she recognised the car.

Ryan.

'Georgie? Are you all right? What's happened to your car?' he asked, climbing out of the car to join her.

'I've got a puncture—and the hole's too big for the repair kit to work,' she said. 'Sorry, I know I'm blocking the track, but I'm afraid it'll be another couple of hours before the assistance company can get to me.'

'Do you want me to change the tyre for you?' he asked.

'Thanks for the offer, but there isn't a spare—just a repair kit,' she said.

'Ah, the joys of modern cars.' He rolled his eyes. 'Which tyre?'

'Front left.'

He went to inspect it, then came back. 'You're right— the repair kit definitely won't work on that. Look, I know the track well so I can avoid the pot holes more easily. Do you want me to drive your car back to the cottage for you?'

She bit her lip. 'Isn't that going to—well—cause problems with the car if you drive it on a flat tyre?'

'Not if I take it very slowly and carefully,' he said. 'Why don't I drive it back and you follow me in my car? Then you can wait for the assistance guys at the cottage.'

The offer sounded genuine rather than grudging, and he wasn't sneering; so it would be sensible to accept. It meant she could have a hot shower and dry clothes and a cup of tea. 'Thank you. I accept.' What she really wanted was a hug, but she was pretty sure that asking Ryan for a hug would be a step too far.

Without further comment, he handed her his car keys, then drove her hire car down the track.

Georgie followed him in his car—and discovered that Ryan listened to really loud rock music when he drove. He'd seemed so closed off that she'd expected him to drive in silence, or listen to podcasts on developments in paediatric medicine. But rock music... That was something they had in common, even though she preferred the poppier end of the spectrum. Maybe that would help them connect better and make the house-share easier.

Back at the cottage, she rang the assistance company to tell them she'd moved the car. When she came downstairs from the shower, Ryan was standing by the kettle.

'Thank you for rescuing me,' she said.

'No bother. Go and sit by the fire and keep Truffle company. I'll bring you a cup of tea. How do you like it?'

Just for a moment, she was really, really aware of the curve of his mouth. How sensual it was. How soft his lips looked. Then she shook herself, realising that he was waiting for an answer. An answer about *tea,* not about how she liked to be kissed. Oh, for pity's sake. She needed to get a grip. Ryan McGregor was the last person she should be fantasising about. 'Medium strength, a bit of milk and no sugar, please.'

'Done. Sit yourself down.'

When Georgie sat on the sofa next to the fire, Truffle curled up by her feet, as if to try and warm her up a bit. Georgie reached down to stroke the top of the dog's head, and the dog licked her hand.

This was so far from her life in London.

And, now she was safe and warming up again, she was beginning to think that maybe there was something good about the wilds of Scotland. Something that would help to finally heal the sore spots in her heart.

Ryan busied himself making two mugs of tea.

Georgie had looked so lost, so vulnerable, when she'd got out of the car. And he'd really had to stop himself from wrapping his arms round her, holding her close and telling her that everything would be OK.

He already knew that she hated pity.

Though this wasn't pity. It was something else. Something he didn't want to explore too closely, because he knew there could be no future in it. Georgie was going back to London in six months' time; and in any case he wasn't looking for any kind of relationship. That would be the quickest way to get his heart broken again—well, not that he had much of a heart, according to Zoe, because he hadn't been sympathetic when her biological clock had started ticking unexpectedly. He'd reminded her that they were both focused on their careers; she'd countered that people could change their minds.

He couldn't change his. He just couldn't see himself as a father.

And deep down he thought there was something wrong with him. Something unlovable. OK, so his mum had only left him because she'd been knocked off her bicycle by a car and hadn't recovered from the head injury; but after she'd died her parents had rejected him, and none of his foster parents had been prepared to work with him.

The only two real constants in his life were his best friend—Clara, whom he loved dearly, but as a sister rather than as a life partner—and Truffle.

He was quite happy as he was, just him and his dog.

Nobody to desert him again. He wasn't lonely, deep down. He *wasn't*.

Ryan shook himself mentally and took Georgie's mug of tea over to her.

'Thanks. You've no idea how much I fantasised about this when I was standing in the rain, staring at the hole in my tyre,' she said.

Not as much as he'd been fantasising about what her mouth might taste like.

He pushed the inappropriate thought away. 'What's the news on Jasmine?' he asked. Work at least was a safe topic.

'She's holding her own. Hopefully she'll start to turn a corner now. And thank you again for your help with the case.'

'No problem.' He paused. 'You're good with parents. Reassuring.'

'I hope so.' She grimaced. 'Though I let them down with the diagnosis.'

'This was rare—it's only the second case I've seen,' he said. 'And you came straight to me and asked for help instead of putting your patient at risk.'

'Of course I did. Our patients should always come first,' she said. 'So I'd always ask someone with more experience rather than trying to muddle through and getting it wrong.'

Ryan liked her attitude.

He liked *her*, too. And he was going to have to squash the feelings that were starting to seep through every time he looked at her.

Thankfully they were interrupted by the roadside assistance company, who'd brought a spare wheel and sorted out the car for her. By the time she came back in, he'd got his wayward feelings firmly back under control and compartmentalised everything. And now life was just how he liked it: with no complications.

CHAPTER FOUR

THE NEXT MORNING, Georgie made coffee and bacon sandwiches for breakfast, to thank Ryan for rescuing her the
previous evening.

'I hope my dog hasn't been pestering you,' Ryan said,
eyeing the Labrador sternly.

She had, but Georgie didn't want to drop the dog in it.
'I hope it was all right to give her a tiny bit of bacon. She
looked so pleading—and I can't resist those big brown
eyes.' She didn't think she'd be very good at resisting a
certain pair of grey eyes, either; but that would mean
trusting someone again, and finding out about Charlie's
betrayal had really knocked her ability to trust, so it was
better not to start something she couldn't finish.

'A little bit of bacon's fine,' he said with a smile.
'You're getting used to her, then.'

'And she's getting used to me.' Georgie was surprised to realise how much she was enjoying having a
dog around. Why had she never thought of getting a pet
before?

Then, when she reached to take another sandwich
from the plate, her hand brushed against Ryan's—and
it felt as if she'd been galvanised.

'Sorry,' she muttered, pulling away. But, when she

looked up, there was a slash of colour across his cheek-bones—as if he, too, had been affected by that brief touch. For a moment, her brain felt scrambled and she didn't know what to do or say. They were almost strangers. Most of the time they'd spent together so far, they hadn't even got on well. But she was very, very aware of how good-looking Ryan was—especially when he smiled.

He'd already told her he was divorced and he wasn't looking for a partner. She wasn't looking for a partner, either. So it was disconcerting to find herself wondering, *what if?*

She pulled herself together—just—and said lightly, 'I'm on a late shift today, so I'm going in to see the car hire people this morning to ask if they'll swap the car for me.'

'Good idea,' he said. 'I'll organise dinner.'

'It's OK. I'll have something at work,' she said.

'I promised Clara I'd do you a welcome dinner,' he said. 'I'm not planning to make it myself. I'm buying it from Janie's.'

Refusing would be throwing his welcome back in his face. And, as they were just starting to get on, she didn't want to risk going back to how it had been on her first night here. 'OK. Thank you. I don't have any allergies or major dislikes.'

'So that's haggis for two, then?'

The Scottish national dish: Georgie knew haggis was a kind of pudding made from sheep's heart, liver and lungs, mixed with onion, oatmeal and suet. She'd never tried it, but she wasn't sure she could bring herself to eat it.

'I, um…' She bit her lip.

He grinned. 'Don't tell anyone, but haggis isn't really my thing, either.'

He'd been teasing her? She looked at him, outraged. And then that awareness crept back in. The little nudge of her subconscious, wondering what a candlelit dinner with him would be like, The cottage would be all romantic and gorgeous in the soft light; and maybe then he'd put some music on and they'd dance together...

Oh, help. She was really going to have to get a grip. Fantasising about her housemate was a bad idea.

'I'd better go,' she said. 'I cooked breakfast, so you're on dish duty.'

And that little bit of sassiness was enough to break the spell and stop her blurting out something stupid.

She managed to sort out the car; and her shift was calm until late afternoon, when a mum rushed in with her four-month-old baby, looking distraught.

'Lewis has got a temperature, and a rash that won't fade, and...' She dragged in a breath.

'Let's have a look,' Georgie said gently, recognising the signs of panic and wanting to calm her patient's mum down. 'Hello, gorgeous boy.'

The ear thermometer confirmed that he had a fever, and when she gently undressed him the rash was obvious—but it didn't look like the meningitis rash that his mum was clearly worrying about.

'So how long has Lewis been ill?' she asked.

'I've thought he was coming down with something for the last three or four days,' Lewis's mum said. 'He went off his food, he's got a bit of a cough and he's been grumpy. I thought it was just a cold starting, but then I saw the rash and I just panicked.'

'I can tell you now it's not the meningitis rash.' Though

Georgie wasn't going to worry the poor woman further by pointing out that meningitis wasn't always accompanied by a rash. 'Did he have any spots in his mouth yesterday? Greyish-white ones?'

'I don't think so, but I'm not sure.'

'OK. Did the rash start at his head and neck?'

Lewis's mum nodded.

'I think he has measles,' Georgie said. 'Do you have any other children?'

'Yes, a two-year-old and a four-year-old.'

'May I ask if they've had the vaccination?' She crossed her fingers mentally, hoping that the answer was yes; otherwise there was a strong chance the poor woman would have three under-fives at home with measles next week.

'Yes. My gran had measles when she was small and it left her deaf in one ear, so I had the boys vaccinated and made sure they had their boosters. Lewis was going to have it when he's old enough. I...' She shook her head. 'How can he have *measles*?'

'Measles has come back in the UK over the last couple of years,' Georgie said. 'It's a mixture of people not giving their children the booster vaccination, or thinking they don't need it because measles isn't around any more, and then visiting other countries where measles is rife. It's pretty contagious, so maybe you've been somewhere with other children and one of them was coming down with it and their mum didn't realise because the rash hadn't come out yet.'

'It must've been at the wear-'em-out play place we went to on Saturday. I let Jake and Ollie run about and do all the slides and the ball pit, and Lewis was asleep in his pram.' She bit her lip. 'So Lewis could end up deaf, like his great-gran?'

'Hopefully not,' Georgie said.

'Can you give him anything to stop it? Antibiotics?' Lewis's mum asked.

'I can give him immunoglobulin, which will give him a short-term boost of antibodies and then hopefully the virus will be less serious,' Georgie said. 'Measles is a virus, so antibiotics won't do a thing to help, and I'm afraid you just have to let it runs its course. The good news is that Lewis should be better in about a week, but try to keep him away from others if you can for the next three or four days, to avoid spreading the infection. How much does he weigh?'

'Seven kilos—dead in the middle for his age.'

'That's great. It means he's big enough for you to be able to give him paracetamol to help get his temperature down; and you need to give him lots of cooled boiled water to drink,' Georgie said.

'What about his cough?' Lewis's mum asked.

'He's too young for honey and lemon, and frankly cough mixture won't help him—your best bet is to put him in a steamy bathroom for a few minutes, or put a wet towel over the radiator in the room,' Georgie advised. 'If his nose is blocked, you could try giving him nasal saline drops—that'll help thin the mucus, so he'll find it easier to drink. But not all babies tolerate the drops well, so you might find it makes him worse.'

Lewis's mum looked anxious. 'And you think he'll be all right in a few days?'

'Yes,' Georgie said. 'But if you think he's developing an ear or eye infection, or he's got diarrhoea or vomiting, go to your GP—ring them first, though, to warn them he has measles, because it's really contagious. And if he's struggling to breathe or it's painful, or he coughs up blood, then bring him straight back here.'

She sorted out the immunoglobulin injection and administered paracetamol, then printed out an information leaflet for Lewis's mum to take home.

The rest of her shift was less eventful, and she drove back to Hayloft Cottage; once she was out of the city, away from the lights, she could see the stars; they were so much brighter than they were in London, and she couldn't remember the last time she'd seen the sheer beauty of the night sky like this. Even though she missed London, she was beginning to see why Clara loved it out here.

When she got back to the cottage, Truffle greeted her with a waggy tail and Ryan actually smiled at her. Her stomach swooped, just as it had this morning when they'd accidentally brushed hands.

'So how was your day?' he asked.

'Fine—apart from a four-month-old baby with measles.'

'Ouch.' He winced.

'I gave him HNIG, so hopefully that will lessen the severity,' she said. 'Fortunately his siblings had had both vaccinations, so they should be OK.'

'It's shocking, seeing measles back in the hospital,' he said. 'Apparently there were four times as many cases in the first three months of this year as there were last year.'

She nodded. 'The poor mum saw the rash and thought it might be meningitis—thankfully it wasn't, though measles is serious enough. Her grandmother's hearing was damaged by measles, so she's well aware of what it could do. Oh, and you'll be pleased to know that Jasmine's responding well to treatment. I popped up to see her before I came home.'

'That's good to hear,' he said.

'Something smells nice.' And it was strange to come home to someone else making dinner. Charlie had always left everything to her. Ryan had said earlier that he only did ready meals, but it was good not to be the one who had to do all the thinking and the planning and the preparation.

'Can I do anything to help?' she asked.

'No, you're fine. Sit down.'

The first course was smoked salmon from the farm shop, served simply with a salad drizzled with honey and mustard dressing. 'It's locally bred and locally smoked,' he confirmed.

It was followed by Scottish beef in beer, a pale yellow mash Ryan told her was 'neeps and tatties'—a mix of swede and potato, mashed with butter and black pepper. And then the last of the local raspberries, with the most amazing salted caramel ice cream.

'It's lovely,' she said. 'And it's so nice to have someone else sort out dinner for me. Charlie never cooked or did housework.'

Which was pretty selfish, Ryan thought, since they'd both been full-time doctors. Yet Georgie didn't seem like the sort who'd let someone get away with behaving like that. She'd definitely bitten back when Ryan had pushed her too far.

'Was he an expert at burning food, too?' he asked lightly.

'No. I don't think he knew where the toaster was kept, let alone how to use it. He just...' She grimaced. 'Never mind. You shouldn't speak ill of the dead.'

That was a really odd thing for a widow to say, Ryan

thought. As if her marriage hadn't really been that happy. There was something in her eyes...

But she'd closed the subject down. If he pushed now and asked her personal questions, then she might ask him personal questions, too; and he didn't want to talk about his past. About the wreck of his marriage. About the way he just couldn't connect with anyone.

They chatted about the hospital and Georgie's replacement car for a while, and then she yawned. 'Sorry. It must be all the country air making me so sleepy. I'll see you tomorrow,' she said.

When she left the room, Ryan sat on the sofa with Truffle sprawled over his lap. 'You like her, too, don't you?' he asked.

The dog licked his hand, as if to agree.

'But I hardly know her, and she has a real life four hundred miles south of here,' he said. 'And I'm not good at relationships. It wouldn't be fair to either of us if I started something. I'd make her miserable and...' He grimaced. 'Better to treat her as if she's just any other member of the team.'

And that was precisely what he did, the next day, when he did the ward rounds with Georgie and Alistair.

'As you've not been rostered together, you probably haven't met properly, yet, so I'll introduce you,' Ryan said. 'Georgie, this is Alistair, our F2 doctor—he's doing his final rotation with us. Al, this is Georgie—she's Clara's job swap partner.'

Once they'd done the social niceties, they started on the ward round. Ryan let Georgie lead, because he wanted to see how she worked.

He was pleased to notice she was great with the children and with any parents who happened to be visiting, greeting them warmly and listening to what the children said about how they were feeling. Before each patient, too, he noticed that she checked Alistair's knowledge of symptoms and treatments, and she let him take the lead on a couple of the more straightforward cases—just as Ryan would have done.

Warm, confident, capable and good at training. She was the perfect paediatric doctor, he thought. And then he had to suppress the thought that popped into his head about how she might be great with him, too. *Not* happening, he reminded himself.

After the ward round, Ryan worked with Alistair in clinic, but he'd made sure to invite Georgie and Parminder to lunch, too, to help Georgie get to know the team a bit better.

'So you don't like football or rugby?' Alistair asked Georgie over lunch.

'I don't like sport, full stop,' Georgie admitted. 'Watching or playing.'

Alistair looked aghast. 'How do you keep fit, then?'

'I make sure I walk ten thousand steps a day,' Georgie said, flashing the watch on her wrist, which doubled as a fitness tracker, 'and in London I did a Zumba class with my best friend.'

'I go to a Zumba class,' Parminder said. 'It's on Monday nights. Do you want to come with me next week?'

'Thanks, I'd love to,' Georgie said, smiling broadly.

'You could come training with me, too, if you like,' Alistair offered.

'Al, you big show-off, of course she doesn't want to train with *you*.' Parminder rolled her eyes. 'He does triathlons,' she told Georgie. 'That's just radge.'

'Radge?' Georgie asked, mystified.

'Crazy,' Ryan supplied. 'It's Edinburgh slang.'

'And Al is the living definition. Miles of running, miles of cycling, and then a freezing cold swim—for miles. Totally radge,' Parminder said.

'Ye've a lot to learn, hen,' Alistair said, hamming up the accent. 'Anyway, I'm not the only one with radge tendencies. There's Ryan tromping through the hills with his wee dawgeh even when it's stoating.'

'Stoating?' Georgie asked, wondering if her colleagues were making up words just to tease her, or if she was going to have to learn a whole new language up here.

'It's stoating when the rain's coming down so hard that it's bouncing back off the ground,' Alistair said.

'And remember this is the dog who chewed Clara's favourite shoes,' Parminder added. '*Three pairs* of them.'

'I replaced them all,' Ryan protested. 'Though it's not my fault if Clara leaves her shoes where Truffle can get them.'

'Just be warned, hen. That wee dog's not to be trusted,' Alistair said in a stage whisper. Then he smiled. 'So what else did you do for fun in London?'

'Music, theatre and history,' Georgie said promptly.

'Well, you're a wee bit late for the Fringe,' Alistair said. 'But there are good theatres and music venues in the city.'

'And there's loads of history,' Parminder added. 'Have you been to the castle yet?'

'On my first morning here,' Georgie said with a smile, 'and I loved it.'

'And there's Mary King's Close—part of a seventeenth-century street that was buried when they built the Royal

Exchange,' Alistair added. 'You might like that. If you don't mind the ghosts…'

Ryan groaned. 'Don't start on about non-existent things, Al.'

'He doesn't believe in Nessie, either, poor man,' Alistair confided to Georgie. 'No romance in his soul, that one.'

'Talking of romance, you have to visit Doune Castle,' Parminder said. 'I take it you've seen *Outlander*?'

'I love that series,' Georgie said. 'My best friend Sadie and I binge-watched it together. You can't get better than a gorgeous man in a kilt.'

A dark, brooding Scotsman. She couldn't help looking at Ryan, who was the epitome of a brooding Scotsman. He was sitting right opposite her. If she moved her foot, she'd be touching his: and the thought made her feel hot all over.

Georgie had going all pink and flustered—and yet again Ryan noticed how pretty she was. His libido seemed to have taken over his brain; he could imagine how *he* could make her all flustered, with little teasing kisses that would make her as hot and bothered as he felt right now.

Think of cool things, he told himself.

Going ankle deep into a hidden puddle.

Trudging across the hills with Truffle when the wind and the rain wouldn't let up.

And how soft Georgie's mouth was…

Oh, help. He really needed to get a grip.

'A kilt and a plaid.' Parminder fanned herself.

'Don't forget a jacket and cravat,' Georgie said.

'And boots,' Parminder added with a dramatic sigh.

'Gorgeous men in period costumes. Totally irresistible,' Georgie said.

Ryan had a kilt. Zoe had bought it for him years ago, to wear at a wedding. Why he'd even packed it when he'd left their house, he had no idea.

He shoved the thought away. He was *not* dressing up in a kilt to bowl Georgie over. They were colleagues. They were at work. *Focus,* he told himself.

Parminder laughed. 'Seriously, Georgie, Doune Castle is spectacular and so are the views. With or without a man in a kilt.'

'It's already on my list,' Georgie said with a smile. 'I was planning to go exploring a bit on my day off.'

So why, Ryan thought, did he have to mess it up by saying, 'Maybe I could drive you at the weekend and show you around the area a bit?'

Georgie's eyes widened. 'I can't ask you to give up your time off.'

Which was his cue to back off. But his mouth seemed to have other ideas. 'Dogs are allowed at some of the historic places, and Truffle's always up for a walk somewhere different. There's the beach, too.'

'Edinburgh has a beach?' Georgie looked surprised.

'Several. There's loads of golden sand at Portobello,' Parminder said.

Shut up, shut up, Ryan told himself. But the words came spilling out despite himself. 'Then maybe we could go to the seaside on Saturday and Doune Castle on Sunday—or whenever our off-duty coincides.'

'I'd like that,' she said, giving him a shy smile.

Oh, help. That smile made him feel even hotter. He needed to get the team involved before he really got out of control. 'I was thinking, we could do with a team night out.'

'If there's dancing, I'm so there. If only to laugh at Al's two left feet,' Parminder said with a grin.

'I'll teach you to dance, Al,' Georgie promised.

And how ridiculous was it that Ryan felt a huge twinge of jealousy?

'You'll be kind to me, hen, won't you?' Alistair asked, clearly trying his best to look piteous.

Ryan wasn't feeling particularly kind towards his colleague, right then. What did Alistair think he was doing, flirting with Georgie like that? 'It doesn't have to be dancing. We could go to an open mic night or something.'

'Dancing works for me,' Parminder said.

'Then can I delegate the organisation to you, Parm?' Ryan asked.

'Sure. I'll find us a ceilidh, so Georgie can go to a proper Scots dance,' Parminder said.

'That,' Georgie said, 'is a brilliant idea.'

'Thanks, Parm. Put the details on the team group chat when you've got them. And maybe we can do a pizza and bowling night or something before then to welcome Georgie to the team.'

'Yes, boss,' Parminder said with a grin.

This, Georgie thought, was the best day she'd had in Edinburgh so far: the first one where she was starting to feel part of the team, accepted for who she was. Nobody pitied her, the way they did in London. And it was all thanks to Ryan, who'd drawn her in to the group.

As for Ryan himself… She was just going to have to damp down the flares of attraction that kept threatening to overwhelm her.

Even if he was gorgeous.

Even if she could imagine him wearing a kilt and plaid, looking incredibly sexy.

Even if she did find herself wondering what it would feel like to dance with him…

Back at the cottage that evening, when Ryan came home from taking Truffle out, he took out his phone and flicked into his calendar. 'I'm off duty on Saturday and Sunday. What about you?'

'I'm off, too,' she said.

'Then we could go to the beach on Saturday and Doune on Sunday, if you like,' he said.

'It's not fair to make you give up your weekend to play tourist with me.'

'It's no bother. Truffle's always up for a walk somewhere different. We can't take her to Doune, but she loves the beach.'

The rest of the week flew by, and on Saturday morning it was unseasonably warm; Ryan drove them to Portobello straight after breakfast. Georgie loved all the Georgian buildings with bay windows and turrets; when they got to the beach itself, the tide was out and there were children making sandcastles, and people on paddle-boards.

Ryan crouched down by Truffle. 'I'm trusting you, mind,' he said. He ruffled the top of the dog's head, and let her off her lead. Georgie took her shoes off, enjoying the feel of the warm sand under her toes and the wind in her hair. It was ages since she'd been to the beach and she'd forgotten how much she liked the faint taste of salt in the air, the scent of the ocean and the sound of the waves swishing over the sand.

As they walked her hand brushed against Ryan's and

for a nanosecond she actually thought about curling her fingers round his. What would it be like to walk barefoot on this beach with him at sunrise, hand in hand? Then maybe they'd stop and watch the changing colours of the sky, and turn to each other and kiss…

The urge to hold his hand grew stronger, but fear held her back. Supposing he rejected her? How awkward it would be. Then again, if he held her hand, that was an even more scary proposition: it would be the beginning of a relationship, and she'd have to take a leap and trust him. After Charlie, she wasn't sure she wanted to risk trusting again.

Truffle circled back to them at Ryan's whistle; she clearly loved the freedom of running around at the beach. Ryan took a Frisbee from his backpack. 'Fancy a game with me and Truffle?' he asked.

Keeping it light and not intense: that worked for her. 'Sure.'

It was the first time she'd seen Ryan look really relaxed, out here with the sun and the sand and his dog. He looked younger, more carefree; his grey eyes crinkled at the corners when he smiled, and he was so gorgeous that she found herself catching her breath. And when he caught her gaze, she felt seriously hot under the collar. She hadn't reacted to anyone like that since she was a teenager.

Right in the middle of their game, another dog came bounding past. Truffle dropped the Frisbee and took off after the other dog, clearly relishing a game of chase, and ignored Ryan completely when he called her name.

'Oh, no.' He took a box from the backpack and whistled. 'Truffle! Come here! Sausage!'

Truffle took no notice whatsoever, until the other

dog's owner called him back to heel. Only then did she seem to remember that she was supposed to be here with Ryan and Georgie and trotted back to them.

'What am I going to do with you?' Ryan asked, feeding her a bit of sausage. 'Well done for finally coming back. But we're going to have to work on recall again.' He glanced at Georgie, his eyes narrowing slightly. 'I'm not spoiling her, by the way. I'm rewarding her for doing what I asked, even though it took her a while. If I shouted at her, she'd associate coming back with being shouted at and that'd make her less likely to come when I call.'

She remembered what he'd said about Truffle being abandoned as a pup. Scaring her off was the last thing he'd want to do. 'Hey, I'm not judging. I know nothing about dog training.' She put her hand out to stroke the top of Truffle's head.

Again, her fingers brushed against his. And this time she noticed the slash of colour across his cheekbones. So did he feel this same wobbly sensation in the pit of his stomach? If so, what were they going to do about it?

'I'll just give Truffle a drink.' He took water and a bowl from his backpack.

Ryan McGregor was a man who truly took care of his own.

So unlike Charlie, who'd seemed so caring when they'd first got together but had turned out to be totally careless with her heart.

The more Georgie looked back on her marriage, the more she wondered how she'd missed all the clues. All the little things—like never making her a mug of coffee when he'd made one for himself—that she'd told herself to ignore because they just meant her husband had a tough day in the Emergency Department: maybe they hadn't been that at all. She'd let herself be blinded by his charm and hadn't seen the self-centred man behind it all. The man who'd lied to her, and who'd lied to his mistress. The man who'd let her down time after time, and she'd made excuses for him because she'd so wanted their marriage to work.

How could she trust her judgement any more?

'Are you OK?' Ryan asked, looking up at her when he'd put the empty bowl back in his backpack.

'Uh-huh,' she said.

'Sometimes you just need the sound of the sea to clear your head,' Ryan said, and she wondered what had made him feel that he needed his head cleared. His ex, maybe? Did he miss her?

She realised she'd spoked aloud when Ryan said, 'I miss bits of Zoe. I miss the good times.' His eyes were unreadable. 'Do you miss Charlie?'

She had a choice: to keep living the lie she'd told in London, or to tell the truth and clear a way for herself to move forward, to finally get over her past. 'I miss him,' she said. Ryan's expression was still absolutely inscrutable. 'But, like you, I miss bits. The good bits.'

Which sounded as if there had been bad bits, too, Ryan thought. 'Sometime the bad stuff gets in the way and you don't mean to hurt each other,' he said.

'I don't think Charlie meant to hurt me. He just didn't consider me,' she said, looking bleak. 'I look back and I wonder if I fooled myself right from the start and saw the man I wanted him to be, not the man he really was. And I wanted my marriage to work, so I ignored things I maybe should've made a stand about.'

It sounded as if she'd been really struggling; as well

as losing her husband she was facing up to the fact that her marriage hadn't been what she'd hoped it would be. And all the while people had been pitying the grieving widow. That was enough to mess with anyone's head.

'Sometimes you need space to think about what you really want,' he said. 'And the sea's good for that. I used to walk here when I was thinking about how things were with me and Zoe. Before I got Truffle.' When he'd seen the children playing on the beach, seen the families, and wondered what was so wrong with him that he couldn't give Zoe what she wanted.

'I'm hoping that distance will stop all the pity,' she said.

Which told him she didn't want him to pity her, either. If he offered her a hug, would she see it as pity? Or would she return that hug, hold him close?

And, if she held him close, what then? Where would it go? There was a lot more to her past than met the eye, and he didn't want to trample on a sore spot—or let her down, the way he'd let Zoe down.

So, even though he had an idea that she too felt that crazy spark whenever they accidentally touched, he didn't know how to deal with it.

'Sometimes you have to learn to leave the past behind,' he said. 'Try and get past the regrets and the might-have-beens. And then you can make the most of tomorrow.'

'When you've made mistakes, it's hard to trust yourself again,' she said, sounding so vulnerable that he wanted to wrap his arms around her and keep her safe.

But he hadn't kept Zoe's heart safe, so how could he be sure that he'd keep Georgie's safe? What she'd just said... 'You're so right,' he agreed. 'I think all you can do is give it time.'

'I've already given it time. It's been more than a year, for me,' she said.

'Me, too.'

They were almost strangers, Maybe they'd be good for each other; maybe they wouldn't. But right here, right now, he wasn't risking it. 'Let's go and grab a coffee,' he said. 'There's a dog-friendly café up the road.' Somewhere with people close by so they wouldn't be so intimate.

The café was right on the edge of the beach, with a slate roof, dormer windows and a turret. Inside, it was all scrubbed wood tables, teamed with bentwood chairs; on the walls were fairy lights and framed old photographs.

'Cappuccino with no chocolate on top, right?' he asked.

Georgie was impressed that he'd noticed what she drank in the canteen at work. 'Thank you.'

The coffee turned out to be excellent. He held up his mug, saying, *'Slàinte mhath.'*

'Slanj-a-va?' she repeated.

He smiled. 'It's Gaelic for "Good health"—and that was a pretty good first attempt at pronouncing it. Anyway, to friendship.'

It was kind of a warning that he wasn't prepared to offer anything more. But she wasn't ready to risk her heart again, so she'd take that. 'To friendship,' she said.

The next morning, Ryan made a fuss of Truffle, promising to take her out later, before driving Georgie the hour to Doune Castle.

It had been a while since he'd last visited, but the building was spectacular: a fourteenth-century courtyard castle with a gatehouse that towered a hundred feet up, made of reddish-brown stone with white quoins.

'That's stunning,' Georgie said, looking awed. 'I mean, I've seen it on TV as the setting for several series, but I still didn't expect it to be this magnificent.'

Part of him wanted to reach out and take her hand—to walk hand in hand through the castle with her. But the idea made him feel edgy; there was so much that could go wrong. So he fell back on the safety of dry facts. 'It was built for Robert Stewart, the first Duke of Albany. It has one of the best-preserved halls in Scotland.'

He was really glad he'd checked his phone the night before and looked up facts and figures, because it meant he could talk to her about history instead of blurting out his feelings as they wandered through the castle.

'Look at that fireplace! It's taller than me, and it's massive. I can just imagine sitting here at a really long table with a trencher in front of me, with dishes of carved meats and flagons of ale,' she said as they walked through the Great Hall.'

He'd always thought that he didn't have much imagination, but suddenly he could see her sitting beside him in a wine-coloured velvet dress, her golden hair long and wavy and topped by a crown, and a choker of emeralds to match her eyes…

Spending time with Georgie made him feel different. It made him see his surroundings through fresh eyes; he'd grown so used to the hills and the sunrises and the sheep that he'd taken them for granted, but Georgie had made him look at things differently, really see them. The wide expanse of Porty Beach, the imposing ruins here, then clambering over the uneven path by the battlement to look out over the river to the Menteith Hills and Ben

Lomond in the distance. How had he forgotten how amazing this was?

Then she tripped, and he grabbed her to keep her safe.

Oh, help. Being this close to her, feeling the warmth of her body against his—it made him want more.

She looked at him, and time seemed to stop. He was oh, so aware of how wide her eyes were, how soft her mouth was, how easy it would be to dip his head and kiss her.

He was at the point of doing exactly that when there was a cough beside them, followed by a plaintive, 'Do you mind letting us get past?'

Saved by the tourist, he thought as he dropped his arms from round Georgie and moved so the man and his family could get past.

'Are you OK?' he asked. Georgie looked shaken. Because of her near trip right next to the castle battlements and a sheer drop, or because of the almost-kiss? He was too scared of the answer to ask.

'I'm fine,' she said, sounding a little breathless. 'Thank you for stopping me falling.'

'You're welcome,' he said, but he was still tingling all over from touching her.

Once they were back on the ground floor, they wandered through the gift shop, and Georgie seemed highly amused by the basket of coconut shells for visitors to borrow—and the children running round in the courtyard outside, banging the coconut shells together and pretending to be horses.

'I still can't quite get over the fact that I'm walking round the Monty Python castle. It's my dad's favourite film. Would you mind taking a snap of me on my phone in front of the castle, so I can print it off and send it to him with some of those coconut shells?'

'Sure,' he said. And her delight in doing something nice for her dad made him feel as if something had cracked in the region of his heart. What would it be like to have that sort of bond with your family, that sort of closeness, all those shared memories? He wasn't envious, exactly; more wistful.

If his mum hadn't been killed, his life would've been so different. Maybe she would've made it up with her family; maybe she would've found a new partner and he would've had a dad, or even a baby brother or sister.

Nobody had loved him enough to want to keep him for long. Then again, he'd had the chance to make a family with Zoe, and he hadn't let his heart open wide enough to embrace a family. So really it was just as much his fault. What was wrong with him, that he couldn't let people close? Why was he so scared of rejection? Why couldn't he move on, away from his past?

He pushed the thoughts away and concentrated on her, taking the photograph as she'd asked.

'You could act a bit out in front of the curtain wall and I'll film it,' he said. 'Then you can send it to him after you've posted the shells to him.'

She laughed. 'Genius. Thank you.'

It was impossible not to laugh as she recreated a bit of the film.

'Did you ever think about acting?' he asked.

'No. I always wanted to be a doctor. And it wasn't just to copy my big brother—I wanted to make a difference and really help people,' she said. 'When I did my rotation, I was quite tempted by obstetrics, because I love those first precious moments of a new life. But I love working with children.'

Was it just working with kids, though? Was her biological clock ticking? He'd decided a long time ago that he didn't want kids. If Georgie did, then that was a good reason to keep things strictly platonic between them—otherwise he'd be letting her down, the same way he'd let Zoe down.

At the same time, the more time he spent with her, the more time he wanted to spend with her. She made him see the world in a different way.

She was here for six months. She wasn't necessarily looking for for ever. Maybe—the base of his spine tingled with longing—maybe they could have a fling. Be each other's transition person. Get this thing out of both of their systems and move on.

'What about you?' she asked.

'I wanted to make a difference, too.' Though he wasn't going to tell her that he'd wanted to help all the children who didn't have anyone else. That was too personal.

'We're on the same side, then,' she said. 'Right—giddy up.' She clicked her tongue and made the coconut shells sound like horses' hooves. 'Come on. You, too.'

How could he resist?

It was utterly ridiculous, pretending to be on horseback and galloping all the way back to the car. He probably looked like a total idiot. But Georgie was laughing and enjoying herself, and he realised that this was *fun*. He couldn't remember the last time he'd done anything like this, if ever.

Her eyes crinkled at the corners as she smiled at him. And it made his stomach swoop.

Once they were back the cottage, he took Truffle out

on a long walk. Georgie joined them, but when they got back to the cottage he noticed how wet her feet were.

'Tomorrow,' he said, 'we need to get you some proper walking boots.'

'I'm on an early shift,' she said, 'and tomorrow night I'm going to Zumba with Parm.'

'We'll nip out in our lunch break, then,' he suggested. 'And Truffle agrees, don't you?'

The dog woofed softly. 'So that's settled, then,' he said with a smile.

CHAPTER FIVE

ON MONDAY LUNCHTIME, Georgie met Ryan in his office and they grabbed a sandwich on the way down to the city to choose some walking boots.

To her surprise, the man in the shop actually measured her feet, got her to try on three different pairs of boots along with thick, comfortable socks, and them asked her to climb over a 'bridge' in the middle of the shop that had an uneven rocky surface before bunny-hopping down a slope to see if the boots fitted properly.

This was definitely not something she'd ever done in London.

She wasn't used to wearing something close-fitting around her ankles and it felt weird; but, if it meant her feet stayed dry when she went out on the hills with Ryan and Truffle, she could put up with it.

'You need to wear them indoors for a couple of hours a night for the next week,' the shop assistant said when she'd chosen them, 'and if they're not comfortable just bring them back and tell us what you don't like about them, and we can find something that suits you better.'

'Thank you,' she said with a smile.

'And make sure you keep them out of Truffle's reach,' Ryan added.

After their shift, Ryan went home to walk the dog while Georgie went out to the Zumba class with Parminder.

'I'm so pleased you asked me to join you,' Georgie said.

'You're welcome. It's not easy to fit into a new department. And everyone loved Clara. It was a bit of a shock when she told us she was moving to London for six months and you were coming here in her place,' Parminder said. 'We had no idea she was so unhappy here.'

'Sometimes it's not so much being unhappy, more that you need a change so you can move forward from a situation,' Georgie said. 'She spoke really highly of everyone in the department. It wasn't anything that any of you did or didn't do.'

'Thanks. Because I just kept thinking that I must've been such a rubbish friend to her, and I feel bad about that. I won't push you to tell me anything you don't want to, though anything you do say to me I'll keep confidential,' Parminder said.

'Thanks,' Georgie said, appreciating the overture of friendship but not wanting to go back to the same problems she'd faced in London. Parminder would be kind, but Georgie didn't want to fight off another deluge of pity. She wanted to be *herself*. 'I just needed a change from London. Let's just say my personal life was a bit…' She wrinkled her nose. How did you describe becoming a widow and then discovering that the husband you'd thought was devoted was actually a cheat and a liar? 'Tricky.'

'Fair enough.' Parminder smiled. 'And at least Ryan's a nice housemate.'

'He's been kind,' Georgie said. At least, after the first couple of rocky days.

'I always used to think that he and Clara would get together after his marriage broke up,' Parminder said. 'But they're more like brother and sister. Clara said she loves him to bits as a friend, but there's just no chemistry between them and she doesn't fancy him.'

Whereas whenever Georgie let her mind wander she found herself thinking about Ryan McGregor. About how beautiful his mouth was. About how her skin tingled every time she was walking somewhere with him and her hand accidentally brushed his. About what it would be like to kiss him—especially since that moment at Doune when he'd stopped her falling and his arms had been wrapped round her, keeping her safe. If that tourist hadn't broken the moment, would he have kissed her? Would she have kissed him back?

'He's such a nice guy. But he's been so quiet since the divorce,' Parminder said. 'I think we all wish we could wave a magic wand and find the perfect partner for him.'

A perfect partner rules me out, Georgie thought. She obviously hadn't been enough for Charlie, or her husband wouldn't have had to find someone else to give him whatever had been lacking in their marriage. And Charlie was the only child of parents who loved him dearly; he'd never had to deal with heartbreak or misery. If she hadn't been enough to keep *him* happy, how could she possibly be enough for a man whose heart was already broken? Plus she was far from perfect.

She changed the subject quickly. 'It's the first time I've shared a house with a dog, too. I live on my own in London. Though my brother lives a couple of floors up in the same building. Our great-aunt left us both money, and we were lucky enough to get the chance to buy the flats when the building had just been renovated. Our parents had just retired and decided to move out of London, so it was kind of nice to still have family really close by.'

'I know what you mean,' Parminder said. 'Mine drive me crazy, sometimes, but it's good to know they're all close by.'

Ryan, Georgie thought, hadn't mentioned having family close by, even though he'd said he'd trained in Edinburgh. Though asking would be intrusive, and she didn't want to gossip about him.

Thankfully the class started then, and there wasn't time to chat any more.

On Thursday, Georgie had another case that puzzled her and led her to seek Ryan's advice.

'Run me through it,' he said.

'Ben's three. He has a fever, a rash and a swollen gland in his neck; the whites of his eyes are red and swollen, and he's got a sore throat. His mum says the family's new kitten scratched him on the face a few days ago and she thinks the scratch might be infected.'

'What do you think?' Ryan asked.

'I don't think it's anything to do with the scratch.' She frowned. 'The rash makes me think it could be scarlet fever, measles or possibly lupus. The swollen glands hint at glandular fever, or it might be the beginning of juvenile rheumatoid arthritis.'

'But?'

She grimaced. 'I've admitted him and put him on antibiotics. But his urine sample and white blood count don't show anything out of the ordinary, he's not responding to the usual treatment and his fever's spiking. I'm missing something. Would you have a look at him for me, please?'

'Of course.'

Georgie introduced Ryan to Ben and his mum. 'Ryan's going to take a second look at Ben for me, because Ben's test results aren't showing what I was expecting,' she said with a smile.

Ryan gently examined Ben, getting him to stick his tongue out. 'See how red his tongue is?' he said to Georgie and Ben's mum. 'And there are vertical cracks on his lips. The skin on his palms is a bit red, too. I think he has Kawasaki disease.'

'I've never heard of that,' Ben's mum said.

'It's quite rare,' Ryan said. 'It's also called mucocutaneous lymph node syndrome. Basically it's a disease where the blood vessels are inflamed, and we don't know what causes it—it might be an infection—but it's not contagious, and we can treat it.'

'With aspirin,' Georgie said, 'and immunoglobulin.'

'I thought you weren't supposed to give aspirin to children under the age of ten?' Ben's mum asked.

'Sixteen,' Ben said. 'You're right, because it can cause Reye's syndrome, but this is one of the very few medical cases where the best treatment for an under-sixteen is aspirin.'

'You might find the skin on Ben's hands peels a bit, over the next few days,' Georgie said, 'but it's nothing to worry about.' But she ordered an ECG and an echo to check Ben's heart, because she knew that one of the complications of Kawasaki disease was swollen and inflamed coronary arteries. To her relief, the tests showed that Ben was fine; and, the next day, his fever had broken.

That evening, there was a team night out of bowling

and pizza. And how good it was to feel part of them, Georgie thought. Everyone seemed to see her for who she was: the London doctor who really wasn't into football or rugby, but who made good brownies. Best of all, nobody saw her as 'Poor Georgie'. They teased her about her accent and she was pretty sure there was a competition between her colleagues as to who'd be the first to flummox her with a new dialect word every day, but she felt that they'd accepted her. Including Ryan.

Though it didn't help that Ryan was on her bowling team, and she was sitting right next to him. There wasn't much room on the benches by their alley, so her thigh was pressed very closely against his. Despite the fact they were both wearing jeans, she was very aware of the warmth of his body. And, a couple of times when she glanced at him, he was looking at her, too. She thought back to that moment at Doune when he'd held her, when they'd been so close to kissing, and her heart skipped a beat. She was pretty sure he felt the same attraction that she did; but what were they going to do about it?

And if they did end up kissing, what then? She didn't want to make another mistake like she'd made with Charlie. And if she got this wrong, things could be very awkward between them at work and at the cottage. Maybe it was better to play safe. So she made sure she was sitting at the opposite end of the table when it came to the pizza part of the evening.

On the Monday evening, Georgie practically bounced into the cottage after her late shift; she'd been quiet for the last few days, so Ryan had been trying to work out how to ask her if he'd upset her. Maybe it hadn't been him at all; maybe it was something to do with her late husband.

'Hi. I'll just heat your stew through,' Ryan said. 'And there's a jacket potato.'

'Thank you. That's wonderful.'

'You look pleased,' he said.

'I am. Ben's definitely on the mend,' she said, accepting the bowlful of stew gratefully. 'And there are clear skies tonight.'

'That's great to hear about Ben, but I don't get what the fuss is about a clear sky tonight.' Ryan said.

'There's a meteor shower tonight, and it'll be amazing because out here it's practically pitch black skies.' Her eyes sparkled. 'Come and watch them with me when I've finished dinner.'

Standing with her under the stars.

Part of Ryan thought this was a dangerous move: he was already finding himself thinking about her at odd moments of the day. But part of him couldn't resist the idea of being close to her—even if she was only offering friendship. 'OK.'

After her meal, they went out to the garden.

'I love the stars out here,' she said. 'I never get to see them so well in London because there's too much light from the city.'

'So you're a star-gazing fan?'

She nodded. 'I've always wanted to see the Northern Lights. I'd just about talked Charlie into agreeing to go on holiday to Finland, to stay in one of those hotels where the rooms have a glass ceiling so you can watch the sky as you fall asleep and hopefully see the Northern Lights.' She shrugged. 'But then he was killed. And going on my own, or even with a friend, wouldn't have been the same.'

That gave him pause for thought. A couple of times

now she'd hinted that her marriage hadn't been completely great. But what she'd just said: did it mean Charlie was the love of her life and she was still broken-hearted over his death? 'I'm sorry,' he said awkwardly.

'Thank you.'

She looked embarrassed, and he wished he hadn't been so clumsy. 'There's a good chance you'll see the lights while you're up here.'

'Wouldn't I have to go to the Orkneys or something, to be far north enough?' she asked.

'No, they've been seen here in Edinburgh.'

'Maybe I'll get Dad to forward his text alerts to me, then,' she said. 'Oh! Look up!'

He followed where she was pointing, and saw a meteor streaking across the sky.

'That's beautiful,' he said. 'I get why you like the night sky. I've never actually noticed a meteor before.'

'They're not hugely common, except when there's a big shower, and then if the moon's bright you might not actually see that many.' She smiled. 'You're supposed to wish on a falling star.'

What would he wish for?

A magic wand, perhaps, to fix things for people when they went wrong.

Or maybe to fix the broken parts of himself, so he actually had something to offer someone. So he'd be able to let a partner close instead of keeping those last barriers round his heart, scared that if he let her closer she'd find him wanting and walk away—just as everyone in his life had since his mother's death, except his dog.

Truffle didn't expect him to talk about feelings; she was happy just to be with him, to walk with him on the beach or over the hills, and curl up by the fire with him.

She accepted him for what he was. Whereas a relationship meant talking and sharing feelings, letting someone see deeper into him and risking that they wouldn't want what they saw.

'What would you wish for?' he asked, to distract himself.

'Ah, no. Telling what you wish for means it won't come true.'

What would she wish for? Obviously to have Charlie back, for him not to have died.

But if by any chance her wish was to fall in love again, could it be with him? Could they find some way to make this work? He had no idea.

But here, with the meteors streaking across the sky, he was starting to think there were possibilities. That maybe they could help each other over their pasts, step by tiny step. He just had to find the right way to suggest it.

Over the new few days, Georgie really felt that she was settling in and enjoying everything Edinburgh had to offer, from the theatre to the pandas at the zoo; and she found herself enjoying the fact that Hayloft Cottage was in the middle of nowhere. She liked getting up and seeing the sheep from next door peering in through the kitchen window; she liked sharing her space with a dog who'd grown used to her enough to curl up on the sofa next to her when she sat reading a magazine, with her chin resting on Georgie's knees; and she liked the feeling of freshness and hearing the birds sing when she walked out of the front door in the morning.

She enjoyed the hospital, too—and she was glad that Ryan was on with her in the PAU when a mum came in, panicking. 'My baby! He's all floppy and he keeps being sick and I can't get to see my family doctor and…'

'It's OK,' Georgie reassured her. 'You're in the right place.'

Ryan took the baby and started to examine him, while Georgie tried to ascertain the medical history. 'Tell us about your little boy.'

'Max is four months. He's never been a good feeder, and my milk's drying up so I've been giving him a few bottles to keep him going,' Max's mum said. 'I thought he'd picked up a bug, because he's been sick and had diarrhoea for the last couple of days, but then this morning I noticed this rash, and he was wheezing, and he's floppy—and all the baby books say if he's floppy it's really serious, and… Please, just help him,' she begged.

Georgie was pretty sure she'd seen cases like this before in London. 'So you're giving him formula as well as breastfeeding? Has he been sick before when you gave him formula?'

'He was sick on the breast, too,' Max's mum said. 'Do you think it's the formula that's made him worse?'

'I think there's a strong possibility he might have a milk allergy,' Georgie said. 'And that's not just the formula—if you've had any dairy, that will go through your breast milk. Are there any allergies in your family, or does anyone have asthma or hay fever?'

'Nothing like that.' Max's mum looked worried.

'I'd like to do a blood test to check my diagnosis,' Georgie said.

'I think she's right,' Ryan said. 'Have you seen any blood or mucus in Max's stools, when they've been solid?'

'Yes. I was so scared it was cancer or something like that.'

'I'm pretty sure it's a milk allergy,' Georgie said again. 'That would explain why he's not feeding well, too. Once we get that sorted out, you'll find he gains weight well and you'll be a lot less worried about him.'

Max's mum bit her lip. 'If he's allergic to formula, what am I going to do? Give him soy?'

'Often there's an allergy to soy as well,' Georgie said. 'We can give you a hypoallergenic formula to try.'

'And a calcium supplement,' Ryan added, 'and a multivitamin syrup with vitamin D.'

'Let me sort out the blood test,' Georgie said. 'We'll see how Max goes on the hypoallergenic formula, and then bring him in to reintroduce a milk feed and see if he reacts. We'll do the test here, so if he reacts strongly we can help straight away. And if we're right you'll need to check the labels for absolutely everything you feed him, to make sure you avoid giving him anything with milk in it for at least the first year.'

'About one in five babies outgrow a milk allergy by the time they're a year old,' Ryan said, 'and most have outgrown it by the time they're three, but some will have an immediate reaction to even small traces of dairy.'

Georgie cleaned Max's heel and took a tiny sample of blood through a heel prick test. 'It's only temporarily uncomfortable,' she reassured Max's mum. 'It'll take a couple of days to get the results back, but in the meantime we'll sort out the formula for you.

'So he's going to be all right?' she asked.

Georgie rested her hand on the woman's shoulder. 'Yes. I know right now everything looks scary, but Dr McGregor and I have seen a lot of poorly babies in our time, and we've made them better. There are lots of things we can do to help Max.'

* * *

That was one of the things Ryan really liked about Georgie: she was calm, kind and practical. While she talked to Max's mum about how to read labels and what kind of alternatives to try when weaning, Max's mum was visibly relaxing and seeming more confident in her ability to manage.

Funny, Georgie made him feel that way, too. Not so much in his job—he knew what he was doing at the hospital—but outside. When he was with her, he saw the world in a different way. He was starting to feel *connected*. It scared him, because he'd never managed to do that before; yet at the same time he wanted more. Much more.

The following night, Georgie was woken by an insistent knocking on her bedroom door.

She grabbed her dressing gown, wrapped it round her and stomped over to the door. 'What?' she snapped as she opened the door to Ryan.

'You need to come outside,' he said. 'Right now.'

'I was asleep and I'm in my pyjamas,' she pointed out, glaring at him.

'Just get your coat and your boots on. Now. You'll really regret it if you don't.'

'Are you insane?' She glanced at her watch. 'It's one in the morning and I'm on an early.'

'I know. Stop arguing, Georgie. It's important.'

Important? How? If it was a fire, she would've heard the smoke alarm. Why was he looking so pleased with himself? Why wasn't he explaining whatever it was? Why was he such an irritating man?

He waited for her to walk before him, not leaving her with much choice.

Scowling, she pulled her boots and her coat on, and followed him out to the garden.

'Look up,' he said.

She did so, and felt her eyes widen as she realised why he'd wanted her to go outside—and why he hadn't explained. He'd wanted this to be a surprise. A delight.

And it was.

Above them, curtains of pale green light rippled slowly across the sky, the stars still visible through the green haze. The thing she'd always wanted to see. *The Northern Lights*.

She'd never seen anything so gorgeous and breath-taking before.

'Oh, my God, Ryan, it's…' Words failed her, and she stood staring up at the sky, utterly entranced.

She had no idea quite how it happened, but then his arm was wrapped round her shoulders and hers was round his waist.

It was just for bodily warmth, she told herself, because it was a cold night and they had pyjamas on under their coats.

And when he stooped slightly so his cheek was against hers, again she told herself it was just for warmth.

But then somehow they ended up facing each other. He rested his palm against her cheek, and she found herself doing the same. Right here, right now, under the glow of the Northern Lights, everything felt like a different world. A magical one, full of possibilities.

He dipped his head, and brushed his mouth very lightly against hers. Her lips tingled at the touch: an invitation, a promise, a temptation. Warmth and sweetness.

A real connection. Things that had been missing from her life for so very long.

And she couldn't help responding, sliding her hand round to the back of his head and urging his mouth down to hers again. His kiss was long and slow, and so very sweet that it made her ache. Asking, not demanding; it made her feel as if she was unfurling under the spring sunshine after a hard and lonely winter, as if the dancing lights in the sky were flickering inside her head, and she didn't want it to stop.

Yet, at the same time, common sense seeped back into her along with the chill of the night air.

She was kissing her housemate.

Ryan was gorgeous, but he'd had a miserable time in the past. And how did she know things would even work between them? Hadn't she learned the hard way through Charlie that her judgement in men wasn't good enough?

She pulled away. 'This isn't a good idea.'

His eyes were dark and unreadable. She didn't have a clue what was going on in his head.

But then he nodded. 'You're right. We'll forget this ever happened. Blame it on the excitement of seeing the Northern Lights.'

Lights that even now were fading away, melting back into the stratosphere.

Just like that feeling of warmth and connection.

Leaving her back in the shadows of loneliness.

'Agreed,' she said, trying to stem the sudden flood of misery.

It was only a kiss.

A temporary aberration.

Not to be repeated.

'Thank you for waking me to see the lights,' she said,

putting as much politeness as she could into her voice. Distance, that was what she needed most right now. 'See you tomorrow.'

'Yeah,' he said, and let her walk back into the house without following her.

What the hell had he been thinking?

Of course it wasn't a good idea to kiss her.

Ryan knew he'd come up with a pathetic excuse. Blame it on the Northern Lights, indeed. He knew precisely why he'd kissed Georgie. She'd switched from super-grouchy at being woken in the middle of the night to almost glowing with joy when she'd seen the display of lights dancing through the skies. He'd found her delight irresistible, to the point where his common sense had been completely bypassed by need and he'd held her close. She'd held him back. And then he'd kissed her, her mouth warm and soft and sweet under his. She'd kissed him back. He'd felt the kind of connection he hadn't thought was possible for him.

And then she'd stopped kissing him and said it wasn't a good idea.

She was right. Of course it wasn't a good idea. It was stupid. She was still mourning her husband, Ryan wasn't a good bet when it came to relationships, and they were only going to be in each other's lives temporarily.

Utterly stupid.

But what was even more stupid was that he wouldn't have changed a thing. If he could rewind time and go back to the second when he'd slid his arm round her shoulders… He would still have done it. He would still have touched her face like that. Still have kissed her.

And he'd lied—to both of them—when he'd said that

they could just forget it had ever happened. Because he couldn't forget it. That kiss just kept replaying in his head, in full Technicolor. When Ryan finally went to bed, he dreamed about kissing Georgie. He woke, aching, because he wasn't kissing her; and then he thought about it all over again. Drifted back into a fitful doze. Dreamed again. Woke again, thinking of her.

What had the actor said in that Shakespeare play Zoe had taken him to, a couple of years back, the one with the magician standing on the top of the stage with his cloak billowing out like a stormy sky as he conjured up a tempest?

When I wak'd, I cried to dream again...

But dreams could be broken all too easily.

Giving up on sleep, Ryan went out for a long walk with Truffle. Thank God he and Georgie were on different shifts today. She'd be gone by the time he got back to the cottage, and he could have a cold shower—and hopefully some common sense would leach back into his head along with the water.

And then somehow he'd have to find his way back to a decent working relationship with her.

CHAPTER SIX

OVER THE NEXT few days, Georgie was pretty sure that Ryan was avoiding her. And it was her own fault, for kissing him. She shouldn't have done it. When he'd slipped his arm round her shoulders, she should've found an excuse to step away, instead of leaning into him and sliding her arm round his waist. She should never have responded.

'How am I going to convince him that it was a mistake and I'm not going to make life difficult for him?' she asked Truffle.

The dog just gave a soft wuff, as if to say that she didn't have a clue, either.

It was fine until the Friday morning. And then she made the mistake of flicking into her social media account and all the memories popped up from six years ago. Her wedding day. Pictures of herself and Charlie in the doorway of the tiny ancient church where they'd just pledged to love, honour and cherish each other.

Forsaking all others.

Had he meant it at the time?

She'd loved him so much. She'd thought they were so good together. They'd got on well with each other's families, they'd got on well with each other's friends, their jobs had complemented each other's, and that day had been so bright and sparkly. The sun had shone all day, and she'd thought they were so lucky to spend such a perfect day with their family and their closest friends, sharing the love and the hope and the joy. She'd graduated and had been halfway through her foundation training, whereas Charlie was two years older and working in the Accident and Emergency Department.

They'd had such plans.

She'd finish her training, do three years in her specialty, and then they'd think about starting a family.

Except Charlie had found a reason to put off having children with her: a reason Georgie had had no idea about at the time. Trisha Hampson, the woman he'd had an affair with. A long-running affair that had started a good year before he'd died and had then continued through every disaster mission he'd gone to help with.

And, just before that last mission, according to what Trisha's parents had told her later, Trisha had found out that she was pregnant.

Had she told Charlie straight away? Or had she wanted to wait until she could tell him face to face, and maybe they'd both been killed before she'd had a chance to tell him?

If they hadn't been killed in the landslide, would he have told Georgie about Trisha and the baby when he came back to England? Would he have chosen to stay with her and give Trisha financial support for the baby, or would he have left Georgie and gone to live with his new family?

And why had he needed to have that affair in the first place? Hadn't she made him happy? She'd never had any real fights with him, and she'd always agreed to whatever he wanted. She'd thought they were good together. What had been missing, for him, in their relationship? Where had she gone wrong?

All that potential, all that sparkle on their wedding day: now she looked at the photographs, and the day just felt tarnished. Her marriage had been a big, fat lie, and she'd been too stupid to realise it until it was too late.

She wasn't even aware she was crying until the kitchen door opened and Ryan walked in with Truffle.

'Georgie? What's wrong?' he asked.

'Nothing.' She rubbed her eyes with the back of her hand.

'It doesn't look like nothing.' He filled the kettle and switched it on. 'I prescribe a mug of tea. And I'm…' He paused. 'I'm not prying, but I'm here if you want to talk about it—and it won't be going any further than me.'

Nobody at St Christopher's knew that she was a widow. He'd kept his promise about that. She really had to stop letting Charlie's behaviour affect every other relationship she had. Just because he'd been a cheat and a liar, it didn't follow that everyone else in the world was, too.

'It's my wedding anniversary,' she admitted. 'Or it would have been.' Would she even still have been married? Charlie's child would've been crawling by now.

'It's the first anniversary since he died?'

'Second,' she said. The first one, though, she hadn't known about Trisha, and she'd still been mourning the man she'd thought she'd married. Now… It was different. She knew Charlie hadn't loved her as much as she'd loved him, or he wouldn't have had the affair.

Ryan clearly thought she was still in mourning; maybe that was why he'd backed off so fast after their kiss. Should she tell him the truth? But then he really might be tempted to pity her—not just poor, widowed Georgie, but poor, widowed, clueless, cheated-on Georgie. She didn't want that.

Georgie looked totally lost, and Ryan had to stop himself walking over and putting his arms round her. Things were still slightly awkward between them since he'd kissed her in the garden, and the last thing he wanted to do was make that awkwardness any worse.

'The photos came up on social media as a memory from six years ago. I should've expected it, but it caught me a bit on the raw.'

'I'm not pitying you,' he said softly, mindful of when she'd told him that her husband had been killed in a landslide while helping people after an earthquake. 'Of course something like this would catch you out. I'm planning to take Truffle for a very long walk by the sea on my wedding anniversary.' It would be the second anniversary for him, too, since the divorce.

'Do you miss her?' she asked.

'Sometimes,' he said. He didn't miss not living up to Zoe's expectations—or his own. 'I wish it could've worked out, but we wanted different things.' She'd wanted a baby. He hadn't. Not that he wanted to go into that. He shrugged. 'She was in PR. We were both busy with our careers and worked ridiculous hours. I guess we grew apart.' That was true: just not the whole truth. 'It was an amicable split, or as amicable as it could be.' After the fights. When they'd sat down and finally been completely honest with each other. When they'd realised that their differences were irreconcilable.

But it had still hurt that Zoe had fallen for someone else so quickly. Someone who'd been prepared to give her the baby she wanted. He was glad that Zoe was happy again; but he hadn't really moved on and found some-one else. Not because he still loved Zoe, but because he didn't want to risk letting someone else down, the way he'd let his wife down. And Georgie had already had too much loss in her life. She didn't need him complicating things for her.

'Things are as they are,' he said. 'I love my job, I love my dog, and I love Edinburgh.'

'You grew up here, didn't you?' she asked.

'Yes.'

'I miss my family,' she said.

Oh, no. Please don't let her ask him about his family. Because he didn't have one. Just a grave he visited on the anniversary of his mum's death. She'd been gone for three decades now; he had a couple of creased photo-graphs of her that had survived the years of foster care, and that was it. 'You're welcome to invite them here. I could sleep on the couch.'

Her eyes glittered with tears. 'That's really kind of you, but I can't ask you to do that.'

'It's no bother. Besides, I wouldn't ask a guest to sleep down here with Truffle. She snores. And she's not above waking you in the middle of the night—that's why Clara bought the stair gate, after too many three a.m. visits from a dog who's bright enough to know how to open a door and will lick your nose until you wake up and give in to her demands for a walk.'

Truffle's tail thudded against the floor at the W-word, and he reached down to scratch behind her ears. 'Yes, you daft beastie, I'm talking about you.'

'I'm fine,' Georgie said. 'I guess…it just caught me a bit unawares.'

'Things do,' he said, feeling awkward.

'I never thought I'd be a widow at thirty. I thought I'd be a mum. I was so looking forward to having a family.'

And here it was. The same issue he'd faced with Zoe. Georgie, too, wanted to be a mum. Ryan hadn't wanted to be a dad. He knew nothing about *how* to be a dad. He'd never had a role model. His mum, until he was six; and then a string of foster parents who'd given up on him.

The one person who'd made a difference was the woman who'd come out of retirement to give temporary cover while his social worker had been on maternity leave: Elspeth McCreadie. She'd sat down with his sulking teenage self and told him that life wasn't fair, and nobody pretended it was.

But he had a choice. He could focus on his past and be miserable for the rest of his life, or he could try making a difference to the world instead. That he was bright enough to do anything he wanted. He was good at science, so he could be a doctor, make other people better—and if he learned some social skills then his future could be better than his past. But Ryan was the only one who could make that difference to his own life. Nobody else would do it for him.

He'd been furious at the time, but her words had sunk in. He'd kept his supermarket checkout job at evenings and weekends, but he'd done his A levels and been accepted at university. Become a doctor. Made that difference to his own life. He'd stayed in touch with Elspeth, and although she'd died before his graduation she'd left him a congratulations card and written that she thought he could change the world and she was proud of him.

He still hadn't completely connected with anyone,

though. He'd tried so hard to love Zoe the way she wanted to be loved; despite all the effort, he'd failed.

Fixing patients, he could do.

Emotional stuff…that was another matter. He didn't have the skill set.

'I'm sorry,' he said awkwardly, wanting to help but not knowing how.

She scrubbed a hand across her face. 'You can't always get what you want. I have a lot to be thankful for. I have my family, a job I love, good friends. I don't have to worry about whether I can pay the rent or afford to eat. Wanting more's just greedy.'

'Sometimes we all want more,' he said. 'Um, I'll make you a coffee.'

'It's fine. I need to get to work.'

A safe place, where she wouldn't have to think about her anniversary because she'd be busy helping patients. It was how he'd used work too ever since he and Zoe had split up.

'I'll see you later,' he said.

But she was quiet all weekend. And every time Ryan thought about giving her a hug, he remembered her words. *I never thought I'd be a widow at thirty. I thought I'd be a mum.*

He wanted her, but he didn't want to let her down. How could he get this to work? But, every time he thought about it, he came up blank.

On Wednesday, Georgie had the day off. She spent the morning cleaning, then nipped down to the farm shop to buy bread and stayed chatting with Janie for a bit. But, when she got back to the cottage, the patter of paws and waggy tail she was used to was missing.

'Truffle?' she called.

The house was silent.

Ryan was on an early shift. No way would he have come home halfway through it and taken Truffle out. So where on earth was the dog?

The stair gate was in place, so it wasn't likely the Labrador had gone upstairs.

And then she heard a creak.

The back door was open. Obviously she hadn't shut it properly and Truffle had gone into the garden. Except, when she looked outside, the dog wasn't there. 'Truffle,' she called. 'Here, girl.'

Nothing.

And there was a pile of dirt by the corner of the fence, along with a hole big enough for a large dog to squeeze through...

Oh, no. No, no, *no*.

It looked as if the dog had dug her way out of the garden. Ryan had said she was an absconder, and here was the proof.

'Truffle!' she yelled, hoping that she was wrong and the dog would appear from round the corner.

Still no response.

How did you get a dog to come back? When Truffle had disappeared to play with another dog on the beach, Ryan had given her slices of cocktail sausage when she'd come back.

OK. Sausage it was. Georgie ran to the fridge and took out Ryan's box of treats. 'Truffle,' she called. 'Sausage!' She rattled the box, and then opened it on the grounds that dogs had a brilliant sense of smell and Truffle would know there were treats on offer and come to get them.

But the dog didn't appear.

Oh, God. *She'd lost Ryan's dog.* She didn't even know where to begin looking for Truffle. And she didn't know the countryside around here well enough to know where the dog might have been most likely to head for. Panicking, she called the ward.

'Is Ryan there, please?' she asked. 'It's an emergency.'

What seemed like ten years later, Ryan came to the phone. 'What's the emergency?' he asked.

'It's Truffle. I went down to Janie's and I must've not shut the back door properly. There's a hole by the fence and I think she's tunnelled out of the garden. I can't see her anywhere and I've called and called and I've offered sausage and—'

'Stop gabbling and breathe,' he cut in. 'You're quite sure she's not there?'

'I'm sure. Where do I start looking for her?'

'You don't,' he said. 'Stay where you are and I'll go and find her.' He banged the phone down.

This was all her fault. And if the dog was hurt, or had been hit by a car and was...

Oh, God. She cut the thought off, feeling sick to her stomach. If Truffle was injured or worse, she'd never forgive herself.

Not knowing what to do, but feeling that she had to do something, she put her phone on charge, put the kettle on to make a flask of coffee and stuffed a first aid kit and a towel into a waterproof bag, together with a torch and a bottle of water and the box of sausage slices. Then she laced up her hiking boots and got her coat ready.

Ryan was back at the cottage sooner than she'd expected, which told her that he must've broken the speed limit all the way back from the city.

'Ryan, I'm s—' she began.

'Save it. I need to find my dog.' His face was a mask of suppressed anger and worry.

'I'll go with you. I've got a bag. A towel, first aid kit, coffee, water. My phone.'

'Half the time there isn't a signal out there.'

'I'm sorry. I'll—'

'Save it,' he said again.

'Look, I know you're furious with me and don't want me around, and I hate myself for being so careless with her, but two pairs of eyes are better than one when you're looking,' she said. 'I can't just stay here doing nothing. Let me come with you.'

He scowled at her; but then, to her relief, he nodded.

Please let Truffle be all right.

Please let her not be badly hurt, or worse.

Please.

It was raining, the sort of rain that looked deceptively light but seeped into every fibre and weighed you down; Georgie was glad of the waterproof coat she'd bought the previous month, and even more glad of the drawstring hood.

'We'll start this way,' Ryan said, gesturing diagonally to the hills, 'and we take it in turns calling and listening. We'll walk for fifteen minutes, then turn ninety degrees and walk that way.'

Half an hour of trudging, and she was freezing but she wasn't going to admit it. Worse than the physical discomfort was the coldness and fear inside. She knew that Ryan loved his dog more than anything. If anything had happened to Truffle...

Ryan had never known fear like this.

He was used to losing people. His mum, her family,

a string of foster parents. But losing the dog he'd loved since he'd first met her, the only one in his life who hadn't deserted him… The more he thought about it, the worse it was. It wasn't blood pumping through his veins, it was adrenaline; and it wasn't air in his lungs, it was pure solid fear. All that was left was a shallow space that kept him functioning. Just.

Gone.

His dog couldn't be gone.

Truffle was all the family he had.

Was this how the parents of his patients felt, when they sat at their very sick child's bedside? As if the whole world was being sucked into a black hole, every speck of light diminishing?

It was unbearable.

Just putting one foot in front of the other was such an effort that he didn't have the energy to run. Every time he called for his dog, his throat hurt. Every time he listened for an answering bark, his ears felt as if they were buzzing. And every time he glanced at his watch to see if it was time to change direction, he found that only seconds had passed.

How could time move so slowly?

How could this hurt so much?

What if they didn't find her?

Ryan didn't even speak to Georgie. Not that she blamed him. What she'd done was the worst thing ever: she'd lost his dog.

Clara would never have made such a stupid mistake.

If anything had happened to Truffle, Georgie knew she couldn't stay at Hayloft Cottage. She wasn't even sure that she could still work in the same department as Ryan. He'd never, ever, ever forgive her.

The friendship they'd been developing, the attraction they'd both been struggling to ignore—that would turn to sheer hatred in a nanosecond.

Please let them find the dog.

Another ninety-degree turn, more calling, more listening, and still nothing.

They trudged on.

And on.

And then finally she heard a bark. Or was it the wind and she just thought it was a bark because she so desperately wanted to hear the dog?

'I think I just heard something. Call again!' she whispered urgently.

Ryan did so.

It was faint, but this time there was a definite answering bark.

Oh, thank God.

Truffle wasn't dead. Though she might be hurt. They were walking in the direction from where they'd heard Truffle bark, but it didn't sound as if the dog was coming to meet them. When Georgie scanned the area in front of them, she couldn't see any glint from Truffle's reflective collar—a glint that should be there, even in this low light.

She grabbed the torch from her bag and switched it on. Although it was small, the beam was really powerful as it swept the ground in front of them, and finally she caught a glimpse of something reflective. 'Look. I think that's Truffle's collar.'

Except it wasn't moving.

If Truffle had heard them, why wasn't she coming towards them?

Ryan was moving faster than she was, but she didn't try to run after him; the last thing he needed was for her to sprain her ankle or something and need his help getting back to the cottage. She made her way carefully behind him, and when she finally reached him he was on his knees next to the dog, and Truffle was covering his face with licks and making little whimpery noises.

'She's stuck in a rabbit hole,' he said, and she realised that he was digging the dog out with his bare hands. 'Daft beastie. You're not going to disappear into the hills again like that in a hurry, are you?'

The dog wuffed gently and gave a feeble wag of her tail.

'I'm so glad she's all right.' She dropped to her haunches and stroked the Labrador. 'You've been out here for ages, poor girl. I'm so sorry. It was all my fault. You're cold and you're wet, but you must be thirsty.' She took the flask from her bag, removed the lid, and tipped cold water from the bottle into it so the dog could lap at it.

Truffle drank two whole cupsful.

But when Ryan had finished digging her out, it was clear that Truffle wasn't going to be able to walk back to the cottage with them because she was limping badly on the leg that had been trapped in the rabbit hole.

'I don't know if it's a fracture or a sprain,' he said. 'But I'm not risking it getting any worse.' He bent down and lifted her up.

Nearly thirty kilos of wriggly Labrador, but he'd lifted her as if she were a feather.

And his eyes were wet.

Georgie hated herself. Hated that she'd been as careless and thoughtless as Charlie had been towards her.

'Can I do anything to help?' she asked.

'I think you've done enough.'

'Ryan, everyone makes mistakes.'

'Yeah.' A muscle twitched in his jaw. 'This dog is my *family,* and you put her at risk.'

The pain in his voice stopped her biting back any more. 'Do you want me to call the vet?'

'You won't have a signal out here.'

She looked at her phone anyway. But it was a vain hope: of course he was right. He was the local, and she was a stupid, dizzy city girl.

When they finally got back to the cottage, she sat next to Truffle, stroking the top of the dog's head and comforting her while Ryan phoned the vet.

'They're staying open for me so they can take her in,' he said. 'I don't know when I'll be back. Don't wait up.'

She took a deep breath. 'Truffle's clearly in pain and scared, and I'm sure she'd rather have someone sitting with her in the car. So I'll drive you while you're next to her. Don't argue. It's the very least I can do.'

The very least?

If she'd been more careful in the first place, Truffle wouldn't be hurt now.

Part of Ryan wanted to snarl at Georgie, to tell her to go back to London and leave him the hell alone, but the more sensible part of him knew that she was right.

'All right,' he said, and gave Georgie his car keys, though he couldn't quite bring himself to thank her. 'We'll take my car. It's bigger and she'll be more comfortable with more room.'

'OK. Is the vet's address in your satnav, or do you want to direct me?' she asked.

'I'll direct you.' He carried the dog out to his car and laid her gently on the back seat while Georgie locked the cottage, then told her where to turn to get to the vet's in the next village.

'Well, young Truffle, haven't you been in the wars?' the receptionist said when Ryan carried the dog into the surgery. 'Linda told me you were coming in, Ryan. Go straight through. She's expecting you.'

'Thanks, Carol.'

Linda smiled at him when he entered the exam room. 'Hello, Ryan. Do you want to bring her over here to the table?'

'Thanks.' Gently, he laid the dog down. 'Stay here, sweetheart. Linda's going to take a look at you.'

Linda checked Truffle's range of movement on all her legs, soothing the dog and talking to her in a low voice as she did so.

'I can feel movement on this leg that really shouldn't be here,' she said. 'I'll do a scan to check that it's definitely a soft tissue problem and not a fracture, but I'm pretty sure It's a grade two sprain. That means she's going to need surgery to stabilise the joint properly. How did she do it?'

'She tunnelled out of the garden, took herself off in the hills, and got stuck in a rabbit hole,' he said. 'I dug her out.'

'Don't be too hard on yourself,' Linda said.

Not so much himself as on Georgie, but anger was still warring with guilt, so he said nothing.

'I've known dogs who've sprained a leg by jumping

off a sofa, so it's easily done,' Linda said. 'When did she last eat?'

'This morning.'

'That's good. Do you want to carry her over to the scanner?'

He was glad to have something to do. Waiting really didn't sit well with him. 'Sure.'

He stayed with Truffle, soothing her, while Linda did the scan.

'Good news,' Linda said when she'd finished. 'It's not a fracture, but I do need to stabilise the joint so I'll operate now. She's going to be fine. Though don't look up the operation or anything on the internet,' she added with a smile, 'because you'll panic yourself—just as I'm sure you tell your patients' parents not to look things up while they're waiting.'

He did. And now he knew how it felt from their perspective. Utterly, utterly horrible.

It looked as if there was nothing he could do other than go into the waiting room and—well, *wait*. His eyes prickled and his throat felt full of sand as he stroked Truffle's head and saw her deep brown eyes looking anxious. Oh, dear God, this was unbearable. He looked at Linda. 'Can I stay with her while you give her the anaesthetic? I don't want to leave her—I don't want her to worry about what's going to happen.' Most of all he didn't want the dog to think he'd abandoned her, the way her first owners had.

Linda, who knew Truffle's background, nodded. 'But then I want you out of here so I can concentrate on doing the surgery and not be worrying about you, OK?'

'OK.' He nodded. 'I love you,' he whispered to the dog.

When had he last said those words to a human?

When had someone last said those words to him?

He hated every second that he stood there by the examination table, trying to keep his voice calm as he soothed his dog, stroking her head and then seeing her eyes grow dark as the anaesthetic took over.

If she didn't make it through this he'd never, ever forgive himself.

'She'll be OK,' Linda said again. 'It's a routine operation and I do this all the time.'

Just the sort of thing he said to his patients' parents.

'Go and tell Carol I said to make you a mug of tea with two sugars,' she said with a smile.

'Thanks.' But he felt too sick to drink anything.

Georgie was sitting in the waiting room, her face white and her expression forlorn. 'How is—?' She stopped and covered her hand with her mouth when she realised he was alone. 'Where is she?' she whispered.

'In the operating theatre. It's not a fracture, it's a sprain. Grade two. Linda—the vet—needs to operate to stabilise the joint,' he said.

'I'm so sorry.'

Despite his misery, Ryan knew it wasn't fair to take out his fear on her. 'Linda said she's seen a dog sprain a leg like that just getting off a sofa. It happens.' He sat down heavily next to her. 'I just have to wait.'

'I'll stay with you,' she said.

Yeah. As if anyone stayed with him for long. 'You don't have to.'

'I want to. There's nothing worse than waiting on your own.'

To his shock, she took his hand. His skin tingled where it touched hers; and it left him feeling even more mixed up. He didn't have a clue what to do now, so he just left his hand where it was, with her fingers curled round his.

She didn't say anything; she was giving him space, he realised. And supporting him at the same time, by just holding his hand. Being there.

And eventually the words started to spill out. He couldn't look at her, but he could talk. Just.

'I'm sorry for snapping at you.'

'It's OK.'

'No, it isn't. But Truffle…' How did he explain? 'She's not just my dog. She's my family.'

'I know.'

She didn't seem to be judging him. 'My *only* family,' he clarified.

Again, she didn't say anything. Didn't ask, didn't probe, just gave him the space to think and talk when he was ready. Although Georgie hadn't promised to keep everything confidential, he was pretty sure that she would: just as he hadn't said anything to anyone else in the department about her being a widow. She understood how excruciating it was to be gossiped about.

'My mum had me when she was very young,' he said. 'She was sixteen. I don't know who my dad was. She didn't put his name on my birth certificate. And she wouldn't tell anyone who he was, so her parents kicked her out before I was born.'

Georgie said nothing, but her fingers tightened around his. And suddenly it was easy to talk. Easy, for the first time ever.

'She got a flat and a job, and we were doing OK together. But then Mum was killed in an accident when I was six. Someone knocked her off her bike when she was on her way from work to pick me up from school and she wasn't wearing a helmet. She hit her head in the wrong place, and that was it.' He shrugged. 'So that left just me.

And her parents—well, they hadn't wanted to know me when she was alive and they told the social worker they didn't want to be lumbered with me. So I went into care.'

Ryan had been abandoned by his family after his mother had died at the cruelly young age of twenty-two?

Just like his dog had been abandoned by her first owners.

Now Georgie understood just how deeply Ryan identified with his Labrador. No wonder he considered the dog his only family. They were two of a kind.

There were no words. So she just kept holding his hand and giving him the space to talk. He wasn't looking at her; she didn't think his gaze was focused on anything, because his expression was so far away.

'I was an angry six-year-old. I missed my mum and I didn't understand why the hospital couldn't make her better, why she'd died. I couldn't settle anywhere. I wet the bed. I kicked doors and walls. I threw things. I stole. I smashed things up.'

A small, frightened child's equivalent of Truffle and her anxious chewing, Georgie thought.

'So the foster parents didn't tend to keep me for very long. I went through a few sets and then I ended up in a children's home.'

'Your grandparents never changed their minds?'

'No.'

She still couldn't get her head round this. 'And your mum was their only child?'

'Aye.'

How sad. Georgie couldn't understand why any parent would throw their only child onto the street like that. Her parents had been there for Joshua after his wife had died and they'd even offered to come back to London to help, despite the fact they loved their retirement in Norfolk. Just as they'd been there for her after Charlie had been killed, given her a space to stay and to grieve.

If Georgie had fallen pregnant at sixteen, maybe her parents would've been disappointed that her options were narrower than they wanted for her, but they would've supported any decision she made. And they would've helped out with childcare, so she could go on to study and have the career she'd always wanted as well as a baby. And if anything had happened to her, she knew without a doubt that they would've stepped straight in to give her child a home and make sure the child felt loved and wanted. Her elder brother Joshua would've helped, too.

Ryan hadn't had any of that support. He'd made it to where he was completely on his own.

Since his divorce and Clara doing the job swap, all he had was his dog.

'I'm not pitying you,' she said. 'But right now I'm pretty angry on your behalf. And your mum's.'

'There's no need. The McGregors don't deserve any emotion from you,' he said. 'They'll face a lonely old age, instead of having their daughter and their grandson to look in on them and brighten their day with a visit. They were very keen to tell my mother that "as ye sow, so shall ye reap"—the letter they wrote her was in the box of stuff that social services kept for me for when I was old enough. And now they'll perhaps learn the truth of that themselves. I've thought about facing them, but I decided they're not worth it. The best revenge is living well.'

'That's true,' she said. 'And, just so you know, everything you've just told me is going nowhere.'

He looked at her then. 'Thank you.'

'Does Clara know?'

'Yes. She was the one who suggested I get a dog in the first place, when I split up with Zoe.' He gave her a wry smile. 'She said much the same as you. She also said I should try to find my father. So did Zoe. But, as my mother refused to name him, there isn't anyone left to ask.'

'Maybe your mum's best friend from school?' she suggested.

'That's what they suggested,' he said. 'But I don't know who she was. And, even supposing I found someone who was at school with her, someone who remembered her and might help trace her best friend, what if Mum never told anyone at all? And if she did...' He shook his head. 'If my father didn't want to know when she was pregnant or when I was born, he certainly won't want to know thirty-six years later. And I don't want another person in my life who'd let me down.'

So he expected nothing from relationships. Nothing at all.

It was a warning.

And, at the same time, it made her want to weep for the sad, lonely, abandoned little boy he'd been. The lonely, abandoned man he was right now.

It didn't have to stay that way.

But he gently disentangled his fingers from hers, as if to make the point that he was absolutely fine on his own and he'd prefer to keep it that way.

Well, she'd wait with him anyway.

Carol on the reception desk insisted on making them both a mug of tea. And then finally Linda reappeared. 'Do you want the good news, or the good news?' she asked with a smile.

'She's going to be all right?' Ryan asked, sitting up straight.

Linda nodded. 'I've fixed the sprain. She's got a splint and she'll need painkillers, and a strict regime of rest. Walks only on a short leash, and that includes going out to the loo. No running, no jumping, no rough-house playing. And when she's not with you she'll need a cone on.'

'She's going to be bored out of her mind,' Ryan said.

'Get some different puzzle boxes,' Linda said. 'And do lots of mental training with her—stay, nose-touch, and low-activity "find it" games, that sort of thing. And give her toys stuffed with food so she has to work for it—it'll help to keep her occupied.'

'Got it,' Ryan said. 'What's the other good news?'

'She's come round from her op. She's a little bit woozy and a little bit sorry for herself, but you can take her home.'

'Thank you.' Ryan actually hugged Linda, to Georgie's surprise. 'Thank you for making my dog better.'

'Bring her back to see me in a week. Or before that if you think she's got an infection and she's running a temperature, or you're worried about anything at all,' Linda said.

Georgie waited for Ryan to go and collect the dog, and Ryan's eyelashes were suspiciously damp when he carried Truffle back into the waiting room.

'Let's go home,' she said softly.

Then she realised what she'd said. *Home.* Since when had she thought of Hayloft Cottage as home? But she realised it was true. Despite growing up in London and studying and working there ever since, she'd started to think of the wilds of Scotland as home.

CHAPTER SEVEN

RYAN SAT IN the back of his car with Truffle, who seemed woozy and exhausted. There was a patch of shaven skin on her paw where she'd been anaesthetised, her leg had a dressing on it and Ryan had a plastic cone to attach to her collar when he wasn't supervising her, to stop her being able to chew the dressing or nibble at her stitches.

Georgie didn't push him to make conversation; she had a feeling that he was already regretting spilling his heart out to her. Now she knew why his dog was so important to him, it made her feel even worse.

Back at the cottage, she opened doors for him while he carried the dog inside. He set Truffle down on her bed, and the dog's head flopped down between her paws. For a moment, before he masked it, Ryan's face was full of anguish.

And there was nothing she could do, nothing she could say, to make things better.

She fell back on practicalities. 'I'll cook dinner. I bought salmon yesterday.'

'I'm not hungry,' he said.

'Tough. You're eating. You're not going to be any good to Truffle if you keel over. You need food.'

She took his silence as consent and chopped vegetables

ready to stir-fry them; she also pan-fried the salmon and put a packet of rice into the microwave.

Ryan looked reluctant to leave the dog when Georgie put their plates on the table.

'She'll be fine. Sit down and eat,' she said.

He made a noncommittal noise but at least he joined her, though he pushed the food around his plate. He ate about half the salmon and rice, and let the rest cool on his plate before going to sit on the floor next to Truffle, hand-feeding the dog some flakes of fish and rice.

Georgie wanted to hug him and tell him everything would be all right, but she thought he'd probably push her away. So she busied herself doing the washing up and pottered round in the kitchen, while the silence stretched out further and further between them.

Eventually she put the kettle on, made them both a mug of tea, and collected his empty plate.

'Sorry,' he muttered. 'And thanks.'

'No problem. Is there anything else I can get you?'

'No.' He took a deep breath. 'I'm going to stay downstairs with her tonight in case she has a delayed reaction to the anaesthetic.'

Oh, no. Georgie hadn't even thought of that, and the idea made her feel sick. Of course they weren't out of the woods yet. The operation was just the first stage. 'Then I'll stay with you to keep you company.'

'There's no need,' Ryan said. 'You've got work tomorrow. I swapped my shift so I've got a day off.'

'I'm still staying with you,' she said. 'Apart from the fact it's my fault Truffle escaped into the hills, two bodies are better than one when it comes to looking after someone who's sick. So I'm going to change into my pyjamas and bring my pillow and duvet down here. And I'll sit with her while you do the same.'

Eventually, he nodded. 'All right. Thanks.'

Once she was downstairs, he went up to change and collect his bedding, and meanwhile Georgie sat talking to Truffle, resting her hand lightly on the dog's side for comfort. 'You're going to be all right, girl,' she promised softly.

When Ryan came downstairs, he put his duvet and pillow on the other side of Truffle. It reminded Georgie of sleepovers as a child, when a whole bunch of them would sleep in a room and chatter until the small hours. Though Ryan didn't talk. He just lay there, looking worried, and Georgie didn't want to babble platitudes and make things worse for him.

If only she'd double-checked the door.

And, if Truffle developed complications after the operation and the worst happened, Georgie would never forgive herself for taking away the thing that meant most in the world to Ryan.

Eventually, after Ryan had fitted the cone to Truffle's collar, Georgie fell asleep; the next morning, the alarm on her watch woke her, and for a moment she was disorientated. She wasn't in bed: she was lying on the floor. And somehow, during the night, Truffle had moved. The gap between Georgie and Ryan was no longer there: instead, they were lying wrapped in each other's arms.

She kept her eyes tightly shut.

What did she do now?

She hadn't woken in someone's arms since Charlie's death. She was willing to bet it was the same for Ryan, since his divorce.

This closeness had happened while they were asleep. Neither of them had planned this.

Like that kiss in the garden, under the Northern Lights.

If she wriggled out of his arms, the movement would wake him and she'd have to face the embarrassment and awkwardness. If she stayed where she was, she'd have to pretend to be asleep after he woke; given that her breathing was shallow, he'd know that she was awake. And that would lead to awkwardness, too.

There was no easy way out of this.

And then Ryan stirred, and gently disentangled himself from her arms.

OK. He was awake and he'd decided to move first. She'd take her lead from him. She opened her eyes, though she didn't quite dare look him in the eye. 'Morning.'

'Morning,' he said.

But he didn't comment about the way they'd woken up. That was good. He clearly wanted to avoid the awkwardness, too. 'How's Truffle?' she asked.

The dog's tail thumped on the floor as she responded to her name.

'She looks OK,' Ryan said, and took the cone off. 'Want to go out, girl? I'm afraid it'll have to be on the lead. I can't risk you rushing about and knocking your leg.'

Georgie sneaked a tiny glance while he took Truffle to the kitchen door and pulled on his boots and a coat over his pyjamas. Dishevelled from sleep, he was utterly gorgeous. And it made all her senses hum with longing. But right now they still had fences to mend between them so she needed to put a lid on that reaction.

She got to her feet. Keeping busy was the way she usually dealt with things.

By the time he came back in with the dog, she'd made coffee and laid the table for breakfast.

'You didn't have to do that.'

'I wanted breakfast, and it's as quick to make it for two as for one,' she said.

He looked exhausted. The worry and the emotions from yesterday had clearly taken it out of him.

'Thanks.'

She didn't push him to talk, but after breakfast when he went to have a shower she finished the washing up, then sat on the floor with the dog.

'I'm so sorry about what happened,' she said, stroking the top of Truffle's head. 'It was totally my fault and I shouldn't have been careless with you. I know what it feels like when someone's careless with you.' She bit her lip. 'I feel bad that I hurt Ryan as much as Charlie hurt me. I don't know how I'm going to make it up to him, but I'm just going to have to try harder.'

I hurt Ryan as much as Charlie hurt me.

The words echoed in Ryan's head and he couldn't quite make sense of them.

From what Georgie had told him, Charlie had been a hero. He'd been killed in a landslide while he'd been out helping in an earthquake disaster zone. And she'd been crying a few days ago on her wedding anniversary, which told Ryan that she was still deeply in mourning for her late husband.

But now he wondered. How deeply would you mourn someone who'd hurt you?

She'd said that someone had been careless with her,

and that Charlie had hurt her. Were those two statements related or separate? What had happened?

Not that he could ask. He'd have to wait until Georgie was ready to talk about it—if she ever was. But, with this and the couple of things she'd already let slip, it seemed everything hadn't been quite as wonderful in her marriage as he'd originally thought.

He walked more heavily down the stairs so she'd be aware of his presence; it would give her time to get herself together if she needed to.

'Thank you for keeping an eye on Truffle for me,' he said when he went into the living room.

'It's the least I could do.' She paused. 'I've been thinking—maybe we should look at the roster again and try to move our shifts so one of us is on an early while the other's on a late, so Truffle has company as much as possible. And if you can teach me what sort of things to do to keep her occupied, I'll do my best.'

She really was trying hard to make up for what she'd done.

And, now he was pretty sure Truffle was going to be all right, his anger had dissipated. 'Thank you. And I'm sorry I took it out on you yesterday, when I was worried about Truffle. It wasn't fair of me.'

She lifted her chin. 'I deserved everything you said. You'd warned me she's an absconder. I should have checked the door properly. The stupid thing is, in London I would've double-checked; I know it's no excuse, but here it feels safer.'

'Here, it *is* safer,' he said.

'But I still should've checked, and I'm sorry. And I was going to say to you yesterday, I'll cover the vet's bill because it was my fault.'

'She's insured,' he said. 'But I appreciate the back-up for keeping her occupied. She's going to be bored.'

'Just tell me what the doggy equivalent to reading a gazillion stories and doing art stuff is,' she said.

'Is that what you do with your niece?'

'That and dancing,' she said. 'But you want Truffle to rest physically as much as possible, right? So not the doggy equivalent of dancing.'

He could imagine Georgie sitting with her niece on her lap, reading stories, or at the table, drawing and making models from play dough. And from there it was a tiny step to imagining her doing that with her own child. A little girl who was the spit of her mother—but with grey eyes and dark auburn hair, like his own.

Oh, help.

He'd never imagined himself as a father before. Not with Zoe, even though he'd loved her. But maybe that was because he and Zoe hadn't been quite the right fit.

Was he the right fit with Georgie?

The idea sent him into a flat spin. He was worried sick about the one constant in his life, the dog he regarded as his entire family. Right now, he didn't have the head-space to face the ghosts of his past and work out whether he could deal with them.

Knowing that he was being a coward, but doing it anyway, he said, 'I'll just go and get some more bread from the farm shop before you leave for work, if that's OK?'

'Sure. Truffle and I are going to watch a rerun of *Friends*,' she said.

She was actually sitting on the floor with the dog now, taking as much care of her as Ryan would himself, and it made him feel as if something had cracked around his heart. Something that started to let the light in.

* * *

The feeling intensified over the next couple of days. Georgie was really, really good with Truffle. She was patient, she kept the dog amused and helped tire her out so she wasn't fractious. He could trust her with his dog; so maybe, even though the idea of letting anyone that close to him terrified him, he could trust her with himself. Trust that even when her six-month job swap was up, she'd work with him to find a way for them to stay together.

But she was behaving more like a best friend than anything else. How could he explain to her that his feelings towards her were changing—that he was starting to want things he'd always believed he didn't? And that he wanted them with her?

Sharing a house with Ryan was driving Georgie crackers. He'd made it very clear that he wanted nothing more than friendship from her—that he didn't want to get involved with anyone again, and he wasn't going to act on the attraction between them, despite that kiss.

Maybe a mad fling would get him out of her system.

But Georgie didn't want a mad fling. If anything was going to happen between them, she wanted more than one night; she wanted to see where it would take them.

Which left them at stalemate, because Ryan McGregor was one of the most stubborn men she'd ever met.

She was working in the PAU at lunchtime on the Saturday when a four-year-old girl came in. Jennie had had a cold, which had then turned into a cough that wouldn't go away. Her mum said it was worse at night but thought all colds were like that; and now Jennie was struggling to breathe, her chest was wheezy and she'd complained of chest pain. There was obvious sucking in at the base of her throat.

All the signs told Georgie that this was probably asthma, but she wanted to run an ECG to check the little girl's heart. She went in search of someone to help her do the ECG while she did a full examination, and Ryan just happened to be in the corridor.

'Everything OK?' he asked.

'No, I have a patient with suspected asthma and I want to run an ECG, so I need someone in with me to do that while I help her with her breathing.'

'I'll do it,' he said.

He was too senior for this, really, but she wasn't going to argue; she wanted to help her patient *now*.

She took him back to the treatment room and introduced him to Jennie and her mum.

'Is there any asthma or hay fever or allergies in your family?' Ryan asked.

Jennie's mum shook her head. 'Not in her dad's, either. Is that what you think it is?'

'It's possible,' Georgie said. 'But we'll concentrate on getting Jennie breathing easily before we run some tests.'

'Can you sit up straight for us, Jennie?' Ryan asked. 'That'll make it easier for you to breathe.'

The little girl nodded, a tear running down her face, and sat up straight.

'That's really good,' Georgie said. 'Now I'd like you to breathe in through your nose and out through your mouth. Take it slowly. All the way in, all the way out.'

She guided Jennie through the breathing; once the little girl seemed calmer, she fitted a blue inhaler into a spacer. 'This is special medication to help you breathe,' she said. 'I want you to hold the tube for me, and put the mouthpiece in your mouth. I'm going to press this bit on the end to put the medicine in the tube and I want you to breathe in to make the tube whistle for me. Can you do that?'

Jennie nodded again, and did what Georgie asked.

'That's brilliant,' Ryan said. 'You're being so brave.' He glanced at his watch and counted off a minute. 'Another big breath in of the medicine?'

They repeated a puff of the inhaler per minute for ten puffs, then checked Jennie's oxygen saturation levels. Ryan distracted Jennie with a series of terrible jokes while Georgie took bloods, and then Georgie put sticky pads on Jennie's chest so they could run an ECG.

'The pattern on this paper is a picture of how your heart is beating,' Ryan said. 'And that's beautifully normal.'

Jennie's mum looked relieved. 'So is it asthma?' she asked.

'Coughing and wheezing can be caused by things other than asthma,' Georgie said, 'and Jennie's too young to do some of the tests to show how her lungs are working, so I know this is going to be frustrating but we'll need to do a trial of treatment for the next few weeks.'

'We can give you a blue inhaler and a spacer like this one for her to use when she has bad symptoms,' Ryan said. 'The inhaler will give Jennie a dose of corticosteroids—they're the ones the body produces naturally, not the ones you hear of bodybuilders taking—and using it in the form of an inhaler means that the medicine goes straight into her airways. It'll open them up and help keep her safe while we're trying to work out what's causing the problem.'

'And we'll need you to keep a diary for your doctor,'

Georgie said. 'So when Jennie has symptoms, write down what they are, the date and time, what the weather's like and what's happening at the time—so if there's a pet nearby, or it's really cold, or she was running about. I can print something out for you to make it easier to remember.'

'Thank you,' Jennie's mum said.

'This is going to sound a bit callous,' Ryan said, 'but when she's wheezing or coughing, if you record her on your phone it will really help your doctor or the asthma nurse hear what her symptoms are like.'

'And then if you can write down how many puffs she takes of the inhaler, and whether that helps her, it stays the same or it gets worse,' Georgie said. 'The more information you can give, the more it will help your doctor to spot the patterns and make a firm diagnosis.'

'I'll make sure I do that,' Jennie's mum said.

'That's great,' Georgie said. 'I'll give you an action plan for the next couple of months so you can share it with Jennie's nursery, your family and friends, so then they'll know what to do if she gets any asthma symptoms. The action plan tells you how to spot the early signs of problems and what to do.'

'If she needs to use an inhaler more than three times a week,' Ryan said, 'then your asthma nurse will give you a brown preventer inhaler, which Jennie needs to take every day to help stop her getting the symptoms in the first place. But let's see how we go in the next couple of months. Obviously, if you're worried, see your doctor; and if the inhaler doesn't help, bring her straight back here.'

'Thank you,' Jennie's mum said.

Ryan crouched down so he was at Jennie's level.

'You've been really brave.' He produced a sparkly 'I was brave' sticker from his pocket. 'So I think you deserve this.'

'Thank you,' Jennie said shyly.

Georgie printed out the action plan and asthma diary for Jennie's mum, and helped her fill it in. 'We'll obviously send all the details to your family doctor, but do go and make an appointment to see the asthma specialist in eight weeks' time.'

'I will,' Jennie's mum promised, and took her daughter's hand.

Why was it, Georgie wondered, that she and Ryan were so in tune at work, virtually able to finish each other's sentences—and yet when it came to their personal life, he backed away from her? She really thought they could be good together.

But if Ryan wasn't prepared to give them a chance, there was nothing she could do to change his mind. She'd have to give up. And next year, when she went back to London, he'd fade out of her life.

CHAPTER EIGHT

'ONLY A MEAL for one tonight?' Janie asked, looking surprised.

'It's the departmental night out,' Ryan explained. 'I'm staying at home with Truffle so Georgie can go.'

'If Truffle hadn't had her accident, would you have been going?' Janie asked.

Ryan grimaced. 'Probably. Though only because I wouldn't have had a good excuse *not* to go.'

'What's the problem?' Janie asked.

'It's a ceilidh.' If he didn't dance with Georgie, people would notice and start speculating; if he did dance with her, he'd end up thinking of the night he'd kissed her and the morning she'd woken in his arms. Which would be a bad idea for both of them, because he still hadn't sorted his head out.

'Dancing's good for you. You're a doctor, so you should know that,' Janie said with a grin. 'What's the real problem?'

His head was completely mixed up when it came to Georgie: though he wasn't telling Janie *that*. 'I delegated the organisation to one of my colleagues. She says all the men have to wear kilts.'

'And you don't have one?' She smiled at him. 'No problem. My Donald's about your size. He can lend you one.'

'I have a kilt,' Ryan said.

'Then there's no problem, is there?' Janie said. 'Truffle can have a sleepover with me and Donald, so you don't have to worry about getting back early for her. You work hard enough. You deserve a break. A night out will do you good.' She took the foil tray of casserole from his basket. 'I'm not selling you that. You go dancing in that kilt. And no arguments from you, or I'll text Clara and she'll nag you.'

Ryan knew when to give in. So he duly dropped Truffle at Janie's, showered and changed into his kilt.

When he came downstairs, Georgie was ready. 'I'll drive us, if you like.'

For a moment, he couldn't answer because his tongue felt stuck to the roof of his mouth. Georgie looked amazing. Her hair was up, and she was wearing just enough mascara to make her green eyes look huge, and red lipstick that made her mouth look temptingly kissable. She was wearing heels, making her legs look as if they went on for ever; though her sleeveless red dress was very demure, with a skirt that came down to just below her knee and a rounded neckline that just skimmed her collarbones. And he was filled with the urge to take her into his arms and do one of those complicated dance moves that would spin her out and let her skirt swish round, then spin her back so she was in his arms again.

'Ryan? Is everything all right?'

He gathered himself together. 'It's fine. No, I'll drive and you can have a glass of wine or whatever,' he said.

'All right.' She coughed. 'You look very nice.'

He took a deep breath and hoped that his voice sounded normal when he said, 'As do you.' He gestured to the door. 'Let's go.'

'Very nice' didn't even begin to describe how Ryan McGregor looked in a kilt.

Georgie had only ever seen men wearing kilts on TV or in the movies. She wasn't prepared for just how good the outfit looked in real life. She had no idea what the black and grey tartan was—she planned to look it up surreptitiously online, rather than embarrass herself by asking him—but it suited him, particularly as it was teamed with a Prince Charlie jacket with ornate buttons, a waistcoat, a sporran, a wing-collar shirt and a black bow tie. His shoes were highly polished, his socks showed off very well-formed knees, and she went hot all over when she remembered all the suggestions about exactly what a Scot wore under his kilt.

Oh, help.

The last thing he needed was her behaving like a schoolgirl with a huge crush.

Even though she *did* have a huge crush on him.

More than a crush. She was more than halfway to falling in love with this dour, difficult man—a man who had a huge heart and had so much to give, but kept himself closed off.

He didn't say much on the way into the city, and she walked beside him to the club where they were meeting the rest of the team, not having a clue where they were going.

Parminder and the others were waiting outside; and, as Parm had decreed, every single one of the men was wearing a kilt. Some were wearing a casual ghillie shirt, and others had chosen the more formal option of wing collar and Prince Charlie jacket, but not a single one could hold a candle to Ryan in the gorgeousness stakes.

'I have to say I'm very impressed,' she said with a smile. 'Excellent organisation on your part, Parm, and what a handsome team we have. You all scrub up rather nicely.'

Alistair grinned at her and did a pirouette. 'Some of us more so than others.'

'You look very pretty in your skirt, Al,' she teased.

'*Skirt*,' he huffed, laughing. 'I'll have you know that's my clan tartan and an eight-yard kilt you're talking about.' He gave her a lascivious wink. 'If you're very good, I'll tell you what I keep in my sporran.'

'Yeah, yeah,' she retorted, laughing back because she knew Alistair was completely harmless and just teasing her.

'Now we're all here, let's go in,' Parminder said. 'The first half of the night's a proper ceilidh, and then it's general dancing.'

The hall was wonderful; the overhead lights were turned down low and fairy lights draped the walls and the columns, making the place seem magical. A band was playing on a stage at one end, and there was a caller to organise everything.

Their team joined the dance floor for the next set of reels, and Georgie enjoyed herself hugely. Then, while the band had a break, the caller acted as a DJ and streamed music through the sound system.

Alistair turned out to be as terrible a dancer as he'd told her he was, but Georgie and Parminder helped him as much as they could. And at least dancing with Alistair stopped her making a fool of herself by falling at Ryan's feet, she thought. She danced with all the men from their ward; she danced with what felt like everyone in the whole room for the next few sets of reels; and the only person she hadn't danced with properly was Ryan.

Was he avoiding her?

But then the band left the stage and the caller went back to playing recorded music, this time slowing things down. Couples took to the floor, dancing cheek to cheek, and loneliness flowed over Georgie like a wave.

She'd loved dancing with Charlie.

But Charlie wasn't here any more. Even if he hadn't been killed by the landslide, he probably wouldn't have been with her. He would've been with his new family—the family he hadn't wanted to have with her.

She was lost in thought when Ryan walked over to her.

'May I?'

Her head was suddenly too jumbled to find words, so she nodded.

He drew her into his arms and held her close, dancing cheek to cheek with her. Just as they'd been that night under the stars, watching the Northern Lights. Georgie thought of the way he'd kissed her then and it felt as if all the air had hissed out of her lungs.

This was just a dance. Just a dance. If she told herself that often enough, she'd believe it.

Yet he seemed to be drawing her closer still, and her arms were tightly wrapped round him.

Everything around them vanished; all she was aware of was Ryan, the warmth and tautness of his body and his clean masculine scent.

She wasn't sure which of them moved first, but then his lips were brushing against hers, light as a butterfly's wing and sensitising every nerve-ending. And she was kissing him back, tiny nibbles that segued into something deeper, more sensual.

When he broke the kiss, his grey eyes were almost black in the low light. 'Let's get out of here.' His voice was husky, almost rusty, with desire.

They were by the door. Nobody would notice them leave; nobody would gossip. Their colleagues would assume they'd gone back early to check on Truffle. 'Yes,' she said.

To her relief, they didn't bump into anyone from the department when they collected their coats. And Ryan didn't chat to her as they headed back to his car; though he held her hand all the way, and every so often he stopped to kiss her beneath a lamp-post. And he held her hand all the way back to the cottage, only breaking contact when he needed to change gear.

By the time they were back at the cottage, Georgie was almost quivering in anticipation.

Maybe this was an insane thing to do. Or maybe this was what both of them needed, to help them move on. Maybe actually giving in to the way they reacted to each other physically would sort both their heads out and they'd find this whole thing wasn't complicated after all.

He shrugged his coat off, then removed hers. 'Dance with me again?' he asked.

She nodded, and he found something slow and sweet on his phone before taking her back in his arms.

This time, when he kissed her, she didn't have to worry about who might see and gossip about it. It was just the two of them in the low light of the single lamp he'd switched on.

This time, when he broke the kiss, his eyes held a challenge. 'So where do we go from here?'

'My room.'

'Are you sure?'

Meaning that if she said no, he'd back off. He wouldn't push her into anything she wasn't ready to do. 'Very sure,' she said. 'I've wanted this since the night you kissed me under the stars.'

He stroked her face. 'I made a wish on a falling star.'

That this would happen? 'Good.' She reached up on tiptoe and kissed him again.

His pupils dilated a fraction further. 'I want to turn caveman and carry you to bed,' he said. 'But a spiral staircase isn't the best idea and I don't want to drop you.'

'I've got a better one,' she said, and kicked off her shoes before taking his hand and leading him up the stairs.

At the doorway to her room, he kissed her again.

'That dress. Since I first saw you in it, I wanted to do one of those flashy dance moves that makes your skirt twirl out, then spin you back into my arms.' His breath caught. 'And I want to take it off you.'

'That kilt and that jacket,' she said. 'It makes you look hot.' She felt her face grow warm. 'And your wild hair.'

'It's wild because I can't be bothered to visit the barber every month.'

She stroked his face. 'It makes you look like a Scottish chieftain.'

'I'll run with that,' he said. 'Which means I get to do this.' He slid his hand up her spine, making her arch her back, then slid the zip down very, very slowly. His gaze was intense as it held hers, and he pushed the material gently off her shoulders; her dress slid to the floor in a puddle. Colour slashed across his cheeks and he drew in a sharp breath. 'Well, now, Dr Jones.' He scooped her up in his arms, clearly with the intention of carrying her to her bed.

'Not so fast,' she said.

'No?' He went very still.

'No. Because you're wearing too much,' she said. 'We need to even that up first.'

Then he smiled. 'What do you suggest, Dr Jones?'

'There are two ways we can do this. The first,' she said, 'is that you set me back on my feet and let me undress you. The second is that you carry me to my bed and then strip for me.'

His smile grew more sensual. 'And your preferred course?'

'I don't know,' she admitted. 'I'm greedy. I kind of want both.'

'Compromise, then.' He set her back on her feet. 'Do the jacket.'

The buttons on his jacket weren't fastened, so it was easy to remove; but the matching buttons on the waistcoat were incredibly ornate and it took her a while to undo them. His bow tie was next—a proper one, she noticed, not a pre-tied one that clipped on. As she undid the buttons of his shirt, his breathing grew quicker and more shallow. She untucked the shirt from the waistband of his kilt, then slid the material over his shoulders, letting it fall to the floor.

Bare-chested, he was beautiful. There was a light sprinkling of hair on his chest, and his abdomen was flat. But there was no vanity in him: he simply looked after himself properly. 'Perfect,' she whispered.

This time, when he scooped her up into his arms, her skin slid against his, and desire flickered low in her belly.

He kissed her again, hard, and laid her down against the pillows.

'So you wanted me to strip for you.'

'Partly because I have no idea how a kilt fastens,' she admitted.

He chuckled. 'Buckles, Dr Jones. Buckles. And a kilt pin, to preserve your modesty when you sit down.'

Was he telling her that he wasn't wearing anything underneath the kilt?

She went hot all over.

'First, the sporran,' he said.

'What exactly is a sporran?' she asked.

'The word's Gaelic for "pocket",' he said, 'and that's exactly what it is. It's where I keep my keys and my wallet. Putting a pocket in a kilt would spoil the line.'

'Uh-huh.'

He undid the buckle at the back before dropping it on the floor with his jacket.

'Then the kilt pin.'

'Give me a twirl,' she said.

He grinned, and did so—meaning she got to see the perfect musculature in his back.

'Then the buckles,' he whispered. 'Except I need to do some tidying first.'

'Tidying?' She couldn't think straight. She was still trying to work out what he was wearing under that kilt.

'Aye. Tidying.' He picked up her dress and hung it neatly over the back of the chair, hanging his jacket, waistcoat and shirt over the top of it.

Now she understood.

Ryan McGregor was a man who took care of things.

Next, he took off his socks. 'Because there's an order to underwear,' he added.

And a man wearing nothing but socks wasn't sexy. 'Excellent idea,' she said.

He held her gaze, then, and undid first the lower buckle on his right hip and then the upper. He held it with his left hand, while he crossed his left hand over to his right hip to undo the final buckle.

'And once the buckles are done,' he said, his voice low and sexy, 'you take the kilt off.' He turned away from her, and removed the kilt...

...to reveal soft black jersey shorts that clung to him.

'So a Scotsman *does* wear something under his kilt, then,' she said, her voice shaky.

'This one does, aye.' He placed the kilt neatly on the other clothes on the back of the chair, and gave her the most scorching look. 'But close your eyes and hold that thought.'

He was going shy on her, after looking at her like *that*?

OK. She'd run with it.

She closed her eyes. But when the bed still didn't dip under his weight, she opened her eyes.

She was alone in the room.

Clearly he'd changed his mind.

She was about to get up and close the door, when he reappeared. 'You were supposed to keep your eyes closed and hold that thought,' he said. 'Because there's something important I needed.'

Then she saw the little box in his hand. Condoms. Again, he was being careful with her, and she appreciated it.

'Since you opened your eyes,' he said, 'I think it's my turn.'

'Your turn?'

'For the show. You're wearing more than me.'

'Taking off my tights isn't sexy.'

He raised an eyebrow. 'Are you asking me to do it?'

She sucked in a breath. 'Yes.'

'Then your wish is my command,' he said, giving her a deep bow.

He placed the box of condoms on her bedside table, then sat on the bed next to her and slid his fingers underneath the waistband of her tights before gently drawing them downwards. With one hand, he urged her to lift her bottom from the bed so he could take the nylon down further; and then he peeled the tights off achingly slowly, caressing every bit of skin as he uncovered it.

By the time he'd finished, Georgie was quivering.

She wasn't sure which of them removed which bit of clothing next, because by then everything was blurred by desperate need; all she was aware of was how badly she wanted him and how her temperature felt as if it had risen a thousand degrees.

Ryan kissed her, his mouth sensual and persuading, until she was a quivering mess; but it still wasn't enough to sate her desire. She wanted more. *So much more.*

She must've said it out loud, because at last he moved between her thighs.

'Are you sure about this?' he asked.

'I'm a bit out of practice, but I'm very sure,' she whispered.

He reached over to take a condom from the box.

She curled her fingers round his. 'Let me.'

'Of course,' he said, and his smile was so sexy that she felt the pulse beating hard between her legs.

The past didn't matter any more. All that mattered was this man, here and now, and how much she wanted him.

She undid the foil packet and caressed his hard length,

making him gasp with pleasure, then rolled the condom on.

'Now?' he asked.

'Now,' she whispered.

He eased inside her, gaze intense and focused on hers. It should've been awkward and faintly embarrassing, the first time, but it just felt so *right*.

Then he began to move. 'Keep your eyes open,' he said.

And she did. Instead of closing her eyes and giving up to the sensations shimmering through her, she watched his eyes, his face. She could see her own desire reflected there, the need.

And then she felt her climax splintering through her, felt his body tighten against hers and heard his answering cry.

He held her for a few moments longer, then went to deal with the condom.

When he came back, he went to pick up his discarded clothes.

'Don't go,' she said.

She could see the emotions running through his expression—longing, as if he wanted to stay, and regret, as if he thought it'd be a bad idea to let her this close.

'Just for tonight,' she said. They could deal with the fallout tomorrow. But she wanted tonight first.

As if he guessed what she was thinking, Ryan nodded and slid into bed beside her, drawing her into his arms. Georgie curled against him, feeling warmer and happier than she had for a very long time, and finally fell asleep.

The next morning, Ryan was the first to wake.

He didn't regret last night—he was so glad he'd had

that moment of closeness with her, because it had been everything he'd hoped it would be—but this whole thing made him feel seriously antsy. If he got this wrong, they'd both end up hurt.

He shifted so he could see her as she slept. She was so sweet, so gorgeous and so giving.

Maybe he should get out of the bed without waking her, and then they could face this when they were both fully clothed; but he couldn't bring himself to abandon her.

And then her eyes opened.

'Hello,' she said, all pink-cheeked and shy and adorable.

He desperately wanted to kiss her, but that would complicate things. 'Hello,' he said softly.

His feelings must have shown on his face, because her eyes narrowed slightly. 'You're not OK with this, are you?'

'It's not you. It's me.'

'Uh-huh. That's what men say when they want to make themselves feel less guilty.'

He raked a hand through his hair. 'I'm not trying to make myself feel less guilty. But I shouldn't have even kissed you last night. It wasn't fair to you.'

'Because you're still in love with your ex and you're not ready to move on?'

'No. I'm not still in love with my ex.'

'Then why?'

'Because,' he said, 'I'm not good at relationships and I shouldn't have led you on.'

'Uh-huh.'

He grimaced. 'I need to be honest with you. It's my

fault my marriage broke up. I loved Zoe, and she loved me, and I honestly never meant to hurt her.'

'You cheated on her?'

Why on earth had she assumed that? 'No. I would never have done that. But I still hurt her. She wanted me to let her close. She wanted to have children. And I couldn't do either of those things.'

The expression on her face told him she was assuming he meant he was infertile, and she could think of plenty of solutions. He needed to tell her the truth.

'Not that I couldn't—I wouldn't,' he corrected himself. 'Since I was six, I'd learned to rely on myself and not let people close. Zoe couldn't change that. Neither of us wanted children when we got married—we were both focused on our careers. But then things changed. Her biological clock started ticking, and mine didn't.' He shrugged. 'Having children or not having children isn't something you can compromise on. One of you has to lose. But I never pretended to be someone I wasn't.'

'Charlie pretended,' she said, surprising him.

'How?'

'He was seeing someone else,' she said. 'Every time he went somewhere to help after a disaster, she was there as well.'

Ryan stared at her, shocked. Now he knew why she'd leapt to that conclusion earlier: because it had happened to her before. Her husband had cheated on her. 'That's horrible. I'm sorry.'

'He lied to her, too. He told her he wasn't married.'

He knew it was rude and intrusive but he couldn't help asking. 'How did you find out about it?'

'Her parents wrote to me at the hospital. He'd told Trish that I was his sister. They wanted to know if they could come to his funeral, or if I wanted to go to Trish's. They talked about him, said how much Trish had loved him. I hadn't had a clue.' She swallowed hard. 'I think I broke their hearts even further when I called them to explain that Charlie was an only child and I was his wife. And they kind of broke mine a bit more when they told me Trish had been expecting his baby.'

He remembered she'd said something about expecting to be a mum by this point in her life. 'Had you been...?'

She shook her head. 'We'd planned to. But then, when we got to the point where we'd planned to start trying, Charlie changed his mind. He kept coming up with reasons why we should wait a bit. So clearly he didn't want to make a family with me.'

Which had clearly hurt her. He was glad he hadn't kept Zoe hanging on a string like that.

'I don't know whether he even knew she was pregnant. She might not have had a chance to tell him, because they'd only been out there for a couple of days when they were killed, and she might've wanted to wait for the right moment before telling him.' She dragged in a breath. 'She was four months gone. If they'd lived, the baby would've been crawling by now.'

'That's tough,' he said. 'I'm sorry he cheated on you and I'm sorry you found out that way.' He paused. 'How did his parents react?'

'I didn't tell them,' she said. 'I thought about it. But what was the point? Everyone thought Charlie was a hero. And he was. He was a brilliant emergency doctor, and he went out to help in disaster areas.'

'And he cheated on you and lied to his mistress,' Ryan pointed out. In his view, the way Charlie had treated his wife pretty much cancelled his hero status.

'That wasn't relevant to anyone else,' she said. 'His family, his friends—they were all mourning the man they loved, the man they'd respected. What was the point of making them all feel worse? What would it achieve, telling his parents that their only son had been about to give them a much-wanted grandchild but oh, by the way, said grandchild was killed along with his father?'

'How did you live with that, though? Knowing Charlie wasn't the man they all thought he was, and pretending that you agreed with them—when really you weren't just mourning the man you married, you were hurt by his betrayal?'

She spread her hands. 'He wasn't there to defend himself or explain himself. It wouldn't have been fair to tell everyone the truth.'

'It wasn't fair to you, *not* telling the truth,' Ryan pointed out.

'That's really why I wanted to get away from London. Not just because I was sick of the pity, but I was near to cracking and blurting it out, and then the pity would've been so much worse.'

'And you didn't tell anyone at all? Not even your best friend?'

'I didn't know how.' She bit her lip. 'I told my brother. But only because he was so upset that I was bailing out on him, so I thought I owed him the truth. He was so angry on my behalf. But I swore him to secrecy.'

'I think you're a nicer person than I am. I would've told people the truth.'

'What was the point?' Georgie asked again. 'It wouldn't have achieved anything except hurting people who were already hurting. His parents had suffered enough. And they're nice people. They didn't deserve to have their illusions shattered.' She sat up and wrapped her arms round her knees. 'I still wonder what would've happened if Charlie and Trish hadn't been caught in that landslide. Would he have left me for her? Would they have brought up their child together?'

'Don't torture yourself,' Ryan said. 'You'll never know and it didn't happen.'

'No, but I have to face that I wasn't enough to keep Charlie happy. Otherwise he wouldn't have looked elsewhere. There's obviously something wrong with me.'

Ryan was outraged on her behalf. How could she possibly think that she was the one at fault? 'There's nothing wrong with you.'

'No?' But Georgie didn't quite dare voice what was in her head. If there wasn't something lacking in her, then she would've been enough for Charlie and she would be enough for Ryan—and she clearly wasn't enough for him, or he wouldn't be backing away from her right now at the speed of light.

'There's really nothing wrong with you,' he confirmed. 'Nothing at all. Any man would be lucky to have you in his life.'

Did he include himself in that?

She'd ducked the issue last night, because she'd really wanted to be held, to sleep in his arms. She'd wanted to make love with him. She had no regrets at all. But she wasn't a coward. She knew the reckoning came now, and she was going to face it. 'So where does that leave us?'

He looked haunted. 'I like you, Georgie. I like you a lot. I think we could be good together.'

Hope leaped in her heart. Was he going to give them a chance?

'*But.*'

The hope came crashing back down again. Stupid. Of course there was a but.

He took a deep breath. 'This whole thing scares me spitless. You want children. I never thought that was where my life would take me. It's so easy to get things wrong, to make a mistake. We've both been hurt. And taking a risk with you… I'm not sure I can do this.'

She looked at him. 'Can I ask you something?'

He gave her a wary look. 'What?'

'I accept that you don't want children. But can I ask *why*?'

He raked a hand through his hair. 'You know about my background. After my mum died, nobody wanted me. I don't want to put a child through that.'

'Understood,' she said. 'But if your mum hadn't been knocked off her bike, she would've loved you. She might have met someone and you would've gained a ready-made family.'

'But that didn't happen.'

'And,' she said, 'there's another difference. If you had a child—if anything happened to you, that child would still have a mum and a family who loved him or her. Or if anything happened to your partner, your child would still have you.'

'True,' he said. 'But I don't remember what it's like to be a son. I didn't grow up with a male role model. How do I know I'd be any good as a dad?'

'Because,' she said, 'I've seen you at work. You care for your patients as if they're your own flesh and blood. I've seen you sit with a young child in your break and read stories, or just chat to one of the older ones.'

'I'm merely keeping them from being bored, so they don't disrupt the ward,' he said.

She thought there was more to it than that. She'd noticed he spent time with kids who didn't have a family. That wasn't the act of a man who didn't like children. 'And Truffle.' His rescue dog. 'You love her. You make sure she's fed and exercised and feels loved.'

'That's different.'

'It isn't, Ryan. You treat her the way that other men would treat their child. You've told me yourself that she's your family. So don't try to kid yourself. You're putting all these barriers in the way, but they're not as big as you think they are. And you're not going to be on your own if you try to get over them.'

He shook his head. 'I don't want to hurt you, Georgie. But you need to know I'm really not good at relationships.'

Pain lanced through her. He was giving up on them that easily? He didn't think she was worth the effort? 'So you're saying we call it a halt?'

'I think that's the best thing.'

'Because you're too scared to take a chance.'

His eyes widened. 'So you think I'm a coward?'

'No, I don't think you're a coward,' she said. 'I think you're scared and you're stubborn and you've decided that everything's set in a certain way. But life isn't like that, Ryan. It's flexible. Things change. It's not about being perfect and getting things right all the time. It's about trying, about learning to compromise and realising it's OK if something goes a different way from the way you'd planned it.'

Did she have to spell it out for him?

Maybe. It was a risk. But, if she didn't take it, she

knew she'd always regret it. 'All you have to do is reach out.' Reach out, and she'd be there.

'All you have to do is reach out.'

Did Georgie have any idea how hard that was?

She'd clearly grown up being dearly loved. To the point where she was careful with other people—even though Charlie had hurt her badly with his affair and the baby, she'd still thought about his family and friends and protected their happy memories rather than tarnish them with the painful truth. Ryan wasn't sure he could've been that noble, in her shoes.

And he didn't think he could reach out and grab what she was offering. Deep down, he didn't think he deserved it. Otherwise someone would've tried to keep him before, wouldn't they? His grandparents, his foster parents—all the people who hadn't wanted him enough. Zoe had given up on him. Why would it be any different with Georgie?

'I can't,' he said.

She looked sad. 'You're not even going to try, are you?'

'No,' he said. He felt guilty and miserable, but he couldn't change who he was. He knew he'd only disappoint Georgie. It was better to back off now and keep his heart intact than to let himself believe that someone could really love him, and then learn the hard way that he'd fooled himself again.

'Thank you for being honest.' She lifted her chin. 'I'll find somewhere else to live for the rest of the job swap.'

'No. I'm the one causing the problem, so I ought to be the one to move out.'

She shook her head. 'As you told me, landlords don't like renting places to someone with a dog, particularly a dog who chews. So it'll be easier for me to be the one to go.'

This was when he was supposed to agree. She was giving him what he'd asked for. He couldn't give her what she wanted, so he should just let her go.

So why did his mouth open and the words, 'Don't go,' come out?

She just stared at him.

Maybe this was the best compromise. 'Don't go,' he said again. 'We can be adult about this. We can ignore the—' Well, he had to admit to that much. 'We can ignore the attraction between us, just as we do at work.'

'Says the man who made love with me last night and even now is sitting in my bed,' she said wryly.

'I'm sorry. I wish I could be different, I really do. But I can't. I've tried in the past and I've never really been able to let anyone close to me. If that's what you want from me, all I'll do is hurt you and I don't want to do that.' He took a deep breath. 'I don't regret last night, and I definitely don't regret being with you. But I am what I am. I'm sorry I can't be who you want me to be.'

'Thank you,' she said, 'for being honest.'

So why did he feel like the biggest bastard in the universe?

'I'm sorry,' he said again. And, because the emotional stuff was getting too much for him and he needed to escape, he added, 'I'd better go and get Truffle.'

Georgie stayed curled in bed until she heard the front door close.

Ryan McGregor was strong, silent, stubborn—and oh, so stupid.

Why did he have to be so difficult about this?

Why couldn't he take that leap of faith and just *try* to see where things went between them?

It seemed that friendship was the most he was going to offer. Take it or leave it.

He'd been honest with her, unlike Charlie. Ryan hadn't lied to her, and she knew he would never cheat. But she was also pretty sure he wouldn't budge. He wasn't going to give them a chance. And that hurt so, so much.

What was so wrong with her that he didn't feel comfortable taking a risk with her? Was she right about there being something lacking in her—the same thing Charlie had obviously picked up on when he'd turned to Trisha?

And how were they going to deal with the rest of the job swap?

He'd asked her to stay. But not because he wanted her: because, she thought, he felt guilty about letting Clara down.

Perhaps she'd been right in the first place to think about finding somewhere else to stay. Though asking someone at the hospital where she could find somewhere else to live—that would make it obvious there were problems between herself and Ryan. And everyone would jump to conclusions and gossip, and once the truth was out everyone would start to pity her—the very thing she'd tried so hard to avoid in London.

What an idiot she'd been.

She should've said no last night. Gone to bed on her own, instead of giving in to the temptation to make love with him. It would still have been awkward between them for a while, but at least the situation would've been salvageable. Whereas now she knew what it felt like to make love with him and fall asleep in his arms. She'd lied to herself that it was just for comfort, just for fun, that her heart wasn't involved.

But her heart was involved. Somewhere along the way, she'd fallen in love with the dour Scot who was great with his colleagues and his patients, but who kept a huge barrier between himself and the rest of the world because he was too scared to let himself get close to someone again and be let down. A man who trusted his dog and his best friend, and steadfastly refused to open his heart to anyone else.

If she'd been enough for him, then he would've taken the risk and let down his barriers.

But she wasn't.

She hadn't been enough for Charlie—the man she'd married but who'd made a baby with someone else, instead of her—and she wasn't enough for Ryan.

And the rest of the job swap was going to be the same nightmare she'd tried to leave behind in London: where she'd be lying to everyone, saying that everything was absolutely fine, when in reality her heart was a wreck.

She'd get through it. There was no other choice.

But she was never, ever going to let herself fall for anyone again.

CHAPTER NINE

RYAN AND GEORGIE spent the next few days being super-polite to each other, careful to keep the topic of conversations to work and Truffle. At work, it was easy to focus on their patients and their colleagues, deflecting conversation away from their feelings, but at the cottage it was more and more awkward. Apart from sharing meals and chores, Georgie spent most of her time at the cottage curled on her bed with a book.

And it was horrible.

She missed the old easiness between them. She missed cuddling up on the sofa with Truffle. She missed the way Ryan teased her about trying everything Scottish.

It was starting to be a struggle at work, too, and she was terrified that one of their colleagues would notice that things were strained between them. She was just glad that the situation with Truffle meant they'd already moved their shifts round so they were on opposites for as much as possible.

But she was glad of Ryan's arrival when she called for the crash team on the day when she was on an early and he was on a late.

She was performing chest compressions on a ten-month-old who'd stopped breathing in the middle of tests, pushing down on the little girl's breastbone with the tips of two fingers, then giving two breaths after fifteen compressions, her mouth sealing the infant's nose and mouth.

He grabbed a mask and bag. 'I'll compress, you bag,' he said.

After a minute, he asked, 'Any cough or gag response?'

'No.'

'OK.' He checked the brachial pulse. 'Nothing. We'll keep going.'

It took them another ten minutes of chest compressions and breathing via the mask and bag, but finally the little girl responded.

'Let's get her on a ventilator,' Ryan said. 'And then we'll talk to her parents. Run me through the case.'

'Mollie's ten months old. She had an unsettled night, and her mum took her to the family doctor, who said it was just mucus. Then she got hiccups and was struggling to breathe, and the doctor told her mum to bring her here. I'd put her on oxygen, inserted a cannula and taken a blood test, but then she crashed on me. The rest of it you know.'

'OK. You did all the right things,' he said.

Once Mollie was on the ventilator, Georgie introduced Ryan to Mollie's mum.

'What's happening?' Mollie's mum bit her lip. 'Today's been a nightmare. Mollie had that shocking cold and the doctor said it was just mucus, but then she started hiccupping and she couldn't get her breath. I called the doctor...' She shuddered. 'Thank God my neighbour was home and could drive me here with her. And then the nurse asked me to come out of the room. Is Mollie going to—going to—?' Her face crumpled as she clearly couldn't bring herself to voice her worst fears.

'That's why we're here to update you,' Georgie said gently. 'Mollie's heart stopped, which was why the nurse asked you to come away—it's really not very nice for parents to see, but please don't worry because I'm glad to say we got her heart started again.'

Mollie's mum had a hand across her mouth in horror. 'Her heart *stopped*? Oh, my God. Is she going to be all right?'

'We hope so,' Ryan said, 'But at the moment we need to keep her sedated and cooled down, to make sure her brain doesn't start swelling. We've got her on a ventilator, which makes sure she breathes properly, and we're keeping a very close eye on her.'

'A ventilator?' Mollie's mum gasped, her eyes widening in horror. 'She's sedated? So she—you're keeping her asleep?'

Georgie squeezed her hand. 'It sounds scary, and it looks scary, but it's the best way to keep her safe right now. In a couple of days, we'll wake her up and see how she manages or if she needs further support.'

'My baby.' Mollie's mum was clearly having trouble processing what had happened. 'Can I see her?'

'Of course,' Ryan said. 'Because we've sedated her, I need to warn you now that she won't respond to you the way she normally does, but she'll still be able to hear you if you sit and talk to her, and she'll definitely know if you're holding her hand.'

'Can we call anyone for you?' Georgie asked. 'Mollie's dad?'

'I… He's away working on the rigs. He'll be devastated.'

'We're happy to talk to him if you need us to,' Georgie said. 'Is there another relative or friend who could come and be with you? Your neighbour?'

'No—he had to go to work after he dropped us here.' Mollie's mum looked anguished. 'I'll call my husband but I don't know when he'll be able to get here.' She shook her head as if to clear it. 'Everyone's at work or they're miles away and won't be able to get here for ages.'

'I'm due off duty shortly,' Georgie said, 'so I'll stay and sit with you until someone can join you.'

'But you've been at work all day.'

'I'll sit with you. Come on. I'll make you a cup of tea, and introduce you to the nurses in the intensive care unit, and keep you company for a bit. I'll sit with Mollie while you call her dad and whoever else you need to call.'

'That's—that's so good of you. You're a kind lass,' Mollie's mum said.

'And I'm due a break around tea-time,' Ryan said, 'so I'll come and have my mug of coffee with you, too. And you can ask us anything you want and we'll do our best to answer.'

Mollie's mum looked close to tears. 'Mollie's our only one, and we had three rounds of IVF to get her. If anything happens to her…'

'It's much too early to start worrying about that,' Georgie said, giving her a hug. 'And your Mollie's a fighter. We got her back after her heart stopped, so let's take it one day at a time for now.'

Mollie was still touch and go the next day, but her father had flown in from the oil rig to be there with his wife and baby. On her breaks, Georgie went in to see them with coffee and sandwiches.

'Thank you, that's kind of you, but I can't face anything,' Mollie's mum said.

'I know you're worried sick,' Georgie said, 'but you need to keep your strength up. Both of you. You'll be no good to Mollie if you keel over, will you? *Eat*.'

Though there was a nasty moment later in her shift in the ward round, when Georgie was checking Mollie's obs and the little girl's heart rate started dropping; thankfully, by the time she'd grabbed Ryan to come and help, Mollie's heart rate had gone back to where it should be.

'Sorry. I wasted your time,' she mumbled when they left the room.

'No, you did the right thing,' he said. 'Is there anything else?'

Yes. I want you to stop being so ridiculously stubborn and give us a chance.

But she knew it was pointless even trying, and she wasn't going to let him reject her again. 'I don't think so,' she said coolly, and went back to doing her ward round.

Normally, Ryan didn't take his work home with him.

But he couldn't stop thinking about little Mollie. The terror in her mum's eyes when she'd realised how serious the situation was. The way Georgie had been so calm and so kind, patiently going over things again whenever either of Mollie's parents asked her to explain something.

And it wasn't just being a good doctor. Georgie, he thought, would make a great mum. He'd watched her on the ward with their sick patients, and she seemed to have a knack for knowing just when a little one wanted a cuddle or a story. She made time to do it, too, even if it meant she missed a break or had to eat her lunch while she was catching up with paperwork.

Georgie would be at the heart of any family she made.

She was good with Truffle, too. Even though she'd had little contact with dogs before coming to Scotland, she'd made an effort with his Labrador, learning how to play games to distract the dog and tire her out while she was on enforced rest. Just as she'd be with a fractious child.

'You treat her the way that other men would treat their child. You've told me yourself that she's your family...'

Her words to him, that awful morning, came back to haunt him.

Did he treat his dog as if she was his child?

And did it follow that maybe, just maybe, he might know how to be a dad?

'You're putting all these barriers in the way, but they're not as big as you think they are.'

Was she right about that, too? Was he worrying too much? Could he overcome his resistance and just let himself be loved, be part of a family?

Every time he'd tried it, it had gone wrong. And he knew he was at fault, because he couldn't let people close.

But was Georgie right in that all he had to do was reach out? Was it really that simple?

Did he want a family?

This felt like picking a scab. Sore, stupid and a waste of time. He had to stop thinking about it, he told himself.

Except he couldn't.

He kept wondering. Did he want a family? Did he want a family with Georgina Jones?

He was beginning to think the answer was yes.

And he needed to find the right time to tell her. Reach out. Ask her to be his.

* * *

Two days later, Ryan reviewed Mollie's obs. 'I think we can try taking her off sedation today,' he said. 'If I'm not happy with the way she reacts, I'll put her back on sedation for another day or so, but let's give this a try.'

Georgie joined him for the procedure and checked that Mollie was managing to breathe adequately on her own; and between them they monitored her while she woke.

Had there been too much damage before she'd gone on the ventilator, or had she turned a corner? Ryan's heart was in his mouth. After Truffle had gone missing, he had a much better idea of how hard situations like this were for parents.

Yeah. He knew now that Georgie was right about that. For him, Truffle was just like the child he'd refused to make with Zoe. He'd worried himself as sick over a simple operation as Mollie's parents had over something much more complicated.

Like it or not, he was a dad. Of sorts.

Finally, the baby opened her eyes.

'Talk to her,' he said to Mollie's mum.

'Mollie? It's Mama,' she whispered, her voice thick with tears.

When the little girl smiled, Ryan felt tears of mingled relief and joy pricking his own eyelids. He looked over at Georgie and saw that her eyes were glistening with unshed tears, too.

He knew there was still a way to go, but it looked as if Mollie was going to make it.

If only, he thought, he and Georgie could make it. Because seeing the love between Mollie's parents, seeing how they'd supported each other in a crisis and watched over their precious, desperately wanted child…it had made him think. Made him *want*. Made him think that maybe he'd been wrong to keep that distance between himself and Georgie, that maybe he should've given them both a chance.

She'd be an amazing mum. And maybe she could teach him to be a good dad. A good partner.

Could he let Georgie close, the way he hadn't been able to let Zoe close?

But she was so professional with him, at Hayloft Cottage as well as at work. She kept her distance. How, then, could he find the right words to tell her that he'd changed his mind, that he'd made a mistake and wanted to try things her way?

Maybe he needed to make a huge gesture. Hire a sky-writer to say, *Forgive me, I was wrong, I want to make a go of it.*

He wanted to tell her. He just didn't know how. And the thoughts just kept spinning in his head.

Mollie progressed so well during the next week that she was able to go home. Georgie had just finished the discharge process when she realised that she was feeling odd. There was a weird metallic taste in her mouth. Was she going down with some kind of virus?

She shrugged it off, but a bit later on she noticed that her breasts were feeling tender.

It took the rest of her shift to realise that, actually, there might be a different reason for feeling that way. Her periods were regular almost to the hour, and she was late.

She took a deep breath. How ridiculous. Of course she wasn't pregnant. She and Ryan had used a condom.

But the only completely reliable contraception was abstinence. And a teeny, tiny proportion of condoms failed.

Telling herself that she was being utterly ridiculous, she drove home via a supermarket she didn't normally use. Thankfully she couldn't see anyone she knew in the aisles, but even so she hid the pregnancy test in her basket underneath a magazine.

Ryan was on a late, so she had time to do the test, reassure herself that everything was fine, and get rid of the evidence.

Once she'd made a fuss of Truffle, she went up to the bathroom and did the test.

Of course it was going to be negative. She'd bought the sort that would give you a result even before you'd officially missed a period, just for that extra layer of reassurance.

She washed her hands, then stood and watched the screen on the pregnancy test; the hourglass flashed to show that the test was working.

According to the instructions, it would take up to three minutes to see the result.

It felt like the longest three minutes of her life. Every time she checked her watch, only a few seconds had passed.

And then, finally, the words came up on the screen: but not the ones she had hoped for.

The black, bold type told her the truth very clearly.

Pregnant 1-2 weeks

She went cold. Ryan, who was absolutely adamant that he didn't want children.

What was she going to do?

She'd wanted a baby with her husband, a man who hadn't wanted a family with her but had made a baby with his mistress. And now she was accidentally pregnant by a man who'd told her all along that he didn't want children.

There were no guarantees that she'd carry this baby to term. She had a twenty-five per cent chance of having a miscarriage. Or she could choose to terminate the pregnancy.

She wrapped her arms around herself. Now she knew she was pregnant, the yearnings she'd suppressed were back in full force. So maybe this baby wasn't a disaster: maybe this baby was a gift.

From Joshua's experience, she knew that being a single parent wasn't an easy option. But she also knew that her family and friends would support her. She wouldn't be alone.

But she would have to tell Ryan. She was barely halfway through the job swap, and there was no way she could keep her pregnancy a secret. She'd be showing by the time the swap came to an end. It would be obvious to everyone.

How was he going to react to the news? He was a good man, a man with integrity, so she knew his first instinct would be to support her. But he'd said he didn't want children. So would he walk away from her and be a father in name only, or would he give them a chance? Would he give himself a chance to be part of a family, something he hadn't had for thirty years?

Numbly, she went downstairs. Truffle pushed her nose into Georgie's hand, as if to comfort her.

'He's not going to be happy about this,' Georgie said softly. 'Not happy at all.'

Truffle moved closer.

'How am I going to tell him?'

Truffle gave a soft wuff, which made Georgie smile

but also made her sad. Because there wasn't an answer. She didn't have a clue how to tell him.

She thought about it as she made chicken and apple stew for dinner.

She thought about it a bit more as she baked some brownies, on the grounds that the scent of vanilla and chocolate helped to relax her.

But she still hadn't come up with an answer by the time Ryan walked in.

'Hi.' Georgie took a deep breath. 'I made stew.'

'Thanks, but I'm not hungry.'

Meaning he'd had a rough day? Well, she was about to make it even rougher. 'I think you should eat.'

He frowned. 'Why?'

'Because we need to talk.'

He looked at her. 'You're moving out?'

Very probably, after what she was going to tell him. She said nothing, but heated the stew through on the hob and put some rice in the microwave.

Ryan didn't make it easy for her, either. He ate in complete silence. Well, he ate half of it, probably because he didn't want to be rude, she thought.

He pushed his plate away. 'So what did you want to talk about?'

'There isn't a nice way to say this,' she said, 'so I'll tell you straight. But, first, I want you to know that I don't expect anything from you.'

He frowned. 'You're not making much sense.'

Tell him.

'The night of the ceilidh.' She swallowed hard. 'There were consequences.'

She watched the colour drain from his face as he absorbed her news. 'But we used a condom.'

'You're a medic. You know as well as I do that the only absolutely certain method of contraception is abstinence. Yes, the chances making a baby when you use a condom are tiny, but they exist. And we made a baby.'

Ryan stared at Georgie, utterly shocked.

Had she just said...?

'We made a baby?' he echoed, knowing he sounded utterly stupid, but he couldn't get his head around this. The words felt like some kind of white noise in his head, making no sense.

She inclined her head.

Pregnant. With his baby.

'When did you find out?'

'Today. After my shift. I've had a couple of hours to think about it. And to talk to Truffle.'

'She's a good listener.'

'She's not so great on the advice, though. Her answer to everything is "woof".'

Ryan knew that Georgie was trying to lighten the mood, but he could see the tears glimmering in her eyes. One slid over the edge of her lashes and trickled down her cheek. Before she could scrub it away, he reached out and wiped it away gently with the pad of his thumb.

'Say something,' she said.

He didn't know what to say. Her news had fried his brain. 'What do you want to do?' he asked.

'I didn't try to trap you into getting me pregnant—' she began.

'They were my condoms and it was my responsibility,' he cut in, 'so of course you didn't get pregnant on purpose. If anything, it was my fault.'

She shook her head. 'It takes two to make a baby.'

He was pretty sure he knew the answer, but he asked anyway. Just to be clear. 'Do you want to keep it?'

She nodded. 'As I said, I don't expect anything from you. I know my parents will be supportive, my brother will be supportive and my niece will love the idea of having a cousin.'

Her parents. Her brother. Her niece. He worked it out. 'So you're going back to London and having the baby there?'

'That,' she said, 'depends on you.'

'How?'

'What do you want?'

'I…' All the way along, he'd told her that he didn't want children. He'd been starting to think that maybe he'd been wrong, particularly when he'd seen her with little Mollie and thought about what Georgie had told him about the way he treated Truffle. And now she'd just told him she was expecting his child.

He was going to be a dad.

There was a tight ball in his chest. 'You know my marriage broke up because I didn't want children and Zoe did.'

She was silent, as if working out what his words meant for her. 'Supposing Zoe had fallen pregnant accidentally—what would you have done?' she asked. 'Would you have insisted that she have a termination? Or would you have walked out on her?'

What kind of man did she think he was? 'No, of course not. I would've stood by her.' He looked at her. 'So there's your answer. I'll stand by you. I'll support the child—and you—financially.'

'What about emotionally?'

And that was the rub. 'I don't do emotions.' Well, he

did; but he didn't know how to do them the way other people wanted them.

'Oh, but you do,' she said. 'When Truffle went missing, you were devastated. You love that dog.'

'We're not discussing Truffle.'

'Yes, we are. I've said before, you love that dog as if she were a child.'

He'd come to realise that, thanks to her. 'All right,' he conceded. 'I love my dog.'

'And she loves you,' she continued, utterly remorseless. 'Look at her now—she can see you're worried and upset, and she's right by your side.'

And she was. Truffle was sitting as close to him as she could possibly get, leaning against him, with her chin on her knee as if to say that she was there and she'd never desert him.

'So you *do* do emotions. Truffle's the walking proof of that.'

Where was she taking this? 'I guess,' he said guardedly.

'But I think you use her to deflect your human feelings.'

That was probably also true. But he didn't know what to say.

'And you told me you loved Zoe.'

'I did.'

'So,' she said. 'Maybe you could learn to love our child.'

And he could see in her eyes the thing she didn't dare to say. *Maybe you could learn to love me.*

He thought about it. When Truffle had gone missing, Georgie had been there by his side and helped him find the dog. She'd been there by his side at the vet's. She'd listened to him, and she had still been there by his side afterwards to help him look after Truffle.

At work, last week, she'd sat with Mollie's mum when it was above and beyond the call of duty. She'd refused to leave the poor woman to wait alone until a family member or friend could come to support her. And he'd seen Georgie do that with other anxious parents too, over the last three months.

So it followed that she wouldn't abandon him or their child.

He could trust her.

And he liked the way he felt when he was with her. He liked the way she made him see things differently.

Could he see a baby differently? A baby of his own? The baby he'd always told himself he didn't want—but, if he was honest with himself, the baby he thought he didn't deserve because he wasn't lovable enough?

He'd told himself that he didn't know how to be a father. But Georgie seemed to believe he could do it.

He thought about it some more. What about the practicalities? Would she expect him to move back to London with her? Truffle would hate that and so would he; he'd feel hemmed in, in the city. But would she be prepared to stay here with him?

There was only one way to find out.

Ask her.

He'd never, ever felt this nervous and unsure before. He'd never told anyone the deepest, darkest secret of his heart. Maybe it was time to be totally honest.

'What if I fail? What if I'm a rubbish dad and a rubbish partner and I let you down?'

Hope bloomed in her eyes. 'I don't think you'll fail. I'm not looking for perfection, and neither is our baby.

Just for someone who'll love us all the way back.' She reached out and took his hand. 'And you won't let us down. Just keep being you. A bit less of the silent and stubborn would be helpful, but I don't want to change you.' She took a deep breath.

'So I'll take the risk and say it. I love you, Ryan McGregor. Even if you were Grumpy McGrumpface when I first met you. I love everything about you. The way you notice things and sort things out quietly and without a fuss. The way you insist on seeing everything rationally, yet you can still see the magic in the Northern Lights—and the way you kissed me under them made me weak at the knees. I think that's when I started to fall in love with you. And the night you danced with me at the ceilidh—that was when I realised I wanted you. For keeps.'

She loved him.

'And, just so you know,' she said, 'I wasn't necessarily planning to go back to London. Actually, if you turn me down, I'm going to camp on your doorstep until you agree to let me into your life. The way I see it, you and Truffle are mine, just as the baby and I are yours.'

Camp on his doorstep?

Those were the words of a woman who wasn't going to abandon him. A woman whose family and half her friends would be four hundred miles away if she stayed here in Edinburgh, but she wanted him—loved him—enough to make that distance work.

'So I'm yours, then,' he said.

'Uh-huh.'

'Ryan Jones,' he said, testing out the name.

She shook her head. 'That's Charlie's surname. If you really want to take mine, you'd be Ryan Woodhouse.' She looked at him. 'Though if we're talking name changes, I think Georgina McGregor has a nice ring to it. All those Gs, softie southerner first name and tough Scots last name. That's us all over.'

Only Georgie could have come up with that.

And it felt as if the barriers round his heart, the ones he'd thought were impenetrable, were dissolving. Melted away by the deepest of emotions: love.

'Are you asking me to marry you?'

'If that's what it takes, sure. I'll drop down on my knee and propose. Though a piece of paper isn't going to make the slightest bit of difference to the way I feel.' Her face lit up as she looked at him. 'You're not Charlie—you're not going to be careless with me. You're stubborn, but I think you love me too and you just don't know how to say it.'

How could she see inside his head like that?

'So I'm happy to be the one to say it first. I love you, Ryan McGregor, and I want you to be my family.' She nudged the dog. 'Your turn to speak. Tell him you want to be a family with me and the baby, too.'

'Woof,' Truffle said obligingly.

A baby. A family. A woman who really, really loved him.

Things he'd never thought to have.

He remembered what she'd said to him before. *'All you have to do is reach out.'*

He'd told himself it was too hard; but it wasn't. What was hard was trusting that it would be easy. But he trusted Georgie. The calm, capable, professional doctor who put his head in a spin and put fire in his heart. The one who'd shown him that the world was a kinder, warmer place than he'd thought it was.

All he had to do was reach out.

'I'm traditional,' he said. 'So I'll be the one to do the

asking.' He dropped down on one knee and took her hand. 'You barrelled into my life on a horrendous day, and you brought the sunshine with you even though it was stoating. Since I've met you, I've seen the world with different eyes and I might even think now the Loch Ness Monster is possible. You taught me to wish on a falling star. I made one wish with you—a wish that came true— so I'm hoping the second one I made will come true, too.' He dragged in a breath.

'A wish I barely admitted even to myself. I don't remember what it's like to be part of a family because it was so long ago. But I do know my mum would've adored you as much as I do. And I want a family. A family of my own. A family of you and our baby. You've a heart the size of the world, Georgie, and you make the world a better place. You make *my* world a better place. I love you. Will you marry me, Georgina Jones, be my love for the rest of our days? You, and our baby?'

She leaned down to kiss him. 'Yes. I'd be honoured. I'm absolutely not going to promise to obey you,' she warned, 'but I'll love you, I'll honour you and I'll cherish you until the end of my days. I don't care where or when we get married, and we have plenty of time to sort out where we live. I'm thinking anywhere that has a decent-sized garden for Truffle and the baby and incredibly good fences Truffle can't dig under.' She coughed. 'But there is one thing that's less negotiable.'

'One thing? What's that?' He held his breath. What did she want?

Her face went pink. 'I'd rather like you to marry me in a kilt. The one you wore the night we made our baby.'

The heat in her expression made his blood sizzle. 'I think I can manage that.' He paused and gave her a look that he hoped made her blood sizzle, too. 'Provided you take it off me on our wedding night.'

'That's guaranteed,' she said. 'But those buckles looked a bit tricky. I might need some practice.'

'Just as I need some practice in telling you I love you,' he said. 'I think lessons should start now, Dr McGregor-to-be. I love you.'

'I love you, too.'

'Good. Let's make a start on those buckles,' he said, getting to his feet and scooping her up.

'Hang on. I thought you said carrying me up the spiral staircase was a bad idea?' she said as he strode towards the middle of the room.

'That was then. Now you're my family—and I know I'm not going to drop you, because you believe in me. With you, I'm not going to fail at anything. You're my world, Georgie, and I love you.' He kissed her. 'I really, really love you.'

She kissed him back. 'For now and for always.'

* * * * *

FAMILY FOR THE CHILDREN'S DOC

SCARLET WILSON

MILLS & BOON

This book has to be dedicated to my fellow author
and partner in crime, Kate Hardy.

Thanks for the fun of doing a duo together
and making it such fun.

PROLOGUE

CLARA CONNOLLY SMILED and tried to keep the awkward expression plastered on her face as she watched her ex, Harry, affectionately put his arm around the waist of Gerta, his latest girlfriend, and brush a kiss at the side of her temple as they walked into one of the lifts together.

She could sense a few sets of curious eyes turn towards her in the busy main foyer of St Christopher's Hospital in Edinburgh; hence the plastered smile on her face. She wasn't quite sure what message she was trying to send. Indifference? Happiness? The truth was either would do. She'd only dated Harry for a few months— and he certainly hadn't been the love of her life. He'd been more like a pleasant passing phase. In a way she was glad he'd met someone who made his heart leap up and down. And even gladder that he'd managed to tell her, before the rest of the world found out.

That was the trouble with dating someone from work. The constant possibility of running into each other when the relationship ended. And while she was happy enough for Harry and Gerta, it reminded her that the ticking of her biological clock had started to amplify in her head. She pressed her lips together, letting the smile slip from her face as she waited for the next lift to arrive and take her up to the paediatric ward. It was weird. She was only thirty. But just about everyone she knew had met their 'happy ever after' by now. Clara just seemed to flit from one unfulfilling relationship to another. No big drama. No heartache. Just a general feeling of…emptiness.

It wasn't as if there was no one in her life. She had her best friend Ryan—who was just as unlucky in love as she was. She had a good group of friends, most of whom were now married, pregnant or with at least one child. It amplified her feelings. She had her own place—a cottage in a village on the outskirts of Edinburgh, surrounded by gorgeous farmland and countryside. It was usually her saving grace after a busy shift, but in the last few weeks she'd become more conscious of the space around her, and how quiet her life had become. Last night, after a single glass of wine, she'd found herself looking into sperm donation and seriously considering it. She'd always wanted to be a mother. Sure, she might have thought she would find someone to share the joy of parenthood with, but the more she looked, the less she found any real candidates.

Why not? She was a successful woman with her own place and a good job. There was no reason she couldn't bring up a child on her own. The question was—did she really want to?

Family was important to her—and she had a good one. Her mum and dad had retired to Spain a few years ago and had a better social life than she did. Her brother, Euan, was an engineer in Australia, married with three kids under five. She'd honestly never seen him look happier. Every time she video chatted with either her parents or her brother, there was always that little question— *Have you met anyone yet?*—and she understood; her family just wanted her to be settled and happy, because they knew she wanted that too. But the question was starting to ruffle her normally good nature. It wasn't as if she could just magic Mr Perfect out of nowhere.

She knew that her mother had always wanted a large, chaotic family. But pre-eclampsia had put paid to that idea, with Clara being told that both she and her mother were lucky to be alive. It had weighed on her mind throughout her life. With her brother being so far away, it felt as if the pressure was on to provide grandchildren her parents could see frequently. And the truth was, she might have had similar hopes to her mother—a life filled with children was always what entered her brain when she dreamed about the future.

The doors to the lift slid open and a few minutes later she was on her own ward. She could see the city landscape through the windows. The familiar sights of the edge of the castle in the distance and the Scott Monument usually made her feel grounded, but today they just left an uncomfortable feeling in her stomach. She quickly checked over the patients, reviewing the diagnoses for those who had been admitted overnight, and rechecking the children who'd already been on her ward. She had just finished talking to some parents about their baby son, who'd been admitted with a chest infection, when her colleague, Bea, came into the office with coffee in both hands.

She slid one over the desk to Clara. 'You've still got that look on your face.'

'What look?' Clara glanced up from the screen where she was ordering tests.

'That look that seems to say *I'm trying to pretend to the world I'm fine when I'm really not.*'

Clara took one sip of the coffee then wrinkled her brow. 'What do you mean?'

She'd worked with Bea, one of the senior nurses here, for the last five years. They were friends. Bea wasn't known for playing her cards close to her chest. Clara liked straight talkers. It was probably why they got on so well together.

Bea sighed. 'Ever since we had that kid—Ben Shaw— you've had a look about you. One that makes it seem like you come here because you *have* to—not because you want to. You never looked like that before. Something has to give, Clara. And I'm just worried it's going to be you.'

Clara swallowed back the immediate lump in her throat. Ben Shaw had been admitted overnight a few months ago. Clara had been out sick with norovirus. Any occurrence for a member of staff meant an automatic ban of forty-eight hours from being in contact with patients, and a locum doctor had covered the shift. Ben had been admitted with abdominal pain, for review in the morning.

But as soon as Clara had stepped onto the ward she'd known immediately what was wrong with the toddler. Bowel obstruction was uncommon in kids—and hard to spot for someone inexperienced.

Ben had been rushed to surgery, but had ultimately lost part of his bowel. The delay in diagnosis had been life-changing, and Clara just couldn't shake that *what if* feeling.

Bea reached over and squeezed her hand as Clara stared at the screen in front of her, watching it grow a bit blurry. All the stuff about Ben had affected her, left her feeling a bit numb. Flat, even.

It had happened more than once to her before. She'd first been diagnosed with depression as a teenager and it had remained in her life ever since. Sometimes she was good. Sometimes she was bad. Sometimes she needed someone to talk to, and medication to make her feel a bit better. Most people who knew her had no idea. Clara had always played her cards close to her chest, especially about her mental health. It didn't matter that one in three of all doctors were supposedly affected by mental health issues at some point in their life, it was still something that wasn't really discussed. When she'd had to take a few months off from medical school her family and tutors had been extremely supportive; she'd even got to delay an important exam and take it at a later date. But she still didn't like to tell anyone about it.

She bit her lip and sat back, reaching for the coffee with both hands. 'It's just been a hard few months. What with Ben, then the break-up with Harry, and stuff going on with Ryan.'

'What's going on with Ryan?' asked Bea.

Clara ran her hands through her hair. 'Can you keep a secret?'

Bea nodded. Ryan McGregor was a fellow doctor in the hospital and Clara's best friend and she knew he liked to keep things low-key about his disastrous love life.

'He's having a really hard time. He's going through a difficult divorce and just can't seem to get out of the hole he's dug himself into. He's having to come and stay at mine for a few days until he gets things sorted.'

Bea frowned and Clara added, 'They've sold the house and he's having trouble finding someone who will rent to him until he can find something he wants to buy.'

Bea gave a brief nod. 'Because of his dog?' She took a sip of coffee as Clara nodded in return. 'He adores that dog, doesn't he? But lots of places up for rent around the city won't allow pets. He might be at yours longer than you think.'

Clara blinked back the tears that had brimmed in her eyes. 'I just don't know what to do to help him.'

They exchanged glances and Clara could tell Bea knew she wasn't talking about the housing situation or the dog.

Bea gave a thoughtful nod and leaned forward. 'It's hard to support your friends emotionally, when you don't feel safe in that place yourself.'

It was as if someone had just thrown a blanket over her and given her a giant hug. The guilt that had been playing on her mind over these last few weeks finally had a little outlet. She could hardly push her pathetic worries onto Ryan, not when he had so much to worry about himself—it would be selfish of her to try and talk about it. But that glance from Bea felt like enough. Even saying the words out loud felt like a slight easing of the dark cloud that had settled around her.

Her mood had been low recently and she hadn't really wanted to admit it to anyone. But last week she'd done a postnatal depression questionnaire with a young mum she'd been worried about, and some of the answers to the questions had made her stop and think about how *she* would answer them. Not that she had a baby, or anything. But just that simple act had made her suck in a breath and take a long, hard look at herself.

'I should be fine,' she said determinedly. 'I should be getting on with things and pulling my life together. I'm not dependent on anyone. I have a good job, my own place. I should be happy.'

'But you're not,' said Bea matter-of-factly. 'Who are you trying to convince—me, or you?'

Clara heaved in a deep breath. 'No,' she admitted, 'I'm not.'

They sat in silence for a few seconds while Clara thought about what she'd just said out loud. It hadn't been quite as scary as she'd thought. Maybe it was Bea—maybe it was her intuition and understanding, mixed in with her ability to get straight to the point. Bea didn't know that Clara had actually taken the step of visiting her own GP a few days ago. Her hand went to her pocket and fastened around the packet of tablets she had in there. She hadn't decided yet whether to take them or not. She recognised that she probably needed them. When life started to seem a bit black around the edges she knew she had to do something. She couldn't quite believe how much the young mum's face had mirrored her own. This conversation was giving her a bit of clarity, a sign. The reassurance that she needed. Her fingers tightened around the meds a little more. She could do this. Depression wasn't a sign of weakness. Lots of her friends and colleagues in similarly stressful jobs had suffered throughout the years. Recognising it, seeing her GP and accepting the prescription were only the first steps. It was time to take the next one. Clara gave a half-smile and gave Bea a grateful look. 'I love working with you. You don't let me get away with anything.'

Bea licked her lips and gave a gentle shake of her head. 'This conversation isn't over. I'm not going to let you leave it here. We're friends—it's my job to tell you that you need to give yourself a bit of space to decide what you really want in life, Clara. You're young, you're a beautiful girl. You're a great doctor. But is that enough? Maybe you just need a change of scenery. A chance to get away from things.' She held up her hands. 'Sometimes we get in a rut. Sometimes we need to try something new.' She pointed to a flyer on the noticeboard to the side of Clara. 'Why don't you think about that?'

Clara wrinkled her nose and turned to look at the slightly crumpled flyer that had been on the board for a few months. She'd seen it but never really given it much thought. It was advertising the opportunity to do a job swap elsewhere in the UK for six months.

She laughed. 'What are the chances of another paediatric registrar wanting to job swap for six months? And the chances of the job being in a place I might actually want to go?'

Bea stood up and lifted the cups, raising her eyebrows. There was a slight glint in her eye. 'Well, you won't know if you don't try,' she replied in her mischievous manner, before giving Clara a wink and heading out of the door.

For a few minutes Clara just sat there. She'd actually vocalised how she was feeling, and everything Bea had shot back at her had been true. She wasn't feeling great, and she couldn't put her finger on exactly why. There wasn't one big thing, just a whole host of little things that were bubbling under the surface and giving her a general sense of unhappiness and discontent. She hated that. It made her feel not like *herself*.

But she didn't really feel entitled to be unhappy. Most of her friends would give her a list of reasons why she should be delighted with her life, and in most cases they would be right.

But the fact was, she couldn't help how she was feeling. She slipped the first tablet out of its packaging and swallowed it. There. Baby steps. But maybe she should try something else too?

She bit her lip as she put in all the orders for the tests

required for the patients on the ward. Then she opened another window on the computer and automatically typed in the website address from the flyer. She didn't even have to look up at the poster—it seemed to have imprinted on her brain.

It only took a minute to put in her details: name, job, home address and a few clinical details. She uploaded a few photos of her house she had on her phone. She'd taken them just the other day to send to her brother in Australia. The next box was the hard part. Where was she looking for a job? She shook her head and just left it open. Fate. She'd leave it to fate.

The spinning egg timer of doom appeared on the screen in front of her. She groaned. Chances were the website had just died, or the search was too wide and the system couldn't cope. Any time the whirling egg timer appeared on a computer screen in front of her, it generally meant bad news.

She pushed her chair back, ready to go back out onto the ward, as the screen blinked and then changed.

Her mouth fell open. There was a match. One.

She leaned forward and read everything on the screen. London. In the Royal Hampstead Free Hospital. *No way.* That place had just as good a reputation as St Christopher's. Why would anyone want to job swap from there?

Her heart gave a flutter. Fate. She'd left it to fate. And fate had answered. One job opportunity in a place with a fabulous reputation. Pictures of a flat that looked very swanky. This was just too good to be true.

There was a big button on the screen, inviting her to find out more. For the first time in a long time her heart gave a little leap.

She hesitated for only the briefest of seconds before reaching out and clicking on it.

London. Get ready for Clara Connolly.

CHAPTER ONE

Two weeks later

SHE WAS CRAZY. She was definitely crazy. Yesterday she'd been finishing her last day working in Edinburgh, going back to her cute cottage with a view of the Scottish countryside and being disturbed by one of the sheep pressing its face up against her kitchen window. All entirely normal.

Now, she was circling the same confusing streets of London over and over again, sweat trickling down her back as she realised there was absolutely nowhere to park.

She hadn't thought to ask about parking. It hadn't even crossed her mind. She'd assumed that there would be somewhere convenient and close to the flat to leave her car…and was learning quickly just how wrong that assumption was.

Some of the streets had no parking at all. Others only had parking for permit holders. One car park charged thirty pounds a day. Thirty pounds? She wanted to laugh out loud.

The drive down from Edinburgh had started well. She'd left plenty of time in case of delays—and there had been many. A collision on the motorway near Newcastle had slowed traffic, followed by horrendous roadworks near Doncaster. By the time she'd hit London her timing had been way off, and it was clear she was in the rush hour. It didn't help that her satnav seemed to have forgotten a vital update and had a completely different idea of which streets were one-way and which streets were totally blocked off. By the time the tenth black cab driver tooted at her, shaking his head, she was close to tears.

Clara had always prided herself on her driving skills. Touch wood, she'd never been in an accident or even had a near miss before. One hour in London and she'd almost had one head-on collision and more near misses than she wanted to admit. By the time she finally saw the sleek tower block near Canary Wharf that had the correct address, her nerves were more than a little frayed.

She pulled up outside the building, ignoring all the signs that told her not to stop, and got out, slamming her door and sucking in a breath of the warm, clammy air.

A man leaving the smart building frowned as she strode past him, trying to see if there was anyone who could give her some directions about where to park. Her car was stuffed full of her possessions. Surely she was allowed to unload?

The front wall of the foyer was completely glass, with the building at a slight angle, facing towards Canary Wharf. There was a bank of small boxes to her left and she scanned them, finding 14C and keying in the appropriate code. She sighed in relief at the sight of the silver key, a cream key fob and the slim electronic card—apparently both the key and the card opened the door to the flat.

She glanced back at her car, wondering if she should go back and grab some things before heading up in the lift, but curiosity got the better of her. She wanted to see her home for the next six months.

The silver doors glided open and she barely felt the lift move before they opened again on the fourteenth floor. A short walk down the corridor took her to the flat and she scanned the card in front of the round pad, letting the door click open.

As she pushed inside her breath caught somewhere in her throat. The sun had lowered in the sky and the whole apartment was bathed in warm light.

Everything was so clean-looking! The entrance hall had smooth cream tiles, leading to a matching immaculate kitchen on her right that opened out to a largish sitting room furnished with three curved cream sofas, a glass table and TV set into the left side wall. But it was the view that was the most spectacular. Windows took up the entire facing wall, showing all the beauty of Canary Wharf, just a stone's throw away. Her feet moved automatically, carrying her over to the windows, and she realised quickly they weren't windows but, in fact, concertina-style doors. She fumbled for the button then pushed them open, stepping out onto the balcony beyond.

It wasn't quite on the edge of the dock, but it was close enough that she could see the activity on the dockside. There was a row of restaurants and bars, boats bobbing on the water. The busy noise of people finishing their day at work and hitting the bars and restaurants below floated across the air beneath her, along with the aromas of food, making her stomach growl.

She looked out across the London skyline, spotting the event arena and the snaking river beyond. She really was here. She'd done this. She'd left Scotland behind and made a change. For a few seconds she closed her eyes, leaning against the balcony barrier and breathing in the warm air again, letting the different sensations surround her. It was certainly warmer than it was back home, but her skin prickled.

She opened her eyes again and almost jolted at the view again. Several of the tower blocks around the dock were dotted with lights, sending a purple and pink glow shimmering back upwards from the water. It was beautiful, but could take a bit of getting used to. She spun back around, putting her hands behind her and looking back inside the flat.

This place wasn't like any flat she'd been in before. It was like a show home, decked out in gorgeous pieces of furniture, all ergonomically placed. If it wasn't for the few scattered cushions and the row of books in a nearby bookcase, she might believe no one even lived here.

Her stomach curled as she thought of her inelegant squishy sofa back home, dark stone walls and temperamental fire. She prayed that Ryan had tidied up the way he'd promised and left the welcoming note and food before he left.

Clara left the doors open and wandered through the rest of the flat. The bedroom was just as immaculate as everywhere else, with white bedlinen and a big comfortable pink throw at the end of the bed. A space had been cleared for her in the closet and Clara resisted the temptation of looking to see what clothes her counterpart had left behind.

There was a nice writing desk looking out at the view across London, with a bottle of champagne sitting on it, tied with a big pink ribbon and note.

*I thought if you were anything like me you'd need
some of this after your long journey.*

*There's a secret chocolate stash in the drawer
on the right and I did an online order for food
that, hopefully, Louie the concierge has left in the
kitchen for you.*

*Any problems, give him a dial on 01 and he'll
be happy to help.*

Other than that, enjoy London!

Georgie xx

Clara couldn't resist; she slid open the drawer on the
right to see a whole array of chocolate. Dark chocolate
mints, milk chocolate orange, foil-wrapped caramels and
a huge sea salted caramel bar.

Things were definitely looking up.

She frowned. Concierge? She hadn't noticed anyone
behind the desk in the foyer. She walked back to the
kitchen and opened the gleaming fridge. Sure enough,
milk, butter, eggs, cheese and bacon were waiting for
her, along with a variety of fruit and vegetables in the
cool drawer. In one of the cupboards she found bread,
some pasta and a few jars, enough to make dinner for a
few nights. Her stomach growled loudly. It was so nice.
So considerate. But what she really wanted right now
was pizza.

Clara sighed and made her way back downstairs to
gather the rest of her possessions. It would probably take
her at least an hour to lug everything back up and get
unpacked.

The foyer was still empty and a traffic warden was
frowning outside. She ran out, muttering excuses and
opening her car door before he had a chance to start

scribbling. He raised one eyebrow and pointed to a slim, almost hidden downward ramp directly on the right of the building. 'Emergency vehicles only out here,' he muttered. 'Why don't you use the parking underneath?'

Underground parking. Of course a place like this would have parking for residents. But the angle of the building meant she hadn't been able to glimpse it from the road. She gave a flustered nod and climbed back in, starting her car and swinging it in an uneven arc as she tried to line up her large four-by-four with the narrow lane.

Clara sucked in a breath as she edged her car down the narrow ramp. She knew it was ridiculous—as if she could actually make her ungainly four-by-four smaller! For the first time in her life she regretted being behind the wheel of the wide, sturdy vehicle. It was perfect for farm roads in Scotland, but not exactly ideal for slim underground parking entrances.

It was dark—much darker than seemed normal. Weren't there lights down here? Shouldn't they at least come on when a car entered? This was like something from a horror movie. Any minute now the weird axe man would jump onto the bonnet of her car.

She flicked on her car lights and came to an abrupt halt at the low-slung gleaming red car in front of her. Her breath caught in her throat. Darn it—that was close. What was it about London and driving for her?

She turned her head from side to side, trying to scan the underground parking area. It didn't seem the biggest in the world, and with no other lighting it was going to be hard to manoeuvre her large car. It was too old to have parking sensors, and she didn't even want to think about what kind of luxury vehicles could be hidden down here.

She edged forward, seeing some white lines, and tried to swing into a space. Her headlights lit up the side of another car and she let out an expletive as she moved forward and back, trying to get into the space. It was like being a learner all over again.

These weren't the biggest spaces in the world, she couldn't see properly and she was tired after her long journey. All she really wanted to do was grab her stuff, get back upstairs and open that bottle of champagne.

She finally stopped edging forward and back and shimmied out of her car, taking care not to touch the neighbouring car with her door. Sweat was running down her back. The capital was much warmer than back home. She hadn't really thought about that when she'd planned her wardrobe.

In the dark, she fumbled around the car and opened the boot, grabbing her boxes in the low light within. She was only taking the boxes that carried the bare essentials—she had no intention of coming back down here tonight. Clara wasn't easily intimidated but being alone in a strange dark car park would unnerve anyone. She stuck one box on top of the roof of her car as she grabbed another three. In the far corner of the dark parking space she could see a small blue square glowing—that had to be the lift. At least she'd be able to get back upstairs. Hopefully, tomorrow she'd get a chance to talk to the concierge about the lighting down here. Or at least find somewhere to buy a flashlight.

As if by magic, the lights came on all around her as she reached up to close the boot. She jerked. The box at the top of her pile teetered then spilled onto the concrete floor.

Clara groaned as another car glided down the ramp.

The driver paused, scowling at her, before sweeping into a space opposite. Friendly type then.

She dropped to her knees, stuffing toiletries and underwear back into the box as fast as she could. Last thing she wanted was Mr Grumpy getting an uninvited view of her smalls.

There were a few muffled sounds next to her. She looked up. The guy was carrying a sleeping bundle in his arms, the scowl still firmly in place as he swept past her.

'At least try and park in your own space,' he muttered as his long strides ate up the ground under his feet.

She blinked from her position on the ground. Now the lights were on, she could see that each parking space had a number. The parking space she was in was labelled 24F. Oops.

She glanced down the long slim space, trying to work out the numbering. If she'd got this right, 14C would be right down at the other end. Great. Further to carry her boxes. Should she move her car? Maybe not right now. Now there were some lights she could do it when she came back down to collect the rest of her things. She jumped up quickly and hurried after the man.

He was tall, over six feet, with broad shoulders and an irritatingly quick stride. The doors to the lift slid open and he stepped inside.

'I'm sorry,' she said quickly, still walking towards the lift. 'I couldn't see what I was doing. The lights didn't come on when I came down and I haven't had a chance to speak to the concierge yet and—'

She was babbling. She knew she was babbling.

He spun around and she sucked in a breath. Darn it, he was handsome. *Really* handsome. Dark hair, tall, muscular structure, a shadow around his jaw line and penetrating eyes. And it struck her that it had been a while since she'd noticed something like that.

For the last few months all men had just merged into one. This was the first time she'd actually *noticed* someone in a long time. Her brain gave a hopeful flicker of recognition. Too bad it seemed that he was as arrogant as he was handsome.

It didn't help that she was still babbling—and she hated appearing nervous. Especially in front of a man whose sole intention seemed to be to frown at her and look at her as if she was something on the bottom of his shoe. How dare he? Wasn't he even going to try and be slightly friendly?

This was a horrible situation. He clearly lived here—last thing she wanted was to make an enemy of someone who'd be her neighbour for the next six months. But, on the other hand, he could clearly see that she'd just arrived. Couldn't he give her a break?

No. Those dark blue eyes were still glaring at her. There was a noise behind her—a sliding sound, followed by an ear-splitting car alarm that made them both jump. The child in his arms gave a start and instantly started crying.

She turned around to see the box she'd left balanced on the roof of her car had now vanished, and the car next to hers was the one with the screeching alarm. The words formed on her lips, 'Oh, sorry...' and she turned back just in time to see the lift doors slide closed and the man turn his back on her.

Clara heaved in an enormous sigh. 'Welcome to London, Clara,' she muttered as the lights flickered out around her and plunged her into darkness. Again.

CHAPTER TWO

JOSHUA WOODHOUSE WAS not having a good day.

Correct that. He wasn't having a good week. Not since his sister had sprung the fact on him that she was transferring her post for six months and disappearing to Scotland at short notice. He still couldn't get over it. Had Georgie been unhappy? Depressed? Bored? Why hadn't he realised? She'd denied all those things, just telling him she needed a change of scene for a while. The truth was, he couldn't blame her. Her husband had been killed in an accident a while ago, and Georgie just seemed to have carried on. In fact, she'd continued working in his paediatric department in the Royal Hampstead Free, *and* continued to help him out with his young daughter, Hannah.

He'd kept pressing. And so Georgie had told him the real reason she was leaving and he'd wanted to slap himself. Her husband had been having an affair. Joshua had been shocked. He'd had absolutely no idea, and neither, apparently, had Georgie, finding out only after her husband had died. At first, he'd felt a flare of anger that she'd kept secrets from him. But she'd quickly put him in his place, letting him know that it was her business, and up to her to decide if she wanted to share. Guilt had swamped him. He should have been a better support to his sister, instead of just thanking her for continuing to show up at work and helping out at a moment's notice with Hannah. He should have realised something else was going on. But he hadn't stopped to ask. And now his sister had decided she needed a change of scene for six months.

What could he say when he'd apparently already let her down so badly? Of course, he had to see her off to Scotland with his complete blessing, no matter how he felt about it.

He had too many balls in the air at once. He knew that. Being Head of Department at one of the busiest hospitals in London, as well as being sole carer for his young daughter, sometimes made him feel as if he couldn't think straight.

There had been a nanny. But two days after Georgie had told him about her job swap, he'd got a tearful call from her to say her father had been diagnosed with terminal cancer back in Sweden. It had struck a chord, and he'd booked her a flight home with his blessing, and the knowledge that she wouldn't be returning. It had added yet another ball to juggle and he'd had to hire someone at short notice who he hoped would work out for himself and Hannah.

His parents kept telling him to move closer to them in Norfolk—they loved their granddaughter and would gladly help out. As it was, they came to London frequently to help when they could. But part of him didn't want to push his responsibility onto them.

Hannah was *his* daughter. He had to be the constant in her life. Her mother had died three weeks after delivering their new baby, having been diagnosed with acute myeloid leukaemia. It had taken him a while to come to terms with the fact that Abby had realised she was sick while she was in the late stages of pregnancy, and waited until she'd delivered before telling anyone. Hindsight was a horrible thing. The tiredness. The paleness. The few bruises.

He'd spent the first few months blaming himself while caring for a brand-new baby. But time had given him perspective. Anyone who'd known Abby would have known that she'd never have put her life before her child's. They'd lost a pregnancy the year before, and so she'd been determined to do everything possible to make sure their little girl arrived safely. Her determination was one of the many reasons that he'd loved her.

Her leukaemia had been so aggressive that her chance of survival had been virtually nil. Conversations with colleagues had helped him understand that no matter when she'd admitted to knowing about her illness, the outcome would have inevitably been the same. And the sad fact was, they would have doubtless spent the last few weeks of her pregnancy arguing, with him pushing her to deliver early and seek treatment—of any kind—in an attempt to stretch out their time together.

Instead, they'd spent the time looking forward to the birth of their daughter, with only a few anxious weeks after she'd arrived to consider the future. The ending had been inevitable but peaceful, and whilst Joshua had been angry at the fragility of life, he'd had the opportunity to tell his wife how much he loved her and listen to all her hopes and dreams for Hannah in the future. Abby had even written a diary for their daughter, a list of instructions for him, and some letters to give to Hannah in the future. Whilst lucky wasn't a word he would choose to describe their situation, he'd been a doctor long enough to know that many families didn't get a final opportunity to talk and plan and he should count his blessings that they had.

Hannah was the image of her mother with the same pale blue eyes and fine brown hair. Even though she'd barely met Abby, she had some of the same habits and tendencies. If Josh didn't witness it on a daily basis he wouldn't have believed it, and it had changed his thinking countless times on the nature or nurture debate.

His phone buzzed and he pulled it from his pocket. Georgie, letting him know that things had been 'interesting' when she'd arrived last night and that she was looking forward to her first day.

Something flickered in his brain and he groaned as he walked out onto the ward. He'd been so rushed last night—picking up Hannah from after school care and taking her straight to ballet lessons. No wonder she'd fallen asleep in the car on the way home. But now he had a horrible inkling about the strange woman in the garage last night. And, as if life was trying to teach him a lesson, standing at the nurses' station was a girl with tied-up dark brown hair. His stomach gave an uncomfortable squeeze. *Please don't let it be...*

She turned around, her eyes widening and her face falling as the same recognition that he was experiencing evidently washed over her.

'Oh, here he is.' Luan, one of the regular staff nurses, waved. 'This is Dr Woodhouse, Clara. Josh, this is our new Georgie.' She winked at him. 'I was just telling her all about your sister.'

Joshua kept his expression as neutral as possible as he walked forward and extended his hand. He hadn't exactly been friendly last night; his mind had been on other things. It had taken an age to settle Hannah back down after the car alarm had jerked her out of her sleepy state.

The woman was tall, slim with dark hair and brown eyes. She was dressed smartly in black trousers, a bright red shirt, flat shoes and her white lab coat. He tried to stop his gaze fixating on her high cheekbones and bright red lips. She was pretty—more than pretty. Something he'd failed to register last night in the dimly lit car park. 'Dr Connolly, I presume?'

Had he really just said that? Darn it. She was Scottish too. Would she think he was making a fool of her and mimicking the famous quote *Dr Livingstone, I presume?*

But, all credit to her, Clara Connolly gave a little tug at the bottom of her bright red shirt then held out her hand to his. Her handshake was firm—a little too firm. Maybe she was still annoyed about last night.

'Yes, I'm Clara,' she said, then her lips turned upwards as if someone had just reminded her to smile. 'Nice to meet you.' Was she nervous?

Okay. Those words were definitely said through slightly clenched teeth. He was going to have to make the best of the fact that he'd totally forgotten his new doctor was moving into his sister's flat last night. He didn't even know if Clara had known that he lived in the same building. Well, she did now. And probably thought he was one of the rudest men on the planet.

There really wasn't much recovery from this at all. He decided to get straight down to business. 'Let me show you around and tell you how we do things here,' he said, gesturing for her to follow him down the ward.

He was proud of his department and the reputation for excellence that it held. He was always very careful about recruitment, taking up multiple references in order to get a good idea of whether someone would fit in appropriately with his team. This time he hadn't had that opportunity. The job swap had happened so fast. He'd seen her CV, of course. It was impressive—as was the list of hospitals she'd worked at throughout her career. He'd even recognised the names of some of her supervisors, all colleagues he respected. He knew Clara was at the same stage of her career as his sister—but what he didn't know was what she was made of. It irked him; he couldn't help it. Qualifications were all very well, but could he trust Clara Connolly to fit into his team? This woman with the dark brown hair and brown eyes almost seemed as if she'd tricked her way in here.

She pulled a pair of glasses from her white coat and slid them on. They were red-rimmed, with a cartoon character on the legs. He pretended not to notice. He wondered if red was her theme. 'This is our general admissions assessment unit. We have fourteen beds. We don't leave kids in A&E; they come straight up here once they've been triaged and had any X-rays that they need. Ultrasounds can be performed on the ward, and we have a system where they get anaesthetic cream put on their arms downstairs, so if we need to take bloods up here we can do that straight away. If they don't need anything, we just wipe it back off.'

Clara gave a nod. He handed her an electronic tablet from a stack on the wall. 'You should have received a passcode this morning.'

She nodded and he pointed at it. 'We keep all records electronically, and order all tests this way too. You can log into any device at any point in the hospital.'

He looked around the ward and kept walking. 'We have a general surgical ward, a medical ward, a twelve-

bed paediatric oncology unit for treatments, and six paediatric beds in ITU—all on this floor of the hospital.
You'll be expected to participate in a number of our paediatric clinics, all based on the ground floor, and carry
a paediatric arrest pager.' He cleared his throat a little
and spun around, lowering his voice. 'I see from your
CV that you have experience in all these areas. I take it
you're happy to cover them here?'

There was an edge of challenge in his tone, and one of
her eyebrows gave the slightest hint of lifting. She tilted
her chin towards him. 'I think you'll find I'm competent
in all areas, Dr Woodhouse.'

'Well,' he said slowly, 'we'll see.'

'And just what does that mean?' There was a flash of
anger in her eyes and she planted one hand on her hip.

'Exactly what I said. We'll see.'

He could tell she was trying to rein her anger in. 'I
don't like the implication. I'm sure you can tell from
my CV that I'm more than competent at my job. Anyone who knows me, or has worked with me, could also
tell you that.'

He started walking towards his office. 'Well, that's
just it. I don't know you and I've never worked with you.
I've just had you thrust upon me without much warning.'

Clara had kept pace next to him as he'd started moving
again but stumbled for a second over his last sentence.

She kept quiet until they were in his office but, before
he had a chance to do anything else, she closed the door
firmly and leaned against it, folding her arms.

'Why don't you tell me exactly how you feel then, Dr
Woodhouse? Is this how you treat all your new starts?
Because I hate to break it to you, but you really need to

work on your welcome.' She paused for a second then glared at him. 'In both your personal and your professional life.'

For a second he was stunned. He'd been prepared for some comeback, but it seemed that Clara Connolly gave just as good as she got.

This might actually be interesting. He liked working with people who were straight talkers. It saved time.

He sat down in the chair behind his desk. 'This is my department, Dr Connolly. And I'll run it my way.' As much as liked her direct approach, he needed to make sure she knew who was boss.

'I'm surprised you have any staff at all.' The words shot out of her mouth and then she blinked. Was that a flash of regret in her eyes? Now they were out of the ward environment and he was looking at her full on, he could really get a sense of her. There were a few fine lines around her eyes, a smattering of freckles across her nose and she was wearing impeccable make-up. Maybe it was the make-up that kept drawing his gaze to her dark brown—currently stormy—eyes. Her bright red lips matched her glasses. And her hair—tied in a high ponytail—was bouncing as she spoke.

He took a breath. 'I wasn't familiar with the job swap policy. I hadn't even heard about it until Georgie told me she'd matched with you and was moving for six months.'

Clara looked him square in the eye. 'Any idea why she wanted to leave?'

He flinched. He wasn't quite sure if it was sarcasm or a genuine query. He ignored the remark. He hadn't told a single person the real reason Georgie had left.

'I normally recruit staff into the department myself.

I like to make sure they're the kind of people who will fit into the team. I didn't get that opportunity with you.'

'So, what is this? A "go back where you came from" speech?'

Josh could think of a hundred things he wanted to say right now, none of them very professional. He hadn't been entirely himself these last few weeks, and even he could reflect that he might be taking out his frustrations about his sister's quick departure on the people around him.

Was he actually being fair to this doctor? At first glance, she was smartly turned out, punctual and appeared interested in the role. Should he be looking for more right now? He'd already gathered she'd had a long journey and her arrival at the apartment hadn't exactly been smooth.

He stared at her for a few moments longer. She seemed happy to wait out the silence—there was no compulsion to fill the gap with panicked words. It was almost like a stand-off.

He cracked first but kept his voice steady. It didn't matter that this woman had already annoyed him. It didn't matter that he couldn't quite decide how he felt about her challenging attitude. It really didn't matter that her light, unusual perfume was weaving its way across the room towards him, or that now he'd actually stopped for a few seconds he realised just how pretty she was. None of that mattered at all. He had a department to run.

'No. It's not a—as you put it—a "go back where you came from" speech. It's a "wait and I'll tell you how you'll fit in with my team" speech. Everyone who joins is supernumerary the first week. Watch and learn our systems. From next week, you'll be on the on-call rota like everyone else. Get to know the staff. Say hello to some of our more regular patients. If there are any procedures you haven't done in a while—speak up, ask to observe again. Familiarise yourself with them. Feel free to spend the day with the paediatric surgeons if you want to. Visit our day surgery unit and introduce yourself. Dr Morran, our paediatric oncologist, will have a whole host of protocols she'll want to go over with you, to ensure you can handle any emergency in her absence. Hans Greiger is our chief paediatric anaesthetist and our go-to for NICU. Make yourself known to him. By the time I hand you the page next week, Dr Connolly, I expect my patients to be in good hands. I expect you to be wise enough to identify the gaps in your skills to function in this role and find your own learning opportunities in the next week to increase your competencies.'

It might sound harsh. The truth was, at this stage in her career he didn't expect her to have many gaps in her knowledge. But he treated every member of staff who worked in his department the same. He was a strong believer that all medics should be able to identify and seek out learning opportunities where they could. They were responsible for their own learning. He wanted a team to be able to reflect on their skills, and to know where their limits were.

She stayed remarkably silent. It was almost as if she'd expected something entirely different. Instead, after a few moments, she folded her arms across her chest and gave him a half-smile. 'Fine.' She paused and took a breath. 'Now, are we going to talk about the elephant in the room?'

He almost wanted to spin around and check behind him to see if one had just escaped from somewhere and actually appeared. She was still half smiling, and he recognised the tension in his muscles that had probably translated to his face. She knew she'd rattled him, but from the gleam in her eye he just wasn't quite sure that she cared.

'What do you mean?'

Her head gave a tiny conciliatory nod. 'I mean, we obviously got off to a bad start last night.'

Hmm. *That* elephant. 'You could say that.'

'Are you that mean to all the new tenants?'

'Most new tenants don't park in my space or set off a car alarm and wake up my sleeping child.'

She held up one hand, 'First—those parking spaces are ridiculously small. I probably did you a favour. How on earth could you have got your kid out of the car if you'd parked there?' She didn't wait for him to answer. 'But you're right, and I'm sorry. What's wrong with the lights down there? Are you all just supposed to fumble around in the dark? It's hardly safe. I couldn't see a thing and didn't know the car parking spaces were numbered until you came down the ramp in your car and the whole place lit up like a Christmas tree. Don't worry, I won't make the same mistake again. Was your little one okay?'

She was babbling again. This time it was his mouth that turned up in a half-smile. The more she spoke, the quicker she got, and the thicker her accent became. He shook his head. 'Hannah settled back down once I got her upstairs. Hope you didn't damage the car though; Len Brookenstein inspects that thing on a regular basis. It's basically his surrogate child.'

She pulled a face and sighed. 'Great. No, I didn't. At least I don't think so. It was just a cardboard box containing some clothes. And it barely touched his car. The alarm must be extra-sensitive.'

She was looking him straight in the eye, but the smile still dancing around her lips told him that they both knew the box had hit with a thud.

She shook her head again. 'Honestly, I did check—not a mark.'

Joshua frowned. 'Didn't Georgie leave you keys?'

Clara fumbled in her pocket and pulled out a familiar set. 'Yeah, but what's that got to do with anything?'

He stood up and stepped closer. 'And you didn't have these on you when you were in the garage last night?'

Her nose wrinkled. She tilted her head up to his. 'No, why?'

He touched her outstretched palm, turning over the cream plastic fob that was on the key chain. 'This is the sensor for the garage. If you drive your car down the ramp, or exit from the lift, the sensor automatically activates the lights.' He couldn't help but give a grin. 'And no, you're not supposed to—' he met her gaze '—fumble around in the dark down there.'

A little colour flooded her cheeks and she quickly tore her eyes away from his and looked down at the keys in her palm. 'Darn it,' she said as she lifted her other hand to turn the cream fob over. The movement made her fingers momentarily brush against his and a little shiver shot down his spine. He pulled his hand back. Recognition was obviously dawning. 'I just left the keys upstairs last night.'

'You didn't lock the door of the flat?' he asked incredulously.

'No.' She shook her head. 'Why would I? I was just planning on carrying all my boxes up in the lift. Doors and keys would just get in the way.'

He took a step back. 'I hate to break it to you, but

you're in London now, Clara. You leave the flat—you lock it.'

She frowned. 'But isn't there supposed to be a guy at the entrance—a concierge? People can't just wander in.'

Josh rolled his eyes. 'I kind of assumed that you might have picked up on the fact that most of the residents in the building call our concierge 'the happy wanderer'.'

Clara was still frowning. 'What do you mean?'

'You haven't met Louie yet?'

She shook her head.

'Ah, then let's just say, Louie doesn't much like sitting behind a desk. He's officially retired and took the concierge role after his wife died because he didn't like being in the house by himself.' Josh gave a smile. 'He likes to chat. If you can't find him, it's because he's chatting somewhere. It doesn't do much for the security of the building, hence why you shouldn't leave your door open.'

Clara looked as if she wasn't quite sure what to say. He guessed she was already feeling sorry for Louie, even though she hadn't met him yet. 'Does he get into trouble for that?'

Josh shook his head. 'No one has the heart to complain, and he's really obliging. He'll accept deliveries for you, sort out any issues in the flat, let repair men in if you need them and supervise if necessary.' He glanced out of the window for a second as a few memories surfaced in his brain. 'He tells Hannah great stories. She's his biggest fan.'

Clara's voice was hesitant. 'Hannah—is that your daughter? The kid I saw last night?'

The question gave him a jolt and a flash of annoyance again as he remembered how the car alarm had jerked

Hannah from her sleep. 'You mean the kid you woke up? Yes, that's her.'

Clara wrinkled her nose. 'Sorry. Just an accident. I'm sure it won't happen again. Hope she didn't keep you and your wife up all night.'

It was like a bucket of cold water being dumped all over his head. It had been a while since someone had made a casual comment about a wife or partner around him. Most people that knew him were well aware that his wife had died years before. His mouth opened to automatically form the words 'I'm a widower', and then he stopped. He hadn't invited this woman into his life. He still had no idea if she'd be much of a team player. The old feelings of irritation washed over him. He didn't need to share personal information with her. It was none of her business.

He didn't even form a reply, just picked up a file that one of the secretaries had left for him containing induction paperwork for Clara. 'Here,' he said. 'This is yours. There's a million online training courses you need to complete—health and safety, manual handling refresher, anaphylaxis etc. HR want you to complete some of this paperwork and drop it off. They're on the top floor. There's an office across from here that you can use— and introduce yourself to Helen, my secretary, and Ron, the ward clerk. They can pretty much tell you everything else you need to know.'

He moved behind her, catching a whiff of that perfume again as he opened the door. It was nice, unusual. But her words had irritated him. He didn't want to have to explain his situation to this new doctor. Not when he'd seen the flash of sympathy in her eyes when he'd told her Louie the concierge was a widower.

It was an odd thing when that familiar flash in someone's eyes sent all the hairs on his arms in an upward prickle. He didn't want pity. But for the last five years he'd seen it time and time again. He'd rebuilt his life, focusing on Hannah. He was busy at work, with most evenings spent taking Hannah to a wide variety of activities—none of which she seemed to want to stick at.

There wasn't a place for sympathy in his life. He and Hannah were good. They were solid. Plus, he didn't want the naturally inquisitive and uncomfortable questions that sometimes followed from the widower label being revealed. As he'd reached for the door handle he'd glanced at his hand. He'd taken his ring off two years ago. It had been the right time and right move for him.

Not that'd he'd met anyone serious. Sure, he'd dated. Georgie had encouraged him, babysitting Hannah on occasion. But there had never been anyone who gave him that…spark…that thirst and curiosity to find out so much more about them. Maybe there would never be.

If Abby had lived, he liked to think that their marriage would have endured and they would have grown old together. It wasn't that he didn't think future love wasn't a possibility; it was just that no one he'd met seemed to fill that space.

'I'll leave you to get on with things,' he said briskly to Clara as he strode out of the room. He had intended to take her with him on this introductory ward round. But he needed to get away. She had enough to be getting on with, and so did he.

Clara stared at the broad back striding away from her, and wondered what on earth had just happened. When she'd spun around and seen her new boss she'd tried her best not to let her chin bounce off the floor.

Typical—Mr Grumpy. He didn't like her at home, and it was clear he didn't like her at work. Clara had always shot straight from the hip. She'd hoped London would be a fresh start. But already things were rapidly going downhill. It didn't help that she'd hardly got a wink of sleep last night. Maybe it was being in a new bed, or maybe it was the unfamiliar creaking. What certainly hadn't helped was the low background noise from outside. The restaurants and bars had seemed far away when she'd been on the balcony, but in the middle of the night the raucous laughter and shouts had drifted all the way up to her room. That would teach her to leave the balcony door ajar.

A guy behind the desk gave her a wave. 'Clara?' he asked.

She nodded. 'Come over here,' he said, 'and bring your file. I'm Ron.' He pointed to his badge. 'Some people call me a ward clerk—' he lowered his voice '—but other people call me a magician.' He pointed to the seat next to him. 'I have coffee and doughnuts and I can help you with your paperwork and your online learning.'

A friendly face. Thank goodness. She smiled and walked over. 'Coffee would be great, thanks.'

She sat down next to him, spending the next hour completing the necessary paperwork and flying through the online learning packages. Ron printed her a pocket-sized list of hospital extensions she'd need, along with a reminder of people's names. He also seemed to know everyone's schedules and could tell her where to find the people she wanted to introduce herself to.

He ran down the list as only someone who'd worked in

a place for years could. 'Hans Greiger. Fantastic. Has encyclopaedic knowledge of superheroes and always speaks to kids about their favourite hero as he's sending them off to sleep. In ICU he's so up-to-date with his research. The unit here has trialled lots of new life-saving interventions. Dr Morran, the oncologist, is similar. Research is a big thing here. Dr Morran has two teenage kids of her own and coaches rugby.' His eyes sparkled and he held a finger up. 'She's the tiniest woman you'll ever meet, but she could take someone down twice her size. Now...' he pulled over another list, running his finger down it and pointing at various names '...he gets cranky if he hasn't eaten. She always has a book in her coat pocket. Marlon can make balloon animals for kids—always handy to know. Fi—she can find food anywhere. If you're hungry, ask Fi. The cupboards might look bare, but she'll spirit some food from somewhere. And if you're phoning for a scan try and get Ruby. She's the most obliging.'

Clara nodded as she listened, writing the occasional note. Ron was clearly a mine of information. She bit her lip and hesitated for a second 'Er...what about Joshua? You didn't mention him.'

Ron gave her a surprised look. 'Best guy on the planet. Without a shadow of a doubt. Shame he's never met someone. He deserves to.'

'What do you mean?'

Ron frowned. 'Georgie didn't tell you? I thought you two had been in touch and swapped houses and things.'

'We have. I mean, we did. But she didn't mention her brother at all. I didn't even know he lived in the same apartment block...' she lowered her voice '...and that turned out well.' Ron raised his eyebrows and she shook her head and gave a smile. 'Forget it. And the apartment—it's some place. Absolutely gorgeous.'

Ron nodded. 'Yeah, when Georgie first moved in, she couldn't stop showing us all pictures of the place. She felt so lucky. She and Joshua both inherited money from an elderly aunt. Turns out she'd a huge nest egg from something her late husband had invented that no one had known about. Georgie and Joshua were stunned. But it all worked out in the end. At least Josh doesn't have to worry about a mortgage alongside everything else.'

Another curious comment. She tilted her head slightly. 'What do you mean?'

Ron gave the smallest shake of his head. 'I just assumed Georgie would have mentioned it. Josh is a widower. His wife died a few weeks after Hannah was born; he's brought her up on his own.'

Her skin turned cold and she groaned and thudded her head down on the desk, putting her hands over it. 'Oh, no.'

'What?' asked Ron.

But Clara hadn't quite finished thumping her head on the desk as her stomach gave a whole array of uncomfortable twists. That explained the look on his face. She had almost seen the shutters banging closed across his eyes and hadn't for the life of her understood why. Darn it. Georgie might have mentioned it.

Ron nudged her. 'Okay, new girl, spill. What have you done?'

Clara pulled her head up, well aware that her hair was now all mussed around her head. 'When I got into the flat last night it was a series of disasters. I ended up in the pitch-black car park, parked in Joshua's space, spilling my clothing everywhere and then setting off a car alarm as he was carrying his sleeping daughter to the lift.'

Ron cringed but shook his head. 'Okay, poor start agreed, but what's that got to do with Josh being a widower?'

She closed her eyes tightly and silently pointed to the office at the side. 'When we were in there, I mentioned the bad start between us last night. I might have said…' and she paused, dying a little inside '… I might have said that I hoped it didn't take long for him and his wife to settle Hannah back down.'

Ron sat back, hands outstretched on the desk in front of him. 'Oh,' he said slowly, pulling a face. He paused for a few seconds, then gave a tentative reply. 'Well, you weren't to know.' He turned to face her. 'But Josh never said anything?'

She shook her head and put her hands back over her face. 'He just kind of shut down. Told me to get on with things.'

She pulled her hands back and stared down the ward. He was nowhere in sight. 'I should apologise,' she said, pushing herself up. But Ron was much quicker.

'Oh, no,' he said, shaking his head and putting one hand over hers. 'You shouldn't mention it. I know him. I know what he's like. Take a breath. File the information. And, please, don't do it again.' She met Ron's gaze and could see a whole host of emotions written all over his face. Pity, wariness but, above all, sincerity.

'Really?' She felt uncomfortable. Her first reaction—the one she usually acted upon—was to apologise. 'I don't want to get off to a worse start than I already have.'

Ron's eyebrows lifted so high they practically merged

into his hairline and this time he gave her a half-smile. 'Seriously?'

She let out a nervous laugh. Ron pushed another doughnut towards her and she shook her head. 'No way. I can't afford to buy a new wardrobe of clothes. I need to get my bearings and find a gym nearby.'

Ron put his hand on his chest. 'And this is why you have me. There's a gym in the hospital, free for staff, though it's used for patients during the day. But there's also a fancy gym in your apartment block, and a swimming pool. Didn't Georgie tell you?'

Something clicked in her brain. 'Oh, it might have been on the house swap details. But, to be honest, once I saw the view from her flat I stopped reading.' She tapped her fingers on the desk. 'I'd like to say that I wish I had an ancient rich aunt but, honestly, I didn't love the place last night.'

'Really? Why not?'

'Noise,' she said simply and then shrugged her shoulders. 'I live in a cottage in the middle of nowhere. The only noise I ever hear is a hooting owl or the baaing from the sheep in the next-door field. London? Well, that's a bit different. And it's warmer down here. At least it feels that way to me, so last night I left the door open on the balcony to let some cool air in.'

Ron let out a laugh. 'And instead you got the fun and pleasure of Canary Wharf and the docks?'

She sighed and pushed her glasses up on her head and rubbed her eyes. 'Something like that.' She stretched her back. 'Maybe it was just the bed, or the unfamiliar creaks. But, whatever it was, I felt like I hardly slept a wink.' She leaned on the desk. 'And, between you and me, a no sleep Clara is a cranky Clara.'

'I'll file that as a warning,' said Ron and pulled a large envelope from the drawer next to him. 'Here, take your things upstairs to HR. At least then you'll know you're getting paid at the end of the month.'

She slid her paperwork into the envelope and stood up, catching a glimpse of Joshua again. He was talking with another doctor at the end of a patient's bed. Her stomach flipped. Was it odd that the boss hadn't taken her on his ward round to get them used to working together? It had kind of been the norm wherever else she'd worked. First ward rounds were generally a mine of information on a colleague's work style. As she watched him talk seriously with someone else she wondered if she should be offended.

Every ounce of her felt uncomfortable. Maybe he doubted her competencies since he hadn't had the chance to select her himself? She'd never had her competence questioned before; she prided herself on being a good doctor.

But he'd mentioned team stuff too. Had the debacle last night meant he'd already judged her, and she'd failed? Did he think her personality wouldn't fit with his team? What on earth did that say about her? Was she awkward? Unlikeable?

So much uncertainty. And so *not* what she needed right now. Nothing like making her confidence slip all the way down to her boots. Or, in today's world, her comfortable shoes.

She looked down and wriggled her toes in the American shoes her friend had introduced her to. She now had them in six colours. Nothing else would do for long days on her feet, and in a job where she could literally walk for miles.

She took a deep breath. The first nurse she'd met, Luan, had seemed really nice. And Ron was obviously the font of all knowledge here. They didn't make her feel as if she didn't fit in.

She stared at the names on the list in front of her. Would all these people like her too? Maybe her directness would be her downfall. She'd never had to adjust her personality type to a job before, but there was always a first time.

She looked up again, just as Joshua looked up from his end of the ward. His forehead creased and she turned away quickly before he scowled at her again.

Ron caught her reaction. 'Best not to say anything,' he reminded her. 'It's been a few years, but I doubt he wants old wounds reopened. It's not exactly a good first conversation to have with your boss.'

She swallowed and nodded, painting a smile on her face. 'Yes, of course. You're right.' The envelope crinkled in her hand. 'I'll take this up to HR then start trying to meet some of the people on this list.'

Ron nodded as the phone started ringing. She walked away as he picked it up.

Although she'd been tired this morning, she'd still been enthusiastic about starting a new job. But in the last two hours all that enthusiasm had slowly drained from her body. Maybe this had all been a big mistake.

As she walked along the glass front corridor she stared out at the London skyline.

Why on earth had she wanted to leave home?

CHAPTER THREE

CLARA HAD KEPT her chin up. First, she'd learned to sleep with the balcony door closed. Second, she'd spent hours at the hospital meeting, and hopefully charming, everyone on the list Joshua had given her. There had been no problems. She'd practically memorised Dr Morran's protocols. She'd familiarised herself so completely with the staff of Hans Greiger's ICU that she knew what they all took in their coffee. But it was worth it. Even though she was officially supernumerary, she was still allowed to work and assist if appropriate. It meant that Hans had been around when she'd intubated a small baby and put in a central line. Two tricky procedures, particularly on a small child. She knew he was observing her—he probably did that with any new doctor at her level, but she'd felt her heart swell in her chest when he'd not only complimented her on her skills, but also how she'd dealt with the family.

Thirdly, she'd also managed to spend a bit of time in day surgery, and she'd met the physios, occupational therapists, speech and language therapists and dieticians who were all assigned to paediatrics. The only thing that had appeared tricky was the electronic systems. Occasionally she'd found herself logged out, irritating when she was in the middle of ordering tests or chasing results. She'd called the IT help number and asked them to get back to her. It wasn't a problem she could solve on her own.

By the end of the first week she was exhausted, but also slightly relieved. Her time felt well spent. She'd only caught an occasional glimpse of Joshua at work, and none at all at home. The only downside of the week had been the complete obliteration of the 'chocolate drawer' at home—but at least she'd found the gym. It had good equipment, excellent views and she'd only seen one other person in there. Perfect. Sweaty and breathless wasn't her idea of socialising.

Today was her first official staff meeting—something that Joshua did on a daily basis. She was interested to see how it went.

Ron nodded her into the kitchen when she arrived. 'Get coffee. Kettle is boiled.'

She glanced at her watch. The staff meeting started at seven-thirty and it was only seven o'clock. He gave a gentle shake of his head. 'They're all already in there.'

She gulped. 'Did I get the time wrong?'

'No. It's just how they are.'

Her feet were itching to race into the room. Her cheeks already felt warm with embarrassment at being the last to get there. But she took a breath and headed into the kitchen, filling her cup with coffee and a splash of milk. The meeting was due to start at seven-thirty. She wasn't late—and she wasn't going to act as if she was.

She pulled her shoulders back as she walked the few steps over to the meeting room. Her hand wavered, wondering if she should knock, but then she tilted her chin upwards and opened the door, keeping her back straight as she glided into the room with a smile on her face.

Joshua was midway through talking. He stopped and glanced over at her, irritation evident. 'Oh, good, you're here. Sit down and we'll continue.'

'Continue?' Clara glanced at her watch. 'I didn't think we were due to start for another...twenty-seven minutes. Did you forget to tell me about the time change of the meeting?'

She kept her voice light, but her words were carefully chosen.

One of the other docs in the room snorted into her coffee. She lifted her cup to Clara. 'Welcome, and I like you already. I'm Lucy and, if you don't know it yet, these morning meetings are like a race to see who can get here first.' Lucy looked at Joshua. 'Although the boss usually waits until everyone is in the room.'

Lucy connected her gaze with Joshua's frown and stared him straight in the eye. There was an unspoken implication there, and Clara appreciated it.

She sat down in one of the chairs. 'Well, I'm sure if I've missed anything significant Dr Woodhouse can fill me in later.'

There were a few seconds' silence and then Joshua shifted on his chair before he started speaking again. The meeting went quickly and was over in thirty minutes. Joshua briefed the staff on a product recall, new dosage instructions for a drug used commonly in paediatrics, sick leave cover and alerted them to a few patients he wanted closely monitored. Dr Morran followed up, highlighting a few of her own patients with special instructions. Other members of staff jumped in with general information about delayed results, special consults awaited from other areas and new admissions. Now Clara knew why Ron had told her to bring coffee. The amount of information crammed into that thirty minutes was huge, but crucial for a safe, smooth-running department.

She scanned the room, putting names to faces she hadn't met yet. Her phone vibrated in her pocket and she tilted it sideways to see who it was. Ryan. Guilt swamped her. She hadn't really had a chance to have a real conversation with him since she'd got here. They'd left messages, but kept missing each other. She knew there had been a complication about him moving out of her place—and she had emailed Georgie an apology—but the reply had been short and sweet.

No problem. These things happen.

She wondered what Ryan was making of the mysterious Georgie. Everyone here talked about her with real affection. She couldn't help but hope her colleagues back in Scotland had been a bit more friendly than Joshua.

'Dr Connolly?'

She jumped at the stern-sounding tone, embarrassed that her mind had wandered off while the others were leaving the room.

But, before she got a chance to respond, her pager sounded in her pocket.

She glanced at the pager. 'Duty calls,' she said with an uncomfortable smile on her face, before disappearing out of the ward towards the stairs.

As she hurried down the stairs to A&E she wondered if she'd already got herself in trouble. The doctor in A&E had asked her to attend. She already knew that the protocol stated that all children got fast-tracked up to the assessment unit, so they weren't left in the A&E environment which could, on occasion, be stressful for children.

But Clara liked to have a little faith in her colleagues. If an A&E consultant was asking for the paediatric page holder to attend, then she would go.

She pushed through the swinging doors and made her way to the nurses' station. Joe Banks, a guy she'd met briefly the previous week, gave her a wave. 'You on call?'

She nodded.

'Good. I've got an unusual one for you; feel free to ask for a second opinion.'

Clara flinched, wondering if he was questioning her skills. But her rational brain made her take a deep breath. The guy had barely met her. If this was an unusual case, it wasn't strange to ask for a second opinion.

He pointed to the screen in front of him and pushed a chart towards her with his other hand. She scanned the screen. A seven-year-old girl with fever, tachycardic and itchy rash. It could be any one of a hundred things, and not that unusual a case.

Joe lifted his hand as if he'd read her mind. 'Wait until you see the rash. I've put this kid in a side room mean-time, until you decide if she's infectious or not.'

Ahh… Now she understood. If the triaging doctor in A&E thought a child could have an infectious disease, they wouldn't send them up to the assessment unit. That could result in a whole host of other children and rela-tives becoming exposed to whatever virus they carried.

Clara picked up the notes and gave him a smile, 'Thanks,' she said as she walked towards the side room. Outside were some basics—gloves, masks and aprons, along with hand sanitiser. For an airborne infection, masks like these weren't effective, but old habits seemed to die hard. Clara used all the equipment provided and went in to make her own assessment.

'Hi there, I'm Clara, the paediatric doctor.' She smiled at the anxious-looking mother and the little girl, who was lying sleepily on the bed. 'I'm going to ask you a few questions and take a look at Jessica, if that's all right with you.'

The woman nodded. 'I'm Meg.' Her eyes ran up and down Clara's body. 'Should I be wearing those?'

Clara shook her head. 'We're not even sure if Jessica has anything infectious yet. If she does, we'll take the right precautions.'

She proceeded with a list of questions, gathering the background and history of Jessica presenting at hospital today. She also asked Meg a few questions, checking to see if she was pregnant, or if she, or any other members of the family, had any symptoms of their own. It was all just precautions. Some infectious diseases spread easily between close contacts, and some were risky if a woman was pregnant.

Once she'd asked all her questions, she rechecked Jessica's temperature, her heart-rate, and gently removed the hospital gown to get a better look at the rash.

Her pager sounded and she glanced down to where it was clipped to the pocket of her coat. The number was for the ward upstairs. She had a horrible feeling in the pit of her stomach that someone was checking up on her.

There were so many conditions that this could actually be—measles, meningitis, or even just a viral infection. Although some rashes were distinctive, many—in the early stages—were indistinguishable. As she kept examining Jessica she turned over one of the palms of her hands and stopped, turning back. There, on the side edge of her hand, was a strange mark. Clara leaned a bit closer. Was that a bite, or a scratch?

Either way, the area around it was slightly red and inflamed. It wasn't completely obvious, and could easily be missed.

'Do you have any pets?' she asked Meg.

Meg nodded. 'Two cats, an ancient tortoise and a rat.'

Clara gave a small nod in reply and made some notes. 'First of all, I'm going to prescribe something for Jessica to bring her temperature down, and then I'm going to order some tests. I'll try and ensure they happen as quickly as possible. Let me do that, and then I'll come back and talk to you again.'

Meg gave a half-smile, looking semi-relieved. Something was flickering in Clara's brain—a condition she'd only seen once before. She wanted to check some of the details before she asked any more questions.

It was odd. She absolutely knew that she had to rule out all the normal things that could cause a fever and rash. The list was almost endless, but something deep down inside her was just telling her not to ignore that tiny bite mark.

She'd seen a case before of a disease caused by a rat bite. But she had to check the details. She had to be sure.

A voice appeared at her back. 'What's the problem down here?'

Her muscles stiffened. She hadn't even had a chance to chart her preliminary findings. Last thing she wanted was her new boss looking over her shoulder while she ordered some unusual tests.

'Don't you realise that all children go straight up to the assessment unit? It's a well-known fact that A&E environments can cause unnecessary stress for both children and their families.'

She bristled, trying at first to bite her tongue, and then

deciding to just go with how she felt. She spun around, keeping her demeanour entirely professional. 'Of course I know that. I'm not some half-ass student. If I'm keeping our patient down here, I have an entirely good reason to do so.'

He flinched, obviously not expecting her answer to be so direct. But he was acting so pompous, talking to her as if she were some kind of inexperienced idiot. She heard a gentle cough next to them both and turned to see Alan Turner, the head of A&E, raise one eyebrow and give her a half smile.

She tried to restrain her flare of anger back into a less flammable state. 'Don't worry, Dr Woodhouse,' she said quickly. 'If I need your expertise I'll be sure to let you know. Everything is under control.'

Joshua stared at her, long and hard. She could almost see his brain whirring, trying to decide whether to reprimand her or leave it for the time being. He glanced sideways at Alan, who was pretending not to listen to them both—even though he clearly was.

'I expect to hear from you soon,' Joshua said through clenched teeth.

'Of course,' she said with an enforced breeziness in her tone and watched as he spun around and strode down the corridor so fast he looked as if he might break into a sprint.

Alan moved over next to her, looking down at the forms in her hand. The blood test she'd been looking for hadn't appeared on the IT system—probably because it was so unusual, so she'd written the order by hand.

He made a surprised nod. 'Haven't seen that one before.'

She pulled an uncertain face. 'I know it's a long shot.

But I have seen it before, and my gut is just telling me to check.'

Alan glanced back down the corridor. The door at the end was swinging from where Joshua had just disappeared. 'You do know that any test like that—I mean one that's completely unusual for our lab—has to be signed off by the Head of Department?'

Clara's heart sank. Her fingers crumpled the form a little. 'Please tell me you're joking.'

He shook his head and pulled the slightly bent form from her fingers. 'I'm not so sure that now's a good time to go chasing after Josh,' he said carefully.

'Me neither.'

Alan gave a slow nod. 'Okay, so let's just say that on this occasion I'll sign it off for you. I'll be interested to see what comes back. Let's just call it professional curiosity.'

Clara heaved a huge sigh of relief. She hadn't realised any unusual requests had to go through the Head of Department. It made sense. Sometimes inexperienced doctors could order a whole host of expensive tests that might not be necessary. This was the NHS. They had to be careful of costs and she understood that.

She knew that Alan signing off on this test might cause friction between him and Joshua at a later date. She held the form close to her chest. 'Thanks, Alan, I appreciate this.'

He held up his finger as he moved away. 'It's a one-time-only deal.' He looked back over to the swinging door again. It was clear he'd sensed the friction between her and Joshua. She'd need to think about that. It wouldn't do for other areas to think that staff in Paediatrics didn't really get on. 'Just until you get settled in,' said Alan as he gave her a nod and disappeared behind a set of cubicle curtains.

Clara sighed and looked at her forms again. *Please don't let this be a wild goose chase,* she prayed.

Joshua was trying so hard not to explode. Yes, he was a control freak. Yes, he always had been. And no, that didn't always work well for a Head of Department.

But he also tried to mentor his staff. He wasn't the type of doctor to leave a colleague without support, or in a situation they couldn't handle.

But somehow he knew Clara Connolly wasn't that type of doctor. He'd been asking around. Paediatric circles were surprisingly small. Everything he'd heard about her in the last week had been reassuringly, but annoyingly, good. He couldn't quite understand why this attractive woman seemed to irritate him.

Just her jaunty, slightly lopsided ponytail seemed to annoy him.

When he'd known she'd been called down to A&E he'd hung around the ward, wanting to check up on the assessment notes she'd written. It wasn't intrusive exactly—just a way of reassuring himself that he could trust her skills. But neither the patient nor the notes had appeared. And eventually he'd run out of patience and gone down to the A&E department. He might have been just a little snappy with her, but her response had been equally snappy and not one he would expect from a new start doctor.

He'd had to bite his tongue. Georgie's voice had echoed in his ears as he stormed back up the stairs to Paediatrics. Would he have checked on her? Of course not.

How would he feel if he'd been in Clara's position and someone had checked up on him?

But, ultimately, all paediatric patients who were ad-mitted were his responsibility. He had a right to ask ques-tions. To check up on his staff.

He waited an hour. Then another hour. His fingers were itching to check the electronic record, but he stopped himself.

'Any word from Dr Connolly?' he asked.

Ron looked up from the computer. 'Just to get her a tuna sandwich from the canteen when I'm going. She's caught up in A&E.'

She'd been there for more than two hours. This was getting ridiculous.

No. He wasn't going to wait a minute longer.

When he reached A&E five minutes later he could see how busy it was. Alan Turner was walking out of Resus and pulling off a pair of gloves. He fell into step alongside.

'Josh, twice in one day? I didn't realise we'd paged you.' He was smiling, but Josh could tell from the words and tone that he knew exactly what was going on. He gave Josh a tiny nod. 'Your new colleague—I like her. She's smart—I would never have picked up on that case.'

Josh's footsteps faltered. Both men knew exactly what he was thinking. He bit his lip then asked the question. 'What case?'

Alan gave him a knowing smile. 'Rat-bite fever.' He shook his head. 'What a call.' He walked into the nearby treatment room and started washing his hands. Josh couldn't help but follow him. Rat-bite fever? He'd never even heard of it.

'I had to look it up' Alan smiled. 'But the diagnosis has just been confirmed.' He pulled a bit of a face. 'Oh, apologies, I signed off on the test for her.' He waved one wet hand. 'You weren't around.' He paused for a second and then added carefully, 'I told her not to bother you.'

He was lying; Josh knew he was lying. He liked Alan. He respected Alan. But he wasn't about to stand by and let the Head of another department conspire with a new member of his staff—at least that was what it felt like.

He kept his voice steady. 'I'd appreciate if you didn't do that again, Alan.'

The implication was clear and as Alan grabbed some paper towels to dry his hands he gave a conciliatory nod. 'Sure.'

It was a truce. Alan had successfully let Joshua know that his staff member had performed well, while equally trying to keep him in check.

The annoyance that had been flooding through Josh's veins had diverted slightly, but not disappeared completely. He would have expected Clara to give him a call and update him, particularly around an unusual case. But he couldn't help but be impressed that his new doctor had diagnosed a condition he'd never even heard of.

He pulled out his phone, ready to look it up, just as Clara walked out of the nearby room, a wide smile across her face.

'Oh, Joshua,' she said. 'I was just about to call you.' She waved back towards the side room. 'I know you like to treat children on the assessment unit, but I've just started Jessica on some IV antibiotics. She's got streptobacillary rat-bite fever. I'm worried about septicaemia.'

He lifted the chart from her hands and scanned it before picking up a nearby tablet and pulling Jessica's file. Clara's cheeks flushed and she pulled a piece of paper from her pocket. 'My notes. I'm a bit old-fashioned. Haven't put everything on the electronic record yet—

just her obs and what I've prescribed. It seemed more important to get the antibiotics started once I had the diagnosis.'

The words prickled down his spine. 'How did you manage to run a test like this without my sign off?' It didn't matter that he knew the answer to this question; he wanted to see what kind of excuse she gave.

As she moved he caught a waft of something. He had no idea what kind of perfume she was wearing, but it was like a shockwave to his system. It reminded him of a garden after a rainstorm—sweet, sensual and enticing. It was delicious.

He blinked and breathed in, letting the scent permeate his body. For a second all he could focus on was the smell. He'd never had a reaction like this before to a perfume. Every female colleague that he worked with wore a different scent. All were indistinguishable. But this? This was entirely different. He looked up. Clara was talking. He could see those signature red lips moving. But for a few seconds he couldn't concentrate.

The noise in the busy A&E faded to a dull hum. There was a roaring in his ears, as if parts of his brain were awakening after they'd been snoozing for the last few years. His eyes focused on Clara's eyes. He could see a tiny flare of panic in them. Her voice started to permeate. 'So, I know it wasn't the usual turn of events, but this case, it wasn't usual either. I knew time was of the essence and the lab test takes a few hours. It seemed imperative to rule it out as soon as possible. As I was with her, the petechial rash changed—it became more pronounced around the bite wound. She started to experience rigors and a headache and joint pains.' She licked her lips and stopped talking for a second, pausing to catch her breath.

The roaring in his head hadn't stopped. His eyes couldn't move from hers. There was something about them. Not the colour. Not the mascara on her dark lashes. Something in the depths of them.

He had to stop this.

He held up one hand. 'Dr Connolly. Let's draw a line under this. Don't do it again. If you want to run specialist—and very expensive—tests, run it past me first. NHS is public money. I like to keep a check on things. As Head of Department that's my right.' He took a breath, 'If, however, I'm not here, then I'm fine with you running it past, for example, Alan. But *only* if I'm not at work.'

Right now he wanted to walk away, to try and sort out what was wrong with his head. But his professional mind was listing all the things he should be doing right now. Supporting his team member. Reviewing the patient. Ensuring the correct diagnosis had indeed been made. He also didn't want to admit that he was dying to pull his phone out of his pocket and read exactly what rat-bite fever was.

He spoke quickly before Clara had a chance to start babbling again. Why was she babbling anyway? Was she nervous around him? Worried he would give her trouble for going behind his back and ordering tests? He didn't need to say the words out loud—they both knew that was exactly what she'd done. Once, he could let go—particularly when Alan might have been encouraging her—twice would be a reprimand.

'Why don't you introduce me to the patient and her family? I'm interested to see Jessica and make arrangements to get her upstairs. Maybe I can do that while you finish your notes?'

She twitched. And he wondered if the words he'd meant to sound helpful had actually sounded as if he was implying she hadn't done her job. He waved his hand towards her. 'Dr Connolly?' He gestured towards the side room.

She gave a nod. 'Sure, follow me.' And she walked ahead, leaving a trail of enticing scent for him to follow.

He smiled to himself as the children's story of the Pied Piper who'd lured children away by playing music came floating into his head. This wasn't exactly music but it felt close enough, and he shook himself as he followed the trail that she'd laid.

CHAPTER FOUR

THINGS FELT AS if they were settling down. She'd been here a month. The noises from inside the flat and out were annoying her less and less. She'd managed to familiarise herself with all the regular staff at the hospital and her first few on-call shifts had gone well. Children always came in overnight so she'd decided just to stay when she was on-call overnight, sleeping in a comfortable room next to one of the wards.

Joshua was always in promptly the next morning to review all new admissions and seemed to grudgingly agree with all decisions that she'd made. She couldn't pretend it wasn't a relief.

Since their first few encounters she'd more or less managed to stay out of his way. But he was a curious kind of guy. Any staff member she met seemed to love him. Unlike most hospitals, people at the Royal Hampstead Free Hospital seemed to work here for years, not quite as transient as other places she'd worked in, and most of the regular staff had nothing but praise for Joshua.

On several occasions she'd come across him sitting with a child. Playing a game with them. Laughing with them. Reading a book to them because he'd sent a weary parent to grab something to eat and they didn't want to leave their child alone.

Clara had done the same herself on many occasions—she loved those moments with the patients—so she wasn't quite sure why watching him from afar, rubbing a kid's hair as they fell asleep against him, had tugged at her heart in a way she didn't want to admit.

It had been six weeks since she'd started her meds and she definitely felt a little better, not quite so flat as before. She'd registered with a GP here in London, who'd asked her to come in when she needed a repeat prescription.

Her GP had been lovely and readily acknowledged the stress and strains on fellow doctors. She'd offered to also refer Clara to one of the counsellors in the practice and Clara had surprised herself by accepting.

Now, as she pulled her legs up on the chair she'd positioned next to the window at the balcony, she could finally admit to starting to like this place just a little. Sure, there were no sheep banging their noses against her bedroom window, but sitting here watching the sunset spill orange and red light over the water was pretty mesmerising. She cupped her hands around her mug of coffee and reached for a biscuit. There was beauty here, and she wanted to take the time to recognise and enjoy it.

Now she was starting to feel a little better she could recognise that the incident back home with the toddler, Ben, had been the trigger for her. It wasn't always like this. Sometimes depression just seemed to sneak up out of nowhere; other times, there was some kind of event or trigger that started her down that path. The truth was, it was likely that depression would always be in her life.

A noise at the door made her jerk, spilling coffee down her jumper. She sat up as the main door to her flat opened and a sleepy-looking child walked inside clutching a book in one hand and a card in another.

'Auntie Georgie,' she murmured, blinking her tired eyes.

The words made Clara's limbs unfreeze from their automatic defensive position. She jumped to her feet and moved quickly across the room. Her brain was working overtime. Had she left her door ajar? No.

The card in the child's hand was a slim key card—the same that opened the door to the flat. Hannah. This had to be Hannah.

Clara dropped to her knees in front of the child. 'Hannah?' she said gently.

She wasn't quite sure if the little girl was sleepwalking or not. She knew better than to suddenly wake a child who was sleepwalking.

The pale-faced little girl blinked. Her eyes were slightly glazed. She was wearing pink and white pyjamas covered in the latest trendy cartoon character and was clutching a popular kids' book with a bear and a group of kids on the front. Her fine brown hair was mussed. It was clear that at some point she'd been sleeping.

'Hannah,' Clara said again softly, not wanting to startle her, but clear that somewhere around here Joshua Woodhouse would be in a state of panic.

She gently took the key card from Hannah's hand. It made sense that while Georgie lived here Hannah had gone freely between her aunt's flat and her own. But now? The thought that Joshua Woodhouse owned an entrance card to the flat she was currently staying in left her feeling a little odd. Invaded even.

She looked over at the phone and realised she'd no idea what Joshua's phone number was. She scanned her brain. Was the whole apartment block a bit like a hotel? Could she just dial someone's flat number to get them on the phone? Then she groaned. Of course not. All the flats had A, B, C and D after them. She squeezed her eyes closed for a second, willing the number of the space she'd parked in downstairs on the first day to spring into her head. Nope. Nothing. She couldn't even guide Hannah back up in the lift to her father's flat.

'Book,' said Hannah, holding out her book to Clara.

She hesitated, then took it from Hannah's hand, leading the little girl gently towards the comfortable sofa that was close to the nearby phone. As soon as Clara sat down, Hannah climbed up onto her knee and settled there, pulling the book down in front of them both.

Now Clara was torn. She wasn't sure that Hannah was actually sleepwalking. Maybe just not yet fully awake? She opened the first page of the book and had a brainwave. Louie. What had Joshua called him...the happy wanderer?

She picked up the phone and dialled, sighing with relief when Louie answered. 'What can I do for you, Dr Connolly?'

She spoke quietly. 'Thank goodness. Louie, Hannah Woodhouse has just wandered into my flat. I don't have her father's phone number and can't remember the flat number either. Do you have a way I can contact him? He must be out of his mind. She seems really sleepy and I don't want to startle her awake.'

Louie gave an easy sigh. 'Ah, let me do that. Hannah used to go easily between the two homes. Give me two minutes and I'll get a hold of him.'

Clara put down the phone, breathing a sigh of relief.

Hannah nudged her. 'Story,' she said in a still sleepy voice, leaning back and laying her head on Clara's shoulder.

It was such an easy move for the little girl, as if she did it every day, and it made the breath catch in Clara's throat. There was an aching familiarity about this little girl.

The heat coming from her body as she sat in Clara's lap seemed to permeate right through to her soul. She'd thought about having kids for a long time. She'd even made enquiries a few months ago about using a sperm donor and having IUI.

Part of her had wondered if it was just how she was feeling, so she'd stalled on the decision. But, even now she was beginning to feel better, the loneliness in her remained, seemed fastened to her in every way.

She'd spent many a long hour and restless night with kids on the wards. She'd seen the tears, the temper tantrums, the heartaches and the pain. She didn't have an unrealistic view of what being a parent would be like.

But, as this little girl sat on her lap and urged her to turn the pages of her book, Clara couldn't help but wonder if this was what life could be like. There were always tiny doubts niggling in her brain. Could a person with depression really be a good single parent? Would her mood ever affect her relationship with her potential child? No matter how many doubts she had, just this simple act was filling her with hope.

She started to tell the story in a quiet voice. The words had a rhythm to them, making it easy to get into the swing of the short story. Within less than two minutes they were almost at the end and Hannah's head was nodding, as if she were falling completely back asleep.

The door banged open and Clara started. Joshua stood in her doorway, his face dark with rage. 'What are you doing?' he demanded, striding in as Clara put her finger to her lips.

She took a deep breath, trying to ignore the way her heart was thudding erratically against her chest at the initial fright. He'd crossed the room in a few long strides and stood towering over her.

She refused to let herself be intimidated. 'Shh,' she said quite openly now, nodding towards the sleeping Hannah, who'd been unperturbed by the banging door.

Joshua opened his mouth and then stopped, clearly collecting himself. Clara waited. She tried to put herself in his position—realising Hannah was missing from their apartment and being thrown into a blind panic.

She couldn't imagine how terrified he'd been, and she tried to reassure herself that his blundering into her apartment was just the reaction of a panicked father.

She kept her gaze locked on his and nodded to the space on the sofa beside her.

He paused for a second and then sank down next to her, his sigh of relief audible.

'I guess that Louie never got you,' she said in a low voice.

'Louie?'

She nodded, her hand rubbing gently at Hannah's back. 'I phoned him when Hannah appeared.' Her gaze didn't waver. 'I didn't know your phone number, or your mobile number. And, despite you drawing my attention to the fact I'd parked in your space that first night, I couldn't remember that number either, so I couldn't bring Hannah back up to you. I had no way to get in touch with you, Joshua, and, to be honest, I wasn't quite sure if she was sleepwalking or not. I didn't want to startle her.'

Joshua had the good grace to break their gaze as a

sheepish expression flooded over his face. He let out a low curse. 'I'm sorry, Clara. I'd put her to bed, went in to check on her after a phone call and she was just…gone.'

He ran his fingers through his rumpled hair. 'My heart almost stopped. The door was open, and I hadn't even noticed.' He thumped his head back against the sofa and groaned. 'My five-year-old walked out of the flat and I didn't even notice,' he repeated. 'What kind of a crap dad am I?'

She could almost see the breakdown happening—see the pieces of the puzzle slotting into all the worst-case scenarios he could imagine—as he sat next to her. She reached over and tapped his hand with hers. 'She's fine. And she's lovely, by the way.'

For some reason Clara didn't move her hand from his.

He shook his head. 'No, Louie didn't get me. He'll probably appear up here any moment to make sure everything's okay.'

Clara nodded. 'At least you knew to check here first.' Her eyes glanced towards the key card for the entry panel to her flat. 'I take it Hannah used to come up and down between you both?'

Joshua sighed. 'Yes. She wasn't ever supposed to use the lift by herself and she did know that. But often she would ask if she could come down to Georgie's, or Georgie would phone and say to send her down. Then one of us would either go up and down with her, or put her in the lift, and the other would meet us at the door.' He took a long, slow breath. 'But on a few occasions, particularly around bedtime, Hannah would sneak down to Georgie's.' He gave Clara a smile. 'Apparently my sister's story-telling skills far outweigh my own.'

'I'll keep that in mind,' said Clara, then raised her eyebrows at Joshua. 'We should really talk about you having a key to what, essentially, is *my* flat right now.'

'Ah…' He bowed his head a little just as there was a knock at the still open door.

They both turned their heads. Louie caught sight of the scene, clocked Hannah still in Clara's arms and gave a slow nod. 'Just checking all was well. I'll be back downstairs.' He gave Clara a knowing smile.

Before either had a chance to say anything, he'd disappeared again.

It took her a few seconds to realise that she still had her hand on Joshua's and she pulled it back. It was odd—having him here in her place. At work he was her boss. Here, he was someone entirely different—a worried parent. And the first man she'd had in the apartment—invited or not.

Joshua leaned forward, putting his head in his hands and squinting a sideways glance at the sleeping child in Clara's arms. 'I sometimes think I'm making a complete mess of all this,' he said.

Clara blinked. She hadn't quite expected the admission. 'Why do you think that?' she asked cautiously.

He raised one hand. 'Well, first off, I have a child who wanders out of our place and down to a relative stranger's apartment, climbs into her lap and apparently asks her to read her a story.'

Clara nodded but gave a loose shrug. 'Exceptional circumstances. I'm not entirely sure if she realised I wasn't Auntie Georgie.'

'Oh, she knows,' he said. 'She's been asking when we could come down and meet you.'

'She has?'

He nodded. 'I told her it wasn't appropriate. That you

were a new workmate and couldn't be expected to have us down here.'

'Seems a bit tough.'

'You think?'

She nodded. 'I don't mind. You could have just asked, you know.'

He pulled a face but didn't answer.

'You said first off. What's second?' It might be intrusive to ask, but he'd started the conversation and she could see that now he'd relaxed around her a bit he did seem as if he wanted to talk. Maybe she could finally get to see the man that everyone at work told her about.

He leaned back again. 'Secondly, I have a daughter who seems to start a million activities but doesn't want to stick at any one of them. She gets bored within a few weeks and wants to quit.' He sighed. 'I don't like to complain. But I just get my schedule to fit around one thing then she wants to swap to another. She's tried ballet, gymnastics, baton twirling, Brownies and tap dancing so far.'

Clara wrinkled her brow. 'And you've let her quit everything?'

'Shouldn't I?' A worried expression crossed his face.

She gave another shrug. 'Well, it is up to you. You're the parent. But maybe you should try something different.'

'Like what?'

She took a few moments to consider before she replied. 'Let's think about an activity which could be an essential—swimming, perhaps.' She adjusted her position on the sofa so she was facing him a little better. 'That's an activity you wouldn't want her to quit. Safety—every parent wants their child to be able to swim.'

He gave a slow nod. 'Okay...'

'Okay, so you tell Hannah that she's going to start swimming lessons and it's really important. You let her know that she'll probably be going for a few years, and that she can't stop until she can swim up and down a big pool.' Clara was thinking back to her own swimming lessons as a kid. She gave a careful shrug. 'Of course, there could an occasion where she doesn't gel with a particular instructor, and you might swap her to someone else.' She held up her finger. 'But you let her understand this is a non-quit activity. You let her know this is important.' She looked out of the window at the orange setting sun. 'You tell her that once you know she can swim safely the two of you can have lots of fun on holiday, somewhere with a big pool.'

His eyes narrowed a little as he thought about her idea. 'You think I should try something like that?'

Clara nodded. 'I'm not a parent. And I must have had a different temperament as a child, because once I started something I became a bit obsessed about it. But lots of my friends were like Hannah,' she said reassuringly. 'They tried lots of things over the years.'

She reached a hand out again and touched his arm. 'You know, this has to work for you too. It can't be easy having to change your schedule all the time. Maybe some kind of stability would be good for you both.'

'Are you saying I don't offer Hannah stability?' He was instantly on edge and sat up straight with a flash of anger in his eyes.

Clara let out a sigh and shook her head. 'Why are you so defensive? Why is everything I say a fault?' She rubbed Hannah's back again, enjoying the way the little girl was snuggled into her. 'If I didn't see this gorgeous little girl on my lap, and know you must be finding this tough, I'd think you hated me, Joshua Woodhouse.' She gave a sad smile as he flinched. 'Maybe you're just not used to someone who talks as frankly as me—and calls a spade a spade.'

He waited a long time before he spoke. He gestured with his hand between them. 'I don't do this.'

'Do what?'

'Talk about things… Talk about being on my own with Hannah…. Talk about how I wonder if I'm doing things right all the time.' He leaned forward and pressed his hands into his face. 'Talk about if I'm letting her down.'

'You're not letting her down.' The words were out instantly. 'Why do you think that?'

She could see something flit across his eyes. Guilt. Doubt. This was clearly a man who felt he'd let someone down before. The first person to enter her head was his wife. He was a widower. No one had really told her any details. She just knew his wife had died from some kind of terminal disease just after having Hannah. Why would he think he'd let his wife down?

He hadn't answered and she tried to push past what she'd just seen in his eyes. 'You put too much pressure on yourself, Joshua. Every friend I've got who's ever had a child spends their time endlessly worrying that they're getting it wrong. Haven't you realised yet that the whole world is just muddling through?' She gave a little laugh. 'Even the ones who have pre-made meals for a month and a huge blackboard with everything written on it in their kitchen.'

Joshua's face relaxed into a smile and he visibly shuddered. 'Okay, I've never done that.'

'See?' Clara smiled. 'You're not doing too badly then.'

There was something nice about seeing him a little

more relaxed than normal. He seemed to settle into the contours of her sofa. 'I'm sorry you got a fright tonight,' she said. 'Why don't you give me the number of your flat, and your mobile number, so if Hannah ever appears again I can let you know where she is.'

He pulled a face. 'It won't happen again. I'm sorry. Keep the key card. I shouldn't still have it. Of course I shouldn't. To be honest, I'd just forgotten about it.' He looked at his daughter and Clara's heart panged at the clear look of love in his eyes. 'I'll talk to Hannah tomorrow. I'll tell her she shouldn't come down here.'

Clara shook her head. 'You don't need to do that. She's welcome to come down here if I'm in.' She gave him a smile. 'To be honest, I liked the company. London's kind of lonely. And it was the best book I've read in ages.'

'You're finding London lonely?'

'Kind of. You know, we're in a busy hospital, it's a busy city, you can't turn around without bumping into someone but...' she let her voice trail off for a second while she collected her thoughts '... I miss my best friend, Ryan. I miss my old cottage with the sheep that press their faces up against the window.'

Joshua let out a loud laugh. 'What?'

She grinned. 'Text Georgie; she's been there over a month. She'll know all about it by now.'

His smile stayed for a few seconds, then faded. 'I guess Hannah's missing her auntie. She spent a lot of time here. Georgie was Hannah's partner in crime; the two of them used to gang up on me.'

Clara raised her eyebrows. 'Sounds like a job I could embrace,' she said cheekily. 'No, honestly, she can come down any time. If you think she needs to hang about with a female for a while or—' she chose her words carefully

'—if you need a break and I'm not working, just give me a call.'

She could see the conflict in his eyes. Joshua Woodhouse didn't accept help easily. He was wavering. After a few seconds his eyes connected with hers. The setting sun was streaming oranges and reds through the glass across the room. It was like being held in some kind of spell. Her breath was stuck somewhere inside her chest. It was the first time in for ever that she'd felt some kind of connection with someone.

And she knew it was ridiculous. Joshua was her boss. And, apart from work, she didn't think they had anything in common. But seeing him like this—exposed, worried, vulnerable—it was a far cry from the confident, smooth consultant she saw at work. This was a normal guy. One who was juggling a million balls in the air and trying to stay afloat. Maybe she hadn't given him enough leeway. Maybe she'd been too quick to take offence at some of his words.

'That's a really kind offer,' he said. His gaze hadn't left hers. It was steady. And though it was only a few words, it felt like so much more.

He paused then added, 'My nanny left around the same time as Georgie and my short-term replacement isn't working out as well as I would have hoped.'

Clara nodded. 'Well, think of me as another option. It's not a problem.'

She wasn't sure if this was her imagination or not, but she could swear there was something in the air between them. A weird kind of buzz. A smile danced across her face. There was something nice about this, relaxing. There hadn't been much opportunity, between the two of them, to have some quiet time like this. The hospital was so busy—and she found him so frosty at work—that they'd been like ships passing in the night.

Her heart gave a little skip as Hannah adjusted herself on Clara's lap. Clara swallowed, wondering if she was mixing up her feelings about motherhood with what she sensed in the air between her and her boss. That could be dangerous. And confusing.

But Joshua was still looking at her. She wasn't imagining that. And, as his face started to crinkle into a smile, she was sure she wasn't misreading the flicker of attraction in his eyes. She'd never pried into his life before. She hadn't felt the urge. But all of a sudden she wanted to know everything.

'And if you ever need an emergency babysitter for on-calls, remember, I'm just down the stairs.'

He stood up and leaned close, her nose catching the spicy scent of his cologne as his arms entwined with hers to pick up Hannah. For the briefest of seconds the tiny scratch of stubble on his cheek brushed against hers and she sucked in a breath, feeling her eyes widen as they met his.

His hand and arms were against the curves of her body as he grasped his daughter and he halted for the briefest moment. For a second their lips were mere inches apart and she wondered if he was going to kiss her. From this close she could see the tiny flecks in his blue irises and just how long his lashes were—completely unfair for a guy.

'Thank you, Clara,' he said huskily in a voice that seemed to ripple over her skin.

'Any time,' was her automatic reply.

He pulled back, lifting Hannah from her arms and heading out of the door of her apartment back to the lift.

Her legs took a few seconds to move and by the time she reached her own door she only had a chance to give a brief wave.

'Got to stop meeting like this,' she whispered as the smooth steel doors slid closed.

Her heart was thudding in her chest as she shut her own door and leaned against it. Had that all really just happened?

She drew in a few quick breaths as she crossed the room, pausing to pick up the abandoned storybook still sitting on her sofa. Her hand ran over the back of the sofa, feeling the warmth from where Joshua had been sitting.

This *had* really just happened.

She kept moving, sitting down on the modern cream chaise longue next to the balcony and pulling up her legs to her chest. Part of her felt warm and fuzzy, matching the glow streaming in from the sunset outside. But part of her was a little muddled.

She'd started to feel a bit better—about everything. Work, the change of scene, her life, and what the future could hold.

Spending time with Hannah tonight had cemented something in part of her brain. She definitely wanted to be a mother. Whether she had a man in her life or not, if it were possible, she'd love to have children in her future. But was it something she should pursue now, or later? She wasn't getting any younger. Treatments were tough. And expensive. She had to be realistic about things.

But should she really push away the chance of meeting a man she could love and spend the rest of her life with? Would any guy she met want to date a woman who was happy to go and do IVF on her own to have a child?

Things were so complicated. She didn't want to view

any potential dates as father material. She wanted to keep things separate in her brain, and in her life. But was that realistic?

She leaned back on the chaise longue and sighed, letting the warm orange glow bathe her face in its dimming light.

For the first time in for ever she'd felt a spark of *something*. She hadn't even felt that when she'd been dating Harry six months ago. This was different. This was something that made her skin tingle, her blood pulse and the tiny hairs on her body stand on end.

It made her mouth curve automatically upwards.

Could it really be a 'thing'?

She let out a groan. She was going to have to exercise the thing she struggled with most—patience. And just wait and see.

Darn it.

CHAPTER FIVE

JOSHUA'S HEAD WAS in knots. One of his doctors had quit. Well, not actually quit. He'd had to leave due to a family emergency back in Portugal. But he'd made it clear he regretfully couldn't come back, and the space in the rota seemed to be multiplying by the second. Two others had been struck down by the norovirus which was currently storming its way through the hospital, their paediatric anaesthetist had chickenpox—so severe he'd be lucky not to be admitted to ITU himself—and one of his junior doctors was expecting, and it turned out she had one of the worst cases of hyperemesis gravidarum he'd ever seen.

His pager sounded again and he muttered, 'I swear, if that's someone else sick…'

'You'll what?' Clara appeared at his elbow, a smile on her face, even though he knew she was run ragged covering here, there and everywhere.

'I'll probably run and hide,' he admitted. 'We're too many staff down already.' He wrinkled his brow. 'Don't you have a clinic?'

Clara nodded. 'But Ron's contacted them all, and I'm seeing them up here rather than at the other side of the hospital. It means that I can keep an eye on the assessment unit too.'

Joshua stopped walking and looked at her for a second. 'Why didn't I think of that?'

Clara grinned up at him. He breathed in and it was a little shock to the senses. She was wearing that perfume again that reminded him of a garden after a rainstorm. It made him lose the ability to concentrate—hardly good for today.

They'd come to some kind of truce. He couldn't quite understand why she'd started off pushing all his buttons in the wrong way, but now he'd taken time to take a step back, be patient and leave his judgement unclouded, he actually quite liked her.

She'd been so good about Hannah, particularly when he'd burst into her apartment. The conversation that night had seemed to put them on an uneven balance—one that could easily teeter in one direction or the other.

But she'd rapidly proved herself at work. The rest of the staff liked her, and she seemed clinically sound. On the few occasions he'd brought Hannah into work, Clara had gone out of her way to chat to her and spend time with her. Auntie Georgie's flat had quickly become Clara's place, and he wasn't sure if he liked that or not.

But, more than that, she was just…there. It was as if his senses picked up whenever she was around. He could hear her laugh before he walked through a door, sense her presence in the ward before he ever set eyes on her. She was patient with anxious parents. Good with teenagers. Magical with the terrible twos.

His brain was trying to deal with the fact that he was enjoying her being around. Maybe it had been that first glance. The shock to the system, realising he'd noticed how attractive she was. The colour of her lips. The curve of her hips.

Sure, he'd dated a few women over the last year or so. But none that had been special to him. None that had given him that suck-in-your-breath-for-a-moment feeling. He'd kind of forgotten what that felt like and had thought himself incapable of feeling like that again.

Maybe it was his history. He'd got used to being on his own. It was hard to learn how to trust again when his trust had been so badly broken. It was harder still when he'd loved the person who'd broken his trust completely, and she had loved him. He'd thought he was over things; he was sure he was ready to get back out there. But the slightest hint that the person he was dating wasn't being completely up front with him was enough to send him in the other direction without a second's hesitation. It didn't matter that it was ridiculous. Everyone was entitled to their privacy. But he just couldn't shake off the underlying conviction that was buried deep down inside of him—a relationship meant no secrets, no lies. It wasn't just his own heart he had to protect now; it was Hannah's.

But Clara? She was dancing around the edges of those thoughts on a pretty permanent basis. Which was a shame, as she was only here for six months and there was no way he'd introduce a potential girlfriend to Hannah unless he thought she might be important.

So it was easier to keep Clara in a different kind of box—one where he didn't think about her that way.

But sitting on the sofa with her a few weeks ago had pushed hard at those boundaries. She was easy with the touching; it came so naturally to her. She probably didn't realise it had been a long time since someone other than a parent or his sister had touched his hand in that kind of way. With affection. With care.

Clara stopped walking, spinning around until she was facing him. 'You didn't think of it because your brain doesn't function that way.' She gave a good-natured shrug. 'You're a man. Multi-tasking is a whole new language to you.' She gave him a wink as she walked away. 'Anyhow, I'll never admit it was Ron's idea.'

He laughed as she disappeared through the doors. Clara was full of quips. And he liked that. He liked her sense of humour. It reminded him not to take life too seriously, and he needed that when some of the days here were tougher than others.

Half an hour later she was back, her expression serious. She didn't beat around the bush. 'Help,' she said quickly, 'I need a second opinion on a kid.'

He was on his feet in seconds. 'No problem—what's wrong?'

He started walking with her as she rattled off the child's symptoms and her suspicions. 'Lewis Crawley is seventeen months—temperature, abdominal pain, drawing his knees up to his chest, jelly stools, vomiting bile...'

He put his hand on her arm. 'Clara, stop. What is it? This sounds like a textbook case. Why are you worried? You clearly know what's wrong.'

She was the palest he'd ever seen her. Jittery even. Not the cool doctor who'd diagnosed a weird and wonderful disease in the first week he'd worked with her.

'I... I just want a second opinion. And we don't have our normal anaesthetist. Who will take the case? Who will do the surgery?'

Joshua stopped and put both hands on her shoulders. 'Do you know this kid?'

She shook her head, and he could see the gleam of un-spilled tears in her eyes.

He had no idea what was going on here. And he'd have to get to the bottom of it. But, in the meantime, if this toddler had intussusception and the bowel had telescoped inside itself it was a surgical emergency.

'Okay, let's see him.' The examination took moments. Clara was right with every call. He could see she was trying to keep her emotions in check, so he went back over things with the parents to satisfy himself that they understood what was happening. Then he contacted the surgeon on call for the day, and phoned an alternative paediatric anaesthetist.

Clara typed up the notes as he spoke, recording every extra detail. She'd done everything she could—even ordered all the tests and completed the emergency consent form with the parents.

On a normal day, Joshua would have given any colleague a second opinion and then left them to carry on. But this wasn't a normal day. And he wasn't going to leave her.

He waited until both the surgeon and anaesthetist had come up to the ward, and the theatre staff had appeared to take Lewis and his parents down to surgery, then he glanced around to make sure there were no eyes upon them, slid his arm around her shoulders and guided her into the nearest room, closing the door behind them.

The nearest room was the stationery cupboard, not the best venue for a discussion like this. He took his arm away and turned to face her. 'Okay, Clara, you did everything perfectly. Tell me what's wrong.'

She was shaking—her body was actually shaking—

and he watched as she dissolved into tears, muttering a curse under her breath.

Her head was shaking, but her face was covered with her hands. 'I'm sorry,' she said. 'I just…' she took a deep breath and dropped her hands and her gaze '…panicked.'

The word struck him as odd for Clara to choose. She was a member of staff who'd proved herself clinically competent over the last six weeks, and panic wasn't something he'd seen in her before.

'Tell me why you panicked,' he said steadily. He had to unpick this. If she needed support, it was his job to offer it.

She leaned back against one of the shelves in the cupboard, taking a few moments before she lifted her dark gaze to meet his.

'I didn't expect this to happen.' Her hands were still trembling and instinct made him reach out and take one of them in his own.

'What happened?' His voice was almost a whisper, just willing her to continue.

Her eyes closed and she rested her head back. 'I had a kid, older than Lewis, back in Edinburgh. I wasn't at work.' She winced. 'I had norovirus.'

Just like today—two staff off with norovirus.

'By the time I got into work early the next day, I saw there had been a kid admitted overnight. He might have been a bit older, but the symptoms were all there. A locum had been covering for us and had dismissed intussusception and was querying a grumbling appendix and had ordered a scan for the next day.'

She swallowed and a tear slipped down her face. 'I knew what was wrong with him as soon as I saw him. We got him to Theatre as soon as we could, but…' she shook her head '…part of his bowel was necrosed. Dead. He ended up with a permanent stoma.'

Pieces were slotting into place in Joshua's head. It didn't matter that this wasn't her fault or responsibility. What was important was how Clara *felt* about it. What it made her feel inside. They'd all had a case like this—likely, more than one. The *if only* aspect that tormented them in a way it shouldn't.

He gave an understanding nod. 'So, today?'

She gave a huge sigh. 'Today was the first case of intussusception I've dealt with since then. It just pushed buttons in me. Made me feel panic. Even though it felt textbook, I wondered if I was just making things fit because I'm just so scared of another instance getting missed.' Her head sagged and she pulled her ponytail out, shaking her head as if to give herself some kind of relief.

Her dark hair was mussed and full, scattering over her shoulders and around her face. Every time he'd seen Clara she'd had her hair pulled back in some kind of band or clip. He'd never seen it loose before and the effect was quite stunning.

His hand was still holding hers. She hadn't pulled away, but the trembling had finally stilled. He spoke slowly. 'You did a good job today, Clara. You saw a child and diagnosed him with a condition, and got him appropriate treatment. I'm always here for a second opinion. I'm always happy to do that—so don't be afraid to ask again.' He chose his words carefully, wanting to reassure and build her confidence back up. 'But you didn't need it today. Your clinical judgement was spot on. I have confidence in you. You've proved yourself since you got here. I've not heard one query about any of your work. Have a bit of faith.'

Her brown eyes looked up and their gazes locked.

'I understand it brought back bad memories. I get that we all have triggers.'

There was a moment's silence—so much unsaid. It was the first time he'd seen Clara vulnerable—just like she'd seen him when Hannah had disappeared from the flat. She'd been good to him that night, even though she'd really had no reason to be. After the frosty way he'd treated her he couldn't have blamed her if she'd called him out for not noticing Hannah leaving immediately. He would have deserved it. But she hadn't said a single word like that, just invited him to sit down and talk.

He wasn't quite sure how he'd ended up in a cupboard with Clara but, face to face, this was as close as they'd got. Her scent was wrapping its way around him, pulling him in like some magic power. He'd got to the stage now that whenever he got the slightest whiff of that scent he would raise his head to see where she was. There was something about being in a tight space with someone. Being so close that he could see the tiny beating pulse at the apex of her neck, the tiny smudge of foundation on her cheek and the way her red lipstick had started to wear away. He knew he was staring, but it didn't feel awkward or uncomfortable because he knew she was staring too.

He wondered what she was seeing. Could she tell that he was worried about her? Did she know that he trusted her clinical judgement? Would she notice the lines and dark circles around his eyes because he hadn't been sleeping well lately? The little patch he'd missed this morning when shaving? Or might she sense the fact that he still wondered if he was managing to fulfil the role of both mum and dad to his daughter? Hannah deserved so much love and attention. Sometimes he looked at Hannah and his heart swelled so much in his chest that he thought it might explode.

Clara blinked as she watched him then moved slowly, her other hand lifting and resting on his chest. 'Thank you,' she whispered.

It was in his mind in an instant—that immediate instinctive need to move just a few inches forward to close the gap between them. His eyes focused on her lips as she licked them and he had to root his feet to the floor to stop them moving. The heat from her palm was flooding through his thin cotton shirt, warming his chest and spreading outwards. But it was the inward sensation that was making his breath catch somewhere in his throat. In his entire life, he'd never wanted to kiss a woman so badly.

Was it the red stain still on her lips? The way her loose and mussed up hair look completely sexy? Not moving was currently a form of torture.

But then the spell was broken. Clara closed the tiny space between them, stepping forward, sliding her hand up around his neck and pressing her lips against his.

It was like a roar in his ears. All the brakes were off. He slid his hand through her thick hair and pulled her tight against him. She tasted sweet and as he breathed in the fresh garden scent filled his nostrils. One of his hands stayed in her hair while the other pulled her close to his hip. He could feel the curves of her body against him.

Clara Connolly wasn't afraid of kissing. She met him match for match, pushing him back against the shelves on his side. His hand moved, sliding under her white coat and brushing the skin where her shirt met her trousers.

She made a little sound—one of pleasure—and it nearly drove him crazy. It was as if their minds melded.

They both pulled back, breathing hard. Clara let out a little laugh and lowered her head. When she lifted her head back up her eyes were glowing. The warmth from that glow spread all across his skin.

'Should I apologise?' she asked.

He shook his head and let out a small laugh too. 'Should I?'

'Somehow I don't think we'll be the only hospital staff to share a rogue kiss in a cupboard.'

This time he nodded as he smiled. 'I don't think so.'

Clara reached up and grabbed her hair, pulling it back into the band wrapped around her wrist and then straightened her shirt. 'How do I look?' It was clear she was planning on heading back outside.

'Fine.' Was he disappointed?

Staff came in and out of this cupboard all day—the last thing he wanted was to get caught in here. The gossip would spread like wildfire. And, funnily enough, he'd never really been the type to have a clinch in a cupboard or on-call room—no matter how much hospital staff joked about it.

'Oh, wait a minute.' She stood up on tiptoe and wiped one finger at the edge of his mouth. 'I think I left my mark.' She pulled back her finger, examining the minuscule hint of colour. 'That's better.' She smiled as she put her hand on the door handle.

She paused for a second and he could see her taking a deep breath, composing herself. A little buzz of pleasure flushed through his veins. 'You wait thirty seconds,' she shot over her shoulder as she opened the door and stepped outside into the ward.

As the door closed he leaned back against the shelves again, laughing. He had no idea how that had just happened.

Well, no, of course he did. But his idea of trying to ignore the flare of attraction to Clara had obviously failed. A tiny part of his brain waved a red flag. He was her boss. He'd only guided her into the cupboard for some privacy because she was upset.

But Clara had made the first move and they were both consenting adults. Maybe she'd felt the same wave of attraction that he had?

He wasn't quite sure how he felt about that. Clara was only here for a temporary period. He had Hannah to think about. Maybe it was better to keep things neutral. Certainly at work that would be for the best. Last thing he wanted was for it to be common knowledge that something might be going on between them.

He nodded to himself and breathed, giving his face a quick rub to make sure there was no sign of her lipstick. He swung the door to the stationery cupboard open and stepped out onto the ward.

As the door swung back into place he jumped. Ron was standing—cool as a cucumber—behind the door. He lifted the cup in his hand and grinned. 'Made you a coffee. Here you go.'

And then he winked. And walked away.

CHAPTER SIX

SHE WAS DEFINITELY starting to feel better. The view from her bedroom window had stopped looking so alien to her. She'd started to enjoy standing on the balcony and listening to the sounds from below at night instead of pining for her view of fields with an occasional sheep's baa.

She enjoyed both the swimming pool and gym within the apartment complex, and Louie was practically her best friend. He even put her food deliveries from a supermarket in her apartment for her, taking care to put essentials in the fridge.

As for Joshua? She wasn't entirely sure what was happening there. A few more weeks had passed. She wasn't embarrassed at all by their kiss. It had sent a whole host of sensations whirling around her body. Most of all it made her feel alive again.

Joshua was hard to read. He wasn't avoiding her. He didn't seem embarrassed either. But neither of them had even admitted the event had happened. Though, for some strange reason, it seemed to have helped break the underlying tension between them.

He was a bit easier around her, talking to her more like a friend, rather than a stranger who'd sneaked into his department. That, in turn, had helped her relax a bit more.

She didn't need to prove herself at every turn. Three days ago she'd had another baby with intussusception, and this time she hadn't second-guessed herself—wondering if she was seeing symptoms that weren't there. The baby had been diagnosed by her in A&E, assessed by the surgeon and taken to Theatre within two hours of entering the hospital. All without any complications. She'd spent most of the next day hanging around little Abe and tickling his toes. For a baby who had required major surgery he'd been in a surprisingly good mood when he'd come around and made a rapid recovery, eating and drinking normally within a few days.

Joshua had appeared once or twice at her shoulder and given her a reassuring smile, but nothing more.

Part of her was entirely comfortable, and part of her had a longing for more. Her brain frequently told her that maybe he'd just been feeling sorry for her, but the cells in her body remembered his response. It hadn't felt like any kind of sympathy kiss—instead it had felt like a compressed well of passion. One that she wouldn't have minded exploring a bit further...

But she had taken one step forward. She'd finally pressed send on the email to the IVF clinic, making enquiries about treatment options and using donor sperm. It had felt monumental to her, even though it was a basic enquiry. Once she had all the information she could think again. And that made her feel good—good she'd made the decision, and good that she was thinking about what came next. Life wasn't just the place she was now; life was also the world of possibilities in front of her.

It was Saturday, and the day stretched before her. She was toying with the idea of being a tourist for the day. Buckingham Palace, Trafalgar Square, Tower Bridge and the London Eye were all on her radar. The weather was bright and sunny and there was something freeing about the thought of wandering for a while, maybe stopping for a bite of lunch and perhaps even a glass of wine.

She was just pulling on her jacket when there was a knock at the door. She pulled it open to see Joshua and Hannah standing outside. 'Something wrong?' she asked, glancing between them both. 'Do you need me to watch Hannah?'

Her first thought was that Joshua had been called in unexpectedly to work. Why else would they both be at her door?

'No, Auntie Clara. We're going to the Tower of London, and I want you to come with us.'

Clara was stunned but her face broke into an immediate smile. Firstly, at Hannah calling her Auntie, and secondly at being invited at all. Her gaze met Joshua's and he gave a good-natured shrug. 'I think my company alone is a bit boring for my daughter. She wanted to ask a friend.'

Clara knelt down so she was opposite Hannah. 'And that's me?'

Hannah nodded as if it was the most natural thing in the world. 'We haven't gone anywhere together yet and you've been here for *ages*.'

Her eyes gave the briefest glance to Joshua again. She wanted to be sure that Hannah wasn't pushing him into this. He might not really want to spend time with her at all. But the look in his eyes seemed sincere and half amused. 'What do you think? Have you been before?'

Clara picked up her bag and swung it over her shoulder. 'Never. I'd just got ready as I wanted to do a bit of sightseeing today too. The Tower of London sounds perfect.' She pulled the door closed behind her. 'Thanks for the invite.'

Hannah started bouncing on her toes as they called for the lift. 'Told you she would come, Daddy.'

Joshua looked over as they stepped into the lift then leaned over and whispered in her ear, 'Prepare yourself. Hannah will talk *all* day.'

Clara gave a genuine grin. 'Can't wait.'

Because it was a Saturday they had to stand in a queue for a while to get through the entrance to the Tower of London. Hannah hadn't stopped bouncing and waited for her turn to get her picture taken next to one of the famous Beefeaters in their traditional dark blue and red uniform.

The inside of the Tower was busy, but they weren't in any hurry so enjoyed one of the tours, listening to the Yeoman Warder tell stories of the Tower's history, treachery, torture and legends. Hannah was captivated, particularly when they met the Ravenmaster and were able to hear the names of some of the ravens around the tower.

The queue for the Crown Jewels outside the Jewel House in the Waterloo Block was large, snaking its way across much of the grounds. Joshua bought them all ice creams to eat while they stood and waited, entertained by a group of performers who re-enacted a few of the tales about the Tower.

As they moved forward into the dimly lit corridors towards the Crown Jewels Hannah slipped her hand into Clara's. For a second Clara was startled, but the little hand felt comfortable in hers and a smile slid across her face. 'Told you I was old news,' Joshua said in a voice low enough that Hannah couldn't hear.

Clara gave him a cheeky wink. 'Guess you need to up your game then.'

'Sounds like a challenge,' he said with a teasing tone.

'Not sure you're up for it,' she quipped back quickly. As the line moved forward, Clara lifted Hannah up onto her hip so she could get a better view of the Crown Jewels. They couldn't linger too long, as the line was constantly moving. But they got a chance to look at St Edward's Crown, which was used for the Coronation, and the huge Cullinan Diamond mounted in the ceremonial sceptre and rod.

Hannah's favourite was the Imperial State Crown with the huge Black Prince's Ruby set into the cross at the front of the crown, and she was delighted when Clara bought her a hand-sized replica of the crown in the gift shop later.

She toyed with the thin plastic box it was housed in, trying to stick her fingers through the tricky gaps. 'It's okay—' Clara laughed '—it's yours; you can take it out.'

Hannah sighed. 'But it's too little for my head.'

Clara nodded in agreement. 'It is, but you can sit it in your bedroom and look at it when you fall asleep. Maybe you'll have a dream about being a princess, or a queen.'

'Or a unicorn!' said Hannah excitedly.

Clara kept nodding but looked at Joshua in bewilderment. He laughed. 'You'll learn. It doesn't matter what the topic of conversation is these days, it always comes back to a unicorn.'

She shook her head. 'Guess I'm not as up-to-date as I thought I was.' Her heart was feeling full in her chest. She'd had such a lovely morning with them both. Playing the part of a tourist was always going to be fun, but doing it with them had made it so much better. They'd chatted easily today. Hannah was enthralled by the stories and the sights. Any hint of bad behaviour disappeared in seconds with the latest distraction.

As they walked out of one entrance to view the blue and white Tower Bridge, Joshua's hand brushed against hers. He gave her a smile and then put his arm around her shoulder. 'Anyone hungry?'

'Me!' both Hannah and Clara shouted at once.

They strolled along the edge of the Thames until they came to a restaurant that had tables set out in the sunshine. It was obviously popular but, after a few minutes' wait, they were guided to a table and given some menus.

The waiter appeared as they were watching the tour boats on the Thames and took their order. Ten minutes later Clara was sipping a cool glass of wine and eating traditional fish and chips. She let out a sigh.

'What?' asked Joshua.

She smiled. 'Nothing—just a perfect day. Exactly what I wanted to do. I got to see one of the sights in London, and now I'm having a gorgeous lunch and a glass of wine.' She raised her glass. 'I thought I was going to be doing this by myself, so thank you for the invite today.'

Joshua's heart gave a strange kind of flutter in his chest. This morning he'd acted on a whim. Hannah had pleaded to invite Clara on their trip, and he hadn't let himself find a hundred reasons to say no.

Because he hadn't really wanted to.

He couldn't pretend that his stomach hadn't been giving the odd flip-flop as he'd knocked on her door. But Clara had seemed delighted. And his heart might have skipped a few beats.

All morning she'd been great company—attentive to

Hannah, and easy around them both. They weren't dating, so there was no problem with her spending time with Hannah, but the truth was Joshua didn't really introduce any female friends to Hannah. He'd met a few of the fellow mums and dads from Hannah's time at nursery and now at school—children's party invites made that inevitable—but that wasn't a circle of people he would call friends.

Between working and Hannah's activities, there was hardly time to get to know the doctors he worked with, let alone their families.

Now, sitting here with the breeze from the Thames and the sun in the sky, Joshua realised for the first time in years he was actually enjoying himself.

As they ate their food he could see the excitement in Hannah's eyes. It had been there all day. All she wanted to do was impress Clara, and that made his heart ache a little. Had he made a mistake? He knew she was only here for another four months.

Trouble was, Hannah had told him the other night how much she missed her Auntie Georgie. He knew she'd been angling to go down and see Clara instead and he'd made a kind of lame excuse. It wasn't even that he was self-conscious about the fact they'd kissed. He was much more self-conscious about the fact that last time he'd been in her apartment he'd more or less spilled out his insecurities about failing as a parent. He wasn't even sure why he'd put all that into words.

His mind had been on his sister too. Georgie had texted a few times, and he got the impression that more was going on in Scotland than she was actually telling him. He'd tried to call her and left a few messages. But they hadn't actually managed to talk in person for a few weeks. They were normally so close. He worried about her. He wasn't surprised that Hannah had said she was missing her auntie.

He lifted his glass of beer towards Clara. 'It's our pleasure to have you along with us today. We've had fun, haven't we?' He nudged Hannah and she nodded enthusiastically, her mouth full of pasta.

'I probably should have asked you before,' he admitted without thinking.

Clara gave a soft smile and met his gaze. 'Well, I'm just glad you asked now.'

The words and meaning hung in the air between them. For a few seconds the background seemed to fade away and it was just the two of them there. Joshua felt his mouth dry and his skin prickle. Clara's dark eyes were pulling him in, keeping him there. And he liked it. He liked it a lot.

Was Clara someone he could trust? Someone who would be truthful with him?

'Can we go to Buckerham Palace next time?' asked Hannah, her mouth still full of food.

It broke the spell and they both jerked. He frowned a little as he racked his brain. 'I think Clara might be working next week,' he said, but he gave Clara a warm smile. 'I'm sure we can work something out in the future.'

Clara nodded. 'I'd love to visit Buckingham Palace,' she said. 'It's definitely on my list.' She paused and bit her lip for a second. 'But I do have a day off this week. How about Hannah and I check out that film that everyone's been talking about? I'd love to go to the cinema and see that.' She leaned towards Hannah. 'I kind of need to take a kid with me, or people will wonder what I'm doing there.'

Hannah laughed and turned to him. 'Can I, Daddy? Can I?'

Joshua shifted in his seat. In truth, he didn't like being put on the spot. However, Hannah had been talking about this film non-stop and he had no idea when he'd finally get the time to take her.

'As long as it doesn't interfere with swimming lessons,' he said as he caught Clara's look of surprise.

'You started swimming lessons? That's wonderful. It's so important that you know how to swim.' She said the words to Hannah, but he knew her purpose was backing him up.

'I quite like it,' said Hannah quickly. 'Daddy got me a swimming costume with unicorns on it.' Her proud grin said it all.

Clara leaned forward. 'So what have you done so far? Have you held onto the edge and kicked your legs? Or have you been really brave and put your face in the water yet?'

'I did that last week!' shrieked Hannah.

'Wow.' Clara leaned back again. 'I am so impressed. I bet you'll be swimming without a float soon.'

Hannah nodded as the waiter came over to take their plates away. 'Any desserts?' he asked.

'Can I have ice cream?' said Hannah without taking a breath.

The waiter picked up the last plate. 'Better ask your mum.' He smiled at Clara.

Now Joshua really couldn't speak. No words would come out. He saw the instant that Clara sucked in a shocked breath. But she didn't speak either.

'Oh, that's not my mum,' said Hannah without a second thought. 'This is our friend, Clara.'

The waiter pasted a smile on his face and gave a wary and apologetic smile. 'So, who gets to make the ice cream decision?' he asked.

Joshua nodded quickly. 'Absolutely.' He looked at Hannah. 'Chocolate ice cream with chocolate sauce?' She beamed back and nodded.

The waiter disappeared and Joshua looked over at Clara. She still looked as though she was holding her breath. But there was something else—a tiny light of sadness in her eyes that he hadn't seen at any point all day.

He had no idea what that meant. But his heart seemed to give a twist in his chest. She looked sad. And he didn't like it when Clara looked sad.

It wasn't as if he hadn't experienced random people asking Hannah about her mother before. He'd learned to accept it was an easy mistake—even though it was tactless in this day and age, when families came in all guises. He and Hannah had spoken about this before when sensitive times came up—like Mother's Day. Hannah still had the simple reasoning of a child. Her mummy had died and was in heaven, next to the stars in the sky.

Those who did know her were supportive. Her teacher at school had asked her if she wanted to make a card for her auntie, her granny or her daddy on Mother's Day. These things were done smoothly, with no fuss, and Joshua appreciated that.

So, even though it had been a little awkward, he was surprised to see the hint of hurt in Clara's eyes. Was she just embarrassed by the comment? Or maybe it was something deeper. Maybe Clara didn't want to be a mum at any point. Maybe she couldn't have children. Or maybe she was hiding something else.

No. He pushed that thought away for now. Things had

been going well. He had to try and move past the fact that Abby had kept secrets from him. He was jumping to conclusions. He couldn't assume that Clara would do the same. Whatever it was, he didn't want it to spoil their day.

'Another wine?' he asked her.

She gave a gentle shake of her head. 'I'm afraid I'm a bit of a lightweight. One glass is fine; two glasses make me feel a bit wobbly. Not my best time.'

He raised his eyebrows. 'Really?'

She smiled and nodded. 'You don't want to see it.'

'Maybe I do?' he teased as Hannah was presented with her ice cream.

All of a sudden he was struck with the thought that this day would come to an end, and he really didn't want it to. It was only early afternoon. He glanced over at one of the tour boats bobbing past. It was close enough to hear part of its guide's chatter. The guide pointed to a nearby hotel, naming it. 'It's for the rich, the very rich *and* the very, very rich.'

The people on board started laughing and Joshua looked over at Clara. 'Ever done the Thames tour?'

She shook her head. 'I've seen the boats often enough. They come right down to where the flat is.'

'There's a pier just near to here. We can jump on one of the sightseeing boats. They go right past the Houses of Parliament, and the London Eye. Want to give it a try?'

Clara pointed at one of the packed boats. 'It's definitely this kind of boat, and not the speedboat kind?'

They'd seen several of them shoot past in the last hour. Joshua laughed. 'Don't like the look of the speedboat tour?'

She gave him her best haughty glance. 'I'm just thinking about the bumpy ride. Wouldn't want Hannah to lose her crown, would we?'

He signalled to the waiter for the bill. 'Absolutely not. Just so long as you weren't scared.'

He was teasing her again and she seemed to like playing along. She slid her hand across the table to Hannah. 'Girls aren't scared. We're just far too clever to let ourselves get wet. Have you seen the people that come off those boats?'

Hannah squeezed Clara's hand and looked determinedly at her dad. 'Exactly,' she said in a voice that made him laugh out loud.

'Why do I feel as if you're both ganging up on me?'

Hannah gave a little nod as she slid her arms into her jacket. 'Because we are, aren't we, Clara?'

Clara grinned and gave him a wink. 'Absolutely.'

By the time they got back to the apartments Hannah was almost sleeping on her feet.

The boat trip had only been the start of the afternoon. They'd wandered around the shops for a bit, and come across a ticket booth with availability for some shows that evening. After a quick chat they'd gone for a musical about witches that Hannah had absolutely loved.

'I've always meant to take her to a musical,' said Joshua in a low voice as they waited for the lift. 'I just never got around to it.'

He smiled down at the slumped figure in his arms. 'You might have helped me create a monster. Now I'm going to have to take her to the ice one, the lion one, and the one with the genie.'

'I'm game if you are. Musicals are my addiction. I've

always loved them. Did you see the way her eyes lit up while she watched?'

He gave a slow nod and the edges of his lips tilted upward into a sexy smile. She realised the first words that had come out of her lips and how they might have sounded.

I'm game if you are.

She couldn't help the low laugh that came from deep within her.

'You were saying?' he said huskily.

She stepped a bit closer and whispered in his ear. 'I'm not sure I should say anything at all. We have company.'

'I'm sorry I have my hands full,' was his quick retort.

She took a deep breath and looked at him for a second. They were flirting. After weeks and weeks of playing at just being friends, they were definitely flirting. And she liked this version of Joshua. He could be playful. And he could be deeply sexy. Probably not the best thought to have about her boss—who was also a single father—but she really, *really* liked it.

But something had struck at the heart of her today. She was a little bit jealous of the fabulous relationship he had with his daughter. It was something to aspire to. Would Joshua want to have more kids in the future? The offhand comment by the waiter had made parts of her pang even more badly than they had before.

She leaned against his shoulder. 'No, you don't,' she said honestly. 'You're lucky. And you know you are. You have a fabulous child, and you're doing a great job as a parent.'

He turned his head, his blue eyes locking with hers. His lips brushed against her forehead, sending a whole host of tingles shooting down her spine. 'Thank you,' he whispered. 'That means a lot.'

The doors slid open and Clara swallowed. Her floor was first.

'Do you want to come upstairs?' he asked, the words coming out so gravelly it sent a huge array of prickles across her skin.

Every single part of her wanted to scream yes. She knew he didn't do this—didn't ask women up to the apartment he shared with his daughter while Hannah was there.

But something was holding her back. If she closed her eyes for just a second she could imagine exactly what would come next. But did she want to cross that barrier between them? It could make things awkward at work. She, for one, wouldn't regret the next step, but what if he did?'

She pressed her lips together and swallowed before reaching over and touching his cheek lightly. 'I'm not sure that's a good idea. Hannah's had a big day. I'd hate if she was restless and saw something she shouldn't.'

Her stomach coiled. These words weren't entirely true. She really, really wanted to go upstairs to his place. And she felt sure. She just wasn't sure that he was.

Somehow even the touch of his skin beneath her fingertips let her know that she could fall hard and fast for this man, without him doing another thing. She was feeling good right now—her mood was better than it had been for months. Did she want to risk a chance of heartbreak? Particularly when this romance could potentially only last a few months. Her body felt ready to move forward, but did her heart?

She stood on her tiptoes for a second and brushed her

lips against his. 'Thanks for a great day,' she whispered. 'How about we take a rain check?'

She could see the disappointment on his face, but he gave a slow nod. 'Of course,' he said smoothly as the doors slid open and she stepped out at her floor.

All the way to her door she wanted to turn back around and tell him that she'd changed her mind, but there was too much uncertainty there for her. Maybe they could chat about things in a day or so. It could be this uncertainty was only her head—she could well be reading too much into this. A short-term thing might suit Joshua. She just wasn't entirely sure it suited her.

As the door opened she bent to pick up a large envelope from the floor. Wrinkling her nose, she pulled it open as the lights came on around her.

A number of glossy information catalogues fell into her hand. The clinic. The clinic had sent her the information she'd requested. A small card slid out and she picked it up from the floor. A password and code to access the sperm donor catalogue.

Her skin prickled and her mouth dried. This had all suddenly got very real.

CHAPTER SEVEN

IT WAS LIKE living in a permanent state of standing at a crossroads.

He liked being around Clara. Hannah liked being around Clara. And Clara seemed to like being around them. But that was where everything stopped.

They'd been spending more time together. It was easy to be in each other's company. There had been flirting. There had been glances and a bit of innuendo. But he just couldn't seem to take that final step forward. That final...

She was on his mind more or less permanently. But he really didn't want to play this wrong. Yes, they'd shared a kiss in a cupboard. Yes, she'd spent the day with them and several others since. But it was as if he couldn't actually make a move. Ridiculous. If he'd had this conversation with himself he would have scoffed. But taking things further would lead to what, exactly?

Things had been complicated by a call from his sister last night, letting him know that she was pregnant. It had been a complete shock. Georgie had been resolute. No, she wouldn't talk to him about the father. No, she hadn't told their parents yet. Yes, she wanted to have this baby. And yes, she needed some time to think things through.

He'd wanted to get in the car and drive straight up

to Scotland. But Georgie must have read his mind because she'd sent him a text five minutes after their call had ended.

I told you because I know how you are about secrets. I kept one from you before and swore I wouldn't do it again. This is my life. You have to let me live it my way. Don't worry. I'll call if I need you. Trust me.

He'd spent most of the night awake, worrying about her. But Georgie knew her own mind. And she'd be a wonderful mother. He knew it, and he had to give her space.

Joshua sighed as he sat down next to Ron, who was typing away on the computer.

'You're making a mess of things,' came the unexpected comment.

Joshua started. He hadn't expected that. 'What do you mean?'

Ron rolled his eyes and lifted his fingers from the keyboard. He turned to face Joshua. 'Clara. You're making a mess of things with Clara.'

Joshua's first reaction was to look around and see if anyone else could overhear their conversation, but the coast was clear. 'I don't understand,' were the words that came out.

Ron's glare was sharp. 'Well, you should. Forgive the expression Joshua, but I'm assuming this isn't your first rodeo?'

Joshua's brow wrinkled. 'What?' Why on earth had he sat here? Was Ron reading his permanently spinning mind?

Ron gaze softened. 'I'm assuming that you've dated a few women in the last few years.'

Joshua gave a slow nod. 'A few,' he said quietly.

'Then why not Clara? We can all see it. You're both like a magnet to metal—you're pulled together. Quite often I'll see the two of you laughing together, or sitting together, and it looks like the next natural reaction would be to put your arm around her shoulders. But you stop yourself. I can see you. You actually start to make the move and then stop.' Ron gave a half-snort. 'Your body and mind and all your senses are telling you to do it. But you don't. Why?'

Joshua wasn't quite sure how he'd been pulled into a conversation like this. 'It's complicated,' he said, stalling for time.

'Actually, it's not,' answered Ron promptly. 'You need to get your act together. I can't tell you if there are stars and rainbows in your future. But, from here, it looks like you don't want to find out. You can't take that risk. Why, Joshua? Clara's a great girl. Do you think there aren't a hundred other guys in this place with her on their radar?'

That made Joshua sit up a little straighter. He hadn't actually thought about that at all.

Ron shook his head. 'Right now, her eyes only seem to look at you. If you don't get your act together, you could miss out on a few months of fun.' He lowered his tone. 'Or you could miss out on the opportunity of a lifetime.' He gave a wry laugh and shook his head. 'And you're the one that's supposed to have the brains between us.'

Joshua was stunned. Ron hadn't said a single word about practically catching them both in the stationery cupboard. Not to him, and apparently not to anyone else. It was unusual in a hospital this size. Usually the first hint of anything sent the rumour mill going, turning the barest whisper of something into a firework display. But for Ron to be so discreet, and yet so direct today? It made Joshua pay attention.

Not that he hadn't been paying attention before…

The phone next to him rang and he picked it up. 'I'll give it some thought,' he murmured to Ron as he walked away, shaking his head at him as if he was the stupidest man to walk the face of the planet.

His pager sounded as he was on the phone to another hospital, giving a second opinion on a really sick child.

Joshua sighed and glanced at the number. A&E. He'd get to it in a minute. But the minute hadn't even passed before the pager sounded again, this time not stopping.

MIA—a major incident alert. It only happened a few times a year. A code red was a paediatric cardiac arrest. Unfortunately, they happened frequently, particularly with the really sick kids in ICU. But MIA was slightly different and always came from A&E. He glanced quickly around the ward and shouted, something he rarely did. 'Ron! Find Isaiah and Clara. Tell them there's a major incident and to assemble in A&E.'

Joshua ran down the stairs of the hospital, meeting several other senior colleagues heading in the same direction. 'What is it this time?' one asked.

He shook his head. 'Don't know yet.'

As they walked through the swinging doors to A&E there was a momentary lull. All the A&E staff were crowded around the nurses' station. Alan Turner was standing on a chair that looked decidedly wobbly.

Alan gave Joshua and a few other Department Heads a nod as they joined the group. 'Okay,' he said, lifting a hand in the air. 'Five minutes ago we got a call about a major Road Traffic Accident, involving up to an estimated seventy casualties. Two buses have collided. One a tour bus, and one a bus with kids on a school trip. A major incident alert has been declared. Our flying squad emergency team have just left to assist on the scene. The Royal Hampstead is the nearest major trauma receiving centre. Twenty ambulances and two air ambulances are on their way to the scene. If you have patients currently in A&E then clear them out. We need all areas. If you have patients upstairs you can discharge, then get some of your colleagues to do it. Beds will be needed.' Alan started pointing at areas and shouting instructions as Clara ran up to join Joshua.

'What is it?' she whispered.

'Major RTA. Up to seventy casualties. A busload of kids is involved.'

She nodded as Alan turned to them. 'Paediatrics will be led by Joshua Woodhouse, Clara Connolly and Isaiah Orun. They'll be based in Resus One and Area Six. Bess, Reid and Fran will assist.'

Joshua spun around and nodded. 'Let's set up,' he said as the nursing staff joined them. They all moved methodically, requesting any specific paed equipment they might need and setting up their own small triage areas for children. Clara and Isaiah moved like the professionals he would have expected. Once they were set up, the silence across A&E was almost deafening. Patients had been moved to X-ray and short-stay areas. Others had been transferred up to ward areas for further assessment. Walking wounded had been sent to a nearby GP practice who helped in emergency situations. And the rest of the staff were just…waiting in an ominous silence.

It was only a few moments before the shrill ring of the red phone at the nurses' station broke the silence. Alan answered quickly, talking in a low voice and taking a few notes. As soon as he replaced the receiver he shouted to his colleagues, 'First set of ambulances are five minutes out. Eight adults, three paeds—all major trauma.'

Joshua put his hand on Clara's arm. 'Do what you can do—and if you need help just ask. We'll work alongside each other. Hans is on his way down—he's finishing up in Theatre—along with a few of the surgeons. They'll be available to assist.'

He watched her take a deep breath and give a slow nod. He wondered for a few seconds if he should worry about her. A major incident alert wasn't for the faint-hearted. It could be a time of chaos. Lots of professional staff were unprepared for what they might encounter and have to deal with over a short period of time. But as he watched he saw her give him a serious kind of smile. She was just taking a minute, preparing herself for what lay ahead.

As soon as he'd got the page, Clara and Isaiah's names were the first he'd thought of. They were skilled practitioners, and good at dealing with staff and patients. Clara's straight to the point attitude was perfect for a situation like this, and Isaiah's range of clinical skills would complement the teams.

Joshua glanced around again. Isaiah seemed to have attached himself to Bess, one of the most experienced A&E nurses. He was finding himself an anchor for the storm ahead. It made perfect sense. At a busy time, an experienced A&E nurse was worth their weight in gold. 'Reid, with me please, and Fran with Clara. We'll take resus,' Joshua said, knowing that meant they would have the most badly injured children. But he walked to the main receiving door to stand alongside Alan. If he had a chance to triage all the children first, he would do that.

The first few ambulances appeared in a blaze of sirens and blue lights. Joshua stepped back once he realised the first few patients were adults. Then the children started to appear. The first boy clearly had open fractures. 'Clara, stabilise and get ready for Theatre.' The second boy had multiple facial lacerations. 'Isaiah, assess, stabilise and page plastics.'

The third child was a little girl who was being bagged by one of the paramedics. He met Joshua's gaze. 'Flail chest. Natasha is ten. She was standing in the passageway of the bus and hit the central gear controls.' He rattled off her heartrate, BP and respirations, filling Joshua in on her continued deterioration in the ambulance on the way to the Royal Hampstead.

'Resus One,' he said. 'Any more kids on the way?'

The paramedic shook his head. 'We were the first team. The next will be another ten minutes at least.'

Joshua worked quickly. Flail chests were difficult and quite uncommon in kids. Basically a portion of Natasha's ribcage had separated from the rest of the chest wall. As the paramedic continued to bag her, he could see the uneven way her chest was moving.

One of the other nurses moved to take over the bagging as Reid connected the oxygen supply. Joshua was focused on the little girl, ordering analgesia and sounding her chest while the oxygen support continued. 'Portable chest X-ray,' he ordered. He was certain that at least one of the lungs had been punctured by a rib. He kept his eyes on the oxygen saturation monitor as the X-ray machine was wheeled in.

A face appeared in the doorway—Hans. 'Do you need me?'

'Great,' said Joshua, looking up. 'I was just about to

call you. Ventilation may be required. I think there's at least four ribs detached and a strong possibility of a pneumothorax.' He looked down at Natasha again. Even though she was on oxygen her dusky colour was not improving much.

Clara was dealing with her child in the resus bed next to him. She worked smoothly and competently, ably assisted by Fran. He could see he had no need to worry about her.

A lead apron was passed to him by the radiographer and he slid it over his head, nodding to Reid that he would take over while the X-ray was taking place. Reid waited behind the door alongside Hans, Clara and Fran, for the few seconds it took to take the X-ray.

A few minutes later it was on the viewer next to them. Hans shook his head. Three ribs were obviously misplaced, with one clearly spearing the lung, causing a haemothorax. 'This one needs to be done in Theatre,' he said and Joshua nodded in agreement.

'Absolutely,' Clara agreed as she stepped up alongside him. Her patient was already on his way to Theatre.

Clara reached over and took Natasha's hand, taking a few moments to stand next to the child and talk softly.

Joshua quelled his frustration that he couldn't do something immediately to help this little girl. He'd inserted tubes before to drain the blood from a lung and help reinflate, but not while the rib was still causing damage.

'Consent?' asked Hans.

Joshua looked up once. 'Reid?' was all he said.

A few minutes later the nurse returned, shaking his head. 'Police say parents have still to be contacted. They can't find Natasha's bag in amongst the wreckage of the bus.'

'No parents?' Concern laced through Clara's voice as she continued to stroke Natasha's hand.

'Darn it. No other responsible adult who could give us the information? Who was Natasha travelling with on the bus?'

Reid shrugged. 'It's bedlam out there. Police just say they're still trying to identify Natasha and get in touch with family.'

Joshua looked down and touched the young girl's arm, for a moment thinking that could be Hannah lying there. Hans was talking with one of the surgeons, making a plan to take Natasha to Theatre.

'Reid? How did the paramedic know her name is Natasha?' Joshua asked.

Reid was washing his hands at the sink. He looked over his shoulder at Joshua. 'Apparently she told the paramedic before she passed out with the pain. But the only info he got was her first name and her age.'

Joshua couldn't imagine this little girl going to Theatre with no one knowing. In an emergency situation like this, they didn't need to gain consent from a parent. Her injuries were potentially life-threatening. He would make a final check with the police that they had no other way to identify Natasha right now and, as Head of Department, would make the call with the surgeon.

He moved around the other side from Clara and took Natasha's hand, bent down and spoke quietly next to her ear. 'Hi, Natasha, I'm Joshua. I'm the doctor that's looking after you. I know you're scared, and I want to promise you we'll look after you. Can you try and give my hand a squeeze?'

He waited for a few moments, sad when nothing happened. He looked up and saw Clara blink back tears. There was no obvious head trauma. Natasha's eyes weren't opening but he checked her pupils again and they reacted as normal to the light he shone in them. She just wasn't showing clear signs of consciousness. When he checked her motor responses, she flinched when he applied a little pain to her fingertip. That was something positive.

He recorded all her responses, then spoke to her again. 'I know that breathing is really tricky right now and we're going to do something to help you with that. You need to go for an operation, but we'll make sure you're sleeping, and when you wake up things should feel a bit easier. We haven't managed to find your family right now, but we'll do our best to sort that out while you're having your operation.' He put his hand gently on her shoulder. 'I'll come back and see you once you've had your operation, but I'm going to let my friend Hans look after you from this point.'

Hans had appeared at his side and checked over the paperwork and electronic charts. As paediatric anaesthetist, he had the final say on whether Natasha would get taken for surgery or not. He gave a nod and took over from Joshua. 'I'll call you when we're out of Theatre.' As he looked around he said, 'I imagine you'll still be here.'

Joshua could hear sirens again as more ambulances pitched up outside. He hated the thought of leaving Natasha with other colleagues, and he could see Clara felt the same way, but he knew they would take good care of her. On a normal day he'd assign a member of his paediatric staff to stay with her, but right now he didn't know how many more paediatric cases they might get, and it was a decision that would have to wait. The surgeon signalled him for a quick chat about agreement on consent for surgery, and Joshua waved to one of their nearby police colleagues for an update on any family. 'We're doing the best we can, but we still have no way of formally identifying Natasha any further right now.'

Joshua nodded and turned to the surgeon. 'In this case we have to treat her under civil law.'

The surgeon also nodded. 'Agreed. If we find parents or relatives later I'm happy to do the explaining with you.'

Joshua waved his hand. 'It's fine. I'm happy to take responsibility.'

The scream of sirens sounded from close by. He looked quickly over to where Clara was reluctantly releasing her hand from Natasha's. For some reason, it seemed entirely natural to be close to her. 'Need anything?' he said quietly.

She lifted her gaze to meet his and gave him a soft, grateful smile in amongst the chaos. 'Just sad that Natasha doesn't have anyone right now. The orthopods have already taken my patient to Theatre.' She snapped on a pair of fresh gloves as Reid helped them wheel Natasha out the resus room. 'I'm ready for the next one.'

She was doing her best to appear cool, calm and collected, even though he'd seen the emotion on her face earlier, and he appreciated that. Something flitted across her eyes. 'What about you?'

He glanced upwards. 'I'm just thanking someone upstairs for coincidences. Hannah is staying at the house of one of her school friends who is having a birthday party tonight. This will be a late one. I'm glad I can stay without panicking about babysitters.'

'I'll stay too,' said Clara quickly. 'You'll need all the

help you can get and anyway—' she gave a shrug '—what have I got to go home to if you and Hannah aren't around?'

His heart missed a beat in his chest. She'd said it in a light-hearted tone. But it felt like something more. Like the declaration they'd kind of been heading towards, with both of them tiptoeing around.

He wanted to say so much more, but instead he swallowed and smiled. 'Thank you.'

'No probs.'

'Josh!' The shouting voice made them both turn. 'Four paed cases.'

He moved instantly, triaging quickly and being surprised by a nudge at his elbow. Alice, one of the charge nurses from upstairs, was next to him. He lifted his eyebrows in surprise. 'Executive decision,' she said quickly. 'I've called in extra staff. Lynn's already clearing more space in the assessment unit. You triage and give me all the minors and I'll take them upstairs for assessment. Arun's on the ward and can do his thing.'

He should have known his staff would pull out all the stops in a crisis situation. Lynn was the other charge nurse and Arun one of the other paediatricians. 'I was just about to call you.'

She shrugged. 'You don't need to. We have a shared brain.'

It was true. Staff who had worked together for a long time often anticipated each other's needs. Both Lynn and Alice had been charge nurses in the unit when he'd first arrived. He had a great team and as he noticed Clara giving him a smile as she pulled on a protective gown over her scrubs, ready to receive the next patient, he was reminded how well she was fitting in.

The doors rolled open and an array of patients were

brought through. He triaged quickly—one kid uncon-
scious but breathing, another with a crush injury to a leg,
one with abdominal wounds. There were another four
kids with a variety of bruises, scratches and one little
one who was crying. He gave them all a quick check for
any hidden injuries. 'Last four mine?' asked Alice as she
picked up the weeping four-year-old.

'Perfect,' he said quickly. 'And thank you.'

As Alice dashed off with the other children, Joshua
assigned the three more serious kids between himself,
Clara and Isaiah. And so the afternoon, and early evening, continued.

He and Clara continued to work side by side in resus.
They were a good team, often checking X-rays together
or assisting each other when required.

The injuries of the children who arrived became less
severe. But all the children who'd been involved in the
accident still needed to be assessed to ensure nothing was
missed. Several of the parents of the children had also
been travelling on the school bus as volunteers, and they
had a variety of injuries ranging from minor to severe.

The police did a wonderful job of trying to track and
trace the families, considering the tumbling of the bus
had meant that nothing had been where it started. A
whole host of bags and suitcases had been strewn across
the road, some contents unsalvageable.

One of the teachers on the bus had been trapped for
a number of hours and had to be cut out, so some of the
other school teachers from the same school had come to
A&E to help with the children. It turned out that Natasha had been on the tour bus and not, as first presumed,
on the school bus. Her grandmother had accompanied
her as they were both going on holiday to Spain to meet

her mum and dad, but her gran had required surgery for a broken hip. As soon as she'd come round from Theatre she'd started babbling about her daughter, becoming distraught. One of the theatre nurses had immediately recognised the name she kept mentioning and realised the elderly lady was confused from the anaesthetic and managed to join the dots. Both parents were now flying back from Spain. Things were finally starting to fall into place.

By the time Joshua and Clara were finished in A&E they were both tired. 'I need food.' Clara sagged against the nearby wall and wiped her hand across her forehead. She'd needed food about four hours ago but there just hadn't been time.

'Give me five minutes,' said Joshua, the lines around his eyes more pronounced. 'I just need to give Hannah a quick call.'

Clara smiled and followed him into the A&E staff room whilst he grabbed a seat in the corner and pulled out his phone. She poured them both some water from the cooler and sat down beside him. Within a few moments he shook his head, laughing, then spoke for a minute before finishing his call.

'All good?' she asked.

He let out a long slow breath and shook his head and laughed. 'Hannah didn't even want to talk to me. She's having far too much fun. I let the little girl's mum know that I'm likely to spend the night here because of the accident and she can get me on my mobile if she needs me.'

He closed his eyes for a second and rested his head back against the leather chair. It was lumpy, with some ragged tears, but was one of the few chairs in the room that wasn't made out of hard plastic.

She couldn't help herself. She reached over and grabbed his hand. 'Hey, we did good. Things could have been much worse. Everyone who got here got looked after.'

It was true. They'd heard about a few adults on the coaches who had life-threatening injuries. One kid who was seriously injured had been helicoptered to a more specialist hospital, and they'd since heard that the child was serious but stable. But all the kids who had come through the Royal's doors had been assessed and treated as required. Some would have surgical scars, some might need other supports, but all were alive, and as well as could be expected.

He closed his other hand over hers. 'I know, I know.' He shifted position, leaning forward in the chair so they were closer to each other. 'There was that horrible moment today when I had to send Natasha to Theatre. No one knew who she was; there was no family there for her. And all I could think about was Hannah. And how I would feel if that kid was mine.'

'Of course you did,' said Clara quickly. 'That's what makes you, you.'

Their gazes meshed and a few of the barriers he'd had about this relationship started to melt away. Because he'd seen her face. He knew that Clara had felt exactly the same way that he did. He'd seen her stroke Natasha's hand. He'd seen her talk softly to her. Yes, Clara was here for a short time. But there were so many things about this woman he liked and admired. Right now, he wanted to put his hand at the side of her cheek and pull her in for a kiss. He was tempted to throw caution to the wind, and wonder if he should actually try to give this a go.

He'd kept his heart in a box for the last five years.

Losing his wife so quickly and taking over a new role as both parents to their daughter had swamped his time. He'd had a few dates, but was now realising he'd dated, *knowing* he didn't want things to work out.

He'd let lack of trust get in the way. It was easier never to give himself up to trusting someone else. It was easier to tell himself that he required complete honesty in a relationship before he could even consider moving forward.

It was easier to do that than to admit that allowing himself to trust was allowing himself to put his heart at risk again.

His life was ticking along with only the occasional hiccup—only the occasional doubt that he wasn't doing as well as he could. And this was just it. Every single thought about his personal life always revolved around Hannah. Of course it would—they were a package deal.

But for a few selfish moments he just wanted to think about himself. He wanted to focus on this beautiful woman with the dark brown eyes framed by smudged mascara and tiny freckles across her nose. The one who'd tied her hair up hours and hours ago and not given it another thought since then. She didn't know that her ponytail seemed to have adopted a life of its own and was now in a precarious position at the side of her head.

There was so much about this woman that just drew him in. The way she got straight to the point—she always told him exactly what she thought—but it was clear she had a big heart. He'd seen it in her interactions with kids in the ward, with his daughter and today in A&E.

But right now he wanted to concentrate on the attraction—the way the air between them just seemed to glimmer at times. The look in her eyes that could shoot a bolt of electricity through him. The way she licked her lips. The way she spoke, with her Scottish burr getting more heavily accented the more intense things got between them.

'We need to go back up to the ward,' he said slowly, knowing exactly what he wanted to say next.

'Okay,' she said simply, starting to pull her hand away from his, but he stopped her, tightening his grip around hers.

He lowered his voice to a bare whisper. 'And then we need to talk about the sleeping arrangements, because there is only one on-call room.'

He knew he was looking at her intensely. He couldn't help himself; he still wondered if he was taking the right step.

She leaned forward, her lips brushing against his ear. 'Well, I guess we just need to share then,' she said as she stood up, letting her body brush against his.

It was as if every cell in his body combusted. They were in a room with other staff, even if, because of the emergency situation that had just finished, most of the others were exhausted and no one was paying attention to them. And when Joshua slid his hand back into Clara's as he stood to follow her, no one else seemed to notice. Her footsteps faltered, then she tossed him a glance over her shoulder that set him alight.

Seconds later, as they walked through the door to the stairwell, their lips were on each other. Clara wrapped her hands around his neck, her kisses leaving him breathless. His hands were in her hair, her ponytail band snapping in a ping as their kisses became more intense, making them both laugh.

They stopped for a second and just breathed. 'Let's go upstairs,' she said quickly, pausing to put a hand on his chest before she gave him a wicked smile, 'assess the kids…and then find the on-call room.'

She grabbed his hand and they both ran up the stairs. By the time they reached the ward they were both a little breathless, but had managed to keep their hands to themselves. Both put their professional face into place.

Children had to be reassessed, although, because of the stellar work between Isaiah and Arun, most of them only needed a quick check. Parents were another story. Both Clara and Joshua had to spend considerable time with the parents who had arrived at the hospital with fear in their hearts after hearing their children had been in an accident. Even though other staff had reassured them, Clara and Joshua reassured them again that they would both be around tonight and available if required. The night duty staff had started to appear early, and none of them were surprised to know that two doctors were on call tonight. It wasn't entirely unusual after a major incident, or an outbreak of some sort, that more than one doctor would be available overnight.

When the pizzas that Joshua had ordered arrived on the ward a little later there was enough for everyone, including the kids and parents. Logistics in the ward tonight were awkward. Normally the rules were that each child could have a parent stay overnight if they wished. There were special chairs by each bed that could recline so that they could sleep. But tonight more than one parent wanted to stay, and the ward staff had to juggle and negotiate to find enough space for everyone.

By the time Clara and Joshua headed for the on-call room both were exhausted, but as soon as the door closed behind them it was as if a second wind hit them.

Joshua walked through to the tiny shower attached to the room and held his hand out to her. 'Shall we?'

She paused for just a second before she very, very slowly started undoing the buttons on her shirt and walked towards him with her hips swinging. 'Why, I thought you'd never ask…'

CHAPTER EIGHT

IT WAS LIKE a whirlwind. One minute she wasn't sure quite what was going on between her and Joshua, and the next she knew *exactly* what was going on between her and Joshua.

They didn't publicise it. But outside work they seemed to merge into one another's lives. Clara was trying to tread carefully, but her heart was powering along like a steam train. Hannah was a normal little girl. She had moments when she clearly wanted her father to herself and Clara could read that and make a graceful exit. There were also times when she seemed to delight in them being together, and others when she would crawl up onto Clara's lap and whisper in her ear, telling her stories about girls at school.

For Clara, the best times were when she could watch Joshua and Hannah together. Their connection was so special. She loved watching them laughing or even quarrelling together. When Hannah tried to cheat him at a board game. Or when she would try and talk him out of a swimming lesson, getting annoyed when he wouldn't concede.

Weeks passed in a blur. Clara had never dated a guy

with a child before. She was learning every day. But it seemed that Joshua was adjusting alongside her.

Because of workload responsibilities, plus the fact they were both on call at different times in the week, sometimes they felt like ships passing in the night. As the short-term childcare hadn't really worked out, Joshua had long-standing arrangements with friends who could take care of Hannah overnight when he was on call. He didn't like to ask on any other occasion, meaning that often he and Clara spent time together once Hannah was tucked up in bed.

It was a Friday, and at ten o'clock Clara jumped into the lift with a bottle of chilled rosé in her hands. She was wearing a soft pair of lounge pants and a button-down shirt. She even had slippers on her feet. So when she stepped into Joshua's apartment and saw him dressed in a suit she gave a start.

'Are you going out?'

'No—' he shook his head, smiling, as he took the bottle of wine from her hands '—we're staying in.' He gestured behind him, where his dining room table was set with a white linen cloth, candles twinkling and red roses in a vase in the centre.

Clara stopped moving, her mouth open in shock. 'What?'

He walked over and pulled out a chair. 'Have a seat. We're having dinner. I'm conscious of the fact I don't really get to take you anywhere grown-up at night because of Hannah. So I thought I would bring the grown-up to us.'

Clara looked down. She was practically wearing pyjamas. 'Hold that thought,' she said as she turned and bolted out of the door. She was a doctor. She had years of practice of yanking on clothes at a moment's notice. Her top was over her head as soon as she walked back through the door, and her lounge pants pulled down as she walked to the bedroom. It took thirty seconds to change her underwear, and another minute to yank a red dress from the cupboard. She pulled it on and slid her bare feet into black patent stilettos. There were still some remnants of today's make-up on her face, so she brushed on some bronzer, re-coated her lashes in mascara and slicked on some red lipstick. She was back out of the door and pressing the button on the lift in less than five minutes.

By the time she got upstairs, Joshua had poured the wine. His eyes widened as she walked with confidence back through the door. She wagged her finger at him. 'Dr Woodhouse, you don't invite a lady to dinner without giving her some notice. Just as well I can dress just as quickly as I can undress.' She winked at him as she sat down in the chair.

'Wow,' was all he said in response, clearly taking in the tighter than normal red dress and extremely high stilettos. Not exactly daywear. She grinned at the appreciative glance. Ward environments and days out with Hannah didn't exactly let her bring out her sexy side. Now, for the first time since she'd met Joshua, she finally had a chance to bring out what lay beneath the surface. She'd grabbed the first things she could find—which was probably for the best. If she'd known she was coming up for a romantic dinner she would likely have spent all day trying different dresses on. But it appeared her first instincts had paid off.

He couldn't hide the glint in his eye as he handed her a little card. It was inscribed with calligraphy, giving tonight's menu. Her eyebrows raised in surprise. 'This looks as if it came from a starred restaurant.'

He nodded. 'It did. Let's just say I called in a favour that's been offered for a long time. Everything is in the kitchen, ready to be served.'

She licked her lips, taking in his dark grey suit, pale shirt and slim dark tie. He filled it out well. It was much more fitted than any suit she'd seen him wear at work. She wasn't quite sure dinner was what she had in mind.

But, as Joshua disappeared into the kitchen, she crossed her legs and took a sip of her chilled wine. She gave a little giggle as she realised he'd wrapped some white fairy lights around a plant in the corner of the room. That, along with the roses and candles? He'd actually given this some thought.

Her stomach warmed. There was something nice about being planned for. The menu was all food that she loved, and one dish she'd told him that she would like to try. They had been casual conversations, he could easily have forgotten, but it was clear that Joshua either had a great memory or he'd taken notes.

He placed a dome-covered dish in front of her, then lifted the dome with a flourish. She inhaled deeply before looking down at the perfectly formed food in front of her.

Mushroom ravioli in a rich sauce. It was a tiny portion but she knew at a glance what it was, as it was one of her favourites. She pointed to the elaborately shaped napkin sitting on the table. 'I almost don't want to destroy this, but I can't take the chance.'

Before she had a chance to move, Joshua had lifted the napkin and shook out the design, laying it on her lap. She laughed then picked up her knife and fork to try the first course. Every bite was delicious.

'So, tell me how exactly you made this happen?' she asked. Someone had cooked this delicious food and transported it in a manner to keep it at the perfect temperature. She was almost in awe of them for that feat alone.

Joshua sat down opposite her and gave a warm smile. 'I took care of someone's son a few years ago. The little boy had meningitis and had been turned away from the GP surgery twice. His dad brought him to A&E and I realised quickly what was wrong. The little guy was admitted for a few days but recovered. The dad was a starred chef and has constantly been in touch, wanting me to come to his restaurant. This time when he contacted me—' he paused for a second and then gave a half-shrug '—I asked him if there was any possibility the restaurant could come to me.'

'And it did?'

Joshua held out his hands. 'See for yourself. It appears that it does.'

Clara smiled and tilted her head to one side as she looked at her now empty plate. 'That's the thing about these really posh restaurants. They give you tiny portions. It's like they're teasing, and still leaving you wanting more.'

Almost as soon as she said the words she realised her *double entendre* and her cheeks flushed. Joshua started laughing as he picked up her plate, his eyes twinkling. 'Somehow, I think I can relate.'

His skin was tingling with her just being in the room. Something about all this just felt so *right*. And he hadn't been sure that it would. But any lingering doubts were rapidly disappearing.

At first he'd thought Clara might be more comfortable

in her relaxed clothes—and there was something nice about the fact that she didn't worry about how she looked before she came up to see him. But her five-minute transformation had been incredible. She had her trademark red lips in place alongside a matching form-fitting dress that just blew him away. When she'd sat down, her shining brown hair around her shoulders, and leaned forward for her glass of wine, giving him a glimpse of her cleavage, he could have spontaneously combusted on the spot. It didn't matter what had come before. Tonight, he'd wanted it to seem like a proper date. He'd wanted it to be special. And it certainly seemed that way.

The more time he spent around Clara, the more the niggling little doubts just seemed to float away, like clouds on a stormy day. Maybe he was just too cautious. Maybe he'd just been truly on his own for too long. Dating and getting close to someone were two entirely different things—and it was only now he was really appreciating it.

What reason could he have not to trust Clara? She'd never given him one. At work, she seemed upfront and honest. Maybe it really was time to shake off his past experience and truly move on.

Clara followed him through to the kitchen, opening the fridge door and taking out the bottle of wine to top up their glasses while he put the plates in the dishwasher. He turned around in time to see her lifting the edge of one of the silver domes and peeking underneath. He moved quickly behind her, slipping his hand around her waist and resting it on her stomach. 'Hey, you'll spoil the surprise. Some might call that cheating.'

She spun around in his arms, winding her hands around his neck. 'I've never been a cheater,' she teased, 'maybe I'm just impatient.' She blinked her dark eye-lashes close enough to brush against his cheek. 'Maybe I just want to get to the good part.' She held her breath for a second before moving her lips next to his and whispering, 'Dessert.'

His fingers ran down the length of her spine and she trembled at his touch. 'I'm happy to get to dessert if you are…'

The evening passed too quickly. Clara gathered her clothes and disappeared back down to her own apartment before Hannah woke. But Joshua couldn't sleep. He'd wanted to have a conversation tonight—before they both got distracted. And that conversation, which inevitably hadn't happened, made him nervous. Nervous in both a good and a bad way.

There were only two months left of her job swap. He wanted to ask her what her plans were. He wasn't even sure he'd any right to ask questions like that, but things had heated up between them both so quickly that it felt like the next natural conversation.

Trouble was, this was also a conversation he should have with his sister. Georgie still hadn't told him what her plans were. He was allowed to ask after her pregnancy-related health. But he wasn't allowed to ask anything about the baby's dad. It hadn't taken long to guess it was a fellow doctor from work. Georgie had reassured Joshua that no, the guy wasn't married to, or living with, anyone else. All she said was she wanted to be sure. She seemed to be enjoying the job in Edinburgh. But he had no idea exactly what that meant. Right now, he wasn't sure if she was secretly counting down the days until she returned to London with excitement, with dread, or at all.

A bit like how he wasn't sure how Clara felt.

Part of him wanted her to love working at the Royal and want to stay. A definite part of him hoped that he and Hannah might factor in that equation. But maybe those were unrealistic expectations. She had a permanent job and home in Scotland. It could be that she wasn't thinking quite as favourably on things as he was. It could be he was being entirely selfish. Why should Clara give up her life in Scotland for a life in London, just because that was where *he* lived?

But the thought of uprooting Hannah to a whole new city, a new school, a new circle of friends and activities, made his stomach churn. Would he actually consider doing that to his daughter? Was it even fair?

Joshua let out a sigh and flung off his covers. He wasn't going to sleep at all tonight. He pulled a T-shirt and shorts from his cupboard and strode through to the kitchen to switch on the coffee machine.

But his footsteps faltered as he saw the array of silver domes sitting in the kitchen.

Clara was real. Clara had been here. He could still smell her perfume lingering in the air.

He breathed in deeply. Was he brave enough to take the next step? To have that conversation?

He knew right now he'd be able to tell straight away if he was way off mark. If Clara looked shocked in any way, if she said that she'd never even considered staying, then he'd know. He'd know that he and Hannah didn't feature in her future plans at all. And that would be fine.

Well…of course it wouldn't.

But at least it would be an answer of sorts. It had been

a long time since Joshua Woodhouse had opened himself up to the possibility of hurt.

Was he really ready to do that now?

CHAPTER NINE

SHE WAS LIVING the dream. Or at least that was what it felt like.

Every day she spent at least part of her time with Joshua and Hannah. Work was hectic. And she loved that. But the nights she spent on call at the hospital left her with a strange ache in her belly. She missed them. She actually *missed* seeing them.

Last time she'd missed seeing a guy was when she was fifteen and in the first throes of love. That, of course, had lasted around twenty minutes and ended in what felt like a sensationally shattered heart.

This was entirely different.

She'd just finished walking along the Thames before heading back to the flat. The day was gorgeous. The walk had been invigorating. She turned on the coffee machine and walked to open the balcony doors so she could keep bringing a little of the outside in.

She smiled, realising that if she'd been back in Scotland, the outside would probably smell of sheep. Not that she'd ever minded. There were open fields for miles back home, but she was getting used to the view here. She was actually starting to like it.

Clara moved back through to the kitchen, glancing

at the calendar as she finished making the coffee. The calendar was beginning to annoy her. The days seemed to pass so quickly. It was bit like a clock, ticking down, stealing time away from her. With a scowl she snatched it off the wall and stuffed it into a nearby drawer. But it wouldn't quite go in there. She frowned, rummaging around to find out what was stopping it sliding inside.

She pulled out a familiar large white envelope. The information from the clinic. The coffee machine made a little noise to indicate it was finished and she pulled out the filled cup automatically, staring down at the contents of the mug and then letting out a wry laugh.

Her coffee normally had a much sweeter taste—her choice was a caramel latte. But Joshua's choice was a double shot cappuccino, and *that* was what she'd made.

She'd done it without thinking, almost on autopilot, and it struck her that part of that made her happy, and part of it made her sad.

She opened the cupboard and took out some sweetener, adding two to the cup, then carrying the coffee and the envelope out to the balcony.

She slid the information from the envelope and looked at it again. It had been weeks since it had arrived. She'd read it over with more than a little interest, but still a lot of uncertainty. It all seemed so…clinical. And that was entirely what it was.

But the end process could be wonderful. She took a sip of the stronger than normal coffee and thought about the time she'd spent with Hannah.

No matter how much she wanted to skirt around it, having a family had always been a dream. She didn't even know if she could carry a child, or if she had viable eggs. This process would find that out.

But the thing that imprinted on her mind most was the experience of having a child in her life. Even when Hannah was in a horrible mood, there was still something deep down in Clara that reminded her it was a privilege to be around a child.

She wanted that, she did. But she didn't have a single clue how to have that conversation with Joshua.

It should be easy: *Hey, Josh—would you ever consider having more kids in the future?*

But she just didn't feel ready to ask that. To presume that she *could* ask that. Maybe he'd decided that losing one long-term partner was enough, and he didn't want to commit fully to someone else again.

It could be he'd decided that he and Hannah were a unit all on their own, with no room for anyone else.

Her stomach twisted. What if she tried to ask the question in a casual kind of way and he gave her that look, as if to say, *You think we might have any kind of future together? Are you crazy?*

The more she thought about it, the more she wondered if this was still a dream to pursue on her own. If she did this on her own, she wouldn't need to worry about anyone else, about what they might think, or if they approved. This was her wish. *Hers.*

Trouble was, she still wanted the dream. The loving partner to share the experience with. A houseful of kids. And meeting Joshua had left her with a whole host of question marks.

She hadn't expected to meet anyone while she was down here. She'd actually wondered if she would *ever* meet someone she'd want to stay with, and that feeling of taking action on her own had been empowering. But did it feel that way now?

Now, she was just confused.

She left the paperwork sitting on top of the envelope on the table and stretched out her legs so they were hiding everything. Her brain tried to tell her she just didn't want the papers blowing away in the gentle breeze, but it was easier to just try and forget about everything right now.

What she really wanted was some more time. Time to think things through. Time to sort out her own head, before sitting down and having the conversation with Joshua.

The phone rang sharply and she jerked, sending the papers scattering onto the tiled floor of the balcony. She made a grab for them as she ducked inside to pick up the phone.

'Clara?' It was Joshua. He sounded harassed.

'What's wrong?' There was no room for preamble.

'The doctor on call tonight has walked off the ward. I need to go in and sort things out. I hate to ask, but Hannah's already in bed. Could you come up to my place?'

Clara was stunned. 'Who's walked off the ward?' It was unimaginable to her. She couldn't understand why any doctor would walk away and leave their patients.

Joshua mentioned the name of another doctor. 'I think he was threatened by some parents over waiting too long for test results. One of them had him up against a wall. Now no one can get hold of him. I have to go in.'

Of course he did. He was the Head of the Department; this was serious.

'I'm on my way,' she said, grabbing a few things before she closed the balcony doors and took her bag and keys.

Joshua was standing at the door with his jacket on when she arrived and he looked at the pile in her hands.

She shrugged. 'Pyjamas, clothes for tomorrow in case you need to stay overnight.'

'Thank you.'

She could sense his relief that she was there for Hannah. She gave his shoulder a squeeze and brushed a brief kiss on his lips. 'Absolutely no problem. Call me later.'

He nodded and disappeared out of the door.

It was weird being in Joshua's place without him. But Clara dumped her stuff and went to check on Hannah first. Despite what her father had said, Hannah was clearly not sleeping. She'd bundled her bedcovers up and had a variety of dolls and cars playing across mountains and valleys.

Her eyes widened when Clara raised her eyebrows at her from the door. 'Clara! What are you doing here?'

She ran over and gave Clara a huge hug. Clara melted a little, just like she always did around Hannah. She patted the bed to get her to sit back down. 'There's an emergency at the hospital and your dad's had to go and deal with it. So I'm here until he comes back, or maybe for the whole night.' She could see Hannah's school clothes, shoes and bag already laid out for tomorrow. At least there wouldn't be a scramble to find everything.

'Ooh!' There was an immediate gleam of mischief in Hannah's eyes. 'What can we do?'

But Clara was too wise for a bit of manipulation. '*We*,' she said quickly, 'can check the time and see that someone I know should actually be sleeping right now. Let's get these toys away.' She started picking up the dolls and cars. 'Why don't you pick a book and I'll read that to you before you go to sleep.'

Disappointment swamped Hannah's face. 'Okay, pick

two then,' said Clara quickly. 'But you have to get to sleep. You've got school in the morning.'

Hannah slouched over to her white bookcase and took a few moments to pick two. Moments later she was back in bed with both books in her lap.

Clara settled onto the bed beside her and looked at the books. She didn't recognise either of them.

'Okay, let's start with this one.'

She wrapped an arm around Hannah's shoulders, letting her snuggle in and holding the picture book in front of them both. She was delighted to find it was a story about a little girl who wanted to be an astronaut and decided to make herself a suit out of things she found around the house. The story was comical and the illustrations perfect and they chatted throughout.

'Is this one of your favourites?'

Hannah nodded. 'I want to be an astronaut,' she said with the determination of a five-year-old.

'You want to go into space?'

Hannah nodded enthusiastically.

'Why space? Why don't you want to be a deep sea diver? Or an Arctic explorer? Or a pirate?' She pulled random ideas from nowhere as they snuggled together. There was something so nice about just having a little time together.

Hannah turned her big eyes towards her. 'I want to go to space to see if I can catch Mummy. She's one of the stars up there.'

Clara's stomach clenched instantly, but her heart expanded in her chest.

Out of the mouths of babes...

She'd heard the expression many times but never felt a

punch in the gut like now. The range of emotions was over-whelming, and she knew she had to handle this carefully.

'Who told you about Mummy being a star?'

'Daddy and Auntie Georgie. There's a star up in the sky that has Mummy's name. I sometimes look for it at night. But I'm not always sure what one it is.'

She stopped for a second then wrinkled her little brow. 'They told me they gave the star Mummy's name when I was little. Just a baby.'

Clara nodded, trying to choose her words carefully. But she didn't get a chance. Hannah seemed to want to keep talking. 'I don't really remember her,' she said in a small voice, tinged with guilt.

Clara let her hand push some of Hannah's bed-ruf-fled hair back from her face. 'Oh, honey. That's okay. You were tiny. No one expects you to remember. I don't know anyone who can remember things from when they were a baby.'

She noticed the photo frame across the room; Han-nah was staring at it. Even from here, Clara could see the pale-faced woman with brown hair and the baby bundle in her arms. Clara's heart gave a twist as she thought about what Abby had sacrificed to make sure her daugh-ter got into this world safely. But the overwhelming feel-ing she got when she looked at that photo was love. It was clearly written across Abby's face. She knew she wasn't going to see her daughter grow up. She knew she didn't have much time left. And the photo captured the joy and love in her face for her daughter.

'People tell me stories,' said Hannah slowly.

Clara drew her eyes away from the picture. 'What kind of stories?'

'Dad...' Hannah looked down at her hands '...and

sometimes Auntie Georgie. They tell me things about Mummy. Things they all did together. And Daddy says he's got things to show me when I'm older.' Her fingers twisted the blanket on her lap as she shook her little head. 'But I don't remember things—' her voice broke a little '—and I think they want me to.'

A lump formed in Clara's throat immediately and she pulled Hannah up into her lap. The little girl's confusion was palpable. And Clara couldn't help but wonder how long she'd held this inside.

She smoothed down Hannah's hair with one hand as she spoke. 'Hannah, your daddy and your auntie know that you don't remember your mummy. They wish that you did, and that's why they tell you stories. They want you to know things about her. Like how much she loved you, how much fun she was, and how important you were to her.'

Hannah blinked and bit her bottom lip.

Clara felt as if her heart might break for her. She cupped Hannah's face in her hands. 'It's okay, honey. It's okay not to remember. As you get bigger you might want to find out some things about your mummy, and that's when you can ask any questions you like, and your dad, and your auntie, will be able to answer them for you. But this isn't something to worry about. Not at all. The important thing to remember is that you are a very special girl and that you're loved, by lots of people.'

She pulled Hannah into a hug as her own eyes brimmed with tears. Hannah wrapped her arms tight around Clara's neck. After a little while she whispered, 'Clara?'

'Yes?'

'Will you keep cuddling me until I fall asleep?'

'Of course I will.' Clara moved on the bed, letting Hannah lie down next to her and wrapping her arm around her when she moved to cuddle in close.

Her heart was full of love for this little girl, and her heart was also full of love for Joshua. She'd thought the most difficult conversation she'd have with Joshua was about their potential future together. Now, she wondered if the most difficult conversation she'd have would be about Hannah. Was there any way to talk about this delicately?

He was Hannah's father. He deserved to know that his daughter was struggling a little—and that he, however unwittingly, and with the best will in the world, might be contributing to it.

She squeezed her eyes closed for a second as dread swept over her. She'd have to time it carefully. She didn't want to say anything to upset him. But the truth was, if she cared about him she had to let him know. No matter how hard it was.

Her free hand moved back and forth, doing soft strokes across Hannah's hair as she willed her to sleep.

Was this what being a parent was like? Knowing you had to do what was right first?

Through in the other room she could hear her mobile ring. It would be Joshua, telling her how things had worked out at the hospital. She wanted to answer, she really did. But if she moved she might disturb Hannah.

So she let the phone ring, and kept holding onto Hannah tightly.

There would be time to talk later.

She just had to work out when.

CHAPTER TEN

JOSHUA PICKED UP the mail and stared down at the envelope in his hand. It was cream, good quality but looked a bit battered. The name on the front was definitely his—Dr Joshua Woodhouse—but the calligraphy on the front had obviously been written with a fountain pen and had been smeared at some point on the journey, meaning the end of the street address was almost illegible. Someone had scored through the smearing and written an alternative address—*24F Park Road?*—with a red pen, and that had been followed by *Not at this Address*. Another hand had written *24F Park Tower?*, which was where the envelope had finally ended up.

As he tore open the envelope he was amused by the travels of whatever was inside. A cream card with a tell-tale picture on the front fell into his hand. His stomach clenched. From the sketch of a bride and groom on the front it had to be a wedding invitation.

He flipped it open, scanning the words.

Alyssa Hart and David Jenner
would like to invite
Dr Joshua Woodhouse and partner
to celebrate their marriage on...

He let out a groan. Of course. Both Alyssa and David had been on his university medicine course. He knew they were getting married—they might even have sent one of those 'save the date' cards but he'd completely forgotten. In all honesty, he hadn't been invited to many weddings over the last few years. He was sure most of his friends thought of him as the awkward single guest—plus they knew he was a lone parent to Hannah. But Alyssa and David had insisted he come to the wedding. The date made his stomach flip. This weekend. Just how long had this invitation been bouncing around?

He examined the envelope. Sure enough, the postage date was six weeks before. And, since they'd already sent him a save the date, he was sure he wouldn't get out of it with the usual *Sorry, I'm scheduled to work* that he had pulled before when he'd been invited to social events.

His thoughts started spinning. His parents had already offered to come and take Hannah away for that weekend to their caravan just outside Brighton. He had planned to surprise Clara in some way. He'd even toyed with the idea of taking the train to Paris and staying overnight somewhere. But he hadn't booked anything—and now it looked like he had a wedding to attend.

He leaned against the wall for a few moments. Of course, the only person he would invite would be Clara. But would she actually want to go? The wedding would be full of people who'd known him years ago. Some of them might actually have attended his own wedding, and he knew that Clara would get a few curious glances. He paused—was it fair to ask her? It wasn't that his friends would say anything awkward or inappropriate... Then again, it was a wedding, alcohol would be involved, and his friends might say something *entirely* awkward or inappropriate.

But he wanted to get back out there. He *wanted* to introduce Clara to his friends. He didn't want to continue to be the sad, lonely, widowed single friend. Clara was gorgeous. She was funny and smart and he wanted his friends to know that he'd met someone who…

His brain stopped dead. He'd met someone who…? Who he hadn't managed to have the *What do you think about us and the future?* conversation with yet. He looked down at the invite again. RSVP by… Oops. The date had long since passed.

He picked up his phone and sent a text message to David, who replied a few minutes later.

About bloody time. Alyssa's having a nervous breakdown at the amount of people who haven't RSVP'd. You've just got yourself off the hit list by the skin of your teeth. Can't wait to see you!

He smiled. The last few days had been a bit odd between him and Clara. It was as if she was always waiting to say something, but just couldn't get there. The pessimistic part of him wondered if it might be telling him they needed to cool things down as she'd be leaving soon. But the optimist in him hoped she might say she wanted to stay.

Maybe this invite would give her the push either way. It would be the first formal event they'd attend as a couple. Joshua glanced down at the venue. A beautiful hotel towards Essex set in large grounds. The invite included a number for guests to call to book a room to stay overnight if they wished. He dialled it immediately, hoping because he'd left it so late they wouldn't be assigned the broom cupboard under the stairs.

By the time he'd replaced the phone, plans had fallen into place in his head. He'd invite Clara to this wedding—he knew she was free this weekend. If she accepted, then he'd use the opportunity to have the conversation with her that had been stalling these past few weeks. It was time. He felt good about it. He wanted to be honest with her. He wanted to be able to consider a future with her, and with Hannah.

He couldn't ignore the fact that she was always the first person he wanted to talk to—the first person he wanted to see. He couldn't pretend that his heart didn't skip a couple of beats like a crazy teenager when he saw her laugh, or he noticed the wicked twinkle in her eyes.

After a few years in hiding, his heart felt ready to take the next step. To trust someone again. To try and make a go of this relationship and take pleasure in imagining where it might go. Maybe things wouldn't work out, but he was certain he wanted to try. And the only person he wanted to try with was Clara.

It had been an odd kind of day. The wedding had been sprung on her. When Joshua had told her Hannah was spending the weekend with her grandparents she'd hoped they would do something together. A wedding was a little unexpected, and she couldn't pretend that she wasn't a bit nervous. Nervous enough to take herself off to some exclusive boutique recommended by a particularly stylish fellow doctor and try on the contents of the whole shop.

An hour earlier she'd met Joshua's parents as they'd waved Hannah off. If his parents had been surprised to see her they hadn't shown it for a second. Linda and

Alastair were warm and welcoming, both giving her hugs and appearing genuinely happy to meet her. But, more importantly, it was clear they absolutely doted on their granddaughter. It was equally clear that Hannah had them both wrapped around her little finger. It was interesting to see Joshua interact with his parents. It was obvious they were immensely proud of both of their children, and the resemblance between Joshua and his father had been obvious. They both had tall slim frames and a similar gait. But his mannerisms mirrored his mother's, from the way he sometimes talked with his hands to the way he inclined his head a little while listening to someone, and that made Clara smile in amusement.

By the time they'd waved Hannah off, Clara only had forty minutes to get ready before they had to leave to drive to the wedding.

She'd thrown some things into an overnight bag but, because no one could ever predict what the traffic would be like in London, she'd decided just to wear her outfit for the wedding.

It took ten minutes to put her make-up on and get ready. She carried her fascinator in the cute little box it had been packaged in, rather than perch it on her head for the journey. She was just spraying some perfume and touching up her lipstick when Joshua came into the apartment. 'Knock, knock,' came the deep voice. 'Want me to grab your bag?'

'It's by the door,' she said as she stuffed her lipstick into her matching clutch bag.

The women in the shop had been very entertaining. They'd played music and brought out champagne while she'd tried on dresses. With each dress they'd managed to magic matching shoes, jewellery and fascinators to try on. But they hadn't been overbearing. 'Oh, no!' one of them had exclaimed as she'd stepped out in a silver sequin design. 'That colour wipes you out.'

The design of a tomato-red dress had been vetoed too. And it had actually felt like shopping with friends. Now she understood why her colleague had recommended this place. They gave her confidence that, whatever she left with, she wasn't going to look like some kind of fool who'd been duped into buying something unsuitable.

It wasn't her normal kind of thing. But she hadn't wanted it to be. This weekend already felt special. She couldn't pretend she didn't want to make a good impression with Joshua's friends.

She took a deep breath and stepped out the bathroom. 'How do I look?'

He was bending over, picking up her carry-on-size suitcase, and he glanced over his shoulder and promptly dropped the suitcase on his foot.

He straightened, giving her a good view of his dark navy suit, white shirt and pink tie. She'd handed it to him last night with a wink. 'Just making sure we'll match.'

From the expression on his face, the larger than usual balance she'd paid had been money well spent.

'You look stunning,' he said simply as he stepped forward, shaking his head a little. He held out one hand. 'Am I allowed to touch as long as I don't spoil anything?'

She glanced down. Her mid-pink sleeveless silk dress was the sleekest item she'd ever owned. From the deep cowl neck, it clung to every curve, skimming her hips and falling straight to the floor. Only the three-inch heels kept it from touching the ground.

'What's the point of looking but not touching?' she teased.

His hands grasped her firmly as he took her by surprise and bent her backwards as he kissed her. She laughed, grabbing a hold of his shoulders. 'Aren't we supposed to save this for the dance floor later?' she said breathily.

'I couldn't wait that long,' he said as he trailed kisses down the side of her throat.

'You'll make us late for the wedding,' she giggled.

He sighed and tilted her upwards again. 'Spoilsport.'

She shrugged and dusted imaginary dust from his shoulders. 'You don't scrub up too badly yourself.'

He held her for a few more seconds and she could see something flitting across his eyes. Her heart missed a couple of beats. But then he leaned forward and spoke quietly into her ear. 'Let's just have fun this weekend. Deal?'

Relief flooded through her. For half a second then she'd been worried. But then, she'd been thinking herself about the conversations they needed to have and wondering when it would be appropriate. The thought of forgetting about all that and just having fun sounded like heaven.

'Deal,' she agreed as she dropped a kiss on his cheek, leaving a hint of lipstick there. She could have lifted her fingers to smudge it away, but she liked it. That almost invisible mark on his cheek. A sign that he was hers.

They made it to the Essex wedding venue with ten minutes to spare, thanks to the diversions and hideous London traffic. Any plans he might have had to sit for a while, enjoying a glass of wine before the wedding were well and truly blown.

By the time they'd put their bags in the room and Clara

had put some magnificent creation on her head they were almost out of time.

'Wait,' he said as she put her hand on the door.

'What is it? Have I got lipstick on my teeth?' She squinted over at the mirror.

He laughed. 'No. I arranged to get something delivered.' He glanced around the room, spying a cardboard box in a cool spot. He walked over and lifted the lid, smiling when he saw what was inside.

Clara appeared at his shoulder. 'What's in there?' She gave a little gasp and he could swear he could hear the smile in her voice. 'You bought me a corsage?'

She sounded kind of stunned. 'Of course I bought you a corsage.' He lifted the delicate ringlet of flowers for her wrist. 'After you gave me the tie last night, I phoned the hotel to see if they could arrange a buttonhole for me, and a corsage for you in the colour you'd specified.'

He held up the tiny roses that exactly matched her dress, encased in some greenery and entwined around a pearl corsage for her wrist.

'It's beautiful,' Clara sighed. She twisted her wrist one way and then the other, admiring it, before reaching in and taking out his matching buttonhole. His was a single large rose in exactly the same shade of pink. 'Let me.' She smiled as she fastened it onto his suit.

'We're a matching pair,' he said quietly, catching sight of them both in the mirror. His heart squeezed in his chest. This was it. This was what he wanted. A partnership.

Her hand came up to his chest as she turned to see where he was looking.

It was like a moment in time. To the outside world they looked like the perfect couple. Her in her slim, sleek pink dress with shining hair, sparkling eyes and leaning into him. He, in turn, in his smart suit, matching buttonhole, with his arms wrapped around her waist. Both smiling.

People could look. Mention how matched they were. Both paediatricians. Both hard workers.

He didn't have a badge above his head saying single parent and widower. She didn't have a badge above her head saying that she was only here on a temporary basis.

His overwhelming urge was to make this permanent. To make the move, have the conversation and put his heart on the line once more. To take a chance on trusting someone again.

Clara's reflection smiled at him, then her face turned up towards his. 'Are you okay?'

She must have seen something in his eyes. He dropped a kiss on her lips and didn't hide the fact that he inhaled deeply, taking in what he now knew was her signature scent. The smell of summer flowers in the rain.

There was still something burning deep inside him. Doubt. Something he couldn't put his finger on and he hated that. He knew how he felt. He knew what he wanted to do. But, for all that Clara didn't seem to have any reason not to feel the same way, he still felt as if there was something he didn't know. Something she hadn't shared.

It was odd and had never been entirely obvious. Of course, he didn't think there was a hidden relationship anywhere, or something traumatic in her past that she hadn't shared. But there was just something—something else.

He stared down into those deep brown eyes. For right now, he could see nothing. All he could feel was the potential for this weekend. He pushed his doubts aside and smiled, putting his hand into hers.

'Let's go have some fun.'

* * *

The wedding was perfect in every way. They hurried down the stairs into the large, beautiful sunny room set out for the ceremony and slid into some seats next to people who were clearly friends of Joshua's. He leaned forward and whispered to them, 'Ben, Roma, this is Clara.'

Both smiled and stretched their hands to shake with Clara while she tried not to puzzle over the introduction. Clara. Clara who? His workmate? His girlfriend? His casual friend?

She didn't get much of a chance to think about it. 'Gorgeous dress,' Roma whispered to her as the music started and the groom and his best man walked down the aisle, shaking hands with friends.

The ceremony was beautiful and the bride wore a lace-covered cream gown and carried a bunch of yellow flowers. Joshua had told her that these were two of his oldest friends—he'd trained with them, which meant that they must have known Abby. She couldn't pretend that didn't make her nervous. But didn't the fact he'd brought her here in the first place to meet them mean something?

After the ceremony the guests mingled in the grounds next to the outside bar while the wedding party had their photographs taken. Everything seemed very informal. As Clara was standing at the bar, getting her glass of white wine topped up, she felt a nudge at her elbow. She was shocked when she turned around and found herself enveloped in a hug from the bride.

'You must be Clara,' she said as her veil brushed against Clara's cheek. 'I'm Alyssa. I'm so happy to meet you.' She signalled to the bartender, who gave her a glass of champagne.

'Nice to meet you too,' said Clara quickly, a little

stunned. She wasn't too sure that Joshua had specified to the bride and groom who he was bringing with him. 'Your dress is absolutely gorgeous.'

'Thanks. So is yours. That colour really suits you. So, you're working with Joshua and staying in Georgie's flat?'

Clara barely had time to nod before Alyssa continued. 'What do you think of Hannah? Isn't she adorable?'

Clara started to relax a little. Maybe it was the second glass of wine. She answered completely truthfully. 'Hannah is great. I love being around her.'

Alyssa tilted her head. 'I love your accent.'

A voice started calling Alyssa's name in the distance but she waved her hand. 'Oh, they can wait. I want to know more about you. Can we catch up later after dinner? David and I both really want to get to know you.'

It was ridiculous but the hairs on Clara's arms gave an uncomfortable prickle. Why was she nervous? Of course Joshua's friends might be curious about her, but this seemed like a bit of a test—what if she didn't pass?

'You're the bride.' She smiled. 'You're the boss. I'd love to meet your husband too at some point. Joshua told me you all trained together.'

Alyssa nodded and gave a sad smile. 'A long time ago. We're all getting old now.' She gestured across the garden. 'It's taken ten years for David and me to finally organise getting married.' She looked back at her, and Clara could see it in her eyes. The unspoken words. The words about Abby.

She decided to address the elephant in the room. 'You must have gone to Joshua and Abby's wedding then?'

It was easier just to have it out there. She didn't want

Alyssa to feel awkward about mentioning someone who'd presumably been a friend.

Alyssa nodded and put her hand on Clara's arm. 'We're so glad he's brought you. I wasn't sure that he'd bring anyone. I mean, he's dated, but it's never been serious. He's always been so focused on Hannah that I wasn't sure he would ever find room in his life for another person.'

Clara took a gulp of her wine. It wasn't such a strange thing to say. But it still made her feel self-conscious. Alyssa finished her champagne and gave her a smile. 'We'll chat after dinner. I'll bring David over to meet you.'

Clara gave her a smile of relief. 'Can't wait, and again, you look beautiful.'

Alyssa waved her hand and drifted off in a froth of cream lace as Clara let out a big breath. Joshua was crossing the grass towards her from where he'd been in a conversation with someone else. Alyssa met him on the way and he spun her around, laughing, before she whispered something in his ear while winking back at Clara.

But Joshua's eyes stayed fixed on Clara. And as he walked towards her with a big grin on his face she felt as if she was the only woman there.

He slid his hands around her waist and bent to kiss her. If she had any doubts about what role she had here they all vanished in an instant. 'Having fun yet?' he whispered.

The nervous flicker in her stomach dissipated at his touch. 'I'm with you,' she said softly. 'Of course I'm having fun.'

She started to relax a little. Joshua took her over and they sat in the garden with the couple who'd they sat next to at the ceremony. Ben and Roma were old work colleagues of Joshua's too. Ben was a radiographer and Roma a fellow doctor. They laughed and joked easily, telling her tales of work disasters. Several other guests came and joined them from time to time, all welcoming Clara warmly.

The weather was warm and when they were invited back inside for dinner the glass doors that led to the gardens were left open to allow the air to circulate. Dinner was served quickly and the food was delicious. They were seated at a table with some of the groom's relatives, as well as some of Joshua's friends. Chat was light, and by the time the evening reception was due to start Clara was beginning to wonder if this was turning into the perfect day.

As they watched the first dance Joshua's arm was tightly around her waist. 'Hey,' he said huskily in her ear, 'I've never asked you. Do you like to dance?'

'Would you like to find out?' She leaned back against him and he made a low noise.

His lips touched the back of her neck. 'You have no idea.'

As the music started for another tune she took that as a yes and stepped out onto the dance floor, beckoning him with one finger.

One of his friends let out a wolf whistle as Joshua took his cue and followed her. He took her firmly in his arms and swept her around the floor, his footsteps sure and confident. She was surprised at just how good he was. 'Hey, ballroom dancer,' she joked. 'Got any other secrets you want to share with me?'

'What can I say? My sister told me as a teenager I had to find some kind of rhythm and dance. Girls like to dance. So I learned.'

Clara grinned. 'Ah, so this was just some kind of technique to get girls?'

'Absolutely.' He nodded. Then he glanced over his shoulder in some kind of mock act. 'Is it working?'

'We'll see,' Clara teased as she kept spinning around him.

They danced until her feet hurt in her high shoes. She took them off and put on a pair of flip-flops that had been supplied for the women. Evening snacks appeared, cupcakes with *Mr and Mrs* on them, traditional wedding cake, rolls with bacon, rolls with sausage, alongside bowls filled with tomato sauce and brown sauce. Joshua started laughing. 'This,' he said, lifting up one of the rolls, 'this is how Alyssa and David met. David came in late to halls one night. Alyssa had just made herself a bacon roll and ducked back to her room to grab her sauce. By the time she came back, David was eating it.'

'What?' Clara started to laugh, then wrinkled her nose. 'She kept her sauce in her room?'

Joshua nodded solemnly. 'Of course, it was hide or die in those halls. Anything you put in the cupboards in the kitchen disappeared. Literally, in an instant. We all thought some kind of hungry ghost lived there.'

'But, in this case, the ghost was David?'

Joshua nodded. 'He'd gone on ahead when we'd left the pub. By the time I got in, Alyssa was hitting him over the head with a cushion. He offered to give the roll back, but he'd put brown sauce on it, and she hated it.'

'Where did he get brown sauce in the middle of the night if he hadn't gone back to his room?'

'Aha,' said Joshua slowly. 'We—I and a few of my fellow students—had a hiding place for essentials in one of the vents. We would never have left cooked bacon unguarded. As soon as you started cooking food in the kitchen people would appear from nowhere. It was definitely survival of the fittest.'

He pulled her down onto his knee, one hand resting on her leg. 'You've been great today. I know it might have been hard—mixing with my friends and a whole bunch of people you didn't know. But...' he reached up and touched her cheek '...thank you. I appreciate it.' He looked out across the crowded room. 'It's been a long time since I've come to something like this and actually enjoyed myself.'

She breathed in slowly, taking a minute to say the right thing. 'Why?' she asked simply.

His eyes connected with hers. 'Because I hadn't found the right person to come with.' The words made her heart melt. He couldn't have said anything more perfect. She picked up a cupcake and held out her hand to him. 'How about we take some of these things back as room service?'

He stood up and crossed over to the bar, coming back a few seconds later with a bottle of champagne and two champagne flutes. Clara had a little pile of cupcakes on the plate. 'Ready?' she asked.

'Always.' Her heart skipped a few beats as they made their way back to their room.

The service had turned down the bed, put some chocolates on the pillows and left the curtains open, showing a beautiful view of the gardens. At this time of night the gardens were lit by multicoloured lights that glowed on and off, giving the impression of a magical wonderland. Joshua put down the champagne on the table at the window and turned to take Clara in his arms.

'How did you find it today?' She could hear the tinge of anxiety in his voice.

'I've had a great time,' she reassured him. 'Your friends have all been lovely.'

He swallowed and paused for a second. 'A few of them asked me.'

'Asked you what?'

'Asked me if we were serious.'

She felt herself stiffen. Now it was her turn to swallow. 'What did you say?'

In the dim lights his eyes fixed on hers. 'I told them I'd like to be, but wasn't sure what you wanted.'

Her breathing stuttered and skin prickled. The question. The conversation she'd been waiting for. 'What about Scotland?' she breathed.

His gaze lowered. 'That's up to you. I could never ask you to give up a home or job that you loved.'

Something plucked at her heartstrings. She remembered the first time she'd walked into Georgie's flat and thought it resembled a show house instead of a home. Her place was much more low-key. Much more cosy.

Her voice trembled. 'How do you feel about long-distance relationships?'

He tilted his head to one side—a movement that reminded Clara of his mother. 'I think,' he said steadily, 'that it might be worth a try.' A little flare of hope fired inside her belly. He was actually considering it.

'London and Edinburgh aren't that far apart. Four hours by train.'

He must have been checking. More hope.

'And we could talk every day and video chat to catch up.'

His hand slid over the smooth silk of her dress. 'But it's not quite the same, is it?'

Her mouth dried. She knew exactly what he was saying. It wasn't the same. It wasn't the same as being able to climb a few flights of stairs and walk into his flat on a nightly basis. It wasn't the same as seeing him every day at work. How would she feel with some distance between them?

She knew instantly that she didn't want that. 'It's not the same,' she whispered. 'I can't imagine not seeing you or Hannah on a daily basis.'

Her heart was sinking. Hannah was settled at school and Joshua was in charge of a department at one of the best hospitals in London. Any decision to be made had to be hers.

Part of her wished she'd tried to phone Ryan before tonight—to talk things through with him. To see what he would think if she told him she might not want to come back to Scotland at all. Would he be surprised? Angry? Or pleased for her?

Joshua reached up and stroked her cheek. 'I can't imagine not seeing you every day either.' He let out a low laugh and shook his head. 'I've been so worried about having this conversation with you.'

'You have?'

He nodded. 'We haven't had a conversation about the future. I wasn't even sure how you would react if I asked you about it. I was worried I had read this all wrong.'

She pressed her lips together and nodded too, laying her hand on his chest. 'I've been worried too. Worried that you might think I was trying to insert myself into your lives—into a place I might not be wanted.'

'Oh, you're wanted,' he said in a deep voice. 'You have no idea how much you're wanted.'

She moved her hands to his shoulders, trying to take

her attention away from the fact that Joshua had started moving his fingers oh-so-lightly down her spine.

'What about Hannah? What do we tell Hannah?' She knew there was another part of this conversation, but it just didn't feel like the right moment.

'We tell Hannah the truth,' he said firmly. 'We tell her that we're dating and, because your job was only agreed for a short time, we're trying to find a way to make it work.'

Clara was still a little nervous. 'How do you think she'll react?'

He took a little time to answer. 'You've seen her happy, you've seen her having a temper tantrum.' Her stomach flipped because she'd seen other things with Hannah that she'd need to talk to him about. He gave her a smile that was half proud, half sad. 'I have nothing else to compare her to, but I'm sure she's in every way a normal five-year-old.' He took a deep breath. 'But I think she's ready, Clara. I think she's ready to have someone else in her life—' he pulled her closer '—just like I am.' He murmured the words against the skin of her cheek. 'We love you, Clara. We want you in our lives.'

Her heart swelled in her chest. These were just the words she wanted to hear. The reassurance. The commitment. The perfect final piece of the jigsaw puzzle slotting into place.

She answered from the bottom of her heart. 'That's what I want too.'

His fingers continued their sensuous dance down her spine and she let out a little giggle. 'What are you doing to me, Joshua? You're going to drive me crazy.'

He dipped her backwards. 'Exactly my plan.' His grip was firm, making her feel safe and secure.

'I like your plans. And I liked you dancing. You know, letting loose a little. How about some more?'

He pulled her upwards and slid out his phone, filling the room with slow, sensual music. Perfect. She merged her body against his, their curves melding together, as if they were made to be this way.

As they moved in gentle steps, Joshua trailed kisses down her neck. She'd hoped this would be a special weekend. Now she knew the man who had stolen her heart felt the same way she did. Everything seemed to be aligning. Even though she'd need to sort out logistics about her house and her job, it all felt worth it.

Worth it to feel like this for a lifetime.

CHAPTER ELEVEN

THE NEXT FEW weeks kind of floated by. Clara looked online at other suitable job vacancies in London. The job swap had been unique. Most positions at her level were recruited for more than a year in advance and, unless someone pulled out at short notice, there might not be a vacancy.

She toyed with the idea of connecting with Georgie. She had no idea how things had worked out with her placement at the hospital in Edinburgh. Was there even a remote possibility that Georgie might like to continue there?

It seemed too ridiculous, so Clara put it out of her mind.

Joshua was charming at work, easy to be around, and most of the other members of staff had guessed that something was going on between them. Ron had given her a few raised eyebrows, then told her that he was delighted for them both.

She couldn't stop smiling. And she couldn't remember the last time she'd felt like that. Things were going so well she was considering coming off the meds she'd started taking months ago. She didn't want to do it without talking to her GP first, but getting an appointment was proving tricky.

The countdown on the calendar was feeling ominous, the end of the swap creeping closer and closer. Soon, it would be time to pack up her belongings and drive the long road back up to Scotland. She should feel happy to see some of her old colleagues, her best friend Ryan—who she'd badly neglected since she'd been down here—and to see the views from her old cottage again with all the fields and sheep.

But, even though she knew she should be happy, there was still a feeling in the pit of her stomach. Or two actually. One, because she wasn't looking forward to going home the way that she should—and that made her feel a bit guilty. And two, because she still had something really important to do first.

Hannah. She had to have the conversation with Joshua about Hannah. She'd tried a few times, but it had never seemed quite the right moment. But it was beginning to feel that there would never be the right time to have this kind of difficult conversation. She had a duty. To herself, to Hannah and to Joshua.

If there was any chance of them being a family together, she had to prepare herself for times like this. She was still a bit of an outsider—but that might have been why Hannah had confided in her.

As a doctor, keeping confidences was always an issue. Times at work could be tough, and child and family protection issues meant that confidences had sometimes to be broken in order to protect those who needed it.

Of course those kind of issues didn't apply to Hannah but, as a compassionate adult, Clara knew she had to let Joshua know how his little girl was feeling. His wife, Abby, was such a sensitive subject. She had been mentioned in passing, more so since they'd been at the wedding together and Clara had met a number of their mutual friends. None of those people had made her feel uncomfortable. Clara wasn't that type. She didn't expect people who'd known Abby to feel as if they couldn't mention her in Clara's presence.

Joshua had loved and respected his wife. That much was clear. But he was ready to move on. He'd told her that, and she believed him. She didn't have the feeling that she was taking someone's place, or living in their shadow, and that gave her the security in this relationship that she needed.

But it still didn't excuse her for not being brave—for not bringing up the subject before now.

Clara sighed and stretched as she looked out of the window. She'd emptied a few drawers in the kitchen, trying to sort out what she needed to keep and what she needed to get rid of. When she'd arrived here, Georgie had this place as neat as a show home and whilst Clara wasn't quite up to those standards, she wanted to make sure things were still kept tidy.

The door clicked and Joshua walked in, a broad smile on his face. He flung his backpack into a corner and wrapped his arms around her, shuffling her backwards towards the sofa.

She laughed as they both landed on it together. 'Hey, what's this for?'

His body was warm against hers. 'Just missed you,' he said.

He'd been at a hospital management meeting, and she knew that he hated those. It was part and parcel of being the head of the department, so there was no getting out of them.

'Want me to make you some food?' she murmured next to his ear.

He shook his head. 'Just coffee.' He lifted his head. 'Hannah still on her play date?'

She nodded. 'Hunter's mum phoned and asked if she could stay longer. It's an hour before we need to pick her up.'

Joshua let out a groan and rolled off her, changing position so he was sitting on the sofa. 'I don't think I'm cut out for this. What five-year-old girl goes on a play date with a boy? Shouldn't she be hanging out with other girls?'

Clara laughed. 'Stop being such an old guy. Hannah can go on play dates with whoever she likes. She's having fun, she's socialising; that's what's important.'

'Who is this Hunter anyhow?' asked Joshua. 'Do we know his mum and dad?'

She shook her head. 'Oh, no, we handed over our daughter to perfect strangers without a single question.'

The words were out before she'd even had a chance to think about them. But as soon as she said them out loud she froze.

Joshua's head whipped round and his gaze locked on her with such an intensity that her natural reaction was to back away. 'Slip of the tongue,' she said quickly as she stood up. 'I'll get the coffee.'

Her legs were shaking as she hurried into the kitchen and she couldn't ignore the slight edge of panic in her chest.

She knew instinctively within a few seconds that Joshua was following her. She took a few quick deep breaths, trying to calm herself again. It was a genuine slip of the tongue. But it left her feeling exposed.

She stuck the pods into the coffee machine and kept breathing. Maybe this was a sign. Maybe it was time to have that conversation about Hannah that she'd been delaying.

As Joshua came around the corner into the kitchen, Clara spun around and put her hands behind her, leaning against the counter.

'We need to talk.' Their voices sounded in unison.

'Me first,' said Clara quickly.

'Okay.' Joshua nodded, his expression more serious than she'd ever seen before. It felt like being a child called into the headmaster's office. Which was ridiculous. Of course it was. But she couldn't pretend that wasn't how she felt.

'I need to talk to you about Hannah,' she said quickly.

'Okay.' His brow furrowed a little as if he wasn't quite sure where she was going with this.

And she wasn't. Instantly she wanted to delay again because she was sure, no matter how she tried to frame this, Joshua would feel hurt. And it was the last thing she wanted to do. But she had to be truthful. She had to put Hannah first. Before her own wants and needs. And before Joshua's.

'Hannah spoke to me a few weeks ago about something. And I know I should have told you sooner but, to be honest, I've found it difficult to bring this up without hurting your feelings. Because that's not my intention, not at all.'

Joshua just looked confused. 'What do you mean?'

She sucked in a breath, willing herself to ignore the tears that materialised in her eyes. 'She was worried,

Josh. I think she feels pressure—even though I know it's completely unintentional.'

'Pressure about what?' She could see he was starting to get a little annoyed.

'About her mum. About Abby.'

Joshua took a few steps closer. 'I don't understand.' The coffee machine started to make gurgling sounds behind her.

Clara closed her eyes for a second. 'It was bedtime and she was tired. She was talking. She told me she doesn't remember her mummy at all. And she's sad about it.'

Joshua shook his head. 'But she was just a baby—'

Clara put her hand up. 'I know that, and I explained to her that you and Georgie know that too. But she's sad. She's sad she can't remember anything—'

He cut her off. 'But that's why Georgie and I have told her as many stories as we can. So she knows it's okay to talk about her mum, to ask questions.'

Clara paused for a second, letting some silence fill that air between them. 'She feels guilty, Joshua. She feels guilty she can't remember, and she feels pressure to find memories that just aren't there.'

As Joshua's eyes widened, Clara added, 'She thinks it makes you sad.'

He took a step back, leaning against the wall in the kitchen. 'But—'

Nothing followed the word but she could see him trying to process what she'd just told him. His eyes fell on a pile of papers and cartons on the counter top that she'd been ready to take to recycling.

His voice trembled a little as he looked across at her. 'How long ago did she tell you this?'

Clara hesitated, inwardly cringing. 'A few weeks ago.'

'A few weeks ago, and you've said nothing?' There was no mistaking the incredulous tone in his voice.

Guilt flooded over her. 'I know. But I wasn't sure how to tell you. I've thought long and hard about it.'

'Did you think long and hard about how many times I might have mentioned Abby to Hannah over the last few weeks? How I might be unintentionally hurting my daughter without realising it?'

The wounded expression on his face told her everything she needed to know.

'I'm sorry,' she said quickly. 'But I did try and explain to her you didn't mean it. And I told her that maybe when she was older she might want to ask questions, and that you and Georgie would be happy to answer them.'

'You told my daughter all that, but you didn't think to sit me down and tell me too? To let me know that I'm clearly failing my daughter.' The words were spat out, and she knew he was angry, she knew he was hurt. Those words took her back to the first time he'd sat down on her sofa and opened up. Opened up about wondering if he was getting things right with Hannah. It was clear that those underlying fears had never left him.

She stepped forward but something in his expression made her halt. 'You're a great dad, Joshua. Don't doubt it. Hannah is a lucky girl. And she's a real credit to you.'

Even as she said the words she could feel the shift in the air between them. It didn't matter that she was taking steps closer to him, it felt as though they were pulling further and further apart.

He shook his head and rested his hand on the countertop, not meeting her gaze. 'I can't believe you didn't talk to me about this right away. Don't you get how important this is?'

The implication in the words stung. She kept her voice low. 'I know how important it is. Why do you think we're having this conversation now? Do you think I wanted to do this? Do you really think I want to tell you not to talk about Abby to Hannah?' She held up her hands, 'How dare I? I didn't know Abby. I have no right to say something like that. Because I understand how hurtful it is.' She shook her head and looked down. 'I'm new to all this parenting stuff, Joshua. You know that. But I know what the right thing is. And this,' she pointed her finger down to the floor and said the words a little more resolutely, 'is the right thing to do. Because you and I aren't the important ones here. Hannah is.'

'You think you need to tell me that?' His voice was raised, cutting through the kitchen.

Clara threw her hands back up. 'Of course I don't. But you're so angry at me right now I think you need a reminder.'

Joshua turned his back on her, leaning over the counter top, his eyes fixed downwards. Clara wasn't sure what to say next. She was trying to quell the tightness in her chest. A few days ago, everything had been perfect between them. Should she have kept quiet—said nothing at all? But what kind of person actually did that—didn't loving someone mean loving all of them, and not being afraid to talk about the hard stuff?

She turned and pulled out the cups from beneath the machine. She wasn't even thirsty, and if she could pick a drink right now it wouldn't be coffee. But it gave her something to do with her hands. Something for her brain to focus on while Joshua's brain focused on how much he hated her, and what a bad parent he was.

But the next words she heard were totally unexpected. 'Clara, what are these?'

She turned back around. He had an empty cardboard pill box in one hand and a catalogue in the other. The sperm donor catalogue. The things she'd planned on placing in the recycling bin.

Her heart stopped.

Joshua was shaking his head and looking thoroughly confused. 'Are you trying to have a child?' he asked.

The words stuck somewhere in her throat. This wasn't a conversation she'd ever planned to have with him. 'I... I...considered it,' she said finally.

'You considered it?' he repeated, disbelief on his face.

She nodded and swallowed. Coffee might be useful right now. Her mouth had never been so dry.

'And this is another thing you didn't think to mention?'

She shifted uncomfortably, but somewhere deep inside she felt a little flicker of anger. 'I didn't mention it because it didn't affect you. This was something I was considering before I came down here. I hadn't decided if it was a step I wanted to take, but I wanted to find out more, so I did.'

'And you didn't think it important enough to mention to me—even though we were in a relationship?'

When he said those words out loud, it made her feel ridiculous. Even though it all made perfect sense in her head.

Something flickered across his gaze. 'And was IVF with a sperm donor the only way you considered having a baby?' Ice dripped from his words so clearly it made her shiver as the implication penetrated her brain.

'What?' She couldn't help but raise her voice. Surely he couldn't be accusing her of *that*?

He kept his gaze locked firmly on hers. 'Answer the question.'

She couldn't believe it. She couldn't believe his brain would actually work that way. 'You'd better be joking,' she snapped, her temper finally fraying.

Joshua started pacing. 'Why would I be joking, Clara? The person that I've told that I love, that I want to make plans with, has been keeping secrets from me. I thought I knew you—but it turns out I don't know you at all. Maybe this relationship is all just a convenience to you. Charm the local guy and see if you can get pregnant. Is that what I was to you—a convenience?'

Now she was shouting and she couldn't stop herself. She didn't allow herself to start where he had just left off. She started with the whole ridiculous idea. 'Are you crazy? What I feel about you is hardly convenient. How could it be? In a few weeks we'll be parted again. You'll be here and I'll be back in Edinburgh. The job swap will be over. I won't get to see you every day. I won't get to run up the stairs and knock on your door whenever I need a Josh fix. I won't get to pretend to want to use the gym just to see you in those shorts. What part of being hundreds of miles apart seems convenient to you?' She took another breath. 'And then, on top of all that, you make stupid claims. That I'm using you as a potential sperm donor. Words can't even describe how insulted I am. You honestly think I would do something like that? Casually sleep around and try to get pregnant. Just what kind of human being do you think I am?' Angry tears started to spill down her cheeks. She needed to get her temper in check. Her brain wanted to transport her body to the gym upstairs so she could have a go at one of the punch bags. It might be the only way to let all this pent-up frustration out.

Joshua was still shaking his head. He picked up the cardboard pill box. This time his voice was quiet. This time his voice sounded sad. 'And why didn't you tell me about these?'

She blinked, becoming automatically defensive. After a few moments of deep breathing she tilted her chin upwards. 'Because what prescription medication I take is my business. I don't need to share that with you. You've been in this job a long time, Joshua. I know lots of doctors who've taken anti-depressants, now, and in the past. It's a stressful job. Things happen. And sometimes you need to seek treatment. I'm not ashamed. I'm not embarrassed. This has been part of my life for a long time, and I've accepted it. I also don't think I need to explain myself to you. I'd actually just decided that I was feeling well enough to come off my meds, but again, that's nothing to do with you.'

He turned back to the counter and pressed his hands against it, bowing his head. By the time he turned back around she was stunned to see he had tears in his eyes.

'I can't do this,' he said simply.

'What?'

'I've lived this life. It almost broke me. I can't do it again.'

'What are you talking about?'

'I had a wife who kept secrets from me. She knew she was sick. She knew the treatment could harm our baby. She chose not to share with me. She chose to keep it to herself until after she'd delivered our baby.' He paused and she could see the hurt on his face and in his eyes. 'She didn't trust me enough to tell me.'

The words sliced through her. More than she expected them to.

He shook his head again and, although there was a tremble to his voice, it also seemed firm. 'I can't be with someone like that again. Someone who can't trust me with their personal issues. Someone who keeps secrets.'

She knew he wasn't talking about the sperm donor. She knew he was talking about her mental health.

Part of her felt guilty. She'd never thought about this from his perspective before. She'd been so worried about hurting his feelings over the conversation about Hannah that she hadn't even considered this—even though she knew his history. Why hadn't she made the connection? It made her feel stupid.

'Talking about mental health isn't easy.' She started slowly, meeting his gaze again. 'Particularly when the person you're going to talk to is also technically your boss.' His expression remained unmoved.

'If I tell people I suffer from depression then—no matter who they are—a judgement forms in their brain. *She can't cope. She isn't grateful for what she's got. She can't be relied on. Don't give her more than one thing to do. What on earth has she got to be depressed about?* I've heard them all, Joshua. So I stopped talking about it.' She held up one hand. 'How do you explain depression when you can't link it to one thing? How do you explain that you just lose interest in things you previously loved? That you can't find the energy to get out of your chair, let alone do an extra shift? That the edges around your world feel dull and greyish? The first thing people ask is why? What they can do to help. What they can do to make you better.' She sucked in a deep breath as her voice started to shake. 'I guess somehow I thought that you might be like that, Joshua. That you might try to—' she lifted her fingers '—fix me.'

Another tear rolled down her cheek. 'I don't want you to fix me. I don't want anyone to fix me.' She pressed a hand to her chest. 'Because this is me. This is who I am. And I want to fix myself. And you have to take me as I am, Joshua. All of me. Even the parts you don't like.'

He blinked, clearly slightly stunned by her words. One minute both had been raising their voices, now they were speaking in barely a whisper, so much hurt in the air between them.

Clara blinked, trying to pull back the memories of their weekend together and how they'd been so happy. Life had seemed almost perfect. She'd met a man she loved, with a little girl she adored. Work was great, and they were making plans for a future together. Maybe that future could include the large family she'd always wanted?

Now, because of one conversation, everything had become unpicked. Had they ever really known each other at all?

The realisation made her sway and she clutched the counter behind her.

Joshua squeezed his eyes closed for a second. She could almost hear his brain ticking—and she couldn't even begin to guess what he might be thinking.

His voice remained low. 'I thought we were good together. I thought we loved each other and could find a way to make this work. I thought I might have found someone who would love my daughter just as much as I do.'

Those words made the tears start to stream again.

'But I can't risk my heart, or hers, with someone who doesn't trust me. I would never have judged you. I would never have tried to fix you. I wanted to love all of you, not just the parts you let me see.' He gave a hollow laugh. 'I didn't think you were perfect, Clara, but I thought you were perfect for me.' He lowered his head one final time. 'Seems like I was wrong.'

And then he turned and walked out of the door.

For a moment she was stunned. Her first reaction was to run after him. But too much had been said. She still felt as if she couldn't process most of it.

Her heart started fluttering rapidly in her chest and she couldn't quite get a breath. Her legs crumpled under her in the kitchen and her body moved into self-protect mode.

She moved her head between her legs, ignoring the heartbeat she could now feel pulsing in her ears and counted to ten, trying to slow down her breathing.

Her brain felt foggy and muddled. Her first instinct was to look at her watch, but she avoided it, not wanting to become more panicked. She willed her heart to slow. She knew exactly what was happening to her. She'd seen it happen to other people—she'd even treated other people having panic attacks—she'd just never expected to have one herself.

She stayed where she was for the longest time, waiting until her breathing and heart rate eventually slowed. Eventually, with shaking legs, she stood.

She grabbed a glass and filled it with water, taking a few sips before setting it back on the counter. Alongside the untouched coffee cups.

It was as if someone had reached inside her chest and given her heart a sharp twist.

Those two cups. When she'd started the process she'd just had that slip of the tongue about 'our' daughter. Because in a few short months that was how she felt about Hannah. Joshua and Hannah were her family. The people she should be with. The place her heart told her she belonged.

She moved out of the kitchen and through to her bedroom, sagging down on her bed.

Except…it wasn't her bed. It would never be her bed. It was Georgie's.

The view from the window would never be hers. Her view was one of fields and sheep. One of emptiness, bleakness and loneliness.

Her cottage had never conjured feelings like these before. The comfort she usually felt from memories of her own place was gone. Now, it just seemed like a space for someone who'd made mistakes. Who'd lost the people she loved.

And would probably never feel whole again.

CHAPTER TWELVE

JOSHUA DRIFTED FROM one day to the next. It was amazing how easy it was to purposely avoid someone at work. Every time he caught a glimpse of her slim frame or white coat he would find something else to focus on entirely. Whether that was giving the conversation he was having with someone else his full attention or concentrating completely on tests results or case notes, he found he could easily keep his eyes glued on one subject.

It was his other senses that objected. They seemed to scream from every pore of his body. He would catch her scent from across the room or around a corner. He would hear her voice or laughter in conversation with other members of staff. His stomach clenched when he saw a wrapper from her favourite chocolate bar in one of the bins under the desk on the ward. As for his skin? It seemed to permanently tingle. An ache had formed underneath his fingertips. Letting him know they were missing something, mimicking the ache in his heart.

He caught sight of a few curious glances. The other staff obviously knew something was amiss. But no one had dared ask him.

He could hardly blame them. He snapped when anyone second-guessed an order that he gave, changed off duty rotas with little consultation to avoid being on shift with Clara, and didn't have his usual patience for the job.

All the time he was constantly aware of the days ticking past in his head, like some enormous game show timer. She'd be gone in a matter of weeks. And even though his head told him he should be relieved, his heart ached so badly he wondered if he'd ever stop thinking he might actually have chest pain.

His pager sounded late one night and he picked it up and sighed. The call took minutes. He'd have to go in. But he had no one to look after Hannah. On previous occasions he would have picked up the phone to Clara. Before Clara, he'd had his sister or his nanny, but now his options were limited.

He bundled Hannah up in blankets and carried her out to the car. It was less than ideal.

By the time he reached the ward, the doctor who'd called him had started to panic. He was surprised to find Ron at the desk—he normally worked day hours.

Ron held out his arms for Hannah as Joshua strode into the ward. 'My fault, sorry,' he said. 'It's my niece and Reuben seemed out of his depth.'

Joshua nodded. Reuben, the doctor on duty, *had* been out of his depth—he'd known that from the call. Joshua could see what must be Ron's sister and husband crowded around the bed of a small, pale child, wired up to a monitor that showed her heart rate was way too fast.

Joshua took a breath and put his hand on Ron's arm. 'Don't worry,' he said reassuringly. 'I'll look after your niece.'

And he did. The little girl had a high temperature due to chickenpox. The spots came out gradually over the next few hours. But the temperature led to the discovery of an undiagnosed heart murmur, causing lots of extra beats and a worrying ECG. Joshua called in a cardiac colleague who, in turn, discovered an issue with the little girl's heart valve. Treatment was started promptly, and as soon as her temperature started to come down her heart rate came back to normal limits.

It was four hours before Joshua had a chance to sit back down at the desk with a partly relieved Ron. 'Where's Hannah?'

'In a makeshift bed I made for her in the duty room. Clara's with her.'

'What?' It was the last thing Joshua expected to hear.

Ron sighed and shook his head. 'She woke up and, even though she knows me, she was scared. You were busy looking after my niece, so I called Clara. She was here within ten minutes and is curled up with Hannah now.' He ran a hand through his hair. 'Why didn't you leave Hannah with her?'

Joshua was trying to ignore the prickle of anger that he felt. Ron had prioritised. He knew that Joshua needed to focus on his niece. So he'd left him to focus on his job, while sorting out things for Hannah. He knew it was reasonable.

He took his time before he spoke. 'Clara and I aren't together any more. It wouldn't be fair for me to ask her to watch Hannah.' He paused, then added, 'I wish you'd asked me before you called her.'

Ron gave him a hard stare and lowered his head closer to Joshua's. It was still the middle of the night and most of the ward was in darkness.

'Josh, you're my colleague and I respect you. When Kelly was sick tonight, you were the one person I wanted to see her. When I knew that Reuben was panicking, I insisted he call you. For kids, you're the best there is. But for life? You're a halfwit.'

Joshua was stunned. In all the years they'd worked together, Ron had been always been straight talking, but never quite *this* blunt. Ron pushed his chair back. 'I'm not going to give you a lecture because I've no right to. But everyone has spent the last week tiptoeing around you. This place is too busy for nonsense like that. I asked your daughter who she wanted when she was upset. She said one name. Clara. That's why I phoned her.'

He pointed to the duty room. 'You look terrible and so does Clara. Everyone can see it. Whatever is wrong, it's time to sort it out—for all our sakes.' He put a hand on Joshua's shoulder. 'So, for tonight, and for what happens in the future with Kelly, thank you, Joshua. Thank you for coming in and looking after my niece. I trust you. I trust your judgement.' He gave a sad smile as he looked at the door of the duty room. 'But do you trust your own?'

Clara had been surprised when the phone had woken her in the middle of the night. Most doctors had internal radar. The nights they were supposed to be on call, they never truly slept properly, always waiting for a pager to sound, or a phone to ring. But on the nights they weren't on call most slept like the dead.

It only took a few moments to grasp the situation and, even in her befuddled state, she was already out of bed and opening her wardrobe before the conversation was over.

As she'd arrived she hadn't even looked along the corridor to where she guessed Joshua was. She'd gone straight to the duty room where Ron sat with a sniffing

Hannah and gathered her up into her arms, letting her snuggle in to get the sleep she so badly needed.

She'd taken Ron's hand. 'I hope your niece is okay. I'm sure Joshua will get her sorted.'

Ron gave her a worried smile. 'I hope so,' he said before disappearing out of the door.

Clara sat for a while, thoughts spinning around her head. This had become the normal for her. Going over and over what she could have done differently. How things might have gone if Joshua hadn't looked at the pile of recycling at the end of the counter.

It was odd. But somehow it felt as if it was meant to happen. At first she'd been angry and annoyed at his reaction to both things: the potential look for a sperm donor, and the empty packet of tablets.

But time and clarity had made her realise how damaging keeping secrets had been for him. The truth was, telling Joshua earlier would never have changed his wife's outcome. But maybe it would have changed how he lived with himself after.

The door opened, letting in a sliver of light from the ward. She raised her head as Joshua took a few steps into the room and closed the door behind him.

There was silence for a few seconds. Just his presence made her skin prickle and as the familiar smell from his quickly sprayed deodorant drifted across the room towards her she blinked away the damp feeling in her eyes. 'Ron's niece is going to be okay,' he said in a gravelly tone. 'She'll need surgery at some point, to sort her valve. But everything is manageable.'

Clara gave a sigh of relief for Ron, the quiet backbone of the paediatric unit. His family lived on the opposite side of London, but when there had been trouble he'd brought his niece here, to the people he trusted to look after his family. To Joshua.

There were only a few weeks left. Soon she'd be gone from all this. And the startling realisation for her was, no matter how bad things were, she didn't want to be away from this. She didn't want to be away from him, or Hannah. Not ever.

He took a seat opposite her. 'Thank you,' he said in a low voice.

'You should have called me,' she answered quickly.

He sighed. 'I didn't like to. I didn't think I could. Not the way things are between us.'

'We're adults,' she said as a tear spilled down her cheek. 'We can fight all we want. It doesn't need to affect Hannah. We have to do better than this.'

She could sense him holding his breath. The warmth from Hannah's little body against hers was flooding through her. This was the life she wanted. With this prickly, sometimes argumentative man.

'I don't want you to go,' he said so softly she thought she'd imagined it.

'What?'

He raised his head and looked at her across the dark room. She could only see him because the blind on the window wasn't down. 'I don't want you to go,' he repeated thickly. 'No matter what's happened, how I felt about things—I don't want you to go. I love you, Clara. Things are tough, but I've learned enough in this life to know that if you find love, only a fool lets it slip through their fingers.'

She couldn't speak, her words sticking in her throat.

'I want this to work. But I need honesty. I need us to be an open book to each other. I don't want to fix you,

Clara. I just want to understand how you're feeling. If you're struggling, tell me. If you're not, tell me. I just need to know there are no secrets between us. I have to be able to trust you.'

She blinked back the tears in her eyes. 'I don't want to leave either,' she breathed. 'I was wondering how to tell your sister that I don't want to go back to my job in Edinburgh. To ask if she'd consider staying.' She let out a quiet laugh. 'I was looking at jobs in London last night. Wondering where I could find some place down here. I'm sorry, Joshua, I've had some time to think about it from your perspective. The truth is, I'm not used to sharing. I've spent so long keeping things inside. There's still such a stigma around depression—even though we both know lots of our colleagues suffer. I wasn't sure how you would react, or what you would say.' She glanced down at Hannah as her voice broke. 'You might have questioned my ability to do my job. Or you might have thought I wasn't good enough for you and Hannah.'

He was in front of her in an instant, his hands cupping her face. 'No. Don't say that. Not ever. I would never think like that. I love you, Clara, and everything that comes with you. I overreacted before. All I could think about was how hurt I'd been. How I hated the thought of someone I loved keeping secrets from me.' He pulled one hand down and put it on his heart. 'I know I can't live like that. I hadn't realised how damaged I'd been before. How much losing Abby had affected my ability to form other relationships. Before, I always had excuses. I didn't want to get close to someone. I didn't want to find out they'd kept something from me, or lied to me about something, because I wasn't sure I could survive that again. It was easier just to keep myself in a box. To not expose myself to the possibilities.' He took a deep breath. 'You were the first person who made me want to put my heart on the line again. You, Clara.'

She blinked as tears streamed down her face. Her words faltered. 'You were the only person I've ever thought could give me the life I wanted. The happiness. The family I always dreamed of. I just didn't know how to tell you. To share with you.'

His fingers brushed a tear from her cheek. 'I love you. Please tell me that we can both learn how to share. I don't expect perfect—because I know I'm far from perfect. But I've found someone who makes me want to live life again. Who loves my daughter just as dearly as she loves me.' He took a breath. 'And who wasn't afraid to put Hannah before me, before us.' He looked into her eyes. 'I understand that now. I understand how hard that must have been. And I know it was completely and utterly the right thing to do. I'll get better at all this, Clara, I promise.'

Clara took a few shuddering breaths. 'So, you can accept me as I am? Knowing that sometimes I might feel unwell. And you can't fix me. You can love that part of me, just as much as the rest of me?'

He nodded. 'Of course, Clara. It's you. It's part of you. Whatever you need, I'm here.'

She nodded slowly, letting the warm feeling inside her spread. Acceptance. Acceptance for now, and for always. No need to lie about how she was feeling. No need to paint a smile on her face and pretend things were always fine. The feeling of relief was overwhelming. 'And what about later?'

'Later?'

'When I ask you about my other dreams.'

His brow furrowed slightly. 'What other dreams?'

'Dreams about having a big family. Could you see that being part of our future?'

His face broke into a smile. 'If we're blessed with a family, I'll be delighted. If that doesn't happen, we can look at other plans. As long as we do it together, I'm happy.' He clasped both her hands. 'Just promise me you'll stay. You make our lives complete. We don't want to do this without you.'

The tears were well and truly flowing now. She pulled him towards her, so his mouth was only inches from hers, with only Hannah's small body between them. 'I'm only going to say yes if you kiss me and promise to keep kissing me, now and for ever,' breathed Clara, her heart racing in her chest.

His lips brushed ever so gently against hers. 'I can make the promise...' his fingers tangled in her hair as his lips met hers again '...now and for ever.'

EPILOGUE

THEY WERE IN LUCK. It was the one sunny day of the year in Scotland.

It was strange being back in her old house. It was even stranger sharing her old bedroom with Georgie as they both got dressed for their double wedding.

Their dresses were entirely different. Georgie's was more fairy tale with cream lace, slightly off the shoulder and three-quarter-length. She had tiny flowers woven through her hair, and her three-month-old baby lay kicking in the crib in the centre of the room.

Clara laughed as she held her breath and Georgie zipped her into her close-fitting, full-length gown. Outside, the white marquee flapped in the wind. They'd decided on a more informal wedding with a marquee in the field next door. Clara only hoped the farmer had managed to keep the sheep away. She stared down at her gown. 'How long before this is covered in mud?' she said, laughing.

Georgie fastened her short veil onto Clara's head. 'About five minutes, give or take how long it takes Truffle to jump up on you.'

She squeezed Clara's arm. 'I'm so happy that my brother met you.'

Clara held up one finger. 'Don't. You'll get us both crying again. I've never seen Ryan this happy. And as for baby Isla. You're making me broody.' They both turned to where Isla was lying happily kicking in her crib with a big smile on her face.

There was a noise at the door. 'Come on, girls. Let's get this show on the road.'

The door swung open and both fathers were waiting outside. Hannah was jumping up and down in her long pink dress. 'Hurry up!'

Georgie's mum came inside and picked up her tiny granddaughter. 'Daddy's waiting for you.' She smiled, before stopping to give each bride a kiss on the cheek.

'Ready?' Clara asked Georgie. They both nodded and made their way down the spiral staircase without tripping.

The wind caught their dresses as they walked towards the marquee, each on the arm of their father.

Clara's breath caught in her throat as she saw Ryan and Joshua waiting next to an archway of flowers, both dressed in kilts. Ryan had Isla in his arms and was beaming as he waited for his bride. Joshua looked decidedly nervous, but as Hannah tore down the aisle in front of them he swept her up in his arms and shot Clara a grin. 'Gorgeous,' he mouthed to her.

Warmth flooded through her. All their family and friends were here. The double wedding had been her idea. As soon as she'd met Georgie she knew she was perfect for Ryan, and that she had another friend for life.

Three months ago, she and Joshua had sat nervously in the waiting room for news of their niece or nephew. By the time Ryan had emerged from the labour suite, his eyes bright with delight, and the words *'It's a girl!'* she'd known she'd never need to worry about her friend again.

Their friends laughed as Truffle came down the aisle with the rings attached to his collar. There was no way that Ryan wouldn't let him be part of the day.

She slid her hands into Joshua's as they said their vows. No matter the chaos around them, he only had eyes for her. The marquee fell silent as he recited the vows that he'd written.

'Clara, you breezed into my life when I least expected it and swept me away with your sass, your straight talk and sincerity. I didn't know what I was missing until I met you. You embraced both myself and Hannah and made us feel truly loved. I learned how to trust again. Know that I will love you now and for ever. You bring such joy into our lives. On good days and bad I will love you. In joy and sadness I will love you. In old age and wrinkles I will love you.'

The congregation let out a laugh before he continued.

He reached up and touched her cheek. 'Whatever life throws at us, Hannah and I will love you, because we can do anything with you at our side.'

There was a collective sigh around the room and then Clara said her own vows back.

'When I first met you I called you Mr Grumpy. I didn't realise what a big heart was hiding inside that chest of yours. Thank you for loving me and accepting me the way I am. Thank you for trusting me with your heart and with your daughter's. I promise to always take care of them, and any other children that might come along. Thank you for bringing joy into my life and a sense of belonging, a new family, and for letting me experience the joy of parenting a wonderful little girl with you. Thank you for letting me realise that being together takes work, commitment and the biggest amount of love in the world. I'll love you always.'

Joshua let Hannah take their rings from Truffle and pass them over to them, sliding hers onto her finger.

Ryan took a little longer, getting tearful through his vows, before juggling baby Isla and finally managing to slide the wedding ring onto Georgie's finger.

'Finally!' Georgie said gleefully when the celebrant announced they could finally kiss.

Joshua slid his hands around Clara's waist and held her tightly. 'I agree,' he whispered. 'Finally.' His lips met hers and he dipped her backwards as she slid her hands around his neck.

And Clara knew that life was perfect.

* * * * *

MILLS & BOON

Coming next month

FIGHTING FOR THE TRAUMA DOC'S HEART
Rachel Dove

Michelle looked at her boss, but he was oblivious.

'So that's it?' she demanded of Andrew. 'I go abroad for four months, to help people who really need it, and then I come back and have to fight for my job, against him?' She hiked a thumb over her right shoulder at her rival.

There was a challenging look evident in Jacob's expression.

'I'm not worried. I like it here, actually, so I say bring it on. What do you say, Mich?'

Michelle stood up straight, drawing herself up to her full height. She tolerated 'Mich' from people she knew and trusted, but his use of it sent a wave of rage charging through her body.

He mirrored her actions, straightening his tie. She was five ten—more when she was out of her trainers and in a pair of heels—but she still had to look up at her suave rival.

'What do I say?' she said to both men, her arms folded to keep her from flailing them about like a child in the throes of a tantrum. She'd never give them the satisfaction. She couldn't be childish about this.

So she'd left, and the place hadn't been able to run on its own. They'd needed Jacob. But now she needed her job—her normality—back. She needed him to leave so she could burrow back into her comfortable life. That was her plan, and she didn't have a back-up. She had to be the victor in this fight. She wasn't sure she would be able to get up again if she got knocked down this time.

'Bring it on. May the best doctor win.'

'In six weeks I'll make my decision about who gets to lead the new trauma centre as head of department,' said Andrew. 'Don't let me down; I need you both at your best.'

'Six weeks of working together...' Jacob smiled, his pearly whites flashing as they caught the light. 'How ever will you resist me, let alone win?'

Michelle looked him up and down pointedly, ignoring the frisson that his sculpted body produced in the pit of her stomach.

'I'll survive, I'm sure.'

She held out her hand, and he shook it, holding it between them. The warmth from his hand pervaded her bare skin.

'We'll see, shall we? This is going to be fun.'

Continue reading
FIGHTING FOR THE TRAUMA DOC'S HEART
Rachel Dove

Available next month
www.millsandboon.co.uk

COMING SOON!

We really hope you enjoyed reading this book.
If you're looking for more romance, be sure to
head to the shops when new books are
available on

Thursday 23rd
July

To see which titles are coming soon, please visit
millsandboon.co.uk/nextmonth

MILLS & BOON

THE HEART OF ROMANCE

A ROMANCE FOR EVERY KIND OF READER

MODERN

Prepare to be swept off your feet by sophisticated, sexy and seductive heroes, in some of the world's most glamourous and romantic locations, where power and passion collide.
8 stories per month.

HISTORICAL

Escape with historical heroes from time gone by. Whether your passion is for wicked Regency Rakes, muscled Vikings or rugged Highlanders, awaken the romance of the past.
6 stories per month.

MEDICAL

Set your pulse racing with dedicated, delectable doctors in the high-pressure world of medicine, where emotions run high and passion, comfort and love are the best medicine.
6 stories per month.

True Love

Celebrate true love with tender stories of heartfelt romance, from the rush of falling in love to the joy a new baby can bring, and a focus on the emotional heart of a relationship.
8 stories per month.

Desire

Indulge in secrets and scandal, intense drama and plenty of sizzling hot action with powerful and passionate heroes who have it all: wealth, status, good looks…everything but the right woman.
6 stories per month.

HEROES

Experience all the excitement of a gripping thriller, with an intense romance at its heart. Resourceful, true-to-life women and strong, fearless men face danger and desire - a killer combination!
8 stories per month.

DARE

Sensual love stories featuring smart, sassy heroines you'd want as a best friend, and compelling intense heroes who are worthy of them.
4 stories per month.

To see which titles are coming soon, please visit

millsandboon.co.uk/nextmonth

MILLS & BOON
MEDICAL
Pulse-Racing Passion

Set your pulse racing with dedicated,
delectable doctors in the high-pressure
world of medicine, where emotions run
high and passion, comfort and love are the
best medicine.

Six Medical stories published every month, find them all at:

millsandboon.co.uk

Y028681

Kate Ha
read before she went to school. She discovered